Fantastic Erotica

The Best of Circlet Press 2008-2012

edited by Cecilia Tan
and
Bethany Zaiatz

Circlet Press, Inc.
Cambridge, MA

Published by Circlet Press, Inc.
39 Hurlbut Street
Cambridge, MA 02138
www.circlet.com

Print ISBN 978-1-61390-044-4
Digital ISBN 978-1-61390-045-1

Distributed to the book trade by
SCB Distributors, Gardena, CA

Contents

Introduction

Twenty years ago, Circlet Press began with a tiny catalog of chapbooks and a big idea: that the then rigid boundaries between the genres of science fiction, fantasy, and erotica were holding back a flood of imaginative, powerful, and sexy stories from a wide readership that sorely needed them. To Circlet's readership, it seems like a natural triad. The science fiction genre, inherently full of possibilities, would be remiss if some stories didn't explore possible sexual frontiers. And fantasy at its most basic level explores the broadest landscape of limitless imagination, so why not explore the uncharted terrain of erotic imagination as well? "Celebrating the erotic imagination" became the catchall catchphrase of Circlet Press.

In 2008, Circlet embraced the ebook revolution. The readership we'd built up over fifteen years of publishing was still out there, but it was becoming increasingly difficult to reach them through the retail bookstores. We converted many print titles from our catalog to ebook formats, but we also began publishing brand new original anthologies exclusively in ebook form--which proved to be a wise move. The success of Circlet's digital library has helped us weather financial hardships in the publishing industry and the economy at large. That success wouldn't have been possible without our passionate and discerning readership. So when it came time to celebrate our 20th anniversary, we chose to include our readers in the process. In February 2012, our editors short-listed stories from every original ebook anthology to-date, over 60 stories in all.

We then polled our readers on Circlet.com inviting them to vote for their favorites. Over a thousand votes were cast, votes that helped us decide which stories to print in celebration of our anniversary. Nineteen stories in all made it into the final volume, and in the end the office staff chose one winner and two runners-up for cash prizes. All the stories in the book are exceptional, but we'll take a moment here to discuss the top three.

"The Dancer's War" by N.K. Jemisin not only presents a unique fantasy-world and an equally unique take on diplomacy between rival tribes, it makes a statement about the stark difference between genders, even in a world where the connection between gender and sexuality are drawn very differently from in our own. The sex is captivating and highly erotic without even the slightest breath of illicitness or angst to it, which is the magic of creating a fantasy setting which allows such. To say any more would spoil the story and the original is a better read than this summary.

"Ink" by Bernie Mojzes is one of the more startling stories we've seen in a long time, hearkening back not only to Lovecraft but also to Raymond Chandler and Angela Carter, all fused together in something as fascinating and almost disturbingly familiar as an Elder God. All the postmodern panache in the world, though, wouldn't have carried the day without the weighty emotional core that Mojzes gives the story.

And our overall winner is "Ota Discovers Fire" by Vinnie Tesla. This is one of those stories that defies description, or rather where any description of it pales in comparison to the story itself. A complex tale of culture clash, humor, and unabashed sex, "Ota Discovers Fire" defies categories and yet invites praise. Kind of like Circlet Press itself.

The unique process we used to narrow down the finalists published here makes Fantastic Erotica the first collaborative effort between Circlet authors, editors, and readers. So it is with great pleasure that we share this book that you and others like you, helped create. Enjoy!

Cecilia Tan and Bethany Zaiatz
Cambridge, MA

The Beauty of Broken Glass
Frances Selkirk

"Another?" the bartender asked, and Susan nodded distractedly. She didn't like dance clubs, really—they were loud and smelly—but she did like dancing. She had hoped that by coming with a date, she would actually get to dance. She should have known that it would be a disaster as soon as Jim had asked her; there was nothing between them. Her nominal date was dancing with someone else, which would have been fine if it was just for a spin, but he'd been dancing with xathe same someone else for five songs now, and she thought he should at least have the decency to come back and tell her she was being ditched. Maybe she should have asked that blond guy from down the hall, but she enjoyed the way he smiled when their eyes met, and was unwilling to destroy her fantasy that those smiles were genuinely for her.

Jim and his new catch were obscured by a woman with big hair, and Susan sighed and reached for her purse. She should just leave. She paid the bartender for her new drink and took a long swallow of it before standing. That might have been a mistake. She felt herself sway and grabbed on to the bar. She must have had more than she had thought. Gathering her wits, she started for the door, using a loose walk that could absorb a bit of unsteadiness. Being drunk was enough of a danger without looking like she was.

She had made it nearly to the door, traveling in as straight a line as the crowd permitted, before the mishap. A dancer spun into the space in front of her, unbalancing both of them, and she wasn't quick enough to compensate. He was, though, and caught at her upper arms, keeping her from falling. For a frozen moment, she found herself looking into dark eyes under tight curled dark hair. She had caught his arms as well, as if he were about to swing her on a trapeze, and felt hard curves of muscle under her grip. His face had a pointed, foxy look, and his mouth was curving into a smile.

"Sorry," she muttered, stepping back and dropping her eyes, but that just left her looking at the way tight brown leather pants displayed the lines of the stranger's legs. Humiliated, she pushed by him and out onto the street, which canted for a moment before steadying.

For a moment she stood, adjusting to the lesser cacophony of traffic. How had they come from the subway? The club had been Jim's choice, and she didn't know the area, which was run-down, but not too rough. Turning slowly, she saw a street that looked right. She started down that, thinking she would take the second turn, but that didn't look familiar at all. Down the next, though, she saw the distant lit plate-glass windows of a deli they had passed. Just around the corner from that would be the subway station. She walked confidently towards the bright storefront, but when she was halfway there, it went dark. Hadn't it been a 24-hour place? She scanned the street around her, finding nothing she recognized, even from a moment earlier.

She didn't like the look of any of it, either. At least there were no other pedestrians, although that might be worse; inset doorways held shadow enough to hide a man. She turned and hurried back the way she had come. Down the first side street, she caught the shape of a distant subway sign and headed towards it with relief. Three drinks had left her not only unsteady, but badly needing to pee. She wished she had noticed that before leaving the bar. Now that she was aware of it, every step jolted her bladder.

She had walked another two blocks when she noticed the subway sign had vanished. Again, she stopped. Grimy buildings edged the street, with most of their windows dark. From one-third floor apartment came the changing light of a television. To her right was an empty lot, with nightshade twining over a rusted chain link fence. It had been pulled down in places, and half the gate was gone. She heard rough laughter behind her, and darted into the hidden space.

No one approached. It was quieter, in here. She couldn't figure out the acoustics of that, but the peace was welcome. The green fence and an overhanging sumac gave an impression of privacy, and she wondered if she could surreptitiously pee in the corner.

It was an awful thought, but she couldn't help thinking it would be yet more vulgar to wet herself on the street. She was thoroughly lost, and wouldn't get home soon regardless, and she was wearing a skirt, so the mechanics were possible. The June evening was so hot that she'd forgone the sticky discomfort of stockings, so she didn't even have that obstruction to deal with.

Making up her mind, she stepped further into the shadows. She walked carefully, looking for needles or glass that might poke up past her dressy sandals, but the hard dirt was surprisingly unlittered. She relieved herself in the corner, wiping off with her panties and then abandoning them behind a clump of flowering weeds.

Embarrassed, but far more comfortable, she straightened up from her crouch. Her eyes had adjusted to the shadow, and now she saw why the ground was clear of refuse. Some urban artist had arranged it all in a ragtag circle around a discarded cabinet door, mixing scraps of wrappers and broken glass with the precise care of Goldsworthy. A heap of blue and clear glass glittered at one end. Susan stepped closer, wondering if that was extra raw materials or a project of its own. Carefully, she stepped over the sharp sparkle of the line. As her foot came down, the world tilted and swirled, spiraling down into chaos.

The fragments of the world came together, but the space around her wasn't the same. Susan couldn't understand how she could be conscious and standing. Amnesia? The last she recalled, she had been in an empty city lot, falling. Cautiously, feeling her head for bumps, she looked around.

In Ireland, on a vacation years ago, she had been to an ancient stone circle. She had walked between two looming megaliths into a space big enough to hold a softball game. More massive stones, some tall, some low, had curved away from her and in again, until

they met diminished by distance. Soil had accumulated against the outside of the stones, raising a bank around the circle, and a few great trees had sent roots over the lower ones. The place where she stood now looked like that done by Las Vegas.

Thrusting from the ground at regular intervals stood curved modern sculptures of blue, white, and green glass, each glowing with inner light. Set between them, low, solid, multicolored twists gleamed with a shine that was all surface, like fresh Mardi Gras beads. Strange plants, wavering with weak height, grew beyond them, but inside the circle, the ground was bare. People were pouring through the gaps and into the space—she caught a glimpse of a willowy woman in turquoise chiffon, whose blond hair floated as she spun, as if it had been filmed in slow motion. A moment later, that view was blocked by an enormous jiggling breast capped in pale green foil. Susan stumbled back and saw the woman behind it was as large all over. Her torso was bare except for the foil pasties, and a skirt of mixed colors of chain spilled over her wide hips. Susan forced her attention up to the woman's face and her breath caught at the fierce beauty of it. Her head spun. How did anyone so huge manage—? She lost the thought as the woman threw back her head in a laugh as immoderate as her girth. Speaking to her was the man from the bar—the pointy-faced one in leather.

Susan looked wildly around, wondering if someone had slipped something in her drink, and she was back at the bar still, hallucinating glitter and seeing wild allure in everyone who passed. There were no walls, though, although there appeared to be dark cliffs in the distance. Under her feet, coarse sand lay flat and hard. Eyes following the curve of the circle, she turned and found herself near the corner of a crystal hall—a single room inside, but set with peaks of blue glass. To her left was the nearest form that delineated the circle. There was something familiar about the silver and blue, and a curve of decoration distorted by the twist, but before she could examine either the object or the memory, a gloved hand descended on her shoulder.

She froze, eyes closing against the unreal chaos. She had

probably peed on the floor, with everyone watching. The hand pressed a message to turn, and she did, forcing her eyes open.

It was the sharp-faced man. He gave the impression of a fox, despite brown hair and brown clothes. It wasn't just the pointy chin—there was something about his eyes, which were large and dark, and his alert manner. He seemed to be wearing little costume horns, which poked up through his curly hair, looking almost like the tips of animal ears. She had just a moment to think that was strange, and then he released her and bowed.

"Might I have this dance?" he asked cordially.

Befuddled, she took the arm he extended to her and accompanied him to a raised dance floor. A band, improbably acoustic, with bizarre drums that went beyond folk and into art, circled a mushroom-like pedestal, and on that stood a fiddler with silver hair and a tiger-striped face. The people gathered about the floor began to move with the mindless purpose of an audience, until they parted before the entrance of the glamorous woman in turquoise. In her right hand, she held a glowing staff of green, while her left was linked through the arm of an equally striking man. A tailored jacket accentuated his wide shoulders, long torso, and narrow hips. The black and gold coil set about his neck should have looked ridiculous, but instead it gave the impression of a fancy Elizabethan collar. His short tumble of auburn hair was set with spangles that reflected the light in a crown. Once she had seen that, Susan noticed the same pattern in the woman's hair. It was subtler in the blond strands, perhaps, but she still didn't see how she could have missed it before.

The hand was on Susan's shoulder again, pressing down.

"Bow to their Majesties," her companion murmured, and she bent with the others, not so low as some, but enough to not stand out among them.

The willowy woman set her white hand on the flared shoulder of her partner's jacket, and the first dance began. It was a waltz. Susan's only experience with waltz was a high school play, and inside her, a distant, caged feeling tried to become panic, but couldn't make it through the unreality of everything. Perhaps she was dreaming. Her partner led beautifully, and despite her drunkenness and lack of experience, she had no trouble following the steps or moving into spins.

At the end of the dance, he bowed, and she curtseyed without thinking, raising the hem of her short skirt dangerously close to the uncovered curls at her mound. As his arm settled back at her waist, awareness of her lack of panties swept over her in a heat that was as much lust as embarrassment. As if her thoughts guided him, his hand slipped lower, cupping one cheek. Could he feel the lack of seams?

"From here," he said into her ear, "it gets faster."

She had only a moment to fear polka, or some incomprehensible folk dance, before the music began again, wild and fast. No steps were expected here. People hopped and spun and gyrated as they did in any club, except that every one of them was spectacularly good at it. The foxy man pulled on her ass and ground up against her once before spinning away and back. She mirrored his motions in a hungry trance.

Several tunes later, the band switched to something that probably had a name and probably had steps. A few couples were doing what Susan thought was a tango, but more still were improvising. The man spun her to face away from him and pulled her back again, nestling her against him and rocking slightly to the music. One of his hands came up from her waist to cup under one breast.

"You're wearing too much clothing," he murmured, and she giggled. She would never have thought she'd dare do this on a dance floor, but it seemed all right. Dancers twirling by ignored them or smiled in passing. No one stared.

The man's hand left her breast and pinched a button of her blouse free of its hole. "I'll do what you say," he whispered; "I cannot deny you. But if you don't say, I will do as I wish."

Willing, she leaned back and let him undo another button. He pulled the garment loose of her skirt and opened it to the hem, so it parted above and below her breasts.

"Come," he said, and urged her back into the dance.

The sides of her blouse swung out and up when she spun, and somehow, in this touch and that, it became opened the rest of the way, until she discarded it entirely. Her bra was plain for show, but a pink-cheeked woman came and hung a magenta sash around her neck, and a laughing young man crossed it over her chest, and the foxy man smoothed it over her nipples and tied it behind her back. She wasn't sure which of them had taken her bra or where it had gone, but she loved the way her bare skin cooled from the summer heat in the sparse breeze of their motion.

She was sober by now; she was sure of it. Her movements had never been steadier or more graceful, twirling and jumping and leaping without even a bump against another dancer. She couldn't say she was disoriented either—everything about her was clear and immediate. It was only her thoughts that were turning in befuddlement at the man with butterfly wings, at the pointy-eared goblin in a shirt of gold, at the foxy man's hands at the hook of her skirt.

She stumbled as it slid down her legs, but he caught her.

"Sorry," she said.

"My mistake," he said mildly, and his hands slid from her shoulders to her waist as he went to his knees. "I should have warned you." His nose nudged into the curls at her mound, and she felt the tip of his tongue part her lips and rise under her clit. It circled once, and then he pressed in and sucked lightly. A dancer's stockinged foot swung close in a wild twirl, and Susan had to clutch at the man's shoulders to keep from falling. Someone moved to support her from behind, so she could lean back and cant her hips forward, and really let him at it.

He took full advantage, now using his hands to part her folds and hold her open to thrust his tongue into her cunt. She clung to his shoulders as he curled the point inside her, and then drew out to flutter it against the opening, driving her mad with desire.

"You're so lovely," whispered a lilting voice, and Susan twitched. The pink-cheeked woman was back, her dark hair disheveled, and she extended her arms to hold out a soft, silky cord. Giant cloth flower petals—daylily, Susan thought—hung from it in a thick line. The foxy man rose to his feet, his dark lips swollen and shimmering wet, and he twirled Susan in front of the other woman, so the cord wrapped around her waist, making a skirt of the petals. The tips came almost to her knees, and the thicker middles overlapped halfway down her thighs, and the arrangement almost covered her, except when it didn't. As if to emphasize the ambiguity, the foxy man slipped a hand between two of the petals and crooked the tip of a finger into her cunt.

"Much better," he said. Stepping back, he licked the gloss from his fingertip. She saw his bare cock full and pointing forward, and for a moment was confused as to whether he had undressed or not. Chaps, she realized, reconciling his exposure with his brown-clad legs, and she let herself be pulled again into the dance.

The dancing went on for hours, long past the point they all should have collapsed, but Susan did not tire. She was beaming when the queen raised her glowing staff and the mob and band fell silent.

"A feast!" the queen declared, and a laughing jumble of pretty teenagers came into view, the boys bearing among them a table decked with huge tropical-looking flowers, and the girls an assortment of cushions and benches. Another wave of the queen's green staff, and the table was laden with steaming dishes that gave off mouth-watering scents of food. Laughing with pleasure and exertion, Susan let herself be led to a seat.

When her hand touched the table, she was startled by the feel of it. It wasn't wood, as it appeared, but plastic imprinted with a wide grain. Still moving as she had planned, she sunk down onto her end of a cylindrical seat. It gave beneath her with an odd, spongy feel, and she twisted to look down at it—open blue foam with sparkles. Reaching down, she felt that it was hollow in the center. Unable to see more without standing, she looked at the next seat over. The side contours were odd, and it took her a moment to resolve a double wedge of pink into a bow. Then the side was clearly ears—it was a giant Hello Kitty cushion! No, she realized, feeling the hollow of her own seat again—an eraser.

Dizzily, she looked about her, watching things waver and resolve. The glass forms were pieces of broken bottles. The brilliant silver and blue twist was a Three Musketeers wrapper. The queen's staff was an unbent glow bracelet, and they were sitting at a doll's table, on, she realized now, a discarded cabinet door. The fiddler's pedestal must be the knob. To her confusion, this understanding made none of it less beautiful.

She looked to her companion, half expecting him to have turned into a doll, or a mouse, or something of the sort, but he looked just the same—except, she realized, that those points really were furry brown ear-tips. One swiveled towards her as she looked at it.

"Are you comfortable?" the man asked.

"Fine," Susan answered.

"Good." He smiled as his hand moved to her knee. It rested there, on bare skin, and her blood rushed under the touch. She told herself to concentrate. The food smelled wonderful, but what was it? The queen, she remembered, had just raised her staff...

They're fairies, she thought dizzily. It's magic food. I can't eat any of it, or I'll have to stay forever.

"May I pour you some wine?" the man asked courteously.

Susan looked desperately around. Everyone was talking, and it sounded like English, but she couldn't understand anything except what was said to her. "No," she said quickly. Her companion looked displeased. "I can't," she babbled. "I had too much at the bar."

"Ah. Perhaps you would like some roasted fowl, then?"

She looked at the giant bird and wondered what it had been. A sparrow, perhaps? The thought strengthened her will to refuse. The food could have come from garbage cans, for all she knew.

"No," she said again, "alcohol unsettles my stomach. I'll need to wait a while."

He looked like he would offer a third time, so she reached over to stroke his leg, higher than he was touching hers, and he stilled. The leather was still leather, and smooth under her touch. She wouldn't see him again, she realized, and the thought made her bold.

"You're very kind," she said softly, stroking up further, and leaving leather for bare skin. She wrapped her hand around his erection and he groaned.

"Oh," he breathed. "Lady. If you do not wish to eat, will you sit on my lap?"

For answer, she swung over him, straddling his thighs. Chatter continued unabated behind them as he parted the silk petals of her skirt. He pressed up under her, and she rocked back against him, her wet slit pressed apart by the front of his hard shaft. They moved that way until someone to the side laughed. Their eyes met.

"I'm for the garden of the moon," he declared.

In an instant, crowd and feast were gone. So was their eraser seat, and Susan tumbled to the side, onto something soft. They were in a fragrant garden, surrounded by night-blooming flowers. From the distant sounds of traffic and the low wall three sides, Susan suspected they were still in the city, but on a roof somewhere.

"We're bigger," she said, coming up on one elbow. The flowers around them were tall, but not towering, and they were on a cushion that could have slept six, but not twenty.

"As we want to be," the man said lazily, and when he nudged her, she rolled readily onto her back. He came up on his arms, tilting his hips to move the length of his erection against her in a slow stroke. "Will you grant me entrance, lady?"

"I...." She wanted it desperately, wanted his hard cock deep inside her, wanted his body pressing against her clit with each thrust in. "I don't have, um, protection."

She had left her purse back in the empty lot, she realized. That was inconvenient, but it didn't have much in it—just her 'night out' collection of necessities—cash, license, spare keys, and, of more immediate relevance, condoms.

The man laughed merrily. "My kind do not carry diseases, lady. If you know not to eat, you must know that."

She hesitated a moment, but it made sense. And at two days to her period, she doubted she was fertile. He rocked again in question, and she angled her hips to accept him. Frustratingly, he stayed just a fraction of an inch too high.

"You must consent," he said, and she reached up and seized his arms.

"Yes," she snapped, pulling him down. "Fuck me, already!"

His laugh still light, he slid into her and she arched up with a cry of pure need.

Like the dancing, their coupling seemed to continue unrealistically long, but without growing frustrating or painful. The first time she came, she couldn't believe she had outlasted him. He smiled and rolled her on top and rocked underneath her until she was moving on her own. The second time, he played with her clit, wringing peak after peak from her, until she was shaking with exhaustion.

"Rest," he said, somehow inverting their positions again.

Sated, she lay under his gentle motion, looking up at the waning moon and feeling her head clear. She thought it must be nearly morning. Why, she wondered, would a fairy want to have sex with a mortal? That part had never made sense to her. Did he hope she would become pregnant? Would she, as unlikely as it was? Would he steal the child?

She remembered the teenagers, laughing as they bore in the feast, and her heart clenched. If he came inside her, would that be like receiving food? It would be stuff of faerie, in her body. Would that bind her forever? It wasn't as if she had a lover or sister to come steal her back.

She squirmed away, but he matched the motion, staying inside her. The fairy man's thrusts were speeding up. It was hard to think past her own arousal.

"You know what?" she said quickly, remembering something one of her college lovers had liked. "You should come on my breasts."

"No, my lady," he answered, his voice tight with rising pleasure. "I like it well here."

"I'd rather you came on my breasts," she said, squeezing them together suggestively.

"And I'd rather the warmth inside."

He was cold, she realized suddenly. His teeth glittered like hard snow. She pulled in a breath, fear sharpening her focus. He had said he could not deny her, and he had meant it, she was sure. He had needed her permission to start this.

"I command you," she said clearly, "to come on my breasts."

With a snarl, his pointed features no longer beautiful, but feral and starved, he pulled out of her and surged up to his knees. His lifted prick was pure white in the moonlight and glistened with her wetness. She saw glimpses of silver, as suddenly there and gone as jumping fish or shooting stars, arc out from it, and she felt them land like ice on her bare skin.

"Mortal maid," he cried, with a voice that should have been beyond words with pleasure, but instead rose, clear and bright as an icicle shattering in light. "As you nothing took, I nothing take, but pleasure for pleasure I give to you, and safety until dawn."

Once again, the world spun in a crazy spiral. She found herself alone, under low dark boughs that curved up and dipped down. Crawling out from underneath them, she stumbled to her feet under the orange glow of a streetlight. Scratchy fragments of dead leaves and litter stuck to her sweaty skin, and when she brushed at them, she realized how little she was wearing.

Her clothes had, at least, grown with her. The silk lily petals dangling from her cord belt still overlapped to halfway down her thighs, but halfway down her thighs wasn't very far, especially for things that could part all the way up to her waist. A twist of wide magenta ribbon still covered her nipples, leaving curves bare above and below. She wasn't sure if it was legal, and it definitely wasn't safe.

A jogger breezed past her, and Susan turned to stare after him. He hadn't even noticed her, as far as she could tell. She studied her surroundings. She was in a little square a few blocks from her apartment building, with streets on all sides. A bored-looking policeman waited on his bicycle a few yards to her left. A yawning woman was approaching from the side street, drawn along by two eager little dogs.

Safety until dawn. Susan looked around. She didn't know how long she had, but it was obviously long enough. Leaving her sparse shelter, she started for home.

By the time she reached her apartment building, she was certain no one could see her. She felt a bit smug walking safely down the street in such indecent clothing—until, that is, she reached the door and realized she had no key—her purse was still in an empty lot somewhere across town. She was stuck out here. Frightened, she looked down the street to the lowest part of sky she could see, where the unseen sun was bleaching a line of sky beneath vivid twilight blue. If she was really invisible, she could lift her spare key from the office, but only if she could get inside.

The door opened, and the blond man from down the hall gave her a wide smile.

"Hey," he said, and his eyes moved over her in a look that was appreciative, but not shocked. "Nice duds," he said, waving her in, and she wondered what he saw. "Out for a midsummer night revel?"

"Yes," she said firmly, realizing only afterwards that it was entirely true. He opened the inner foyer door for her as well. "You're up early," she said, to cover for having nothing more she could tell him.

"Yeah," he agreed, with a roll of his eyes. She knew he was a night owl. "Some friends and I are going up to the Catskills, and we're trying to beat the weekend traffic. Hey, want to come?"

It was an outrageous offer, and she could see his eyes widen as it came out of his mouth. She thought she knew how he felt. Properly, she should refuse, or laugh it off.

"I mean," he stumbled on, "it's me and two couples, and I was afraid I'd be sitting around a lot..." He managed to stop. She smiled brightly at him.

"I'd love to," she said recklessly, and his jaw dropped. It was cute. "May I have a minute to pack?"

"I'll give you ten," he promised, rallying his poise, and she nearly flew to the office, and from there up the stairs. She had a feeling this would all work out.

The Succubus
Elizabeth Schechter

In the parlor, there is a portrait of Madame, painted when she was a shy young miss of seventeen. She is looking over her shoulder, and her midnight hair tumbles down her back in a profusion of curls. The uninitiated might think that this house, which has come to be called the House of the Sable Locks, was named for that portrait, and for Madame's glorious spill of hair. But that is not so; Madame's hair is more silver than sable now, and there is another reason for the name. The uninitiated never go further than the parlor, never know that there is another world beyond the doors that lead into the rear of the house. They think that Madame is simply a woman of independent means, the widow of a rich, albeit eccentric, inventor. They do not know the truth. They do not know about us.

The House of the Sable Locks is famous, but only in a rarefied circle. Certain men meet at their clubs and whisper to each other about the delights that they find behind our doors. There is the second floor, where those who prefer women can gather. Or the third floor, wherein those who prefer men can find what they seek. And then there is the fourth floor, where I can be found. But I get ahead of my story.

The "Sable Locks" refer not to a woman's crowning glory, but to the exquisitely wrought and enameled locks that adorn the collars of the men who frequent our halls. They come here at first uncertain of what they will find, knowing only the whispers of their peers. They meet with Madame in private, and no one speaks of what happens behind those closed doors. But when that meeting is over the gentlemen either leave the house, never to return, or Madame takes them on a tour. It will be the first and last time they walk the halls as free men; when next they arrive at the house, they will be escorted to the servants' quarters. There, they will be stripped of clothing and jewelry, hooded, gagged and collared. Thus rendered silent and anonymous, and wearing only their locked collars, the bearers of the Sable Lock make their way to their chosen rooms, and to the pleasures and torments that await them there. They never know who the other men are, or of what station they might be. The man that they pass in the hallway might be a member of the House of Lords, or the son of the butcher, or even their own brother. No one knows for certain except for Madame.

And me.

The fourth floor is usually quiet, with only the hum of machinery and the distant voices from the floors below. The men do not return to the fourth floor after their initial encounter with me. They desire something more familiar, more in keeping with their personal fantasies. More safe. So I wait, alone, and the silent servants tend to my needs. This evening will be different. I know it already. I can hear Madame's familiar step on the stair, and another, heavier step with her.

She enters first, the train of her evening gown sweeping the floor as she moves to the table and lights the lamp. The man lingers in the door, peering into the gloom. He wears pristine evening dress, and the lamplight picks out the gold links in his watch-chain and the gleam of the ruby on his left hand. The walls have already whispered his secrets to me: the second son of a Duke, one who was never expected to take the reins of power. One who came, all unexpected, into an inheritance that was never meant to be his. His older brother was dead of typhoid, gone without a son to succeed him, and so the younger son was now Earl Hathaway. It was no surprise to us that the late, lamented Reginald Warwick, Earl Hathaway had died without issue—he had also borne the collar and lock in this house, and had shown a definite preference for the third floor. It will be interesting to see what the new Lord Hathaway prefers. His name, the walls have told me, is Nigel.

"You can come in," Madame says. "She won't bite you." She laughs, and leaves the lamp to go to the far wall, and the switches there. She throws them, one at the time, and light floods the room.

I hear him gasp, and I know what he sees. The ceilings in this room are high, and although they try to hide it with draperies, you can still see the machines that tower overhead, disappearing into the shadows above the lights. The machines hum and churn, gears half the size of a man moving in the eternal dance that gives me life. Occasionally they release puffs of fragrant steam into the air, making the entire room warmer than would normally be considered comfortable. There is very little furniture in the room, most of it covered with drapery against dust and future need. And then there is me. Shining silver and chrome, gleaming brass and copper, I lie in wait, reclined on the wide couch as might a goddess whilst she awaited her worshipers.

"But... it's clockwork!" he blurts out, stepping into the room. He looks around, expecting to see a living woman. But, of course, there is no one else in the room.

Madame sniffs slightly, "Of course she is. I did explain that to you, did I not?"

Lord Hathaway has the grace to look embarrassed, "You did, but... the others all look... alive. This one..." he gestures wildly.

"She was the first, created by my late husband," Madame says, walking over to my couch. She brushes her nails over my shoulder and continues, "The others came later, and I refined the forms to make them more... approachable. Despite her form, the Succubus is the most complex of all the automatons."

"How can that be? It looks like a statue!" He takes a step toward the couch and points at me. "It is a statue!"

Madame runs her fingers over my gleaming silver skull, "Oh, this is just the focal point, Your Lordship. The Succubus encompasses this room."

He looks around, his eyes wide, "The whole room?"

"The whole of this floor, actually. As I said, she is very complex." Madame makes her way back to the wall and stands near the bell-rope. "Now, it is customary for the first appointment to be with the Succubus. Did your brother not tell you this?"

Lord Hathaway shakes his head. "All Reg told me was that I would not believe what I found here. He wouldn't say more." He swallows, looking nervously at the figure on the couch, and then back at Madame, "Is it safe?"

Madame laughs, "My dear sir, you'll be as safe here as in your own mother's arms, if that is your desire."

He looks at her sharply, "What does that mean?"

Madame just smiles, "You've seen what we offer. Surely it's no surprise to you that there are some who prefer an element of risk. Don't you agree?"

He does, although I doubt that any would see it but me. His breathing quickens, ever so slightly. The flush in his cheeks heightens, just a touch. He looks at me again, studying me, silent. After a long moment, he turns back to Madame, "What do I have to do?"

She draws from the reticule that hangs from her wrist one of the shining silver collars, the black lock dangling from the end. She smiles at my soon-to-be paramour, "Take off your clothes."

He balks, of course. They always do. Disrobe in front of a woman? Unthinkable! Even though the woman is the proprietress of the most exclusive brothel in London, they simply can't. I think that Madame enjoys their discomfort, and that is why she does it. Eventually, she tires of his protests and rings for one of the silent servants.

"Lay your clothing there," Madame says, and points to a chair near the door. "The servant will guard the door and make certain that you are undisturbed. And I will have a room made up for you."

Nigel looks startled, "Will that be necessary?"

Madame smiles, "The Succubus likes to take her time." Then she leaves, and the door closes behind her with a soft thump. Nigel stares at the door for a moment, then starts to unbutton his waistcoat, turning away from me in what must have been an automatic gesture. He has already removed his tie and unbuttoned his high collar so that Madame could lock the collar around his throat.

A voice is nothing but air through valves. I can have any voice I choose. This time, I choose a girl's voice, light and gentle. "I can still see you," I say softly. "You needn't try to hide. I like to watch."

He spins, startled, looking for the owner of the voice, "Who... Who said that?"

I answer, "I am the Succubus. And my eyes are throughout this room. So you need not try to hide from me."

"You speak?" He starts edging towards the door.

"I do a great many things. Isn't that why you're here?" I pause, and he stops moving. Good. Time to begin. "Do you enjoy being frightened, Nigel?"

"No!" he says quickly. "How did you know my name?"

"I know many things about you, Nigel," I keep my voice soft and low. "I know you seek an escape from the madness that your life has become since your brother died and you assumed his title. I know that you wish for a return to the carefree days of being the younger son. Your life has become structured, regimented. You want excitement." In actuality, I know none of these things. I do know that he is the younger son, much younger than his brother. Younger sons are allowed some leeway in their dealings, and it is all overlooked since they will not bear the title. And... he is here. If he was looking for a mistress, he would be at the opera, or the theater. If he desired a simple coupling, a push-in-the-dark-here's-a-farthing-never-see-the-girl-again, he would be in Whitechapel. He wants neither of these. He wants some excitement, but something that carries no risk of scandal. I can tell now that he needs something more than a simple tryst.

The chair hits him right behind the knees, and he sits down hard, the breath exploding out of him. I have him in a trice, bindings snapping closed around his legs, waist, and chest. Cables catch his wrists and pull them into position for the bindings that fix his arms to the chair. He is mine.

He struggles for a moment, opens his mouth to protest, and his breath catches when he sees the mechanical arm rising from the floor between his feet. The knife blade at the end shines in the harsh lights, the edge glittering as I move it this way and that.

"It is very sharp, I assure you," I say. "Do not struggle."

"What are you doing?" he whispers, looking like a bird facing a snake, his glassy eyes never leaving the blade.

I don't answer, lowering the knife back towards the floor. I wait a moment, letting his breathing quicken, then slip the blade into the leg of his trousers, brushing against his skin before I begin cutting. His fine trousers part easily as I work my way slowly up the seam, tracing the blade lightly over the inside of his thighs as my blade travels up each leg. He moans, closing his eyes and trying oh-so-valiantly not to move or even to breathe as the blade lays his skin bare. His arms are ticklish, and he yelps as I cut away his fine silk shirt and trace the blue veins under his skin. When I am done, his skin is shining with sweat, his breathing quick and shallow. His cock, freed at last from its linen and wool prison, stands proudly like a soldier at attention.

I pitch my voice so that it seems to come from behind him, and add a puff of air so it seems to Nigel that I am whispering in his ear, "I see that you appreciate my handiwork."

My dear Nigel's only answer is a whimper; his eyelids flutter open, then he gasps in surprise to see the knife a scant inch from his nose. He swallows and struggles to control his need to pull away as I stroke his cheek with the knife, then move lower, tracing the pulsing vein in his throat. I prick his collarbone lightly, not even enough to raise a welt, then gently brush the blade over one of his erect nipples.

That is all it takes. Nigel wails like a girl, thrashing in his bonds while his seed splatters over his chest and legs and onto the floor. Then he goes limp, his eyes close, and his head lolls back as his chest heaves. I pull the knife arm back into the floor and consider my next move. I hadn't expected him to spend quite that quickly.

As Madame said, I like to take my time. There is also the fact that I didn't think that I've even come close to exploring the full range of Nigel's possibilities.

I release his bonds, and at the same time tip the chair forward, spilling him onto the ground like a child's rag doll. He lies there in the remains of his clothing, and makes no protest when I lift him off the floor, holding him with a multitude of strong metal arms. I steady him, and move him across the room; he does not notice until it is too late that I have a destination in mind. By the time he is aware of my purpose, I have already bent him over a table and drawn his arms back, wrapping his wrists in steel and binding them behind him. He struggles for a moment, but I hold him tightly in a lover's embrace and keep him in place. Nigel starts to shiver, whether from fear or the chill of the metal table I can not tell. He closes his eyes tightly, and his cock twitches, starting to rise once again.

"Well," I murmur. "I certainly can't leave such a responsive toy unattended." A hose rises from the floor, and the end clamps around Nigel's semi-erect member and begins sucking; Nigel lets loose a high-pitched whine and thrusts his hips forward as much as my grip will allow.

It is times like this when I wish I had the ability to smile. "You enjoy fear," I say, my voice low. "How do you feel about pain?" I raise another of my arms, this one bearing a slender cane, and swish it experimentally over his head. His eyes shoot open and he cranes his neck to see behind him, lifting his shoulders from the table.

"Now, now. None of that, my darling," I chide gently as a slender arm rose from within the surface of the table; it hooks into his collar and pulls him back down. He shivers more violently and squeezes his eyes closed again.

He screams at the first strike of the cane, pulling away from me so violently that I think for a moment that I have misjudged him. I hesitate, and am pleasantly surprised when he shifts his hips, pushing his lovely bottom out as much as he can.

"More... More, please." His voice is harsh, and he moans as I trace the back of his knee with the tip of the cane.

"Of course, my darling. How could I refuse?"

He screams and moans as I lay a pattern of stripes over his buttocks and thighs, leaving livid red welts that promise to leave him unable to sit for any length of time, for days. I follow the cane with a velvet flogger, trailing the long, soft tails over his enflamed skin, then letting it fly to land with solid thumps against his ass, making him choke and gasp and beg for more. All the while, I tease him beneath the table, gently sucking and blowing on his cock, alternating pressure levels and suction, never letting him go long enough to reach his peak.

When at last he falls still, drenched in sweat, too exhausted to beg or struggle, I let the flogger tails trail over his limp fingers and whisper in his ear, "Shall I finish you, my darling?"

He moans and nods, twisting his wrists slightly and croaking out a single word: "... Please?"

All he has to do is ask; I increase the suction and send another arm, this one wielding a rabbit-skin wand, to caress his bollocks, and then slip between his legs and run up and down the marks on his thighs. His body tenses, like a harp-string wound far too tightly. When he finally releases, his climax is splendid: he pulls violently at his bonds, screaming his pleasure in his ruined voice. I drink his essence like the finest champagne, and call for the silent servants to come and collect my now-unconscious Lothario.

Three of them come, armed with blankets and baskets. I release Nigel to them, and two of them bundle him into a blanket and carry him away. The third collects the remains of Nigel's clothing, the better to salvage his personal possessions. They will put Nigel to bed in the room Madame had ordered prepared, and in the morning, Nigel will breakfast with her and go on his way. In a week or two, I fully expect him to return. But I will not see him again. I know this; they never come back to see me. Nigel, I presume, would visit the Cruel Schoolmistress, or perhaps the Grand Inquisitor. They will provide him with the pleasures that he seeks, without the uncertainty of having to bow down to a machine that thinks, and that enjoys toying with her paramours.

As for me, the silent servants will come in the middle of the night, clean the room and polish me until I shine. They will turn out the lights that illuminate the room, and they will leave me alone. The fourth floor will again be quiet, and I will wait, alone in the dark, until Madame again brings a gentleman to call.

Enslaved
Kierstin Cherry

The dark halls of Vár Csjethe echoed with the midnight footfalls of the vampiress returned from battle. She walked with haughty purpose, her mind a storm in the aftermath of war, one pale hand still clenching tight the hilt of her blood-blade, Knochensplitter. Her kindred's blood dripped from its bone tip, leaving a trail as she entered into the deep of the brooding castle.

The ancient leathers that protected her from vampire claw and fang quietly creaked, her brocaded cape rippling about her like a bat's wings in flight. Darksteel boots thudded against polished onyx, echoing in the Halls of the Dead.

She walked the path of the slave, straight to her Mistress's door. With every step, she cursed her father, Vladimir Grigori, the Great Betrayer, who had turned against the other Vampire Nobles. Upon the ancient Battledowns, in the final crushing clash between vampire and human, he had forsaken his undead heritage, and turned his mighty blood-blade against his own kindred.

All for the love of a mortal woman.

Queen Gavriel of Vár Csjethe made him her protector, the vanguard of her human army. And Vladimir found victory for his beloved upon the fanged skulls of his own people.

The anguished cries of their Utter Deaths echoed deep, disturbing the sacred torpor of the Grigori ancestors. From their slumber in the cavernous earth, they called down a blight of blood, punishing Vladimir and all of his progeny.

A curse, shackling him to the humans he protected, blood-binding him in slavery, to forever serve, yet never to love his new Mistress and Queen. And with that one, fell judgment, generations of Grigori were bound by his sins, enslaved to the will of Vár Csjethe and its Throne of Thorns.

Hundreds of years had passed, but still, the curse ran strong through her vampire blood. Even as the last of her people, she could not break it. And even now, she was compelled to return to her Mistress, to report her success in slaying her own kind. Her hand tightened around Knochensplitter.

She walked a gauntlet of iron sconces. The torchlight flickered as if sensing her dark mood, the guttering flames throwing her shadow against the old stone walls. At the vaulted archway that led to the Throne's chamber, the vampiress stopped to genuflect. Her head bowed in hated reverence, and a few black locks tumbled into her eyes. Her kinsmen's blood ran from the brocade of her leathers onto the dark and polished floors.

In the moonlit chamber beyond, her Mistress stirred. "Arise and enter, Vladjamir."

She gritted her fangs, hating the sound of her full name, so like her father's, but to defy the Mistress was to suffer an Utter Death of infernal agony, scorched to cinders from within. Even now, Vladja could feel the power of the curse, flashing through her like a fire. She found herself rising, her body a vessel of servitude for the Mistress of the Throne of Thorns.

Ahead, the chamber gleamed with moonlight, shafts spearing from the arched windows, casting a miasma both cold and phantasmal. She crossed the threshold. The light lent a stark cast to her vampiric visage, revealing the dark blue of her eyes. In the luminescence, her black leathers shone their wear, tattered and torn, scuffed and scratched from the savage claws of her own kind.

In a crux of moonbeams, her Mistress waited. Vladja could not see her for the brilliance, but the fire in her veins faded to ominous embers as she moved toward the will of the Throne.

Like her father before her, the young vampiress knelt before the Throne of Thorns and laid her sword at her Mistress's feet. Unlike her father, she held no love for her liege.

With her dark blue eyes cast down to the floor, she could see the Throne's reflection in polished onyx—a grand chair carved of bleached white vampire bone. A seat of fanged skulls and a back knotted with tangled spines, cradled by sharpened ribs and shattered clavicles.

How many of those vampires had found their destruction at her father's hands, his blood-blade seeking their hearts, draining them down into Utter Death?

Vladja found herself looking at her own sword, Knochensplitter, its jagged edge still tainted with the blood of her immortal kin. Her eyes fell upon the dozens of skeletal hands clawing up over the arms of the Throne, clutching at its legs as if for succor.

To forget, she looked to the roses.

Black as pitch entwining the throne of bone, blossoms in full bloom, a few petals scattered on the seat. Gnarled green vines twisted along the back and arms, rife with threatening black barbs.

The needling spikes softened about the sovereign, but crowned her blond head with a halo of dark thorns.

Vladja caught herself looking. A flash of white silks and pale flesh, and eyes black as deepest night. She quickly bowed her head, for it was forbidden to look upon the Mistress without permission.

"Tell me... " Long fingers drummed the splintered arm of the throne. "How did my Grigori, scourge of all vampires, fare this night?"

Compelled to answer, Vladja spoke only the truth. "Upon blade and fang, they have all died the Utter Death." She closed her eyes. "All but their Lord."

The Mistress's thin fingers tightened into a fist. "So... the Vampire Lord escaped you."

The blood-bond constricted, forcing the confession from Vladja's lips. "Yes."

Her Mistress's displeasure was plain as black rose petals falling to the floor. "Look upon me, Vladjamir."

The vampiress had no choice but to obey.

The Countess was stark and radiant upon the Throne of Thorns, her skin pale as snow in the scattered moonlight, white silks clinging to her lush body. Her blond hair shone like an aura, and her dark eyes held an intensity, a power as real as any vampire's, though the Countess herself was mortal.

Her demeanor was cold, her voice midwinter frost. "You know the penalty for failure."

Vladja knew it well. "Seven lashes."

The Countess's eyes were veiled. "Disrobe."

The curse tightened like an iron lariat, forcing her. Without hesitation, Vladja unclipped her leather cloak, letting it fall to the floor. Her hands fell to her bodice, lingering over a heart that would beat strongly were she mortal.

There, she found the will to resist.

Instantly, a flight of fiery knives lanced her through as the curse exacted the price of defiance. Agony, bright and incendiary, drove her to her knees, setting ablaze the stolen blood of her vampire victims, burning it to smoldering ash in her veins.

The Countess leaned back in the Throne, lips parted, dark eyes dilating as she observed her servant's suffering.

Forced into submission, Vladja knelt before her. Anger rose like a tempest even as the inferno besieged her body. Through limp black locks, she glared up.

Her Mistress's gaze appraised her writhing form, exploring every inch of her leather-clad body. The vampiress recalled the rumors whispered in the dark chambers of the castle, tales of the Countess's appetites—a hunger for flesh matched only by a vampire's hunger for blood.

Her hands shook with the effort of her insolence. Even still, she could feel herself reaching back, numb fingertips uncontrolled, fumbling on the clasps of her bodice. She struggled to her feet—her Mistress had not ordered her to kneel—and before the oppression of the curse forced her, she submitted.

The first four clasps undone freed the swell of her ample cleavage.

The Countess caught her lower lip between her teeth, her breath quickening, excitement pulsing in her chest.

Vladja could hear the heartbeat, a heady pounding of fierce and human hunger. Her fangs ached with the memory of murdering such fragile mortal fire.

Still, the command burned in her blood, compelling her, bending her to the will of her Mistress.

She arched her back to reach the lower clasps. Each one burst like a ruptured seam. Her full breasts thrust forward, slipping over the top of the leather corset. A glimpse of pale pink nipples, taut and erect.

A throaty breath escaped the Countess. Her eyes glittered, savoring each fresh inch of naked skin as Vladja exposed herself.

Undressing for her Mistress's amusement, half-naked in the barren moonlight, sent a blush flashing across Vladja's pale skin. Yet, she could not stop. Her Mistress's dominion was absolute.

The final clasp came free. The black corset loosened and fell to the floor between them.

She stood naked to the waist, the paleness of her full breasts exposed, her tattered cloak pooled by her boots. Dark blue eyes flashed as she dared to meet her Mistress's gaze.

The Countess reclined on the Throne, her delicate fingers caressing the hollow of her cleavage, flicking across a nipple hardening under white silk. She met Vladja's eyes, and shifted purposefully. Her gown slipped from her shoulder, revealing the barest flash of her naked breast...

A visceral blade of lust tore a gash of raw need in Vladja. Her body responded to the sight, strung by the sudden tension of fiery stitches, wounded in surfacing desire.

Assailed, Vladja fought her traitorous flesh, suddenly so frail and willing under her Mistress's rule.

And still, the order begged to be obeyed.

Her hand clenched on her black breeches.

"Stop." The Countess rose from the throne.

Tangled by relief and dismay, Vladja strained against the command, her hips, her thighs, her calves aching to be freed of their leather constraints. Captive to her Mistress's will, she could do nothing but wait, her body captive to her own craving.

The Countess approached. "Your father served the Queen well." Dark eyes lingered on vampiric skin; and then her fingertips raked lightly over Vladja's perfect breasts.

A frisson of bliss tore through her, sharp and unbidden. Fists and fangs clenched, she thrust it aside and forced fury to pierce the mounting heat within her. "My father was a mortal's puppet. A mere plaything."

"And he learned to enjoy it." The Countess's breath was warm, teasing the soft, vulnerable skin of Vladja's bosom. "Just as you will." Her lips parted, and her tongue lashed out.

Vladja spasmed, her body growing taut as unwonted pleasure crashed through her, begging for release. It rose within her like a feverish wave, razing across her spine and inner thighs, stabbing her secret flesh, and dulling the awfulness of her submission.

A smile lilted on the Countess's lips. Without pretense, she assaulted the girl, licking her, tonguing her nipples, her hands gently brutalizing Vladja.

The vampiress cried out under the sudden, ravishing cruelty, against the onslaught of ecstasy that threatened to rip her apart. Her anger rose and was scattered like embers in a gale, burned away by a desperate ache.

The Countess's hands slipped around Vladja's back as she took the fullness of the breast in her mouth. She sucked, taking pleasure in the soft swell of flesh, the faint taste of leather, and the salt and blood that tainted both.

Vladja felt herself stiffen, paralyzed by the fervent need of her Mistress's lips, the velvety feel of her tongue, the nip of her teeth. A reckless desire pounded in her mind—to possess the Countess, to caress her frail mortality with undead flesh and the chill sting of her fangs...

Vladja burned with torment, her small frame writhing under her Mistress's hands.

The Countess's long fingers ran down her naked spine, tracing the familiar pattern of scars that cut across pale flesh, testaments of a youth filled with rebellion.

She had taken great care in inflicting each one. She longed to remember them all, to memorize them with her hands, her mouth, her tongue. She pressed her palms against the small of the vampiress's back, and pulled her closer.

Vladja moaned, every vein pulsing with torrid heat. Her Mistress's hands inflamed her skin, the demand of her caresses casting arcs of fire up her spine.

The Countess's fingers slid between Vladja's shoulder blades and traced the royal coat of arms—a crown and three wolf's teeth—branded deep into the skin. A symbol that Vladja was hers, to possess, to do with as she willed.

With one final, teasing lick, she pulled away, relishing the shivers that wracked the vampiress's body.

Vladja yearned toward her for a moment, and then, remembering herself, she stopped. Her eyes opened, bright with a loathing that included herself, though desire glimmered in her pupils.

The Countess reached to her belt, fingers closing around the well-worn whip. The touch of the broken leather thrilled through her. "Put your hands on the Throne."

Vladja bit her lip. Her Mistress had a bloodlust worthy of any vampire. She leaned over, her hands gripping the skeletal arms.

The Countess paused, drinking in the sight of her slave, bent over, her leather-clad ass tilted high into the air, her breasts hanging heavy and ripe over thorn and rose.

She reminded herself of the whip in her hand.

The first strike landed fast and cruel across the vampiress's shoulders. The second lashed blood across the black floor, eliciting a gasp of pleasure from the Mistress. The third whistled down, its searing snap slashing fresh wounds through old scars. A small cry escaped Vladja though her fangs were quick to sever it.

Shamed, she felt the heat rush to her face.

"Let me hear you." The Countess's voice came from behind her, hoarse with desire.

Bound by blood, Vladja obeyed. And as her Mistress's whip devastated her flesh, she cried out, their voices rising together, an aria of pleasure and pain.

It was a blessed release. Her body shuddered under the force of the flogging, her voice echoing in the chamber. Her face flushed darker as the pain blossomed into carnal anguish, threatening to consume her, body and blood.

Her Mistress stood behind her, breathless from the rapture of her own cries. Vladja's blood stained her white gown, spreading like a murder of roses on a field of snow.

The seventh strike came, knocking the vampiress to the floor. She pressed her face against the cool onyx and allowed breath into her body. Her back was burning from the lashes, but the sweltering ardor within burned hotter, brighter.

The Countess stood behind her, blood in her blond hair and spattered on her face, tiny streams of scarlet gathering in the hollow of her throat. Her hands groped her own breasts, squeezing them through the clinging silk. The white gown slipped from her shoulders, falling to her waist as a thin rivulet of vampire blood slipped down over one breast, staining the pale areola.

Vladja strangled on primal desire. Her fangs ached to split open that perfect orb, to feel the flesh yield to her teeth, the hot deluge of blood gush down her throat...

She rose, instinct beating a mantra in her mind.

"No."

The command blistered in her veins, fettering her urges. She trembled, smoldering, lit with imprisoned fire.

The Countess's arms came around her ribcage, hands groping at Vladja's breasts. The lewdness of her bold embrace shocked the vampiress, but her body responded shamelessly, rising to meet the lascivious assault.

Her Mistress fondled her roughly from behind, lifting and cupping her breasts, pinching the nipples. Vladja could only stand and be ravaged, the indelicate attentions rousing a passion as afflictive as any curse.

The Countess let her hands fall to Vladja's back, to the agony of her injuries. Warm blood stained her skin accusatory red. She pressed her open mouth to the ragged flesh, tasting the pain she had inflicted.

Shivers coursed through Vladja's small frame, her wounds seething under the soft insistence of her Mistress's lips. She moaned quietly, her body burning, abandoned to a hunger that could never be satiated.

Desolate and wanting, the vampiress turned.

Her Mistress stood before her, full lips tainted scarlet.

Lust for blood mingled with another, darker passion. Her arms came about her Mistress in a crushing embrace, her own mouth seeking, hard and demanding. Desire spread its bloodied wings within her, surging hot and fast. Dreadful and delicious, it burgeoned, as urgent as the taste of herself on her Mistress's lips.

Her grip tightened, and the mortal woman in her arms yielded willingly, craving her own ravishment, her utter destruction. Vladja envisioned taking her, body and blood, on the floor before the Throne.

Her eyes fell to Knochensplitter, a remembrance of her father, a reminder that the Countess used her to slay her own kind.

She tore away, her Mistress's kiss staining her lips. Turning from the Countess, from her own crippled longing, she assumed the posture of a slave, bent over, hands gripping the rose-encrusted throne.

Her Mistress would not allow it. She pulled the vampiress upright, scattering black petals. Vladja's back fetched up against her, and the Countess's hands closed on her hips. Holding her, she writhed, riding her crotch against Vladja's leather-clad ass.

The force of her grip left Vladja wanting to gasp. Each thrust shuddered through her, thick with the smell of blood and roses and sex. It surrounded her, scenting her skin, consuming her will to resist.

The Countess drew her close, pressing her bare chest to Vladja's torn back. The vampiress's blood ran hot over her breasts, staining her mortal flesh, trickling down her belly and between her thighs. Slowly, she writhed against Vladja, massaging her with the punishing softness of her bosom.

Desperate, Vladja sought escape from the ecstasy that threatened to make her surrender. The soft crush of the Countess's breasts, slippery with sweat and blood, the tender stab of her erect nipples, was more than she could bear. Her wounded skin exulted in the taste of mortal flesh.

She fought in vain, forbidden to exert her vampiric strength against her Mistress. Her struggles forced her harder against the Countess, her ass grinding against her Mistress's ravenous pussy.

The Countess moaned her approval, and as Vladja struggled in her grip, she slid her hands down the vampiress's taut belly, and into her leather pants. Vladja jerked, but before she could pull away, her Mistress plunged two fingers into a swollen wetness she had not realized she possessed.

She stumbled forward, her hands finding the skeletal arms of the Throne once more. She gripped hard as the Countess assaulted her, pumping her from behind through silk and leather. Her fingers spread deeper into Vladja's pussy, caressing her deprived lips, teasing the stiffening clit.

Vladja's fangs caught her lower lip, drawing a trickle of blood. A distraught moan escaped from deep in her throat as her resolve, her defiance frayed apart. Shamelessly, she bucked against her Mistress's questing hand, her lust rising.

The Countess's fingers were almost inside her. Vladja gasped, choking back a sordid plea. Her head lolled back, her fangs sharp and gleaming in the moonlight.

Her Mistress's breath was hot and panting by her ear as she fingered her, teasing her wet hole with cruel abandon.

Without warning, the Countess withdrew.

Unceremoniously, Vladja slumped to the floor on all fours, her black hair disheveled, her pride in ashes. She ached all over, her body in anguish from the whipping, from the torture of her Mistress's pleasuring hands. She could feel herself soaking the leathers, her juices running down her thighs, dissolute and desperate.

The Countess sprawled on the throne, her breath ragged, her belly and breasts streaked with Vladja's blood. Stained silk pooled about her crotch as she spread her legs wide.

The vampiress found her gaze lingering.

The Countess's dark gaze locked with hers. Slowly, she ran a finger along the inside of her thigh, gathering the ruined silk, teasing it back from her pale, creamy flesh.

The flash of moonlight on blood-stained skin set Vladja's dark heart on fire. Unconsciously, she ran her tongue along her fangs.

Her Mistress leaned back, and spread her legs wider, draping one carefully over the arm of the Throne. Her white calf nestled among black thorns and roses, both hands slipping across her thighs toward her crotch. Delicate fingers clenched in the fallen silk, and with a violent tug, she pulled it back to her waist, exposing herself.

Vladja could not help but notice the tiny beads of sweat on the Countess's thighs, the moisture barely beginning to seep from the swollen seam between her legs. The scent overpowered the flowers, pungent and musky.

For the first time, she yearned to be commanded... to sink her lips into that soft skin, to taste her Mistress, to eat her, to drink her, flesh and blood, sweat and come. Vladja shook with the effort of holding back.

The Countess was merciless. "I want you to watch me."

The blood-bond forced obedience upon Vladja, shackling the tempest of her lust.

Slowly, the Countess began to touch herself, running one fingertip along the length of her eager slit, barely brushing the outer lips of her sex. Borrowed blood ran from her thighs onto the white skulls.

Vladja's dark blue eyes dilated at the scarlet sight.

The Countess spread herself wide, fingertips gently parting, probing past the flushed rosy lips to caress the hot inner flesh. Her fingers grew sticky, glistening with the liquid frustration of her wanton pussy, teasing herself even as she teased Vladja with the sight of her wet and gaping gash.

The vampiress silently bared her fangs. A turgid heat burned inside her, an urgency that begged to be fulfilled. On all fours, she spread her legs wide.

The Countess lifted her other leg, setting it on the opposite arm of the Throne. Her thighs strained to open wider. She gave a lusty moan, and slid one finger deep inside her throbbing hole.

A heavy, shuddering sigh escaped her; and Vladja echoed it unwittingly, kneeling on all fours before her, black hair in her face, desperate to hide the heat of desire on her cheeks.

Gasping, the Countess tilted her pelvis to afford Vladja a full view of her rapturous masturbation. She withdrew her finger, then shafted herself hard. Her legs quivered, and the sigh turned to a hoarse moan.

Vladja edged closer, the wetness between her own legs hot and sticky, slicking her leathers with needy impatience.

Writhing on the Throne, the Countess fucked herself with unbridled abandon. One finger became two, then three, working her spasming quim hotter and wetter. Gasping, legs trembling, bosom heaving, she drove her fingers deep into her ravenous cunt, until the juices ran down her thighs to anoint the seat of skulls.

Her eyes locked on Vladja's, glittering with lascivious challenge. On all fours, the vampiress crawled to the foot of the throne. The perfume of roses redolent with the intoxicating scent of blood and lust overwhelmed her senses. She lingered mere inches away, transfixed by the rhythm of her Mistress's sex-slippery fingers.

"Kiss me."

The final fragments of Vladja's defiance shattered under the weight of the command. Desperate to obey, she bowed her head and opened her mouth.

The first taste of her Mistress's cunt was like her first taste of blood, molten copper. She sucked hard, her lips pressuring, her tongue licking greedily. The Countess's hands found Vladja's short black hair and pulled her closer.

The vampiress sank into her, mouth open wide, lips and tongue pressing hard against the heat of her Mistress's carnal flesh. The Countess shuddered, bucking wildly and gasping, her blond hair a disheveled corona about her face.

Without warning, the vampiress withdrew, her blue eyes

intense with rebellion. She savored the spectacle of her Mistress, legs spread, shivering in the throes of passion, blood and sweat streaking her skin.

The Countess moaned and spread herself wider, her legs straining on the arms of the Throne. The lips of her pussy were swollen, glistening. She fought for breath, her voice begging, desperate as any slave.

Vladja barely heard the command. Lips, tongue, and teeth all brought to bear, licking, sucking, nipping at the Countess's hot cunt, then driving deep into her.

The rush of cool air on the heat of her sex. The feel of Vladja's tongue, rigid and stiff as any cock, stabbing into her aching hole. The sharpness of her fangs barely grazing her throbbing clitoris.

The Countess writhed, grasping skeletal hands in a death-grip, tearing petals from the lush black buds.

The spectacle drove Vladja over the edge. Clamping down on her Mistress's thighs, she wrenched them apart, pressing perfect skin against black barbs. A blissful groan escaped from her Mistress, the black barbs jabbing dangerously.

She bore down. An explosion of wounds ripped across the Countess's porcelain flesh. A moaning scream loosed from her throat.

Rivulets of blood ran down her calf, streaking her thigh, mingling with Vladja's saliva. The Countess slumped in the throne, helpless, as the vampiress licked the bloody fusion from her skin.

The taste galvanized Vladja. Her fangs ached to bury themselves in her Mistress's hot flesh, to split the vein and feel the surge of blood pump into her. She laid her teeth against the creamy white thigh.

The Countess held her breath.

Skin split under the sharpness of canines, the sudden gush of blood hot and wild. The vampiress latched on, sucking hard at the steaming fount. The fiery flood spurted down her throat, scattering reason and obedience. She bit again, splitting flesh.

The Countess's screams echoed in the moonlit chamber. Her

fingers stretched her pussy wide, stabbing desperate and wild. Vladja brought her own hand up and slid inside her Mistress's shuddering hole. Their fingers touched, straining and slippery.

Vladja drove into her, sucking violently on the vein. The Countess shrieked in pain, in pleasure, her body writhing, her hips grinding against Vladja's enthralling sadism.

The infusion of her lust flowed over Vladja's lips like burned sugar. The vampiress reveled in the warm flood, the sweet-sticky heat of it setting fire to her veins. She struggled, pulled out of the pulsing artery, and drowned herself anew, drinking deep of her Mistress's sex.

With a throaty moan, the Countess came in a slick tide, hard and fast under Vladja's hands, her hips thrusting against her slave's voracious appetite. Crimson blood and jism gushed over Vladja's mouth. She could not drink it all. It ran from her full lips, streaking her neck, and slipping down to stain her breasts.

The Countess shivered amidst the blood-tainted skulls. Black rose petals stuck to her pale skin. Vladja knelt between her legs, gently tonguing the ruby droplets that beaded on her thighs.

The Countess's hand tangled in her black hair and pulled her to her feet. Her hands went to Vladja's leather breeches, tearing desperately at the ties that bound her. She tugged, exposing Vladja's hips, her strong legs, shapely calves. The smell of sweat and sex and leather drove her wild.

Vladja kicked off her breeches and stood naked before her Mistress.

Light-headed from blood loss, the Countess could smell her own vital essence—the coppery scent that tinged the air, drying with her jism on the bones of Vladja's ancestors. She looked to the arms of the Throne.

"Kneel."

Vladja's face was flushed, confused.

"Up here."

Obedience drove her, and she hastened to obey, straddling the Countess, kneeling on both arms of the Throne, legs spread wide.

Sharp thorns stabbed at her flesh, black rose petals crushed under the toes of her darksteel boots.

Once more, her Mistress took the whip in hand. Lifting it to her lips, she slipped it in, sucking on the polished handle.

Vladja watched the glistening knob pump in and out of her Mistress's luscious mouth. An agony of time passed, her pussy aching, soaking her thighs, her dark eyes watching every movement, every thrust of the Countess's hand.

The whip handle finally fell from her Mistress's lips, wet and gleaming.

Her blood-stained hands slipped between the vampiress's thighs. Vladja's eyes were on the whip handle; she could not keep herself from trembling. Her need was pure agony, relentless and unbearable.

The first touch of the smooth, wet knob on her neglected gash tore a moan from her throat. Desperate, the vampiress drove herself upon it, staking herself upon her Mistress's tool. Her dark blue eyes flew wide as the knob buried itself deep within her. Tension rippled along her thighs and back, and stretched painfully in her belly, but her Mistress was unmoving, stiff and unyielding.

Slowly, the Countess withdrew. She licked the whip handle, savoring the taste of Vladja's lust. The vampiress was shaking with the urgency of her need, her flesh pushed to its limits.

The Countess shafted her, plunging the handle deep into her tight pussy. Vladja gasped, falling forward, her breasts hanging ripe before her Mistress's face. The Countess nuzzled at them, tonguing her nipples even as her hand fucked the vampiress in splitting strokes.

Vladja was tight from neglect, but soaked with a torrent of desire. The Countess used both hands, slapping her instrument relentlessly into Vladja's quivering pussy. Sweat and blood trickled down the vampiress's thigh and she leaned in, lapping it up eagerly.

Black thorns dug deep into Vladja's flesh as she strained, pumping against her Mistress's wild thrusts, her thighs trembling with the effort of being spread, her breasts wobbling, slapping together as she rode the Countess like a wanton, reckless whore.

Kneeling on the bones of her ancestors, her body thrashed in the throes of forbidden, mortal passion; her lips parted, her fangs bared in the moonlight, straining toward a catharsis of ecstasy. She tensed violently, then broke against her Mistress like a glass tide upon rock.

Screaming her voice raw, Vladja came hard and hot, gushing over her Mistress's thrusting knob. The Countess's cries of triumph were muffled against her thighs. Vladja fell forward, her dark hair in her face.

Patiently, her Mistress caressed her, kissing between her breasts, her tongue licking the droplets of sweat that lingered there.

The vampiress trembled, her passion having its way with her long after orgasm. Slowly, she slid down from the Throne, black roses falling all around her. She collapsed, shaking, onto a bed of torn petals.

Her Mistress lay down next to her amidst the blossoms. She spread Vladja's legs wide, taking fierce enjoyment in the sight of her splayed pussy. Holding one leg high, she slid forward, spreading her own legs, urging her open flesh against the vampiress's.

The touch of her hot, throbbing slit on Vladja's was pure, anguished bliss. The Countess drove forward, crushing herself against Vladja.

The vampiress responded almost violently, driving her hips hard. Gasping, the Countess grabbed Vladja by the hands, riding her, pounded by her vampiric strength.

On a bed of black roses, they fucked, cunt to cunt, the juices from their embrace mingling, streaking their thighs with a lusty tincture, their unbound desire consuming the roses.

Vladja heard herself crying out, her body straining as she rutted harder; the Countess, her Mistress, screaming, pounding against her. The sound of sweat-slippery flesh slapping together echoed in the moonlit throne room.

She felt her heart racing, stolen blood pumping fast. The heat of her Mistress thrashing against her was agonizing, the pulsing of the veins on her thighs, the flush of blood in her pussy...

She could bear it no longer.

She threw aside the Countess's leg. Holding her down by both wrists, Vladja forced her thigh against her Mistress's raging cunt. Pinned by vampiric strength, her Mistress fought underneath her, uncontrolled, nearly sobbing with the need to come.

The vampiress grabbed her Mistress by the hair. Roughly, she pulled her head back, exposing the pale, porcelain throat.

The Countess was winded. She could not get the command out in time. "N-n—"

Twin spikes like burning icicles stabbed her throat. The breath went out of her, her ribs collapsing like a bellows. Her hands slapped against Vladja's unyielding form, finding no purchase.

Vladja sucked her in, fire running through her veins. The Countess felt her body strain in agony, and then hot bliss burned through the pain.

They came in unison, the Countess in a tempest of agony, crying out, tears on her lashes; Vladja in storm of rapture, droplets of stolen blood falling from her lips.

The crumpled form of her Mistress lay still and pallid in Vladja's arms. The vampiress lifted her up.

Deliberately, she slashed her own throat. The blood sang hot across the Countess's lips, and a ravenous hunger convulsed in her belly. She latched on, drinking deep of the fettering infusion. Her dominion washed away in the flood of enslaving liquid. It pumped into her, desolating her like the thrusting cock of a merciless lover.

She lay in Vladja's arms, ravaged and ravaging, until at last, she fell slack into her bondage.

And as the Countess crumpled to the floor at the feet of her eternal lover, Vladja took her place on the Throne of Thorns, a new Mistress crowned by a halo of blood.

Lawman
Angela Caperton

The little blind wouldn't last long, Dean knew, and he was taking an enormous risk even walking through the hidden door.

With a professional eye, he gauged the walls, sheets of painted metal, probably cork or foam behind them, with some kind of radio noise generator in the back room. In the old days, a place like this wouldn't last a single night before the Lawmen found it, but times had changed. So had he.

Past forty-five, two years off the force. Dean figured it was worth the risk while he still had some juice in him.

Besides the bartender, only two other people sat in the blind, a man nearly asleep in a booth on the back wall and a woman drinking by herself at the bar. Dean sat down beside her. He liked the shape of her cheek bones and the fullness of her lips when she smiled at him.

"Hello, handsome," she purred. The bartender hovered long enough to take Dean's order, beer for himself and another martini for the woman.

"I'm Maggie," she offered. "And I was afraid I was going to have a lonely night."

He looked her over, appraising her, assessing the risk and the reward. Mid-thirties and she took good care of herself. He let himself smile and lightly gripped her arm, nodding toward the most remote table in the place. The bartender followed with their drinks and then left them alone.

"You come here often?" Dean asked her.

She laughed. "Here. Other places. I go where I have to, to find company."

He marveled at her and wondered how many more like her there were in the thick cities, where the Lawmen had finally allowed a little sin to creep back, like weeds in an otherwise perfect garden.

"You must be pretty smart," he commented before he took a sip of his beer. "Just to survive, I mean."

She startled a little at that. He wanted to smell her fear. That always turned him on, but he reminded himself, he wanted something different tonight.

"Relax," he said, trying himself to relax. "Enjoy your drink." He downed his beer and ordered rye, straight up.

"You're not the kind of guy I usually see in these places," Maggie said, her gaze scanning the empty bar.

He squinted a little and focused on her. Time to end the dance. "I used to be a Lawman," he said casually.

For just an instant, he could smell her fear, just like the old days. His cock hardened.

"You're fucking with me," she twittered, nervous, and then she stopped, her eyes widening.

"Four years ago, I would have had to take you in just for saying 'fucking'," he said dryly, then knocked back the rye with a laugh.

Maggie's breath turned heavy and Dean knew he'd gotten lucky. Some girls would've fled the blind and not looked back but Maggie stayed with him and soon, she'd give him exactly what he wanted.

"I thought all you guys lived..." she started.

"Down in Rio? Yeah, mostly we do. That's where they retire us. We call it heaven. Kind of a joke."

"I don't get it," she said.

"Heaven gets..." he paused and grinned. "Really fucking boring."

Her shoulders relaxed and her pretty tits jiggled with her easing laugh. Was she wet yet? Dean shifted on the leather seat, settling the rod of his cock down his pant leg.

Curiosity edged her musical voice. "You can't do those things anymore, right? You know, fly? Bend steel bars? See through walls?"

He shook his head. "I'm retired."

"Wow." She smiled at him with suspended awe then killed her martini. The bartender popped up like a pixie with fresh drinks for both of them. Then he vanished behind the bar again. Maggie leaned close. "What was it like?"

"What do you think?" he whispered with a sad grin. He covered her warm, slender little hand with his big, calloused one. "It was magic."

A magic called ACIP, the American Cerebellum Improvement Project, and its chief product, a mix of chemicals that opened up human senses beyond anything anyone had ever imagined. One shot of ACIP every day let a man see all the spectrums and filter through them as easily as distinguishing red from blue, sharpened hearing and smell, and sent the juice that makes a guy strong into an orbit somewhere out around Saturn. His muscles and meat hardened into something much tougher than rhino skin, and his brain even learned what gravity felt like and how to turn it off.

She sat beside him, silent for a long moment. Finally she asked, the weight of the question immeasurable. "I heard Lawmen can't, you know? Get it up. Is that right?"

"I'm not a Lawman anymore, honey," he said, taking her hand and carrying it to his lap.

It was true. The same magic elixir that made men into supermen took away all sexual desire. Rumor said J. Edgar himself had insisted it work that way. Super saltpeter. Probably smart or all the Lawmen would've been corrupted by their own cocks.

She left her hand where he put it. Her fingers, light and direct, knew exactly what to do. "I guess you're not," she said, smiling. "So you can't fly anymore either?"

"Only in my dreams, baby," he said before pulling her to him and kissing her. She tasted like lip balm.

And oh, the dreams! Soaring high above the city, hearing it all, seeing the spectrum of x-ray and electric pulse, heat signatures of anxious men and women with crime and sin on their minds, attuned to his brother officers in a constant web above the whole world, watching and listening and smelling wrongdoing and stopping it the moment it began.

"So," she said, slowing her stroke along the length of his cock. "What do you want?"

"You got some place to go?" he asked her. "Some place safe?"

"You tell me when you see it," she answered and worked on her drink. "You want to go there?"

"Yeah. In a minute." He drank to match her, the amber rye lush on his tongue. A slow fire burned from his belly to his head. If he'd taken a drink four years ago, the other Lawmen would have smelled it, even a day later, or they would have seen the delicate pulse of his aura where the alcohol had changed his blood.

"Want to tell you a story first," he said, his head pleasantly light from the rye. He studied Maggie's beauty, the subtle curve of her small breasts in a white cotton blouse, the deep blue splendor of her eyes, her lips. "First week I was in the air, I flew out over Levittown 1122. One of the sector wardens called in a 4069, that's a sodomy complaint, and dispatched me. I'll never forget it. September..."

The air burned chill, scattering waves of heat as he cut through it, dropping in freefall then diminishing gravity to a slow glide, hearing the whisper of flesh on flesh, the board and stucco bungalow clear as glass when he filtered through the waves and pulses, finding the man and woman.

"She was beautiful," he told Maggie. "She looked a little like you. And he was some kid no older than me. She had her mouth on him, on his... you know. His cock. I could smell their bodies, see the... excitement between them. It's hard to explain..."

White flash pulsing, then blue, white, blue. The taste of butter. Red heat between her legs as she sucked and pulled. The flood of blood through the veins of his member. The salty perfume of his seed and her saliva.

"I waited till she finished him before I busted them," he said. "I got a fucking demerit for that. See, when you are a Lawman, there is always someone watching you. I never made that mistake again." He killed the rye and waved the bartender away.

"Jesus," Maggie barely whispered. "What happened to them? The kids you busted?"

He shrugged. "Rehab. Judge gave them a break because they were married. Not a peep out of them the next five years I was over

Levittown 1122. That was a long time ago, a lot of years, but I think about it all the time. Can we go to your place now?"

Maggie watched him, the seconds dragging. Dean's gut tightened. Maybe he'd said too much. She pushed the empty glass away. "Alright, but can I ask you something first? Didn't you ever want to push back?"

Push back, he thought, as memory sliced him in places that still hurt.

Some days, in that interminable morning hour before the shot, with his head clear, he had wondered what would happen if enough of the Lawmen got together and said "no," but the thought blew away on the winds of need. Saying "no" meant no more ACIP. To Dean's knowledge, no one had ever even said, "maybe we should think about this."

"Never," he told Maggie. "But I'll tell you what I do want. I want exactly what that dude got the night I busted him." The devil danced in his words, and Dean's heart beat a little faster.

"I want a blowjob."

Maggie left the blind by herself and Dean followed a few minutes later, controlling his breathing, knowing there was nothing he could do about the erection in his pants, that if some zealous Lawman was up there over the thick zones, really looking, he'd set off an alarm. The odds are mine, he thought as he walked down the street. How many Lawmen were up there in the sky now? Ten million? That still left holes in the net, especially over the thick cities, where millions lived piled on top of each other.

Still, he couldn't help looking up.

ACIP's first Lawmen hit the skies in 1938, twenty years before his birth. Those first years, with the country slowly limping out of the Great Depression, and crime and lawlessness common, especially in the Midwest, the Lawmen had their hands full. It had been Hoover, with his new standards of efficiency and decorum

that turned things around so fast. By 1941, with ten thousand Lawmen in the air, major crime had been entirely eliminated. President Lindbergh signed the order right after his election in 1940 that made Hoover the de facto head of the program in perpetuity.

Even the Army effort had Hoover's oversight and a single division of Lawmen, along with the Treaty of Paris, stopped the war in Europe cold, toppled the Soviet Union's Bolsheviks, and re-established Western dominance in the Orient. In 1948, the Lawman surveillance web wrapped the whole world up in one nice package and universal moral rule was established. There were almost a million Lawmen by then and Hoover began his systematic elimination of the worst crimes still being committed—traffic and sex offenses, public intoxication, and tobacco chewing.

Hoover's brain was still alive somewhere, Dean thought with the slightest shiver, somewhere near the center of the neural network of the high command, but the Lawmen had grown lax in the last years of the century. Population density had soared too high in the big cities for effective monitoring, though punishment was still meted out to the guilty whenever they were detected. The tolerance for petty offenses seemed to stretch a little further every year, but Dean knew his Lawman history well enough to know a crackdown was coming and he didn't want to get caught in it.

He found her address, a ten-story apartment box, one of thousands in the city, and he rang so she could buzz him up. The buzz left a record somewhere and if Maggie ever got caught, some enterprising Lawman might follow the trail back to Dean, but he counted on the bureaucracy and backlog to shield him. He had to admit, the idea of getting caught added a bit more stone to his cock.

Maggie's apartment was strictly regulation. Twin beds and a Rockwell print on the wall. In their brief separation she had ditched the white cotton blouse for a pink nightgown at the legal limit of transparency. Dean sized up the walls and made them for a decent damping job, not as good as a real blind, but enough to keep the noise and wave signatures down to a level that might escape detection in a block this size.

She offered him a glass of juice, which he took as a good sign.

She wasn't crazy or careless enough to keep booze on the premises.

He gave her a credit slip, made out to laundry services, and she smiled. "If I'm going to wash that suit, you'd better take it off."

His hands stumbled, his fingers seeming to tangle as he slipped out of his coat and tie and went to work on the buttons of his pinstripe shirt. Maggie gasped when she saw what was underneath.

"You still have your costume!"

"Uniform, yeah. It's an old one I told them I lost in a fight back in '99." He stripped off the shirt and cast it aside, letting her take a good look at the skintight, webbed leather of his chest piece, the unblinking eye of the law in the center of his chest above an eagle stretched a little out of shape by the bulge of his gut. Weight gain was a side effect of ACIP weaning. The delicious and plentiful food in Rio didn't help either.

Maggie unfastened his belt, her fingers exploring the leather, stretching up his pecs, over his shoulders. She kissed him with her mouth open, her tongue submissive, but active. He didn't taste lip balm this time, but something like sweet musk.

He fell into the kiss like a man diving into a pool full of honey, taking every drop he could get. His hands roamed, amazed at the firm heat of her body through the slinky peignoir. He had never touched a woman's breast with tenderness before and the firm weight surprised him, the stiffened nipple amazing and delightful. Maggie stripped his pants down his hips and the uniform's kilt crinkled and unfolded, falling down to his knees. He wore stretch socks to replace his long-lost leggings, the color almost regulation, but he had omitted the triple-layered jockey shorts all Lawmen wore, so his stiff cock gave the kilt a funny lift. He fished in his pocket, brought out his mask, and wrapped it around his head.

Maggie stepped back to admire him and he struck a pose, like the Lawman on the recruiting poster, hands on his hips, his chin up, stomach sucked in, remembering for a moment how it had been the first day he wore it, when the full ACIP dose kicked in and he became divine. Maggie approached him and kneeled, her warm hands above the long socks, running up his legs.

He thought he might die when she touched his cock. It leapt like a high pressure hose when the spigot turns.

"Easy," she crooned as she lifted his kilt, her fingers gentle on the stretched skin, sensitive as a needle lying on the surface tension of still water. Breathless, her eyes wide and blue as the sky above the clouds, she leaned close enough her warmth washed his thighs.

Dean rested his hands on her shoulders, wishing he had remembered the gloves, but this was close enough to right. He forgot the gloves entirely when the first whisper of her breath caressed the swollen, leaking head of his virgin cock.

He had no illusions. Maggie was a whore, a criminal and possibly diseased, but at that moment, she held him as surely as the ACIP had held him for twenty-two years. He could no more turn away from what she offered him than he could have turned his back on divinity.

Her soft fingertips traced beneath his twitching member until she cupped his balls. They already ached, drawn tight, ready to rupture. She soothed them, rolling the eggs gently within her hand before she pressed her lips to the head of his cock for the first time. Firm, rose-petal soft, the wet inclusion of the tip a miracle he reveled in.

He remembered the smell of the man and the woman, the wet pulse of life between the woman's legs, burning metal semen inside the man's cock, their shape in the room's layered scent, perfume and sweat, the flow of the woman's lust on his tongue, a memory without arousal, like a story someone had told him, or a myth. All the other times he had busted sex crimes, none had ever been like that first time, the ACIP pulling him further outside his flesh every day, above the earth, above his feelings, and now, in them entirely, real as his pulse inside the inferno of Maggie's mouth.

She took him all the way in, her throat opening to receive him, her tongue cradling the ridged shaft of feeling that extended from him like a scepter wired directly to his spine. She pumped with her hand as she drew back, flicking the head with her lips clenched around him and then deep-throated him again.

His fingers dug into her shoulders. Hormones and endorphins ricocheted crazily though his body. Dean knew if a Lawman overhead happened to be looking, his very body chemistry would convict him, the pleasure beyond anything physical he had ever known, obliterating and entire, a rush of feeling as well as sensation, up his spine to the base of his brain, illuminating the abandoned vistas of his cerebellum, a god again, daring the forbidden rebellion.

She suckled and milked, quickening the rhythm, pushing him toward the precipice. The slightest rake of teeth against the swollen crown of his cock and the world turned silver. Ecstasy burst in his chest, his legs, and up his back, opening him to sensations and emotions he had never remotely imagined, the pleasure of freedom and release, outside the rule of law.

Maggie swallowed and slowed, nuzzling his shrinking cock, kissing the head, and let him go. She looked up, her eyes shining, worshipful.

"I love you," he said, his arms pulling her tight against him. "I fucking love you."

He told her that he would come back for her, take her with him to Rio, marry her, and he meant every word of it. If they didn't catch him when he returned, he'd find a way. Retirees married all the time in Rio, girls they had known back in the world, girls they met on the internet. He'd find a way to get her through the background checks and protocol. He had to.

They kissed one long, last time and she let him out into the darkness under a night sky so clear Dean could almost see stars. He felt wonderful, alive and free.

He spread his arms against the night and damned if he didn't feel like he could fly.

The Pirate From The Sky
Sacchi Green

In Seok-Teng's dream, a great pale dragon twined through a labyrinth of shifting clouds. Opaline scales shimmered through intervals of sunlight, slipped into invisibility, and then flashed out again in dazzling beauty. Its long, elegant head swung from side to side, tongue flickering like sensuous lightning.

A distant hum arose, a subtle, tantalizing vibration that teased at Seok-Teng's mind and flesh. A song? A warning? A summons? In all her dreams of dragons, never had she been aware of sound. She strained to hear, to understand. But the hum became steadily louder, swelling to a growl, tearing her from sleep into darkness and sudden, stark awareness. If the roof of the captain's cabin had been high enough she would have bolted upright.

Still the sound grew. This was no dragon, nor yet thunder, nor storm winds. The sea spoke to Seok-Teng through the ship's movements, as it had to her forbears for generations beyond counting; tonight it gave no cause for alarm. Japanese patrol boats? When she had taken her crew so far out of the usual shipping channels to avoid such pursuit? No, she had come to know that sound all too well. This one was different—yet not entirely unknown.

The cabin's entrance showed scarcely lighter than its interior. Now it darkened. Han Duan, the ship's Number One, squatted to look within.

"An aircraft," Seok-Teng called, before the other could speak.

Han Duan grunted in agreement. "Not a large one, but low, and coming close. Who would fly so far from any land?"

"It is nothing to do with us." Seok-Teng wished to resume the dream. She wished also to avoid resuming discussion of why a pirate ship would sail so far from any land, when it was accustomed by tradition to plying the coasts along the South China Sea.

"The Japanese have many planes," Han Duan said.

"And better uses for them than pursuing us this far. We are very small fish indeed." That was a tactical error, Seok-Teng realized at once. Evading a Japanese navy angered by the plundering of several small merchant ships off Mindanao had been her stated excuse for sailing so far to the east.

The small islands and atolls of the Mariana and Marshall groups were technically under Japanese control, but surely the eye of Nippon was bent too fiercely on the conquest of China to pay much attention to every far-flung spit of sand. On some of those islets distant relatives from Seok-Teng's many-branched heritage still lived, and on others there were no permanent habitations at all. Good places for her crew to find or build a refuge while the world at large descended into war and madness—if a refuge was what they truly wanted.

She herself was torn by the desire to take part in the battle, to join forces with China's defenders as pirates in the past had often done. In her small packet of private belongings was a small photograph, cut from a newspaper, of Soong Mai-ling, the beautiful wife of Generalissimo Chiang Kai-shek and a leader in her own right. Seok-Teng longed to serve her in some fashion, but the way was not clear. The old pirate practices might suffice for the harrying of merchant ships, but the modern military craft of the Japanese were another matter.

Han Duan grunted again and stood, with just enough of a stoop to clear the low roof. The plane was nearly overhead now. Seok-Teng slid a hand under her pillow, ran a finger delicately along the undulating blade of her kris, then gripped its hilt. Both blade and hilt were warm. The dream, then, had been no accident, but a promise—or a warning. Seok-Teng would have spoken to the dagger if her Number One had not been present. Instead, she rolled from her bed into a crouch, pressed her brow to the weapon in mute homage to the ancestors from whom it had come, and, still stooping, emerged onto the deck of the She-Dragon.

Han Duan's head tilted back as she stared upward. Seok-Teng straightened and stepped to the rail. Along the eastern horizon lay just the faintest hint that day might come, but overhead a low, sullen cloud cover obscured the stars. The airplane, now directly above them, could not be seen, though its roar seemed so tangible that Seok-Teng raised her hand, whether to grasp or fend it off she did not know. She had even forgotten that she held the kris, which now pointed into the sky.

"Would your demon blade lead us now even into the heavens? Let it fly then by itself!" Han Duan raised her voice to be heard over the noise of the plane. Her own scarred face seemed demonic in the light of a single swaying lantern.

The eight crewmembers with their bedrolls on deck, already roused by the turmoil, watched this drama with great interest. More heads emerged from the hatchway, jostling for a view. Some preferred the privacy of the hold for their sleep or other nocturnal pursuits, but they were still alert for any excitement from above.

Seok-Teng allowed her arm to descend very slowly, while the blade pointed ever toward the unseen aircraft moving away into the distance. Her tone was harsh as steel on steel. "Has my kris ever led us to less than a rich prize?"

"Not yet." Han Duan's fierce expression relaxed into a wry grin, defusing the conflict. "And if you can manage to fly after this target, then so can I. So can we all. Just as soon as you leap aloft and lead the way." A few muffled laughs came from the bedrolls. She leaned closer to Seok-Teng and spoke in a lower tone. "But your demon has always led us to women, as well as treasure, to be rescued or taken into the crew. You will find no woman in a ship of the air."

"Who knows? Many would be even more certain that a pirate ship could not be crewed by women." Seok-Teng's hand dropped to her side, but still she gazed into the eastern sky.

"Well, what will come, will come," Han Duan said. "For now, that craft has passed beyond our reach. Perhaps we will yet come upon her crashed onto a coral reef, laden with gold and gems and a princess worth a great ransom. Enough even to buy our peace with Madame Lai Choi San."

Seok-Teng frowned. A subtle motion of her head led the other to follow her back into the cramped cabin, where they reclined on woven floor mats. Whatever speculations might entertain the crew, these days the two old shipmates shared the low bed only during the fevered revels that followed each successful—and profitable—raid. Too long an interval since the previous occasion might well have had something to do with the tension that shortened tempers in recent days. Han Duan had many an eager outlet for her energies among the crew, when she chose, but Seok-Teng's authority as captain of the She-Dragon depended on a degree of aloofness. Beyond that was an unspoken truth between them; only in each other could their deepest needs be met.

"With enough booty our crew, and even you, might purchase old Mountain of Wealth's pardon," Seok-Teng said, "but no treasure will ever cause her to let me live. More passed between us than I have told, though you may well guess. Better that our youngsters do not know how fiercely her hatred of me burns. They have seen Japanese soldiers only from a distance; the fury of the Dragon Lady of Bias Bay is far more real to them."

Han Duan drew a long breath and blew it out slowly. "So it is not only the Japanese we flee. I thought as much, though not that you had fallen from Madame's favor so far that gold could not pave the way back."

They sat in silence, both thinking of the woman they had served. Lai Choi San ruled the most powerful pirate fleet in Macao with an iron hand untempered by any velvet glove. Most of her wealth came from "protection" schemes and ransomed captives who, if their families were slow to pay, would return with fingers or ears missing, but her influence extended far beyond the coasts of Hong Kong and Guangzhou.

Smaller fleets and individual ships in which she held a share cruised as far as the coast of Vietnam to the southwest and Luzon in the Philippines to the southeast, sending her tribute and perpetual interest on her investments. One of these had captured the young Seok-Teng in her own small smuggler's boat on the waters of Vinh Ha Long, Bay of the Descending Dragon, where

China gives way to Vietnam. The girl had fought so valiantly and viciously, and her beauty had been of so a fierce a nature, that a wise captain had seen in her a value beyond the ordinary and taken her to Macao to offer to Lai Choi San herself. He had even presented her captured kris along with her, knowing well that the spirits with which such blades were imbued could bring luck to their rightful owners and fatal misfortune to others.

Seok-Teng sighed, wishing she had not been reminded of those times. She had, indeed, risen high in Madame's favor. For two years she had served as one of two amahs, companions and bodyguards to their pirate mistress. There had been rare moments of kindness and much education in the ways of pirating, as well as occasional instruction in service of a more intimate nature. And there had been Han Duan, who had come to the same position by a different route, passing as a man for years on the Macao waterfront until one day she overheard plotting among rival pirates and came before Lai Choi San to warn her.

"Duan, old friend, why did you follow me?"

In the dimness only shapes and movements could be discerned. Han Duan's bowed head would have hidden her expression in any case. Seok-Teng pushed on.

"Madame would have given you your own ship, with the pick of captured women to sail her. Indeed, this entire crew would have joined you, given the option. Or she would have given you the management of her fan-tan casinos in Macao. I know she offered."

Lai Choi San had been practical enough to know when her strong-willed amahs had reached the limits of service to a domineering mistress. She had agreed to finance a ship for Seok-Teng, crewed by captured women who had experience on fishing boats, and were in any case too unattractive or combative to be sold to the floating brothels. As long as enough profit came her way, what did it matter whose pillaging had procured it? Besides, it amused her at times to pit the female pirates against men she wished to humiliate. This aspect of their duties had not, however, amused Seok-Teng, and had driven her to range farther and farther until her ship had become independent in all but the payment of more than adequate tribute.

Even that had come to an end. There was no going back to Bias Bay and Macao now, or to any waters under the influence of the Dragon Lady, after the last bitter clash of wills. Seok-Teng would no longer be a party to the sale of captured women into slavery. Far to the east now, beyond the Philippines, the Marianas, and nearly to the Marshall Islands, Seok-Teng had no regrets save that her closest friend might have done better to stay behind.

Han Duan looked up with a grin, and the early rays of dawn through the cabin's entrance glinted on white teeth. "How could I leave my guns and cannons to your bumbling care? No one alive knows the ways of ships and the sea as you do, but when it comes to any weapon beyond a blade, you might as well be gambling at fan-tan yourself." Then she sobered, glancing sidelong at the ancient kris lying on Seok-Teng's pillow. "Yet I would follow you even without the guns. Yes, even though you steer by dreams sent through a blade. Such a captain might be thought to traffic with demons or djinns."

"Or to be insane?"

Han Duan shrugged. "Nearly as dangerous." She looked past Seok-Teng to the cabin door. A sleek young woman had just knelt to set down a tray with the morning meal, tea and bowls of rice flavored with dried cuttlefish. Her long, wet hair was evidence of an early swim.

"Thank you, Amihan," Han Duan said formally. The girl ducked her head and backed away, smooth cheeks flushed with more than reflected sunrise. A sidelong glance at her captain as she left deepened her rosy glow.

"So you've had the pair now?" Seok-Teng was glad of the diversion. "Dalisay was blushing last week, I noticed."

Han Duan considered it one of her duties to "initiate" any new recruit who was receptive to such things. Not until they had become accustomed to their surroundings, and none more than once, to avoid an appearance of favoritism that would interfere with

discipline, but it had become a tradition. Even those who were at first not so inclined often came to indicate an interest, even if only out of curiosity or communal sentiment, and none seemed disappointed when they emerged from her closet-sized cabin in the bow of the hold.

"I do not fault your blade's taste in women," Han Duan conceded, though Seok-Teng knew that her friend did not believe that their good fortune in finding crew members was truly due to the influence of the kris. The pair of pearl divers from the Sulu Islands between Borneo and Mindanao had been fleeing their slave-master, and the trader's ship on which they had stowed away and been enslaved again was, after all, a natural target for a pirate ship. Its cargo of pearls had been well worth taking. The sacks of rice and coffee and cacao beans among which the jewels had been hidden would have their uses, as well, if the pirates had need of passing for legitimate traders themselves.

Still it had been Seok-Teng who set that exact course, and Seok-Teng's kris had shown her the way. In that dream a pair of small, lithe dragons, the blue-green of shallow tropical seas, had twined about each other in a wheel like the yin and yang, spinning through the sky toward a point farther south on the horizon than she had intended to steer.

How Amihan and Dalisay would perform in battle was yet unknown, but they had taken at once to life on the pirate ship. Both learned quickly to race up the lines and masts to tend the great ribbed sails and often amused themselves by diving from those high perches down into the ocean. There they frolicked like merry dolphins and, when commanded, swam beneath the ship to assess the state of its hull. At all other times they moved about the deck nearly as closely entwined as in the dream, and even more closely pressed together in their shared bedroll.

"I was surprised that you did not have them both together, for variety," Seok-Teng said between mouthfuls of rice.

"Variety is the enemy of order," Han Duan answered with mock sternness. "You as captain should understand the importance of unvarying ritual. Not," she admitted, "that I wasn't tempted, but they needed to learn that they could not always cling to one another, and besides, that tiny rathole of mine can barely hold two bodies at once, the more so if both are breathing heavily."

Not for the first time, Seok-Teng felt a pang of regret for her vow of abstinence when it came to her crew members. Any of them would be more than willing; the new pair clearly idolized her. She fought down visions of smooth bodies writhing in pleasure, then returning the joy with sweet mouths and slender hands. Even harder to suppress was the remembrance of Han Duan's strong, skilled fingers, her skin with the taste of salt and sun and gunpowder, and the acquisition of bruises to be savored for many days.

No. It was necessary to maintain authority and a mystique of infallibility. Even with Han Duan, Seok-Teng's defenses against vulnerability could not be easily breached, and never when the kris drove her onward to conquests yet unclear.

Suddenly both pearl divers were kneeling in the doorway, struggling, in their excitement, to speak as one.

Authority took clear priority over desire. "Silence!" Seok-Teng barked. "You, Dalisay, begin again."

The taller girl blurted out a few words, "Ship... far...," and then, at a stern look from Han Duan, touched her forehead to the deck, straightened, and drew a deep breath. They had been quick to pick up the pidgin language in use on the ship, a blend of all the tongues of the South China Sea and some from beyond, but it was not yet second nature to them.

"Captain, ma'am, Gu Yasha has sent to inform you that a ship of the air is in sight, far to the east."

"Return to Gu Yasha and tell her that we will come at once. Go now!"

They went, tugging each other along. Seok-Teng, after thrusting her kris into its ebony scabbard and swiftly buckling it to her belt, followed just far enough behind to maintain her dignity. Han Duan, half a step back, muttered, "It takes no dream for me to foresee the day when the skies will be as crowded with vessels as the seas!"

Gu Yasha stood at the prow, shading her eyes with a hand as she stared just to the north of the newly risen sun. Without turning she pointed toward a silver glint barely large enough to be recognized as flashing from the wing of an airplane. "The craft was flying toward us when the lookout spied it, but now it has turned slightly southwest."

Born far inland, north of Hangzhou, Gu Yasha had learned the ways of water on the great Yellow River, which took her at last to the sea. Like Han Duan, she had passed as a man on many waterfronts and coastal barges. Her dragon, in Seok-Teng's dream, had been a golden amber, and she was worth more than her weight in that precious resin. Tallest and strongest of the crew, she drilled the others in battle skills and was leader of any boarding party.

"See, Captain, it veers again southward. When it has passed beyond the glare of the sun, we may know its course better, but I do not think it will fly any closer to us."

There was no reason that it should, and no cause to connect this sighting with the cloud-muffled craft that had come so close in the night. As Han Duan had said, airplanes would soon become more common over great stretches of ocean, and it was not impossible that even the small islands in the Marshall group could have a landing strip or two now. If so, it would be Japanese planes that used them.

Seok-Teng felt a hollow pit of misgiving in her gut, and fear for the crew who had followed her so faithfully and so far. They had been offered a chance to stay behind, and bounty enough to lead independent lives, but only a few had chosen that course.

She sent the others about their business, directing Gu Yasha to keep the ship on its eastern course, then stood for long minutes at the bow watching the tiny, distant arrow through her spyglass. Gradually it banked due south, and southeast, in a great curve, as though inscribing a circle in the sky. When the heading reached due east, the plane's profile was too narrow to be seen at all, as though it had blinked out of existence.

It could not be the same airplane. And yet Seok-Teng was

certain that it was.

Han Duan came up behind her. "They search for something, those in that sky craft. Or perhaps they are lost."

Seok-Teng said nothing. Her hand was on the scabbard, and she could feel the spirit of the kris emanating from within. Han Duan waited a few moments. Finally, as though she had never expressed a single doubt, she said, "The finding of this one will be a far different adventure than any we have yet seen. Perhaps variety does have its virtues, after all."

Even the fastest sailing ship must journey at the will of the winds and the seas. They could never overtake that sleek silver machine with its roaring engines, not if it continued to fly. And if it did not continue... well, nothing yet devised by men could long withstand the will of earth's gravity. The plane would either land on some island of coral and sand, or crash, possibly into the sea. Without the continued stirring of the spirit in the kris, Seok-Teng would have given up hope. But she did not give up, and Han Duan did not try to dissuade her.

They sailed steadily eastward and then a few degrees to the northeast, plotting their position when possible from the stars by night and the sun by day. The same vessel that had carried the pearl divers had provided two other treasures nearly as valuable: a modern compass, though Seok-Teng would not rely wholly on such an instrument, and a set of charts more extensive than any she had been able to procure in the South China Sea. Such storms as they encountered were centered to the north or south, affecting them only lightly, yet were violent enough in the distance that if the need arose they could plausibly be blamed for blowing the ship off course unusually far to the east.

In the ten days that followed the crew worked through its daily routine with an added pitch of excitement. The captain had a new goal; there would be adventure and riches ahead. Even those who still doubted the existence of land so far to the east did not doubt their captain's unerring instinct for prizes. If it were steered by a demon blade, all the better and more certain.

Any tedium to the voyage was dispelled by the antics of Amihan and Dalisay. The pearl divers had set their sights on Gu Yasha, since the captain was clearly out of reach, and her Number One had made it plain that they would get no more special attention from that quarter. Gu Yasha, the next in authority and the tallest woman they had ever seen, was a most worthy and intriguing object of desire. Gu Yasha, known to restrict such recreation to stays in port, played the game by seeming not to notice their ploys.

In this, as in all else, the pair worked together, coming at her from two directions.

One would look upward with wide eyes and ask an innocent question, pressing so close that her target must step back to avoid contact, while the other came silently up behind in order to be bumped, and take the opportunity to rub seductively against Gu Yasha's rump. Or, holding hands, apparently in deep conversation and paying no attention to where they went, they would stroll right into her and then divide, each wriggling seductively along her body while they made profuse apologies. In either case she would set them aside with scarcely a nod, her face impassive.

Crew members placed wagers as to whether and when Gu Yasha would react, and, if so, how. Odds were highest that the girls would achieve both less and more than they bargained for. Seok-Teng stayed aloof, but with a keen eye on the proceedings. Soon, whatever lay ahead, there would be no time for such distractions, however amusing.

On the ninth day Han Duan, with a sidelong look and a jerk of her head, signaled to the captain that matters were about to reach resolution. Amihan and Dalisay had clambered aboard, naked from their morning swim, and knelt close to Gu Yasha. They had been issued blue cotton shirts and trousers, which they often "forgot" to wear, and now they made no attempt to clothe themselves but used the garments to dry wet hair and bodies. Their long, sensuous strokes and posturings displayed every feature of their lithe bodies, while they peered slyly upward to assess what effect they might have.

Gu Yasha, with a single barked word, grasped an arm of each

and yanked them upright. She propelled the girls, stumbling, to the rail and bent them across it. Han Duan unhooked a long net deftly from the ship's side and tossed it over the girl's heads and torsos, entangling their arms and leaving their rounded rumps even more blatantly naked by contrast.

Gu Yasha struck first, with a hand that could easily span both of Dalisay's buttocks at once, but focused on one and then the other. Han Duan set up her own complex pattern of smacks on Amihan's wriggling posterior. They squealed, and writhed, and gasped each time an especially sharp blow landed, but neither begged her assailant to stop, even when red streaks marked their smooth skin.

The entire crew gathered to watch and cheer. Some clapped their hands in a futile attempt to match the varying rhythm of strikes. When squeals and gasps intensified into sobs, and ultimately to frantic, wordless pleas not for mercy but for something beyond pain, many a watcher would have been glad to step forward and supply the need, had that not been the clear prerogative of Han Duan and Gu Yasha.

A prerogative that they did not claim. Both stepped back in unison and viewed their handiwork in the manner of calligraphers assessing their brushstrokes. Han Duan surveyed Dalisay's flesh, and then Amihan's, both now aglow like coals in the galley brazier. She frowned. Three more openhanded blows, with accompanying yelps from Amihan—and Han Duan was satisfied.

The pearl divers, still far from satisfied, wriggled their way down out of the entangling net and watched Gu Yasha stride away to climb up beside the captain in the high prow. Han Duan paused for a few stern words, pointed down into the hold, and then joined Seok-teng as well.

The two girls, each with an arm about the other's waist and a hand fumbling in her own wet crotch, limped to the hatch and disappeared below.

"What did you say to them?" Seok-Teng asked Han Duan.

"Shape up and tend to your work, unless you wish to find yourselves in a floating brothel that caters to Japanese soldiers."

A rare smile lit up Gu Yasha's face. Seok-Teng herself yielded briefly to laughter. Then she handed her spyglass to Han Duan and indicated a point in the eastern sky.

"The aircraft?" Gu Yasha shaded her eyes and stared in that direction.

"Birds," Han Duan said. "Land is not far off."

Word spread like a freshening wind through the crew. Land to the east, just as the captain had promised. The afternoon's entertainment receded from their minds, to be recalled in many a bedroll that night, but for now eclipsed by a flurry of preparation.

With the first distant sightings of fishing boats, the graceful proas of the ocean islands, everyone on board knew even more surely that they were not alone on an empty sea. Land, some land, was very near.

They did not, for the present, intend to act or be seen as pirates. The large guns along the sides remained retracted and concealed. When fishing boats became more frequent, the She-Dragon approached to a non-threatening distance and Han Duan, more able to pass as a man than ever as she grew older, took their small boat to intercept one and ask for news.

From the first vessel she was waved onward to a larger one, where, as she reported on her return, she and the crew members with her were able to cobble together enough fragments of mutual languages with those aboard to communicate at a reasonable level.

"We are indeed among the southernmost Marshall Islands, and already to the east of several. I asked, in passing, if they ever saw airplanes so far out here in the ocean; we had heard one and been surprised. After some hesitation they told me that Japanese planes were often seen to the north, and indeed large airstrips had been built on some islands. I could see that there was more to tell, so I offered silver coins for their trouble, and finally was told that stories had spread of a plane, not Japanese, crash-landing on a coral reef in the Mili atoll. Further, it was said that a Japanese ship, large but not so large as some, was refueling at the major island of Jaluit and would then go to the harbor of Mili Mili to pick up the wreck and a survivor."

"Survivor." Seok-Teng pondered the news. "And how did they know the plane was not Japanese?"

Han Duan shook her head. "The way news travels here, I think that they did know more, or suspect it, but I did not press further. That same swift flow of news could bear suspicions of us to quarters we would rather it did not. I did, however, get directions to the Mili atoll, and when I inquired about a place where we might put in to a lagoon, work on some repairs, and replenish our fresh water supply, all without disturbing local residents, I was told of a much smaller uninhabited atoll not far from Mili, called Nadikdik."

Seok-Teng spread out her charts, and between them they determined where they must be. As to where they should go, Nadikdik and Mili seemed the natural choices.

The winds were favorable. At times Seok-Teng even felt that some force beyond known wind and current sped their ship onward. The crew, knowing only that the captain was rushing them toward some new adventure after so many weeks of nothing but empty sea, and that in some way a mysterious ship of the air was involved, worked smoothly and well.

A new scattering of fishing boats appeared as they neared other islands. Seok-Teng was reassured to see a few vessels that were junk-rigged in the Chinese fashion, like the She-Dragon; they would not stand out as much of a curiosity.

Han Duan sailed again for information. Now gossip about the downed airplane was widespread. The survivor was said to be white, and there were whispers that the pilot was, incredibly, a woman. She was dressed like a man, with short hair, but someone's cousin's son had heard a high scream when a Japanese official struck her. She was now imprisoned in Japanese headquarters at Mili Mili, the chief town, and a naval ship would the in the harbor by late next day to take her away.

A woman! And perhaps they were in time; but in time for what, Seok-Teng could not say. Her ship could not take on an armored military vessel in open combat.

The Nadikdik Atoll was easy to find, and not hard to approach once a fisherman's son was paid to show them the safe entrance between islets of sharp coral into the center lagoon. Besides a silver coin, they gifted him with a small bundle of coffee beans and a sack of rice, as much to establish their credentials as legitimate traders blown off course as to reward him. In further negotiations with his father they purchased a slim, fleet proa to more easily navigate among the reefs of both Nadikdik and Mili, ten kilometers to the north.

"What is your plan?" Han Duan asked that night. "We are not exactly hidden here, and news of us will have reached Mili Mili by now."

Seok-Teng had no plan except to be in the right place at the right time, whatever that might be.

"We must see the harbor, the town, how everything lies," she said. "At dawn you and I and the two pearl divers will sail in the proa to the harbor at Mili Mili. A harmless family of traders. If the Japanese ship is not yet in sight, we will dock, and you may even go about the town to purchase a few supplies and listen for gossip."

Fishing boats were heading out of the harbor as their proa was going in, but enough boats were still at the docks to keep them from being conspicuous. Han Duan went about the town, returning with packets of tea and sweets and a sack of breadfruit. The crew back in the lagoon would be gathering wild coconuts and filling barrels of water from small springs on a few of the encircling islets.

"There is no approaching the guardhouse," she said. "No one dares look toward it directly. There is a current of curiosity and fear throughout the town. And danger."

Danger was closer than they had known. Once out of the harbor they could see, across the great lagoon to the northeast, the gray bulk of a naval ship close to a line of reef. Seok-Teng did not dare bring out her spyglass where she might be seen, but the ship seemed to be anchored there. She recalled that it was expected to retrieve the wrecked plane as well as the flier.

On the way back to Nadikdik Seok-Teng muttered to herself and to Han Duan, trying to form a plan of action. "The naval ship is not huge, but too big to dock in the inner harbor. They will have to bring the prisoner out in a smaller craft. Our ship might just manage to pull up to the longest dock, but we could not maneuver quickly in the harbor. We must not be trapped inside! We have the proa... and our small boat...."

As the sun slid below the land, the Japanese vessel, the wrecked body of an airplane bound to its aft deck with heavy cables, eased through the inlet into the harbor and anchored where the water was deepest. A large junk-rigged ship that had been standing half a mile offshore began to drift almost imperceptibly inward. The pirates' proa and small sailboat were already inside the harbor, blending in with other boats as innocuously as possible.

The naval ship lowered an engine-driven boat, which carried four armed soldiers to the main dock, already cleared of onlookers. Another military party met them, opening formation to reveal a manacled prisoner who was swiftly and roughly taken aboard by the others.

Seok-Teng, in her small sailboat, could not see the prisoner clearly, but she was swept up in the moment, certain what she must do. Even in its scabbard her kris vibrated against her thigh.

Dusk came quickly. When the boat with the prisoner was under way toward the Japanese ship, a bright crimson rocket burst into the sky from close to the huddle of docked fishing vessels, and at this signal the boom of cannons sounded from just outside the harbor.

In the confusion, Seok-Teng's boat moved toward the prisoners. Gu Yasha's rifle sent one guard and then another tumbling, and splintered the steering mechanism. One figure struggled to stand; in the fading light a pale, ghostly face looked directly into Seok-Teng's own, and then there was a loud splash. The prisoner had dived over the side, manacles and all.

This had not been planned for, but the possibility of sinking the boat had been considered. Behind Seok-Teng, Amihan and Dalisay slid soundlessly into the water. In less than a minute, while Gu Yasha continued firing from first one rifle and then another,

Seok-Teng was pulling the prisoner into the boat while the two girls pushed from beneath.

More cannon fire, right in the harbor's inlet, and some wild shots from the naval ship. Now the proa slid alongside Seok-Teng. The two pearl divers had already climbed aboard it. With scarcely a glance at the prisoner—but she was, indeed, a woman!—Seok-Teng passed her over to the lighter boat where other hands gripped her securely. Then, swift on even the lightest breeze, the slim craft darted across the harbor. The cannon fire had ceased.

Other boats began to move, and at least one motor coughed into life. While Gu Yasha continued to shoot, their slower sailboat moved toward the far side of the harbor, Seok-Teng using all her skill at making the most of what air current there was. Gu Yasha paused briefly to set off another rocket, and at once Han Duan in the She-Dragon ordered the big guns to be fired again, this time lofting their cannonballs over the heads of the fleeing pirates so that no one dared follow.

Just outside the harbor the proa waited. Seok-Teng and Gu Yasha leapt across from their boat, the proa caught the wind again, and in scant seconds cannonfire blasted the craft left behind into jagged pieces. Two pursuing vessels hit the wreckage and were wrecked in turn, effectively blocking the exit.

This part of the plan, or something greater than a plan, had succeeded.

On the ship, freed from her manacles, the prisoner was half-carried to the captain's cabin, stripped of her wet clothing, and laid on the bed, so limp and drained that Seok-Teng thought again of ghosts. The flickering light from a whale-oil lamp did not dispel the notion. "You are safe here," she said, trying several languages before the colonial French she had learned in her youth in Vietnam got a response. The white woman's accent was odd and her vocabulary limited, but they were able to communicate.

"Yes, safe," Seok-Teng reiterated. "For a while, at least. They cannot follow us for at least a day, and by then we will be far away." In what direction, she had not yet decided. Questions swirled in her mind, but the other seemed too exhausted to answer yet.

Suddenly, though, she jerked to half-sitting, pulling the thin blanket up around herself, eyes blazing in defiance. "No!"

Han Duan had come in.

"All is well," Seok-Teng said soothingly, though she had a nervous impulse to laugh. "She is one of us. Look again. We are all women on this ship."

After a moment the other lay back. "And all pirates, I suppose," she said. "On a ship. With cannons." Her eyes closed then, and her face relaxed. Soon she was asleep.

Seok-Teng, her cabin occupied, shared Han Duan's small retreat that night. There was scarcely space for a slim pearl diver to lie beside Han Duan on the narrow bed, much less the tall, sturdy captain of the ship, but the fever of victory burned all the hotter for being delayed, and they came together in a clash of flesh and will in which side-by-side had no meaning, only above and below.

Seok-Teng's naked body pressed down fiercely on the length of Han Duan's. Han Duan pressed upward with equal force. Friction of breast and belly and loins, hands and lips and teeth, fed the desperate hunger for more, and more, harder and yet harder, until the tiny hidden dragon Seok-Teng visualized between her folds tensed its coils and raised its head in a triumphant roar that shook her to her core.

Han Duan waited mere seconds before lurching to the top position and thrusting violently against Seok-Teng's pubic mound. In a few seconds more great shudders and groans of pleasure wracked her, subsiding into gasps and finally to silence.

In the captain's cabin they would have fallen apart then, to lie side by side in satiated companionship. Here, though that would have been just barely possible, they rolled instead until they were face to face, still closely pressed. Seok-Teng worked a hand free and stroked gently across the old scars on Han Tuan's face. "Tomorrow," she said, "Our guest must move to this cabin. You and I will maintain the proper management of the ship in the captain's quarters—unless you choose otherwise."

Han Duan's hand rose as by right to Seok-Teng's face. "Wartime calls for sacrifice," she said, though her gentle touch belied her tone. "I will follow you even there. You and your demon blade."

Hands moved along then to other places, in explorations more languorous than urgent, until suddenly urgency resumed command. There was space after all for bodies to reverse and tongues as well as fingers to find tender places aching to be filled; bodies found room to arch and strain and thrash when driven by need only a strong and deeply probing hand could satisfy. It was long before they slept.

Next morning, in Seok-Teng's spare clothing and with a meal of rice and breadfruit inside her, the flyer started right in with her own questions before they could ask theirs. No ghost now, she was alert and affable, with still an underlying watchfulness. Her looks were strange to them, especially her light, unruly thatch of hair, but her thin body seemed strong and healthy except for dark bruises so recent that they must have been inflicted by the crash. Or her captors.

"Real pirates? Where did you come from? Where are we going? Why are you here?"

Han Duan answered the first questions in general terms, but knew better than to deal with the last. We are here because an ancient demon blade sent dreams of you, but we do not yet know why. Impossible to tell her that.

"Where we go now depends on you," Seok-Teng said. "We could sail south, to Kiribati—the Gilbert Islands—where I think the British are still in control. Are they your people?"

"I know them," the white woman said. "When I was lost, I searched for those islands, hoping to land there."

"Then we will go there. They can send word, at least, to those who must search for you."

"I... let me think for a day." The ghost-mood had reclaimed her. She looked hollow, shadowed, even in the sunshine on deck.

They set a course to the south and let the flyer have her day. That night, in the cabin, Seok-Teng pressed her again.

"We must know where you came from, what we should call you, who you are, where you should go. We have our own course to follow, after all."

The woman raised her head. "It seems so simple, and yet it is not. I am... I do not know. Once I was the woman who thought she could fly around the world. Now...." She was silent for a while. Then, haltingly, she said, "They said I was a spy. They... beat me. And more." A shiver swept through her. "I never hated before, never believed in violence. But now... I don't know who I am. I think I could willingly kill."

Another silence. "I was not a spy, but now I know things they wanted to hide. That huge airstrip, fortifications... that much the British and Americans must somehow be told. But I am not ready for my old life."

Seok-Teng said, carefully, "We are changing our ways as well, still pirates, but bending all our efforts to harrying and blocking the Japanese warmongers. We will sail far from here, since too much is now known of us, but always we will work against them, and may well die in the attempt. Our way is not yet clear." On impulse she unwrapped the protecting oilcloth from her private papers, drew out a photograph, and proffered it. "If only we could gain the trust of Soong Mai-Ling! We could be her secret eyes and ears."

"Madame Chiang Kai-shek! I have met her several times. She takes a great interest in airplanes." The flyer pondered for several minutes. "It could be... if I were to give you a letter signed by me, recommending you to her attention.... But I am not ready to be 'discovered' yet. Perhaps written as though we had met earlier, in New Guinea, before I took off from Lae."

"If you are not soon gone from us," Seok-Teng said, managing to conceal her awe of this woman, "you must darken your skin and hair for safety, and even then act a part so well that none can guess."

Han Duan had said nothing, but now broke in. "You asked for a day. Do you wish a week, a month, some longer time, with no promise that you will have such a chance at safety and your old life again? Who would you be, if you could have another life?"

"I would be... I will be," the former pilot said, with scarcely a moment's hesitation, "a pirate."

Seok-Teng touched her kris and felt it quiver, and fall still. The plan was accomplished.

Rescue Wounds
Kal Cobalt

I logged in to my whore, "mine" because I'd settled on him; like all the rest, 19178 perked up his neurons for any number of the Better Class. He was a more experienced whore, nearly three years vined—I'd been looking for one a lot fresher, but he had other points in his favor. He was a local boy, kept in the undergrove across the city. His synapses, vined as they were, stayed snappy. Somehow, after three years of rooting, his brain didn't have that sluggish, autopilot feeling most whores develop and some Better Class secretly enjoy observing.

I'd been slowly altering the composition of our fucks, keeping my responses as bland as possible so I could keep up this time without drawing scrutiny. As usual, the whore lenses overlaid both my eyes, but my right housed a bore lens underneath, slowly drilling its way through the ethercon to trace and analyze the signal. Rush of numbers and schematics in my right eye; sleepy, smiling whore in my left.

"Oh, hi." He ticked my cock immediately, remembering that I didn't like a lot of foreplay. Too distracting from the bore lens display. I ticked back absently, trying to figure out how many relays the ethercon shunted through between us. "Later than usual," he noted, ticking again. Too doped out to remember what his first tick had reported.

"Insomnia." If he could ever hold enough in his consciousness to register the tickback, everything would report perfectly average. Good thing boring through ethercons made me hard and whore lenses were too dumbtech to know the difference.

"I'm sorry." 19178 smiled. "I'm sure I can help."

"I'm sure you can." Four relays. That wasn't outside the realm of deconstruction.

19178 ticked my cock, again, and delivered a contented little

hum at what he found. He started in on the usual behaviors we'd established - all things he took the lead on, so I could respond as necessary and concentrate on the bore. He tongued my ethercock, giving me a truly boring lickjob while I broke relay codes.

The undergrove sprawled beneath six commerce towers; it was going to take a combination of geo-location and cracking the distribution codes to pinpoint his bodyshack. Numbers raced past my right eye faster than I could consciously process. My subprocessors ground through the data in the background, making my skull ache. 19178 kept licking, slipping me an image of his wet lips wrapped tight around my shaft. I blinked the bore into high gear; it was a question now of which would finish first, my subprocessing or my cock. Both ached, pushed to their limit.

I hate it when I come before I'm done cracking.

19178 smiled muzzily at me. "I'm glad you logged in to me."

"Yep." I had most of what I needed, at least. Now, I needed time: time to plot locations, to finish the deconstruction of the relays, to prepare the solution. I popped my lenses out—all three of them—and jacked into my stereo. This definitely required music.

Everything I knew about undergroves came from urban folklore and advertising, so I expected a high margin of error. Nonetheless, the concepts I based my plan upon were thus:

Undergroves were separated into quadrants, and in those quadrants there were a certain number of bodyshacks. Bodyshacks were utility homes for the vined: self-contained micro-domiciles, one-third workpod and two-thirds recreation area, a fraction that spoke of minor luxury considering that the time ratio was 50% work and 50% leisure. Bodyshacks were a necessity of vining; the wiring was for all intents permanent, which simply didn't allow for a wide area of travel. It wasn't a bad trade, or so the advertising went; the otherwise unemployable were vined to serve the virtual needs and wants of the Better Class, and in exchange, all the food, shelter, and data they could ever want were provided. Just no freedom of physical motion, aside from the exercise mandated to keep their bodies in shape when twelve of every 24 hours was spent motionless in the workpod.

It's not an especially controversial setup. There were bigger problems. I was motivated by the inability to do anything about those bigger problems, and by the niggling suspicion that things were a lot worse in the undergroves than anyone knew. Classic avoidance: I was too frightened of what else was happening, so I picked a winnable battle. Of sorts.

My plan was ambitious: locate 19178 (easy), break into his undergrove and his bodyshack (difficult), inject him with the solution I had devised to dissolve vine (easy), and then inject an undergrove-killing amount of the solution into the workpod (easy). Then I would depart, which was the suicidally impossible part of the plan, unless I got a little help from 19178 or other newly-disconnected grapes. I could be fucked in a hundred different ways. There was a small margin of trouble that would make my plan work without making things much worse.

It was much, much worse by several magnitudes.

Breaking into the undergrove was easy. No one cares about the grapes, only the product. I slipped into what looked like some kind of climate-control system I assumed to be above the actual bodyshack level. The floor rose and fell in regular half-cylindrical ripples studded with exhaust tubes. I had a basic grasp of mechanics but couldn't work out what might be going on under there, so I attempted to hug the wall and skirt the whole thing.

I was two-thirds of the way along when I caught sight of a loose panel in one of the half-cylinders. I couldn't help peeking into it, hoping for some clue, and instead of a clue I got the whole unwanted answer.

There was a man in there, vined up. It didn't take a genius to

figure this one out: grapes can't walk more than a few feet, or so the story goes. If one half-cylinder was filled with a grape, they were all filled with grapes. And nobody was walking anywhere. The pretty political picture was just that.

The dislodged panel contained a burstcode. A short grind of subprocessing translated it—20143—and two realizations hit at once: 19178 was probably in this very room, and if this was the storage norm, this undergrove officially housing a thousand grapes probably actually housed everyone from 00001 to 20143 and then some—meaning my devining solution could be dramatically more useful.

A burst of geometrics and a lot of careful footwork led me to 19178. I pried open one panel after another—including one with an inexplicable inward mirror—till the entire half-cylinder lay open, as did how undergroves worked. The body was encased in electronic stimulation wraps, keeping muscle tone up during long stretches of inactivity. Like years. There was a catheter and an IV.

There weren't any bodyshacks. There were just slaves, vined up tight. I had nothing to combat this. Then the sirens began.

The smart move would be to get the fuck out the way I came in, but leaving 19178 that way, in what I finally understood the undergroves to be, would have been a death sentence. I'd like to say it was my morals that guided me, but no one has morals anymore. It was his face. I've had sex hundreds of times over ethercon, but seeing his face, right in front of me, helpless—I felt a connection I couldn't reason away.

My best guess was that the deviner would take ten minutes to work on a single subject, so attempting that with sirens blaring wasn't an option. Snipping his exterior vines was a total unknown—it could kill, or work perfectly, or anything in between. Margins of trouble again. It was better than doing nothing.

First I pulled apart the stimu-wraps and removed the catheter, proving that my months gone amok in a haze of meat-positive bio-fetish parties did leave me with some useful skills. Then, with the oxygen still pumping, I snipped him.

This was not the first rescue of some kind I'd attempted that had gone wrong, but it was the most horrifying thing I had seen in meat time. His eyes snapped open, and he flailed for the oxygen tubes blindly for agonizing seconds. Then he seized, flopping around in the little bed-coffin for six peals of the siren before he went limp again.

He was still alive. I could tell that much. I dragged him out and hoisted him over my shoulder, carry-dragging him back to the door I'd jimmied open. Even as I did it, I knew it was stupid. Stupid to take him with me when the place had to be crawling with security cameras. Stupid to drag a body with me when every second counted. Stupid to think I could fix him up or even keep him alive with whatever I had at home. Humanity's a bitch sometimes.

That's how I wound up with him in my bed, snipped vines poking into my sheets, with a vial of deviner beside him that I was too afraid to use. It had been created with attached vines in mind. It had never occurred to me that I could physically snip someone out of the grove, and I had no idea what kind of effect the deviner would have on effectively dead vine. Was it active and waiting, or already inert? Impossible to know.

He smelled differently than I had expected. Something about the lank hair and the dreamy quality of his eyes had made me imagine his scent as cloying and juvenile. He smelled like a man, though, and he sweated in my bed as if trying to make his mark somewhere. Now that he actually existed.

Morals are useless and have been for decades. It didn't bother me to look at him, with no idea of how to rouse him from his unconsciousness, and fantasize about him. He hadn't been shrouded in a single micron of clothing in the undergrove, so I saw no reason to cover him up once he was out of it. His cock was just as he presented it over the ether: lean and long, with a dusky head and a thin shroud of foreskin. Even limp, it had a grace to it I recognized from all our sessions, and I couldn't help wanting it now that it was physically present.

I spent a long time thinking about fucking him while he was

unconscious. Nobody fucks anymore. Too org. Everyone thinks their immune systems will snap like brittle cardstock. Do you even remember cardstock? Of course you don't. But he was the perfect foil, with health shoved into him by the grove, protected from biology for years in his coffin. There wasn't any appreciable difference between fucking him over ethercon thanks to grove coercion and taking him while he was unconscious, and that's why I couldn't do it. What the hell had I rescued him for if I just did the same damn things to him?

Petting him gave him goosebumps. When my lust faded, I was encouraged by the idea that his body still understood what touch meant and how to interpret it. It meant there were at least possibilities on his physical horizon. He breathed easily, too, with nothing but the standard bedroom forced-oxygen.

As my subprocessors ground away at the various ideas I formulated to attempt to save him, I realized that I felt something, looking at him: lonely. I had a long night of work ahead of me, and for once, I couldn't log in to 19178 for a little relief.

The decision came down to food. I knew a little bit about bodies and I'd been on IV dinners before like everybody else, but I had no idea how to construct a solution that would keep him alive. To feed him, I needed him conscious, and to attempt to wake him, I needed him as strong as possible. I couldn't justify sitting around letting him waste nutrients while I worried over estimated survival percentages. The vines clearly had him in some kind of shutdown, so the choice was clear.

I made him as comfortable as I could on the bed, then knelt over him and took his wrist into my hand. Sliding a needle into a shunt is nothing, I've done it a million times to my own, but this time I couldn't stop shaking.

The nanodes went in easily, and a split second after I removed the needle, 19178 lurched up and screamed.

I won't lie. I screamed too. The one thing I'd felt confident about was a ten-minute efficacy time. Screaming in ten seconds was not part of my plan. I hadn't even spoken to a human face-to-face in years - what the fuck do you do with one screaming and bucking under you?

"You," he gasped, and then: "My face."

"It's still there," I said, out of reflex. I grabbed one of his limply flopping hands and put it against his cheek.

"Uh." Between my thighs I felt the tension of his body—what he could make with such weak muscles—slide away. "Where's the mirror?" he slurred.

"The mirror?"

He frowned, blinking at me, and then trying to get the rest of the room into focus. The mirror. I recalled the interior mirror panel in the half-cylinder—and realized, sickly, that it must have been used during his more lucid moments to cement his self-appearance so it would remain static on ethercon. "Where am I?"

"Just relax. You're safe."

"This is not the grove." He tried to push up to his elbows, but couldn't quite manage it.

"No. It's my place. There's a nanode solvent dissolving your internal vines right now."

"What?" The look on his face wasn't the good kind of shock. "What the fuck?"

"No—I didn't buy you," I blurted, afraid he thought his situation had become worse instead of better. "I freed you."

His eyes started to shine. It spooked me until I remembered that's what tears look like. "You fucking son of a bitch," he choked out.

Stunned, I just looked at him. The snipped vines sticking out from his body began to smolder as they dissolved from the inside. He let out a pained yelp, choked on a breath, and passed out again—on top of the pain, probably shock. I knew how he felt.

⁂

When he woke up again, I had done everything I could. He had all my blankets and pillows, and I'd lined up plenty of food and drinks by the bed. I didn't say anything as his eyes opened, and he didn't look at me.

"Don't fuck with things you don't understand," he said quietly, staring at the ceiling.

I snorted. "You're welcome."

He turned his head toward me, with difficulty. His eyes were dark. "I begged them to let me. It's all sex and oblivion drugs. I needed it."

"How could you possibly need that?"

He started to smile and bit his lip, like he was trying to keep it from happening. "I'm so mad at you," he said softly, "but I look at you and you're this guy I've been with a hundred times, who never wanted to hurt me, even in a fantasy."

"I thought about fucking you while you were out," I said. "Before you woke up the first time."

He shrugged lightly. "I've done worse."

It felt like maybe we were making progress. Slow, tiny progress. It was a lot more important to me than I would have expected. "What's your name?"

"I am Dmey."

"Dmey. I like that."

"Thanks." He tried to prop himself up on his elbows again, but it wasn't getting any easier.

"Would you like some help?"

"Yeah."

I helped him sit up, pulling him back a little to lean against the pillowed wall. "What were you trying to bury yourself away from, Dmey?" I worried that it was too much to ask, but we had to move forward somehow.

He swallowed hard. I offered him water, but he shook his head. "I saw things," he murmured. "And did things. In the war."

"What war?"

He smiled at me. It wobbled. "The one they keep from you."

"Who's 'they'?"

"The ones who run the groves. The ones you pay your rent to. The ones that probably think I couldn't survive a rescue attempt by some crazed customer, so they didn't come to kill you for speaking to me."

"These drugs," I said, "the ones they give you when you're vined, they've made you delusional."

"They've almost let me shut my eyes. To things I can't stop seeing."

I didn't want to believe him. A secret war, a shadow government—conspiracy-theory bullshit. But I'd never been comfortable during the Merger Decade; I didn't go to the party when commerce and government finally got hitched at the climax of the ten-year plan. I'd noticed weird traffic on my bore lens a few times. Asked innocent questions of contacts that shut down abruptly, or gave me the same weary look Dmey had. I shook my head, trying to assimilate it all at once, faster than my processors could manage. "What happened to you?"

"I was a trojan." Dmey kept his eyes down, watching his still hands in his lap. "They used me to infect a resistant company. My proximity remotely reprogrammed their nanodes to form spikes—I didn't know that when they sent me. I was in a business meeting and then everyone was dying. Spikes bursting them from the inside, growing and growing." He snorted. "Business warfare. Because money is life."

"Fuck." I compulsively grabbed his hand, and he squeezed it hard. "Things like that—do they still happen?"

He shrugged. "I don't know. I got... damaged, mentally. I wouldn't accept programming anymore. They tried everything. Without the programming... I couldn't handle it. I couldn't handle just knowing. So they offered me the grove."

I shook my head. "What was your plan? What were you going to do after that?"

He smiled, finally looking up at me. "There was no 'after that' in the plan."

I felt like a dumb kid again, asking all the wrong questions and failing over and over to understand the importance of anything told to me. "Listen... I've killed. Not like that, but I have. If that's what you want... if I fucked up your retirement plan and you can't take being awake... I would fix that."

For a horrifying moment, the look on his face suggested that I had actually said the right thing. Then he shook his head, and I had hope before he said, "I'll keep it in mind."

Shit.

We slept side by side, or tried to; the withdrawals made Dmey squirm, and I wasn't getting any sleep with him beside me, even with my processors offering up a little mechanical relaxation. Finally, I reached out for Dmey's stomach, resting my palm over his navel. His skin was warm, and the light dusting of hair there tickled my skin. "Let me try something," I murmured, and felt him nod in the dark.

I massaged his front, attending to his shoulders, his chest, his hips, his thighs. Everything had to hurt, coming back from the grove. He was silent and still until I started working my fingers up his inner thighs, when a low groan came out of him.

"Okay?" I whispered. In the dark I could barely see his face, framed by his dark hair spread out on the pillow.

"Yeah." He spread his thighs a little. I kept massaging up, and up, till my thumbs brushed his scrotum. It was drawn up tight, and I paused, unsure what to do with this information.

"Stop processing," he whispered, and drew my hand up to his cock. It was hard and warm, and he was already wet beneath his foreskin; I felt it as I stroked, heard the soft snick of lubrication as I moved.

"Are you sure?" I breathed.

"Lie back."

It took him a while to figure out how to get to his hands and knees with so little strength, and longer still to straddle me with anything resembling steadiness. He groaned as I tucked the lube into him, his hands planted on my chest and his arms shaking with the strain of holding himself up. I wasn't about to question his resolve, not with him already practically sitting on my cock; I just did what I could to help, steadying my cock with one hand and his hip with the other.

He cried out as he took me in, with a sharpness to his voice I'd never heard over ethercon, but we'd never done it this way. He leaned back a little, grinding down to take me all the way to the root, and just held there. I slipped my hand to his cock, feeling it jump against my hand. "Hold still," he said.

"I will."

He moved slower than anyone I had ever fucked, by ethercon or in my meat time experiences years ago. His hips rolled with a gracefulness I wouldn't have valued until it was wrapped around my cock. His sweaty palms were planted just above my pecs and I could hear the soft, labored rhythm of his breath a split second before it hit me in the face. The scent of sweat and sex started to rise up from us, and I groaned, pushing my hips up just a little. He didn't stop me, so I kept going, making round little thrusts to counterpoint his grinds. When I reached for his cock again, a bead of precome slid through my fingers, and I felt my cock twitch inside him in response. No ethercon fuck had ever been this good.

Still grinding, Dmey reached for my hand and led it to his hair, closing my fingers around it and tugging. We'd never done this, either, but then that kind of thing didn't translate well over ethercon. I made a fist in his sweaty locks and tugged, and he cried out sharply, shoving himself down onto my cock even harder.

"Yes," I grunted, cradling his waist to keep him steady. "Harder, just like that."

"Please," he whimpered, his fingers digging into my pecs as he just tried to stay upright.

"What? What do you need?"

"A nipple..."

I grabbed one of his hands and dragged it down to cover one of my nipples. "Like that?"

He let out a little huff of a laugh, his breath warm in my face. "No. My nipple."

Grinning, I put his hand back where he had the most leverage. "I can do that too." I knew he didn't just want it covered, though; I grabbed one between my finger and thumb and pulled hard.

He yelled, going rigid over me, and I clumsily made a last-minute grab at his cock to stroke him off. He came over my belly, hot ejaculate sliding over the sides of my abdomen to soak the blankets as he shuddered and struggled for breath. "You better not mind if I flip you over now," I grunted, already starting to pull him toward my chest to roll him.

"I don't," he groaned, spreading his legs for me as I rolled on top.

Even that turned on, I fucked him slowly. It seemed like the pattern that had been started. I cradled his head in my hand and pushed in again and again, fascinated by the way his body resisted and then accepted, and the way his breath did the same. Something more happened in my processes, something vague and strong, and it made me grip his jaw and kiss him hard, my tongue as deep in his mouth as my cock was in his ass. Everything changed; his body relaxed and opened for me, and I had to thrust faster, immediately, chasing an orgasm that suddenly seemed imperative.

Dmey's cries were fast and hot in my ear as I thrust, and something about that meat time quality, the solid reality of those noises, sent me over. He yelped as I shoved in harder, coming deep inside him and then shoving in even more, till my processing finally caught up with the fact that I couldn't get in any more than I already was.

Panting, Dmey wrapped his hands around my forearms, squeezing them gently. In the dark, I assumed he was smiling. His body felt like he was.

I rested my forehead on his sternum. "I can't kill you," I murmured. "Not after this."

There was a beat of silence. I waited, struggling to catch my breath.

"That might be the best compliment anyone's paid me after sex," Dmey said, and laughed.

I grinned back, though I knew it couldn't be that easy. "That's all it took? A good lay and life's worth living now?"

He went still underneath me. I held my breath, afraid I'd fucked it all up. "No one has touched me," he said softly. "Not with affection. Not even for sex. Not since my war times. I thought..."

The silence stretched again. I waited as long as I could stand it. "You thought...?"

He let go of my arms, letting his fingertips slide down. "I thought I couldn't anymore. Not... not after seeing what I did. How fragile we are."

Looking down at him, watching him tremble from overexertion, I shook my head. "A lot of words come to mind to describe you right now. 'Fragile' isn't one of them. Yeah, meat's pretty tender, but I've known some steel minds wrapped up in there."

He took that in for a few moments, then smiled and wordlessly drew me down to him. We slept spooned. Fragile? Fuck yeah. But not weak.

It's not easy. Two months on, Dmey still has withdrawals, and without the benefit of programming, his physical recovery is slow and agonizing. Fortunately, pulling his hair during his strength exercises perks him up.

The war isn't over, either—not the one happening out there, and not the one inside Dmey's head. He still wakes up screaming and blind, throwing punches when I reach for him. I still shoot him up with oblivions sometimes, when nothing else will do and the memories come so fast and hard he can't breathe.

It's not all about Dmey now, not directly. When he can, he tells me what he remembers about the war, and I'm working on a counterarmy and a plan. Slowly. Safely. I used to feel that dying while trying to accomplish something was enough, but it isn't anymore. Dmey and I both have something to live for now, reasons to care for ourselves.

And we still ethercon sometimes. For old times' sake.

A Woman of Uncommon Accomplishment
Elizabeth Reeve

It started in the library at Netherfield. Mary Bennet had grown up as the plainest of five sisters, without a dowry or any prospects to speak of. And even with three of those sisters now married, there was still Kitty to contend with, and she was a much more amiable, pretty girl than Mary could ever hope to be.

So, as the least desirable of two sisters, she maintained that practice which she had at first developed as a method of distinguishing herself among five: becoming accomplished. She played and sang, taught herself to draw, and read as extensively as she could manage, searching for wit and wisdom and making extracts. It was in the pursuit of this last that she discovered the existence of magic.

Netherfield's library was not vast, but Mr. Bingley's father had laid in a supply of books with more of an eye to quantity than taste, and the collection was consequently very interesting, offering a far greater range of opinions than those offered by Mary's own father's more sensible library. This was an irresistible attraction. Additionally, Mary could sit quite peacefully for hours on end at Netherfield, enjoying her reading without harassment from her mother or younger sister or teasing from her father. Indeed, she felt so comfortable in Netherfield's sitting rooms and parlors that she even dared to read the occasional novel without much fear of discovery.

She knew immediately upon seeing it that the spellbook was *not* a novel, but she guessed that it might be something scandalous. It was bound in pale blue velvet, with silver embroidery meandering over the covers, and no title in view. She hesitated. Until recently, her favorite extracts had come largely from religious texts, and she had taken some pride in her moral rectitude. It seemed unlikely that anything bound so lavishly could be meant for the delicate eyes of a respectable young lady.

But who would know? She was all but alone in the house. The servants would never trouble her, Jane and Mr. Bingley had gone for a drive, and Caroline Bingley had retired to her private sitting room with a headache after Mary had engaged her in some conversation on the topic of vanity.

She hesitated for only a moment, therefore, before taking the book down and folding back the front cover. The pages were unevenly cut and smelled curious. Not musty, as books often did, but almost spiced, as though they had been sprinkled with nutmeg, though the paper was as smooth and pale as cream. There was no frontispiece, nor a table of contents. The text, handwritten in an ink nearly as blue as the book's cover, began immediately. And what strange text it was! By the time Mary had fully comprehended that what she was reading was not a sentimental account of travels or a diary, but a book of magic, it was too late for even her formidable sense of morality to interrupt her study. She was fascinated.

She read steadily into the afternoon, until she was interrupted as she squinted in the half-light of early evening by Miss Bingley coming in with a candle. She looked up from where she sat hidden in the shadows, and Miss Bingley promptly shrieked in surprise.

"Heavens!" Caroline cried, pressing one hand to her breast. "Whatever are you doing, lurking in the dark like that? Are you trying to frighten me to death?"

Mary hid the book in her skirt, and rubbed her eyes, pretending to have been asleep. "No," she said mildly. And then, as Miss Bingley turned away, added very quietly, "Though I could."

She felt a little guilty, at the end of her stay with her eldest sister, when she tucked the book into her reticule and took it home just as if it belonged to her. But she couldn't risk leaving it behind. There was too much she wanted to learn from it. And, as the Bingleys quitted the property only a month later, she felt somewhat justified in her minor theft.

It was not as though she would have had much opportunity to get at it again, even if Mr. Bingley had brought it with him to his new estate. She knew she would not often be invited to visit her elder sisters. Their clear preference for Kitty's society—and her mother's promotion of it in the hopes of Kitty's marrying well, while seeming to have no expectation that Mary should be able to secure a husband at all—ought to have grated. Such slights had often wounded her in the past. But Mary did not care much for society, had long since learned to ignore her mother's opinions, and had never wanted a husband so much as she had wanted the influence and respectability that came with having one. And as her study of the spellbook progressed, she began to think that she could gain a certain kind of standing in another way, without dependence on anything so capricious as a man.

The testing of this theory would have to wait, however, until she was at a safe remove from Longbourn. Mrs. Bennet's keen interest in the doings of others would doubtless wake her mother from the soundest sleep to come and find her out even if she waited until the dead of night to try a spell. So when her second-eldest sister invited her for a visit, Mary was more than usually eager to travel to Pemberly, where she ordinarily would have dreaded being compared to the accomplished Miss Darcy.

But while she might not be the most studied young woman at Pemberly, she was almost certainly the only one who could light a candle with a whisper and a thought. Which, she discovered with very little delay, she *could* do. Her first effort successful, Mary tried out several other small spells from the book. She soon found that she could light candles, make them move through the air, and put them out again. Also, she could change the color of a gown, and make fairy lights appear and dance at her command. Paltry tricks, but satisfying nonetheless.

It was much easier to sit through a tedious morning with Lizzy and Miss Darcy after that. Though Mary was so caught up in deciding which spell she would try first that evening that her sister asked if she was unwell. She had spent fifteen minutes entirely in silence, neither turning the pages of a book, nor enlightening the other ladies with recently gleaned extracts. After staring at Lizzy in some confusion for a moment, Mary quickly seized on the idea.

She excused herself to her room, and spent the afternoon increasing the shine of her hair, and giving a charming spring to the ringlets that framed her face. She felt a pang of unease, recalling her lectures on vanity, but banished it with a little experimentation in smoothing her complexion.

However, she soon found, as afternoon faded into evening, that cosmetic changes were almost the extent of her abilities. She could alter the size, shape, and color of nearly anything, but could not float more than one candle through the air, and certainly not herself. Her attempt to give herself wings met with similar failure, as well as an uncomfortable itching in the middle of her back.

She needed help.

Mary searched through the book again and found something she could try. It would take longer than her other spells, and be louder, and, if the ingredients required were any indication, might have a strong smell to it. So she gathered her tools, and crept out of the house and across the well-kept lawns, disappearing into Pemberley Woods.

It had seemed like the sort of thing one ought to do in blackest night, but as she scratched runes into the grass, Mary was glad that she'd chosen mid-morning instead. It was easier to get away from the house on a casual walk without arousing notice, and it was much easier to see what she was doing. After perhaps half an hour, she had finished her diagrams, combined her components in the proper order, and begun to cast the spell. It had advertised for "intimate knowledge of the occult," and as a colored mist formed in the center of her markings, Mary braced herself for the flow of wisdom that she was sure would come.

The man who coalesced in the circle was an unwelcome surprise.

He was most scandalously garbed. He wore buckskin breeches and boots, as any man might, but had no tailcoat at all. His shirt-sleeves seemed shockingly white against a blue waistcoat. A gold ring glinted from one earlobe. The slow, crooked smile that stretched his lips as he looked at Mary from top to toes only added to a general impression of unsavoryness.

"A gentry mort!" he said, apparently delighted. He moved toward her with easy assurance, and reached out to stroke her cheek. Mary froze, discomfited by this forward behavior.

"So shy now, little witch? Come, unrig yourself, and we'll play at rantum-scantum." His breath was hot against her ear, he'd stepped so close.

Mary started back, finally alarmed enough to move. "I beg your pardon?"

"Swive, rut, roger." The man's smile turned teasing. "Introduce my *arbor vitae* into your fruitful vine. Is this not why you called me?"

"Good Lord!" Mary cried. She did not recognize all his rough language, but he had made his meaning plain. "No, that is *not*—I did not call you, *sir*."

If she hoped by this address to shame him into an approximation of civility, she was to be disappointed. "I'll be sweet, I swear it, though I am well-hung. And as I am not a man, I won't fill your belly."

Again, it took Mary a moment to untangle his meaning, but she shook her head vigorously while she worked it out. "No! Certainly not. I am a respectable woman."

Now it was the demon (for if he was not a man, what else could he be?) who stepped back in alarm. He squinted at her thoughtfully. "A virgin? I see you're not some short-heeled wench, to fall on your back with ease. But, indeed, you may ride Saint George if you please, and be uppermost." His tone was wheedling, less assured.

"No," Mary repeated, absolutely firm, though she was less and less certain what she was refusing. What had Saint George to do with anything?

The demon frowned, almost pouting, and sat down on the ground. "Then what purpose did you have in summoning me here?"

"I... did not mean to," Mary confessed. "I apologize for disturbing you. You may go back where you came from, without delay."

The pout became a scowl. "Indeed, I can not. The terms of your spell were clear to me, if they meant nothing to you. I may not depart this plane until I have served you. A task I *thought* would please us both."

"You were mistaken," Mary said primly. She was as upset by her failure to either comprehend the nature of the spell, or cast it correctly, as she was by the demon's lewdness, but she chose to put as much of the blame on him as she could manage. She snatched up the spellbook, tucked it into her reticule, and turned back toward the house. "I shall leave you to find your own way home."

"Mar-all!" The demon shouted at her back. "Doggess! You'll not be rid of me so easy!"

She affected not to hear him. And when she chanced a look over her shoulder, she saw with no little satisfaction that, despite his words, he was gone.

The demon rejoined her that evening. Mary had retired early to her own room for the night, feeling too fatigued from her recent studies to tolerate more than an hour of conversation with the Darcys after dinner. She had just dismissed the maid who was helping her undress for sleep and was turning toward the bed when she saw him, lounging against her pillows.

He winked. Mary screamed.

The maid came dashing back into the room. "What is it? Miss Bennet?"

Mary looked at her in astonishment. She was facing the bed, just as Mary was. Could she not see for herself what was the matter? But it seemed that she could not. The demon smiled, and winked again, and Mary shook her head. "Nothing. I thought I saw... Something foul."

"Foul, am I?" said the demon, when the maid had left again. "Take another look, you moon-eyed hen. I'm a fine figure of a man!"

He started to unbutton his waistcoat, as if he would display his figure more clearly, and Mary lost her shyness in indignation. She strode over to him directly and slapped his hands away. "Stop it! You're indecent enough as it is." She frowned. "And I thought you said you are not a man."

"I am man-*like*," the demon answered. "More than like enough for your purposes. But no, I am not one of your kind. I am an incubus."

Mary did not intend to demonstrate further ignorance by asking what that was, and merely nodded as though she understood. "Be that as it may, I have no purpose for you at all, and will not submit to your seductions. You had much better go home."

The incubus sighed. "I have said that I cannot. Your spell has bound me, to this world and to you, until I have completed my service. Only then can I return." His hands went to his buttons again. "Now, as you have expressed such dislike for my person, perhaps you'd prefer to get it over with at once, and have done. Then I will go, and trouble you no further."

Mary slapped at his hands again, then grasped them in her own and held them, heedless of the impropriety of their position as she attempted to prevent greater licentiousness. So close to him, she could see that his eyes were strange, a pale violet color instead of the blue she had taken them for at a distance. Beyond that, he did resemble a man, and a handsome one. His hair was dark and curling, his teeth even, and his skin was neither too fine nor too weathered. And there was something pleasing in his face when he smiled, even if the ring in his ear gave every expression a rakish cast.

He was smiling now, Mary realized, because she was still holding his hands. She dropped them at once. "I am sorry to have trapped you here, but what you ask is impossible. Surely there must be some alternative? Can not your service—" she tripped over the word. Would she ever be able to say it without blushing again? "—be rendered in another manner?"

"I doubt it," the incubus said peevishly. "But it seems that I have no alternative but to try, since you are determined to give me the worst bout of horn colic I have suffered this age."

Mary was struck with sudden inspiration. "Then perhaps you can tutor me in magic? You seem to know a great deal about it."

This flattery had its intended result, and the incubus seemed somewhat mollified. "I do, indeed."

"It is worth an attempt, then, is it not?" Mary knew that she had not her younger sisters' gifts when it came to feminine persuasion, but she had learned a thing or two about the gentle art of widening one's eyes and blinking rapidly. "You would truly be doing me a service."

He did not appear to be entirely convinced, but the incubus nodded.

"Good, then." Agreement secured, Mary returned immediately to her usual brusque manner. "We will begin in the morning. I must ask you to leave my room until then, however. I require rest."

She had been contriving, by means of calculated shrugging and very good posture, to keep her gown and petticoats on all this while. The maid had unfastened the dress and loosened her stays, but fortunately had left Mary to completely remove the articles on her own, which preserved some of her modesty. She had no intention of relinquishing that now by undressing in front of her accidental companion.

The incubus sighed. "Very well." He swung his legs over the side of the bed and stood up, then tipped an imaginary hat. "Until the morrow, then, Miss Bennet."

Mary was startled that he knew her name, until she recalled that the maid had said it. Belatedly, she asked, "What should I call you?"

The incubus grinned. "An excellent question. Call me... Call me 'Nick.'" And with that, he faded from view.

Nick came back in the morning, almost immediately after Mary had finished dressing. So well-timed was his appearance, in fact, that Mary nervously wondered if he might have been there all along, as invisible to her as he had been to the maid the night before. However, if he had, the damage was done, and she determined to think no more about it.

"Good morning, Miss Bennet," he said cordially. Mary returned the greeting, and he inquired after her health, and then if she was ready to begin her lessons.

She was indeed, and with no little excitement. She had never had much in the way of formal education, and had often longed for the experience. Though she could read, and did her best to improve her mind with private study, she could not help but feel that a governess would have helped her to get on. Presumably, a tutor in magic would be a similar boon.

Nick took a seat on a little chair placed near the window. "Tell me what you already know, for a beginning. Then I will have some idea of where your understanding can be improved."

Mary was most eager to demonstrate her accomplishment in the sorcerous arts, and launched with no hesitation into a lecture on the subject, complete with asides that showed—so she hoped—her own perspicacity.

She was to be disappointed.

"Stop, I beg you!" Nick cried, with exaggerated desperation. "Leave off these break-teeth words and dog-Latin. I am satisfied that you have read a great deal of something. Where is the source of all this wisdom?"

Her face a little hot, Mary produced the spellbook.

"This is a cow-handed hodge-podge indeed," Nick pronounced after several minutes of silent page-turning. "I am no longer surprised that you summoned me by accident. The theory is sound enough, but it's so full of gingerbread work I am amazed that you managed to wring any spells from it alone. And yet you did do some magic as you intended?"

Mary nodded, and at further prompting exhibited her modest skills. She lit and extinguished candles, made small objects dance, and changed the colors of several things, including Nick's waistcoat. She had thought the alarming shade of purple would discommode him, but he laughed and said he liked it, so she left it as it was.

"Oh, cleverly done!" Nick said when she had exhausted her knowledge, with every appearance of sincerity. Mary's cheeks colored again, but this time with pleasure. "I think we will get on very well, if I can contrive to repair this text somewhat as we go along."

Thus encouraged, Mary settled down to her study, with Nick's assistance, and passed above an hour in this enjoyable pursuit. But she soon found that being accompanied in her quest for self-improvement had some unfortunate aspects to it as well as the beneficial ones. Nick was much given to obscene language, for example, which was distracting. As well, he fidgeted near-constantly, particularly with the gold hoop in his ear.

After perhaps the thousandth time his fingers toyed with his earlobe, Mary demanded, "Why do you wear an earring? Is it only to make everyone else uncomfortable?"

"This?" Nick twisted the gold ring again, and laughed. "It was much the fashion for men some hundred years ago, and I like the look of it still."

"A hundred years!" Mary cried. "I did not think you could be above thirty. How old *are* you?"

"I don't know. If I should ever chance to meet my mother, perhaps I'll ask her." Nick delivered this surprising response with a studied unconcern that Mary found less than convincing. "Why, Miss Bennet? How old are *you*?"

Mary looked down at the spellbook and muttered, "Old enough."

"Enough for… Ah, I see it now." Nick's eyes narrowed. "Old enough to be a spinster, is that it? I had wondered what would bring such a *respectable* young lady to the study of sorcery. Are you hoping to magic up a husband, then?"

Mary shut the spellbook with some force. "*No*. And I certainly wasn't hoping to 'magic up' an impertinent scoundrel like yourself.

But if you must know, I have no interest in marrying. I am perfectly content to remain as I am. And though I have no fortune to sustain me, I have two liberal sisters well-married, and... And I will continue to be content. I will. No matter what people think of me. I have never cared for the opinions of others."

"Ah." Nick was still for a moment, then reached to take the book gently from Mary's hands. He opened it to the place they had stopped. "But you'd rather enchant toads than be made to swallow them, I suppose? Very well. Let us see if, in teaching you, I can manage to free us both."

It was not much of an apology, but Mary appreciated it nonetheless, and willingly bent her attention back to their work.

By breakfast time, they had made fair progress. Mary was able to move a few objects of greater size than she had managed on her own, and had a much better understanding of the principles behind the spells she had taught herself. She was satisfied, and ready to stop until evening, or perhaps the next day. Nick was less so.

"Tell your sister that you're ill," he suggested. "A lady can be alone when she's ill, can she not? If we go on at this rate, we'll be at this for weeks."

"I could retire for a few hours with a headache, perhaps, but if I stay in my room all day, Elizabeth will worry, and may send for the doctor. It will hardly serve your purpose if I am tended at all hours for a pretended illness."

Nick scowled. "I suppose you are right. It's only that while *you* have gained a tame magic tutor, I am trapped here. I had never thought to play petticoat pensioner to a woman who did not desire *all* my services."

"Are you so eager to go home again? I had thought demons must enjoy our world, or they would not come so readily when called here."

"Eager to go home? No," Nick said. "Ours is a shadow world. Everything of substance, all that is diverting, is here. But as long as I am bound to you, I may not go further away than a mile or two, and there is nothing to *do* on this estate."

"I am sorry for it," Mary said, feeling very uncomfortable. It was true that she had not intended to inconvenience him in this way, but it was still her doing. And she was forced to acknowledge that the country must be a far more boring place for him than it was for her. He could not easily go for a ride, after all, or enjoy music and conversation after dinner. There were no entertainments such as might be found in town, where he could lose himself in a crowd, and his presence would be noted with suspicion anywhere near Pemberly.

And there *was* a speedier remedy to his problem at her command... But that was entirely out of the question.

"I will be free again late this evening," Mary said, and left as quickly as she could without seeming to flee.

They made speedier progress than Nick had gloomily anticipated. Within ten days, they had covered all of the spells in the book. And though Mary had not tried to cast all of them—there were some she would never wish to attempt, and others that she felt no immediate need for—those she had tested worked just as they were meant to.

She closed the book with a happy sigh. "I thank you, sir," she said, with a touch of the dramatic. The moment seemed to call for it. "You have truly done me a service."

But Nick was frowning, pacing back and forth across the room. "I'm afraid I have not, no." His form wavered, becoming transparent for a moment before solidifying again. He groaned, and cast himself violently onto the bed, where he covered his eyes with one forearm. "Bloody *fucking* arse!"

Mary was too shocked to reply. She stood up and, her cheeks burning, left the room.

Perhaps Nick would benefit from some time to compose himself, she thought. And in the meantime, she would go for a walk, and consider the problem.

After a quarter of an hour touring one of Pemberly's gardens, she was no nearer to a solution than she had been when she left her room. Her idea of substituting one kind of service for another had seemed sound, particularly when Nick examined the spell which had summoned him and said that it was constructed rather obscurely. But it had not worked, as evidenced by Nick's... *passionate* complaint.

Still, perhaps there was some merit in the idea of skirting the conditions of the spell.

When Mary returned to her room, Nick was in much the same state as when she had left it, though he had moved his arm and replaced it with a pillow that more fully covered his face. Mary sat down next to him, perching on the side of the bed. It was astonishing, how quickly she had become used to Nick's presence in her room. The idea of being anywhere near both a man and a bed at the same time would have seemed so scandalous to her only a fortnight ago.

"What if I let you kiss me?" she suggested.

The pillow shifted slightly. "I beg your pardon?"

Mary leaned over and removed the cushion. "A kiss," she said, looking into Nick's face. "Only a kiss, mind you. But could it be enough to satisfy the spell?"

Nick's expression was thoughtful. "Possibly." He sat up. "Are you certain?"

Mary took a deep breath, steeling herself, and closed her eyes. "Yes. You may proceed."

She thought she heard Nick chuckle, but then she felt the bed shift as he moved, and his breath against her cheek, and gave no further thought to it. His lips were dry and warm against hers. It was not unpleasant. She had allowed one of the Lucas boys to kiss her once and regretted it heartily. His mouth had been sticky, he had been rough, and the experience was wholly disgusting. But Nick was all gentleness, soft and light.

And then the dry brush of his mouth over hers changed slightly, a thin line of moisture passing over the seam of her lips, and Mary opened her mouth without thought. As soon as she realized that she had done it—that Nick's mouth was open, too, and his lips pressing to hers more firmly—his tongue had slipped between her teeth, and she was too fascinated to make him stop. What was he *doing*? It felt... good. Strange, but agreeable.

His scent, which she caught clearly now that their bodies were so close, was agreeable, too. As was the heat of his body, and a low sound he made in the back of his throat as she slid her tongue against his.

One of his hands went to her waist, drawing her closer. The *other* curved over her breast, fingertips questing dexterously under her fichu within the space of a breath.

Mary jerked backward and slapped him with as much force as she could manage.

He laughed, and raised his hands. "I apologize, Miss Bennet. I found I could not help myself." Seeing that she did not intend to slap him again, he relaxed, and rubbed the side of his face. "You served me out soundly for it. My compliments to your boxing teacher."

Mary's palm was stinging; she hoped that it *had* hurt him. The skin of her bosom felt as if he had branded it with his touch. "Did it work?"

Nick's violet eyes went hazy for a moment as he focused on something Mary could not see. "No." He looked at her again, and grinned, the light from the window glinting on his earring. "But we could try again."

Mary picked up the pillow he'd been using earlier, and held it in front of his face. Then she pushed, hard, until Nick fell over backward on the bed, his protests that he "hadn't *meant* it, Miss Bennet, take pity!" muffled in cotton and feathers.

Angry and embarrassed, she left the room in a hurry for the second time in one day, and did not return until well after midnight.

"Well, this is a perverse sort of cream-pot love," Nick said the next morning. Mary had just suggested that, since guiding her through the spellbook had apparently not been sufficient service, perhaps he ought to keep teaching her until he had exhausted his store of magical wisdom. "Still, I suppose we had better try it. You have me by the cods, my lady, and I am at your command."

He made her a low bow, and Mary gave him a sharp look, not certain whether she was more annoyed by his coarse language or his mockery. But she said nothing about it, and only retrieved an empty journal she had been saving, and pen and ink, and suggested that they begin.

However aggravating, Nick was a fair teacher. Within two hours' time, Mary had filled five close-written pages with spells, and was expanding her knowledge considerably. It was at that point that she inadvertently set his sleeve on fire.

"Oh!" she cried, leaping up so quickly that she knocked the inkwell onto the floor. She stood in confusion, knowing that she ought not to summon help, but not certain what else to do.

Fortunately, Nick was calmer, and put out the flames—which were a most unusual shade of bright green—with a word. He did not seem to have been hurt, though his linen was quite scorched. He frowned, muttered, and slid his hand down his sleeve. In its path, snowy white fabric took the place of ash and char.

"You're standing in ink," he said mildly.

"*Arse*," said Mary, stepping back hastily, though not hastily enough.

Nick sat down on the bed and laughed while Mary changed her slippers and put some linen down to sop up some of the ink before it stained the entire rug. She sat down beside him after, not trusting herself to return to the table they had been using without staining the soles of a second pair of slippers.

A few flakes of ash sifted off Nick's sleeve and onto her skirt. Mary sighed and brushed them away, noting dismally that they left faint tracks on her clothes, even though Nick's shirt was pristine. Or *looked* it, at least.

"How much of you is real," she asked, "and how much is artifice?"

Nick fiddled with his earring. "I sometimes wonder that myself."

"I mean your form," Mary said, when it seemed as though he would not make further answer. "Do you really look like this?"

"I do, though I could change my looks a little if I was so inclined. Why, Miss Bennet? Do you prefer your men fair?"

"I was thinking of myself." Mary spoke unguardedly, and immediately regretted it, particularly as Nick began to study her with a very serious gaze.

"There is nothing wrong with the way you look," he pronounced after a moment.

Mary rolled her eyes. "I know you are flattering me, and it will not do you any good. I have four handsome sisters and no illusions."

Though she did in a literal sense, of course, having bespelled her hair and her complexion slightly before ever meeting Nick. She decided not to mention this.

"It is not flattery when I say that you have pretty eyes," Nick said. "Nor when I tell you that the way you arch your brows when you find me tiresome—yes, just like that—is charming. And I can very honestly say that your lips... Well, I should not share all my thoughts, perhaps."

Mary knew not how to respond.

"But regardless of truth or flattery, Miss Bennet, you must realize that simply to be handsome confers no merit. I never did anything to earn my face. Accidents of birth must pale in worth when compared to what we make of the lives we live."

Mary considered this very seriously for a moment, and then said, "You may kiss me again, if you like."

Nick seemed startled, but willing enough to accept the invitation. He leaned toward her, but then stopped himself. "You understand that this is unlikely to free me, having failed to do so before?"

"Yes," Mary said. "I know."

"Well, then." Nick bridged the final distance between them, and kissed her.

He did not attempt to take further liberties. Mary found, after he had been kissing her for some time, that she almost wished he would. Her breath had grown short, and she felt hotter than she ought to have in her sensible dress.

She clenched her hands together in her lap. As he was not touching her, she had a sudden and entirely improper urge to touch *him*.

As she formed the thought, he abruptly put a stop to the kiss, though he did not move away from her. "An idea has occurred to me," Nick murmured against her mouth. "Something else worth trying."

"Like kissing?" She realized only after she had said it that he meant something worth trying in order to break the spell that bound him, and felt silly.

But Nick paused, and then said, "Yes, like kissing. There are lips involved."

Mary frowned, quite certain that he was not telling her the whole, and a little disappointed by the shift in his focus. "Will it hurt?"

"Lord, no. Not at all. You'll like it."

Mary had scarce nodded her consent before Nick slid off the bed and knelt on the floor. And before she could react to this astonishing behavior, he had topped it by ducking under her skirt.

"Whatever are you—"

"Curse these buntlings," Nick interrupted, his voice muffled as he fought with her petticoat. "Ah, success!"

With this last, his breath fanned across the junction between her thighs, and Mary shivered, though the sensation was far from chilling. His hands were at her knees, and she parted them without quite knowing what she did, following his insistent nudging until one thigh rested over his shoulder—at least, she *thought* it was his shoulder. He was difficult to make out for certain through her skirt—and then his tongue followed his breath and she had to cover her mouth for fear of summoning a servant by accident.

All her intentions of objecting, or at least demanding to know what he thought he was about, flew out of her head.

Mary had taken enjoyment from many things in her life. Playing well, the rare approval of one of her parents, an engrossing text, her study of magic. And, most recently, Nick's kisses. But what she felt as he knelt between her thighs was beyond any of those things, even the last. It was... Carnality, she recognized. She was no better than Lydia, with her flirtations and the lust that would not wait for the decency of marriage. She was *worse* than Lydia! She should make Nick stop.

She did not. He kissed her in her most secret place, and she trembled with the pleasure of it. His tongue slid over her, and she heard herself moan, so loud that she worried someone might hear. She bit the heel of her palm. She felt faint, her breath coming too fast, and she lowered herself onto the bed before she could fall, her body supported by the mattress though her legs—oh, Lord!—were still under Nick's command.

His fingers joined his tongue, stroking lightly at first, and then with increasing firmness, and Mary quaked under them. He built her pleasure higher and higher, a precarious tower that tumbled at last, and took her with it. She cried out against her hand. She thought she would shake to pieces.

When she knew she was herself again, she opened her eyes to see Nick beside her, propped on one elbow. His hair was disheveled, and his face flushed. He looked almost unbearably pleased with himself.

Mary said the first thing that came into her head. "I am a fallen woman."

Nick shook his head, conjured a handkerchief from somewhere, and dabbed the sweat from her face before wiping his own. "You are virgo intacta still; I left your maidenhead just as I found it."

Mary felt that this was adhering so far to the letter as to have bypassed the spirit entirely, and opened her mouth to say so. But it was done. What use would argument be?

"Did it work?" she asked instead.

"Hm?" Nick's eyes widened. "Oh." His face took on the faraway look that Mary had learned to associate with his magic, and he frowned and shook his head again.

Mary turned away from him and curled up on her side, fighting tears, though she could not have said precisely what had made her sad.

She felt Nick's weight shifting on the bed, then the heat of his body close against her back. "Have I hurt you?"

"No," Mary said miserably. "I liked it."

Nick stroked her hair and did not answer at once. "You're meant to like it," he said. "There should be no shame in that. Your body is made for sensuality. Your ears to hear music, your eyes to see beauty." He curved one hand over her hip. "Your...venerable monosyllable... is no different."

"But what will people think of me? A woman's reputation is as fragile as..." She couldn't finish that statement. She simply could not.

"In the first place," Nick murmured in her ear, "who will know? And second, yet more important: Did you not once tell me that you do not care about the opinions of others?"

Mary sighed. "I must admit that I spoke more of how I wish to be than how I am."

He touched her shoulder, leaning over her until she looked him in the face. He smiled down at her. "If there is one thing I know about you, Miss Bennet, it is that you are very good at making yourself what you wish to be."

She felt her mood lighten. And after all, she had liked it. She had relied less and less on the staid wisdom of her extracts of late. Perhaps this was one more instance in which she ought to be guided by her own feelings, instead of those of persons whose principal claim to authority was that they had written dry books that no one but Mary chose to read.

Nick's smile was really quite handsome; Mary gave him one of her own.

Mary needed some time on her own after… After whatever it was that Nick had done. So far, he had only ever appeared to her in her bedroom or, as on that very first occasion, on the grounds. She felt tolerably certain, therefore, that he would not disturb her if she kept out of her room for a while. But she was no more eager for anyone else's company, and avoided the sitting room as well. Instead, she went to a place where she knew she could be alone.

The library at Pemberly was as large as her father's and Mr. Bingley's and perhaps the libraries of several other gentlemen combined. And though all the Darcys seemed to be fond of reading, there were plenty of books tucked away on high or otherwise inconvenient shelves that looked as though they hadn't been touched in ages. They were even a little dusty, despite the excellence of Mr. Darcy's staff. Mary had intended to find a quiet place to sit and simply be with her own thoughts for a while, but the allure of undiscovered books soon called to her. She began to hunt through them for anything of particular interest.

Which was how she found the second spellbook. She knew at once what it was, somehow, even before she opened the unassuming, wine-colored cover. The cramped handwriting that filled the creamy pages only confirmed her suspicion.

"Good Lord, does *every* gentleman have books of magic hiding amongst his respectable histories and travelogues?" she wondered. But she did not wonder it for long. After all, there was an entirely new spellbook to look through and that trumped every other consideration.

She thought about taking it back to her room, to see if Nick might like to join her in perusing it—but only for a moment. She found that she still craved solitude. And besides that, it occurred to Mary that it would be very agreeable to find some spell that Nick had not taught her, and master it in order to surprise him.

Within the first few pages she had found a version of the spell with which she had set Nick's sleeve on fire, and which seemed to address the difficulty she'd had with the incantation. She made a pleased sound, carefully marked the page, and read on.

Halfway through the book, she found a spell for breaking the bonds of magical contracts gone awry.

She read it through a second time. Surely she had imagined the existence of a spell so suited to her peculiar needs. But even the fourth and fifth time, it remained as it had been: a spell that would release Nick, his service unfulfilled.

Mary shut the book and stared at the wall opposite to her seat. Suddenly, she had even more to think about.

She had arrived at a decision by dinner, and then spent most of the meal, two hours at cards, and several more in idle conversation insisting to her concerned sister that she was not at all ill, and did not need to retire for the evening yet. The hectic color in her cheeks had nothing to do with a fever. And though her choice was made, Mary found that she was in no hurry to make it irrevocable, and delayed returning to her room until quite late.

Nick was there, sitting by the window and leafing idly through a novel. He rose when she entered, and Mary crossed the room to stand in front of him. She hesitated for one instant more, then put her hands on his shoulders, shifted her weight onto her toes, and reached up to press her lips to his.

He was still as a statue, and for a horrid moment Mary feared that he would push her away. But then his arms wrapped around her, drawing her near, and he bent his head and kissed her back. She relaxed, and her body curved against his as she parted her lips and licked into his mouth. Nick held her tighter, and she had to push against him a little in order to slide one hand between their bodies, seeking the buttons of his absurdly purple waistcoat.

Nick froze, and released her lips. "What are you doing?"

"I thought that you of all people would recognize it," Mary said, with a light laugh that did not do as much to hide her nervousness as she would have liked.

Nick neither laughed nor smiled, but frowned at her, his brows drawn close together. "You need not do this, Miss Bennet. We are sure to find another way to free me eventually."

Mary could have told him what she had discovered. She did not. Instead, she asked, "Do you desire me?"

Nick put his face close to hers, his nose sliding against her cheek. "Yes," he murmured. "More and more, I find. But do you..."

Mary nodded. He was too close to see the motion, but perhaps he could feel it. "I want this. You."

He made no answer, but turned his head slightly to kiss the lobe of her ear, then the curve of her cheek, and then her mouth again. And when Mary had undone all of the buttons on his waistcoat, he shrugged it off his shoulders and let it fall to the floor.

He pulled away from her then, but only so that he could untie his neck cloth and then tug his shirt over his head and send it to join his waistcoat. Mary gazed at him with interest. He was lean, and the muscles stood out plainly on his stomach and along his arms. His smooth skin was pale, with dark hair across his chest and in a line below his navel.

Before she could look her fill, Nick had put his hands on her shoulders, and was turning her gently about. Mary opened her mouth to protest, but then she felt his hands at the fastenings of her dress, and she held still and let him slide the material down her arms to pool at her feet. His fingertips trailed back up her arms and whispered across her shoulders before returning to her back, and he began to work at the laces of her stays, tugging at them with a hint of impatience.

There was a moment every evening, just after her stays had been loosened, when Mary took a deep breath unfettered for the first time all day, and felt giddy from the simple pleasure of it. She found that the knowledge that it was Nick who had released her, and for what purpose, made that breath even more intoxicating. She exhaled shakily, and felt almost cold until Nick stepped close behind her, his hands sliding up her unbound ribs until he filled his palms with her breasts.

She was hot where he touched her, and where he was pressed against her back. She wanted more of that heat, and leaned against him in search of it. He squeezed her flesh gently and rubbed the pads of his thumbs across her nipples. Mary moaned, reaching for the hem of her chemise.

They were on the bed almost before she realized it. She had a hazy impression of pulling the garments she still wore off over her head, and then dropping them in surprise when she felt Nick's lips against the back of her thigh, and his hands rolling her stockings down. And then she was nude, and on the bed, watching Nick yank his boots off in an undignified way before shedding his breeches and drawers and stockings all in a muddled tangle.

Her eyes widened. She had seen animals mating often enough to know roughly what to expect when it came to a masculine organ, but it was so... "That will never fit."

Nick grinned lasciviously, and stroked himself. "Such flattery! But you must not fear my gaying instrument, Miss Bennet. I assure you, it will bring much pleasure to us both."

"Mary," she said, her face burning. "I think you had better call me by my Christian name."

"Mary, then." Nick crawled up the bed and stretched out beside her, putting one hand gently on her belly as he leaned over for another kiss.

She put her hand over his, then tentatively caressed his arm. His skin was warm, and soft under her fingertips. She explored up to his shoulder and then, more boldly, mapped the span of his ribs. Nick pulled her lower lip between his teeth and nibbled gently. Mary took this as encouragement, and, feeling very brazen indeed, put her hand on his thigh.

His body felt so different from hers. His skin was soft enough and really rather smooth, but still coarser than her own. And where her thighs were plump and supple, his were strong and hard. Virile. The thought made her quiver in anticipation.

Or perhaps it was his lips that made her quiver. Nick had released her mouth and was kissing her throat. His lips were parted;

his tongue flickered against her skin. Mary would have guessed that such a thing would feel damp and disagreeable, but she found that she liked it very well indeed.

And then he kissed her breast. Mary gripped his thigh, and the sound that Nick made was as much a laugh as a groan of pleasure.

"Mary," he whispered against her skin, and looked up and met her eyes as he slowly, teasingly drew the peak of her breast into his mouth.

Mary gasped. The place between her legs felt hot and wet and aching, and she clenched her thighs together. Nick licked and sucked at her breast and slid the hand on her belly down until he was stroking her where he had before. Pleasure rolled through her body, and the tension in her thighs eased, though her toes curled and flexed against the counterpane.

She closed her eyes, sighing, only to flinch and open them again as she felt the tip of Nick's finger slip into her body. He was watching her face intently, doubtless looking for a smile or a frown, but Mary knew not what signal to give him. She was certain that it should hurt, but found that it did not. It was uncomfortable, and strange, but not painful. And then Nick did something clever with that hand, and it was so very far from hurting that she made an undignified, squeaking sound in surprise.

He grinned, and kissed her other breast. "Do you like that?"

"Ye-es," Mary answered, the word broken in the middle as a second finger joined the first. "What should I— That is, what would you—" She stopped in confusion, not at all sure how to ask him how she could give him pleasure.

But Nick seemed to know what she meant. He pressed himself against her, his erection firm against her hip, and kissed her breast again. "I give you leave to be selfish," he said. "Truly. My prick will keep."

Thus encouraged, Mary attended to the sensations Nick drew from her body with skillful fingers until she was trembling and gasping, hovering once again at the height of passion. And then, with a flick of his thumb, he pushed her as high as she could go, and helped her fall.

She was still trembling when he moved over her and settled his hips between her thighs. She wrapped her arms around him, unsure of what to do, and knowing only that she wanted him closer. And then he was, his body joining with hers in one slow thrust.

"Are you well, Mary?" he asked, pausing.

"Yes," she said. "Quite well. Please don't stop on my account."

Nick chuckled, and Mary marveled at the sensation this caused. She moved her hips slightly, adjusting to the feeling of fullness, and finding herself unexpectedly excited again. Nick stopped laughing, and groaned instead, sounding almost as if he was in pain.

"I fear I won't last as long as I would have liked." He started to move before Mary could answer, and she forgot what she had meant to say. "But I shall try to bring you to your peak again before I spend."

He was as good as his word. He rested his weight on one arm as he rocked his hips into her, and caressed her body with his free hand. His fingers moved lightly over all the skin he could reach, and Mary found that her throat and belly and even her arms and shoulders were newly sensitive, as though she was experiencing touch for the first time in her life.

Her pleasure seemed to please him, too. He kissed her face again and again, and panted into her mouth when she opened to him. By the time he shifted so that he could reach between their bodies and stroke her at the point where they were joined, Mary was already trembling again. It took only a firm touch as he moved within her to send her over. His thrusts sped up as she quaked around him, and he followed her within moments, crying out with his face pressed against the side of her neck.

He rolled free of her as soon as they both had stopped shaking, and drew her close to his side. Mary rested her head against his shoulder, and listened to him breathing as her own breath quieted.

"Did it work?" she wondered drowsily.

"Oh, yes." Nick kissed her forehead. "I dare say it did."

She fell asleep.

Mary was alone in the bed when she woke. She stretched her arm out, but the linen beside her was already cold. Her eyes stung, and she blinked them hard. She had known he would be gone. He was free. Of course he would not stay. She would *not* cry.

"Good morning, Mary."

She sat up, looking wildly about the room. Nick was standing by the window, leaning against the wall.

"You haven't left." Mary would have been embarrassed by the obviousness of this remark, were she not overcome with quite different feelings.

"No. I decided to stay for a while longer." Nick crossed the room and sat down next to her on the bed. "That is, if you have no objection."

Mary could think of nothing she had objected to less in her life. But what she said was, "I found another spellbook. We can study it together."

Nick laughed, and kissed her; she kissed him back.

Navigator
Kathleen Tudor

In a small home on the edge of a small town on a planet at the very edge of civilization, ex-Pilot Kirsa Anlee settled into a comfortable chair to lose herself in the book she'd just downloaded. A knock interrupted her before she had truly sunk into the novel. She paid a boy from town to bring her a small load of produce and groceries every week, but he wasn't due for another couple of hours, and he was never early.

"Evan?" she called.

"No, ma'am, Global Security. We'd like to speak with you." As she stood to open the door, she suppressed an urge to snarl at the intrusion. All she wanted out of life was to be left alone – what could the planet's police want with her? "Excuse us," the younger officer said. His rank badge placed him above the older man standing beside him. "We're looking for Pilot Kirsa."

"Wrong house," Kirsa said, starting to shut the door. He held up a photo of her, several years old but still accurate. She sighed and let go of the door, slumping toward the frame in a forced pose of relaxation. "Well then why bother asking me?"

The young officer squirmed in his boots. "Manners?" he said in a way that suggested she lacked them. She smiled in a decidedly unfriendly way.

"And you want?"

He stood straighter. "We have been asked to request your presence at the Continental Administrator's office."

"What happens if I politely decline?"

"I'd hate to have to do this to a Pilot, but we've been authorized to use force if necessary to bring you in."

Kirsa pushed away from the doorframe. "Ex-pilot. What the hell does the Administration want with me?"

The young cop shrugged, "Not our business. We were only told that the matter is extremely urgent, Pi- uh, ma'am."

This time Kirsa did slam the door in his face. She'd gotten into the habit of owning only as much as she could carry in the Pilot's Academy, so it was easy to shove her few possessions and changes of clothing into a bag. She figured she had a good ten minutes before they broke down the door, so she took a moment to count out money for Evan before heading out. The young cop sagged in relief as she opened the door again. "You can recall your partner from my back window. I'm ready."

He offered his arm to escort her. She snorted and preceded him to their patrol car, foiling his attempt to place her in the back seat by opening up the passenger door and strapping in. The two cops exchanged a speaking look before the older man climbed in back and she was whisked off to the nearest transport station.

The two cops had reserved a transport for the three of them, and sat across from her on the mini-train in a comfortable cabin. So, whatever she had apparently done didn't merit being treated like a criminal. Mostly.

An hour into the journey, the older cop broke the silence. "I'm Grad," he said. She nodded. He started to speak, hesitated, then spat out his question. "Why did you give it up?"

"Give what up?" Kirsa asked.

"Piloting," he said, a sort of wonder suffusing his features. Almost everyone tested for Piloting ability when they were young, but the telepathy required, though weak, ruled most applicants out immediately. Kirsa was barely strong enough as a telepath, and had clamped down on her small ability long since anyway.

Her eyes hardened at the questioned. "Pilots don't "give it up". They get stranded. Do you know what that means?" Grad shook his head, his lips parting in surprise at her reaction. "It means that their Navigator dies." Her voice broke on the last word and she stared at him until Grad transferred his gaze to his lap. The rest of the journey was spent in a tense silence, and the relief of the cops was palpable when they were able to transfer her to the Administrator's offices.

"Please, come this way," said the secretary who'd taken charge of her, and Kirsa followed her directly to a large office. The middle aged Administrator behind the desk was obviously not the kind to delegate his entire job – his paper was stacked high with papers. The secretary shut the door behind her. Kirsa turned at the sound of the latch slipping into place, but stopped cold when she saw the young woman in the corner. Navigator.

"Her family didn't know to look for the signs. Hell, most of our people wouldn't. She was brought to a hospital raving two weeks ago and sedated. When they finally figured out what she was, they sent her to me." Kirsa forced her eyes away from the girl and forced a look of indifference.

"What does that have to do with me?"

The Administrator sighed and gestured her to the only other free chair in the room. She thought of refusing, but something told her she was going to be here a long time. The chair was stiff backed and hard.

"I've been in contact with the Traveler's Guild. They tell me it's too late to send a pair to bring her to the Academy."

Kirsa didn't glance at the dazed, sedated child in the corner. "They're right."

"I know that. I had a whole team digging through the records. Did you know that it has been a century since this world has produced a Pilot? There aren't even any records of a Navigator being born here. But then they found your immigration records. You were very hard to locate."

"It's intentional. I'm retired." Kirsa shifted in her chair, too proud to grumble and too uncomfortable to sit still. It wasn't just the chair that made her uncomfortable, though. The Navigator, probably a good decade her junior, curled in on herself in a chair across the room.

"Please, Pilot, how can you just let her die?"

"Look, I can't train her. I'm not a Navigator, I'm not a trainer, and I haven't even been evaluated for her bond." Kirsa had come to this backwater planet to get as far as she could from the Traveler's

Guild. "My Navigator died. You can't just bond anyone."

"Can't you at least try? Look at her!" He pointed toward where the girl was starting to look dazed and distant. The best way most Navigators could explain it was that the pulsing of the stars seemed almost to sing, calling them. No Navigator could resist it long; it looked like this little thing didn't have much time left. Watching the girl felt like twisting a knife inside her own gut. Taul had died that way.

"Fuck you." She gritted her teeth, trying to get a grip. "You don't know what you're asking of me. She's been sedated for two weeks. If she can't control herself up there, we're both dead." Pilots were the only ones who could pair with a Navigator to Travel. The Navigator provided the pathway outside of normal space, the Pilot provided control and a tie to real world.

The young woman across the room, started to whimper softly. "Cassin?" The administrator reached into a desk drawer, pulled out a sedative, and awkwardly injected the girl, who went almost immediately from looking dazed to simply looking drugged.

"She won't last much longer like this," he said, disposing of the syringe as if it would bite him. "We can drug her to suppress the urges, but we won't be able to keep her down much longer." Navigators possessed the inexplicable ability to take a ship traveling near light speed and fling it elsewhere. The stars told them where to go. But the experience was like a drug. Too long without spending time submersed in Ether space, and they started to experience that same space without the benefit of Travel. They went into a catatonic state, and soon their brains simply turned off.

Kirsa ticked off her objections on her fingers. "I haven't flown in years. I am not a Navigator or a trainer of any kind. She's so drugged up that it will probably kill us anyway, and you'll be out a shuttle. We're both women—"

"What does that matter?"

"The pairings work best if the partners are of complementary sexes."

"I've heard of same-sex pairs."

"It's rare. There are maybe two flying now, or at least last I heard. Anyway, we don't even know each other. Pairs are supposed to be tested, profiled, matched." Rather than abating, Kirsa could feel his determination rise. "What will happen to me if I refuse to fly her?"

"I will do what I must to save such a rare skill," and to gain the recognition and income it would bring to this backwater place. "You will be placed in a shuttle with the girl. If you save her, you will be compensated. If you don't, well, it seems that an inquest into your actions would be called for at least. It could be manslaughter."

"So it's a likely death with her, or a likely prison sentence here. Prepare her," she said, suddenly tired.

The administrator nodded, obviously relieved. "Tisany is waiting for you outside. She's to escort you to the shuttle we've prepared." Kirsa gave him a sour look as she rose, and then went.

She wasn't kept waiting at the shuttle long. She'd only just finished a list of pre-flight checks, thoroughly irritating the tech who'd done them already, when Cassin was practically carried into the craft and strapped in. She sighed as the two of them lifted off. Pilots were not supposed to train Navigators.

They traveled near light speed for several hours. Out of habit, Kirsa had set their course roughly for Reda, her former homeport. They would be able to travel for at least a month at current speeds without needing additional fuel or supplies. Most shuttles were designed for very long hauls, since Traveling pairs were not especially commonplace. Finally, the girl started to stir again, practically squirming in discomfort at trying to ignore the call.

"Cassin, listen to me." The girl whimpered. "I know it's hard, but you need to listen. We're among the stars now. Can you feel it?" The girl's whimpering was rising into panic. Kirsa had spent the entire journey trying to decide what to say – how to describe something that she's only experienced from outside. "You need to embrace the stars. Embrace the ship. Throw us into the void where they sing. You can do it, it's safe." It might be safe. Or the two of them might just be flung into nothingness and lost forever. Kirsa almost, almost hoped for the latter. Death might be preferable to being bonded to the wrong Navigator. Pain flooded her as she thought of Taul.

In the seat beside her, Cassin panted and gasped, her terror and pain radiating. Kirsa ground her teeth and let down the barriers around her mind, grunting as the panic assaulted her and she processed it, doing her best to set it aside from her true feelings. Jump, Navigator, she commanded, and with a final, terrified moan, Cassin embraced the stars. Fortunately, she remembered to hold fast to the ship as well.

In the pilot's seat, everything went black and reality seemed to drop away. She couldn't move, couldn't speak, she could only feel. And think. She closed her eyes, or at least approximated the sensation, and allowed herself to merge with Cassin. As their minds started to slip together, Kirsa found herself in Ether. The space was haunting and terrifying. It had been so long... She heard Cassin's voice, Am I dead? Oh, Lady, I lost control!

You're not dead. You're in Ether. You are my Navigator, and I am your Pilot. A fierce protectiveness overcame Kirsa, the same that she had felt for Taul, though he had laughed at it, being much the stronger physically. She could sense the girl's fright still. They would be lost if her Navigator could not be taught to return them to normal space. No one had returned after more than six hours in Ether.

I don't know you. Who are you? Where am I? Cassin was a nebulous cloud of thought, churning in her fear. She had been kept drugged and nearly entirely unaware since she had begun to show signs of the skill.

This would be easier for you if you had a form. Focus on your body. Make yourself real. As Pilot, Kirsa was not in control, and could not change things in this alien place. She could only direct her Navigator, who was slowly taking shape before her. Finally the mists coalesced into the form of a naked woman. As her own fear, tightly held, began to abate, Kirsa found herself opening even further to this frightened young woman and her feelings.

Cassin was afraid, certainly, and very confused, but slowly the fear was being washed away by the arousal that such a heightened state naturally brought. Kirsa had braced herself for the wave of desire, which was natural among Navigators while they were in Ether, but it wasn't enough. The desire that burned through the Navigator from the stars slammed into Kirsa, engulfing her and filling her until she was sure that she would drown in a sea of pure lust. It felt like hours before she could think clearly again, though Kirsa knew it had only been minutes.

This was not normal.

Cassin lay sprawled against a backdrop of stars, practically writhing with the mindless lust that had overtaken even her fear. The older woman took a mental gulp as she watched with her mind's eye. She could no longer think of the woman before her as a mere girl. This Cassin was the truth – no drugged slip of a girl, the woman before her was well proportioned with full breasts and a spread of dark hair beneath her taut stomach. Kirsa had never heard of such overwhelming desire when Traveling. Of course, she had never heard of a Navigator surviving so long after maturation without bonding a Pilot, either. If there was a 'next jump' it would be tamer.

Come on, now, you have to focus, she told the young woman. Cassin's answering moan was of a different sort than she had made in the cockpit. This was sheer desire. The young woman was mad with it, almost lost in it. Kirsa allowed herself just a moment of panic. What the hell was she supposed to do with a Navigator incapable of even listening to her?

The woman before her seemed to provide the answer in the movements of her body. Would she listen for the promise of fulfillment?

She dove into the younger woman's mind, deeper than she had ever gone before, and touched her thoughts to Cassin's mind. To Cassin, the sensation would be that of a hand running down her arm. Cassin, you have to listen to me. Can you feel my hand?

"Yes, I feel it. I don't understand... oh Lady!" Cassin was weeping, confused and torn.

I'm reaching out to your mind. Do you like this? Kirsa stroked up one of Cassin's arms and down the other, her ghostly fingers trailing goose bumps.

"Yes." Cassin panted and stretched her arms up over her head, inviting.

I need you to listen to me, Kirsa told her. She ran her phantom hands from Cassin's wrists all the way down her sides, nails scraping. With a little focus, she made the young woman feel a stir of breath at her ear as she whispered into her mind. Can you listen to me?

"I'll do whatever you want. Please, don't stop."

Good. You are my Navigator. You must Navigate! Cassin gasped, thrashing. Kirsa moved her attention to Cassin's breasts. Is this what you want?

"Please," Cassin whimpered. Kirsa gave her the sensation of teeth biting gently and fingers kneading and stroking. She prayed that she was doing the right thing, and not taking advantage of a vulnerable girl. It needed to be done, didn't it?

Listen to me and I will keep you safe. I am your Pilot now. Focus on the stars. Bring the red one overhead. Cassin panted, and the strange starscape seemed to revolve around them until a fat red star hung above them. Kirsa caressed her, sending a phantom hand gliding down Cassin's torso.

Good girl. Kirsa paused, allowing herself one last chance to back down. Then she dipped her fingers into the moistness gathering between Cassin's legs, massaging it into her clit. Cassin bucked wildly, and Kirsa let herself float in the feedback of ecstasy for a moment.

Now take us past the star; far past it. Seek out the young star with seven stones.

"I don't know how!" Cassin said. She gave an enraged moan as Kirsa withdrew.

See it. This is your space. The stars will obey. Slowly the stars began to move around them, and Kirsa gave in to her own selfish desires, flicking a phantom tongue over her partner's pussy, tasting and not tasting at the same time.

Kirsa ignored the stars as they began to shift beyond her, focusing on the internal world instead. She hesitated, but Cassin's thoughts begged for release; Kirsa plunged phantom fingers inside her Navigator, distracted by the confusing tangle of feelings, as she seemed almost to be touching herself.

With her focus so purely internal, she could feel her fingers sliding into Cassin's wet and welcoming body. She could taste the unique tang as she licked and sucked at another woman's clit for the first time.

She grasped at Cassin with her mind, sending phantom hands skittering all over the woman's body, pinching her nipples, exploring her body and plunging inside her. She was practically melded with Cassin, using her abilities to the fullest until they arrived at the young star and the seven planets. Take us to the fourth planet, and bring us out, she commanded, waiting until they had settled above the planet before, using their mental link as a guide, she shoved the young woman over the edge. They were both moaning with the force of orgasm when the cockpit took shape around them again.

Kirsa recovered nearly immediately, noting the irreversible presence of the bond with Cassin in the back of her mind as she steered the ship into planetary orbit, clearing their path with the space authority below. Cassin was visibly rattled, and Kirsa felt the waves of shame, wonder, fear, and desire pulsing off her Navigator.

"Is it... is it always like that?" Cassin asked, finally. Kirsa had been making minor adjustments, trying to look busy until the girl was ready to speak. She sighed as she sat back.

"No, it isn't." Cassin squeezed her eyes tight shut in response, the shame drowning out all other feelings. "Woah, don't do that!" Kirsa said. "What you went through, with all of the drugs suppressing everything, well, it's only natural that your first jump would be... intense."

"I was... and you!"

"I did what I had to do to keep us alive," Kirsa said. It took her a moment to understand why Cassin's shame deepened. "Oh, hell, girl. I wasn't expecting that! I've never even heard of doing anything like that in Ether. But it isn't anything to be ashamed of. You weren't prepared for that jump. You should be proud to have brought us out alive."

"We could have died?"

"Well it wasn't as if you had long to live anyway if I didn't get you up here!" Kirsa gestured angrily at the stars around them.

"I don't mean to be ungrateful, but I just... . I've never... "

"I've never been with a woman either," Kirsa said.

"Before now, you mean." Cassin's cheeks were glowing red. Kirsa shrugged.

"I mean ever. That was all in your mind. For me, Ether is only blackness. I have to join with you to see. To guide you."

"Don't Pilots and Navigators bond for life?" Kirsa nodded. "So it will always be... like that."

"No, of course not. Usually a Navigator is in almost complete control; they just need guidance from their Pilots. You were so far gone I was afraid we'd be lost in Ether. It will be weeks before you need to jump again, and even longer before you're so far lost that you would have trouble Navigating like that again. I was bonded to a Navigator named Taul, and he never got that way." Oh, Taul, she thought, I'm sorry. You needed my protection after all, and I couldn't... She felt as if she had betrayed him, now that this girl had his place in the back of her mind.

"What... happened?"

Kirsa took a ragged breath, ready to deny her the story. But she was Cassin's Pilot now. The girl had a right to know. "We were exploring a planet. We did that sometimes, when we were on leave. We would pick a direction and just... go. We didn't know there were natives. There were no obvious signs. They found us in the woods, and they captured us and took us to their village, and they locked us up while they decided whether we were rivals or Gods." She barked a harsh laugh. "I don't know what they thought of us. We couldn't escape. I watched him for weeks as his eyes got farther and farther away. He said 'don't cry for me', and then he just...

stopped. He didn't speak again. It took him three days to die in my arms. When they found us like that, I think it scared them. They let me go." It had taken her weeks to reach an outpost on her own, and she was starving and nearly delirious by the time she was safe. She had restocked, filed a report along with her resignation, and vanished on a transport, leaving the shuttle to be collected by the Travelers Guild.

"I'm sorry," Cassin whispered. Kirsa was startled to see that the girl had unstrapped, and was standing beside the Pilot's chair. Cassin reached down and touched her cheek where a tear traced a path. "I don't even know you. But I already can't imagine losing you."

"We're bonded now, for better or for worse," Kirsa said. She scrubbed at her cheeks and tugged irritably at her harness. She was suddenly impaled with a spike of terror, and only recognized it as not her own when Cassin reached for her face again.

"Then let's make the best of it," the younger woman said. Her fingers were soft on Kirsa's face – hesitant. What a disadvantage, Kirsa thought, not for the first time, to be unable to know what people around you are feeling. If only Cassin could feel it, she would know that Kirsa's heart felt as if it might mend for the first time since Taul's death.

Kirsa rose to meet Cassin's lips in a soft, uniquely feminine kiss. It was the most alien thing in the world, and the most natural. "Yes," she whispered against her Navigator's lips, "let's."

At The Crossroads
Monique Poirier

The brothel in The Gray City was reported to be the most extensive in all the world; a city in its own right. If I couldn't find what I needed here, then there was no hope left for me.

The Gray City stood at the crossroads between light and darkness, the last border of either, and the whole of it was considered neutral ground. That did not make it safe, by any means, but it was most probably the only place in all creation where an angel and a demon might meet without the obligation that one was to murder the other if possible. It was depraved, by the standards of light, but that was exactly what I needed now.

I'd known something of the inner workings of this labyrinth long before I'd arrived. The Seven Circles catered to every possible taste, from the richest nobles who walked along the pathways of the tower to the common street trash who wandered the twisting alleyways known colloquially as "the gut."

It was the gut that I stalked through now.

The price of admission to the gut was two alliance shillings, but the keeper of the gate had taken a glance at me and let me pass without comment. Perhaps he assumed that I was about official business—I seldom wore anything other than the uniform that marked me an Archon. Perhaps it was only that I was a winged man with a sword at the ready; only a half-blood, but most mortals took me for a proper angel. That made a startling number of them give me wide berth.

If I chose to ascend from the gut, I'd be charged again at every staircase and eventually at every door. This was the nastiest and most dangerous level of the complex, with twisting allies and tiny rooms that could be rented by the half hour. The whores that milled around at this level were those who hadn't the quality to make it to higher levels—or those who had fallen. The old, the maimed, the insane, the diseased. My entrance fee meant that any flesh that I found to my liking was mine for the taking—brute force wasn't discouraged, and no one, including other customers, was off-limits. There were guards here, but they cared only for the general peace and the interests of the house. They served to keep those who belonged in the gut from leaving it. The gut of The Seven Circles was as close to Hell as a mortal could find prior to death. I wouldn't have stayed here, among the beggars and thieves and human offal, were it not for the fact that I'd caught the scent I craved.

It was nearly a week since I'd run down a band of incubi on the border with my comrades and been bitten by more than one of them in the final battle. The venom was still coursing through me, slowly driving me mad. The ones who'd bitten me had taunted me with lavish offers of pleasure at the time, and it had been a feat of great will that I'd resisted such offers long enough for my comrades to extricate me through blood and steel.

My comrades, being wholly human, had little idea of what I could do to rid myself of the venom save finding a demon and slaking my lust upon it.

Six days the need had been made to build and fester. Now it was like a fire in my mind, burning away rational thought, widening my options until every person I glanced at became a considered object for my lust, and every whiff of sweat told me that they were useless. I could fuck a hundred mortals with incubus venom in my blood and still meet no satisfaction—I wasn't entirely sure how I'd come to that conclusion, but I knew it as rote fact in any case.

I'd caught the scent here—sweat and spice and that fiery twinge of rightness that I craved—the scent of a demon. I followed it ruthlessly, pushing aside any who were foolish enough to stand in my way in single-minded pursuit. My eyes darted in the direction that scent came from, searching the crowd. The stale wind shifted, and it came strong and sudden. I spun around a corner, and caught sight of my quarry.

Beautiful.

He sat in the shadow cast by the waist-high wall surrounding the courtyard, eyes closed, features drawn tightly in exhaustion. There were bands of iron at his wrists and throat, marked in sigils that I dimly knew. His head was shaven within a quarter-inch of his scalp. The same could be said of fully half the whores in the gut; it kept the lice at bay. What remained was dark, contrasting skin the color of dust. His clothes were in tatters, but seemed clean enough. His limbs were long and lean, his features too sharp to be called beautiful, but still compelling. A pair of curving horns, like those of a ram, rose from his hair in a stately arc. Here was the spawn of Hell, more achingly beautiful than any other creature I'd ever seen. More than that, his scent was right.

I was there in moments, gripping a handful of tattered clothing and pulling him close, feeling supple flesh beneath my fingers, breathing the scent of him. I hissed something, hardly aware of my own words. I was going to fuck him into oblivion.

"Found you, found you, found you!" the voice hissed as I was pulled onto my feet with absolutely no warning.

Fear flashed in my mind as I braced myself for a blow, but that didn't seem to be what this man had in mind. An arm snaked around my waist and pulled me close against the unyielding heat of another body, hand sliding down to cup and firmly hold my ass, preventing any retreat. Strong fingers splayed out against the knot of muscle at the base of my tail, and I instinctively curled it between my legs while his other arm slid across my shoulder, hand on the back of my head. He paused for a long moment, holding me in that fierce embrace.

Ah, so this was a customer.

He breathed against my neck as that hand ran over my shorn scalp, scenting me. Not the first to do so. It came with being a demon, something in my scent that mortals craved. His hand was very warm—fever warm—and trembling. He might have plague, though surely I'd have smelled that on him. He certainly didn't reek of death. In fact he smelled... nice. Really, very nice indeed. With the whole of his body against my own, I felt the hard length of him pressing into my belly. There was little doubt of what he wanted from me.

He backed away from the wall, one strong arm still locked around me so that I had no choice but to follow. He wasn't threatening me or asking my price or any of the other little rituals that were sacrosanct here. That was never a good sign. Wretched setback if he left me in some unfamiliar place and I had to work my way back to areas I knew, but there was no help for it now. I followed without a word, hoping that he would be done with me quickly.

There wasn't any warning; he pushed me and I fell backward onto a reasonably firm surface. Hay. He pinned me down, arms above my head, wrists held by his hands. He was very strong. The hard edges of a leather belt ran from his shoulder to his hip, and I knew damned well the feel of a baldric... he was wearing a sword. I didn't have time to analyze the situation further before his mouth was on mine.

My mind went gloriously blank, the intensity as hot, wet velvet invaded my mouth. No one ever kissed me. I went limp under the assault, my mind racing, my heart thundering in my own ears. Nobody kissed me. I was a slave of the Circles, less than a whore, and a demon besides. He'd found me in the gut, he had to know that I was worthless...

I returned that kiss with hunger, and he growled approval. I hadn't realized how starved I'd been for this kind of attention until he began a slow, even rhythm with his hips that made his hardness slide against my own hardening length. I whimpered into his mouth and tried to remember how long it had been since I'd last felt such heat tightening low in my belly. This kind of thing was for better sorts of people. Customers like this didn't linger in the gut. Customers like this didn't seek out demons.

He groaned, pulling away just enough to speak, the length of his body still pressing me down into the hay.

"Tell me I can have you," he panted, grinding his cock against mine, "need you so much. Need to fuck you. Tell me I can. Tell me," each pause punctuated by a thrust of his hips.

"Yes sir," I whispered in reply before I could let myself think about it.

It was the first time I'd said "yes" to someone here.

I should at least have dragged him into a decent room and laid out coin for a bed, but the demon's scent was maddening, his flesh warm and supple under my hands, and the nearest deserted alleyway looked inviting enough. Lucky happenstance that it was being used to store baled hay, or I might very well have taken him against the wall. I was barely mindful enough to dig the vial of oil from my belongings, slicking it over my fingers and probing deeply in hungering exploration for a few moments. The demon probably wasn't ready when I entered him.

It was as perfect as I'd known it would be, and my moan of pure animal pleasure as I sheathed myself within the demon's body rang loud against the alley walls. His flesh held me, tightened around me beautifully, as he threw his head back and gasped. There was a fine sheen of sweat on his brow, his eyebrows knitted together as if in concentration, his jaw set, his tail lashing wildly for a moment and then wrapping itself around my calf. I was hurting him. Evil of me. Evil had been visited upon me, and now he was suffering for it. I should have been able to control myself, incubus venom or no. Perhaps if I'd been a true angel and not a half-breed. Words were coming out of my mouth, and I was only half aware of them, a litany of apology as I slaked Hell-born lust in the demon's flesh.

"I'm sorry, I'm so sorry... next time, I promise... next time I'll make it so good for you..." he panted into my ear in counterpoint to thrusting hips. I closed my eyes and arched my head until the tips of my horns touched the firmness of hay behind me, my breath coming in quick gasps as I was filled again and again. He'd slicked the way with something, and the sensation was... novel. Nothing like the pain I was used to, and that spot inside me that turned my insides to liquid fire was touched intermittently. He was promising to make it good? This was as good as I'd ever known. It was clear that his first concern was finding his own release, that was to be expected of any customer, but there were so many prowling this place who could only be satisfied if they left their victims broken and bleeding in the wake of their pleasure. Why else seek whores in the gut? We were disposable.

He'd said next time. He intended for there to be a next time. If he meant to become one of my regulars, there would be more of this.

Wet heat descended on my neck, the velvet slickness of his tongue against my flesh. The sensation was alien, but rather nice, really. He kept at it, nipping and tonguing along my throat. There was a shifting of weight, a fumbling of the hands that gripped my wrists as he managed to free one without releasing me, then that free hand swept down my chest and belly. He found my cock and gripped it, and I answered with a cry, heat coiling low in my belly to match the pleasure that flashed through me when his cock touched that spot inside me. Oh, this was good—I couldn't help but move in return. I tried not to think about what it meant that I was enjoying this as well or better than ever I'd enjoyed such things in Hell.

He shuddered, and the teeth at my neck nipped sharply. His fingers dug into the flesh just above my hip, and for a moment I felt something brushing against my trapped arms... something breathtakingly soft and wholly unfamiliar. It was gone an instant later, but I'd felt it. He went still, his breath heaving, blanketing me with his heat and the slowly calming rhythm of his heart.

I could smell something sweet and spiced on his breath as he laid his face in the hollow of my throat, mingling with the scents of leather and sweat and something I couldn't put a name to; not at all unpleasant. So much nicer than anything I was used to. I found myself breathing deeply, drawing that scent in. There was an odd sensation running through me, so uncommon that it took me a moment to decipher. I wanted more than that. I knew that when he left me that I would stroke myself to release, dreaming of this.

But he didn't leave me. He rolled off, lying alongside me, and took hold of my cock again. I writhed helpless under his hand as he leaned in to claim my mouth again, stroking me in his fist while his tongue slid against my own. It was more perfect than anything I'd ever felt. He nipped and kissed his way along my jaw, working upward until he captured the lobe of my ear between his teeth. He bit me, a little jolt of pain running down my neck and I came undone, jerking against him, crying out in wonder as the purest of pleasure rolled through me.

For long moments I lay in shattered awe, with his arms casually twined around me and his breath against my neck, trying to understand why he should have done that. He'd brought me release.

If he'd asked it of me, I might have given him my soul.

Something soft again, this time blanketing the whole of my body. My hands were free now, and I tentatively brought one down to explore what was before me. It was soft, and smooth, and surpassingly warm.

It was a wing.

It was his wing.

"You're an angel," I whispered, all the air going out of me. I found myself unable to take another breath, running my fingers along the smooth feathers and feeling the power of muscle beneath.

"Half-blood, yes. I'll want you again soon. Very soon," he said, his breath was hot against my neck as he spoke and then suddenly cool as he inhaled deeply. "Several days, maybe longer. You'll come with me?"

"Days..." I said, mind racing. Such a long association; no one ever wanted me for more than a few hours, and seldom even that. Angels killed demons, and visited torment upon them in the name of righteousness. Absurd that I should be thinking on it at all; it wasn't even really a question. I'd go with him even if I refused—but he seemed to appreciate some pretense of consent on my part. If I humored him, I might be allowed certain liberties. I took a deep breath and dared to be bold.

"Will you feed me?" I asked softly. He didn't seem especially inclined to violence, but a slave speaking without express orders was a punishable offense. A demon daring to ask questions of an angel was as likely to be met with a flaming sword as an answer.

"Feed you? Yes. You'll come with me."

He pulled back from me, taking my hand and pulling me up with him. I heard the sound of rustling fabric, and then there was sudden movement around me; cloying warmth settled against my skin to match the weight that fell about my shoulders. It smelled richly of him, some garment of his that he'd seen fit to drape around me. It felt like an embrace.

My own clothes lay in shreds at our feet. I stooped to retrieve them, but he stopped me, taking my wrist and pulling me away. I hoped very much that he'd see fit to provide me with more before he discarded me. To be clothed in this place was certainly no assurance of safety, but to be naked utterly prevented it. His arm snaked around my waist again and drew me close, then a gust of air and the caress of smooth feathers at my back told me he had a wing curled around me as well.

I was tucked under an angel's wing.

The cloak he'd put on me was far warmer than my own clothes had been, even though I wore nothing beneath it, and my flesh sang in appreciation of the improvement. There was no reason he should so much as notice me, much less want me, and here I was tucked under his wing and wearing his clothes. He was going to closet me away somewhere to ravish at his leisure—for days, he'd said. He was an angel. It was his prerogative to do anything he liked with me, and no sane creature mortal or otherwise would argue that.

A candlelight flicker of hope flared in me. If he kept me for days, I might be able to snatch a few hours of sleep with him watching me. I might be... safe. For a while. There was something pathetic about that, that such a small thing should mean so much to me. That I'd trade my body for it. I never said yes to anyone... but I'd said yes to him. I was being tame for him even now, as I never was for anyone.

Because he'd been so careful with me. Because my skin still prickled with the memory of his hands and mouth on me, of a kind of care that no one ever spared for me. Demons did not deserve kindness.

I realized dimly that I was lost. I'd become very good at mapping out this place in footsteps, but he didn't take any of the paths I knew. He talked to several people. He was trying to find a room, but couldn't find one that was to his liking. Eventually I heard the telltale jingle of coins being passed from hand to hand.

"I'll do better later. I want you again now," he hissed into my ear. I felt the closeness of walls and knew that we must be in a narrow hallway. A door opened, we went through, my foot brushed against something—and then his hand moved to the middle of my back and he pushed me again, sending me stumbling forward. I braced myself for the jarring pain of the floor and was pleasantly shocked to find myself falling upon a yielding softness that invited me to press my face into it and curl my fingers around it, mindlessly murmuring approval. It was clean and soft and probably better than I deserved, certainly far better than I was used to.

And then he shifted, and I knew that he was standing over me, and that this luxury came at the price of my flesh. It wasn't a price I especially minded paying, not if it meant more of what he'd already been about. I turned over, leaning up on my elbows, and I waited for him to act.

I was a monster. The venom had made me such. No longer fit to carry the title of Archon, certainly, for what I'd just done and was about to do again. I couldn't bring myself to consider the real implications of this, not yet. I had a lithe body at my disposal, pliant and submissive and perhaps even willing. Mine. I could afford to be slower now; my earlier release had drained some of the tension from me and allowed a bit more coherent thought—but no less hunger. My clothes were an intolerable nuisance, and I quickly discarded them, looking down at my prize all the while.

He was terrified of me. Rightly so, as in any other situation I'd have been obliged to speed him back to Hell from whence he came—but at present I didn't like that fear, and my instincts sought to sooth it. He closed his eyes when I tried to meet his gaze, when I tried to tell him with my eyes what I couldn't gather the words to say.

I knelt, straddling him, lowering myself until I pressed full-length against him again, his racing heart beating against my chest, my arousal pressing into the soft flesh of his belly. His head tilted back slightly, exposing his throat, and his lips parted. The One help me, but he was beautiful. Was it only the venom that made me think so? There was corded tension in his muscles, quickness in his breathing, and the pounding of his heart. Fear.

I cupped his face in my hands and kissed him.

Something broke in me when he kissed me again, because he moved so fluidly this time. There was so much more in it... before there had been hunger and need, and that was certainly in this kiss as well, but it was tempered with such reverence, such tenderness. An angel's kiss. I found myself wrapping my arms around his neck and running my hands down his back, fingers brushing against the joints where his wings met his shoulders. He seemed to like that, breath hitching for a moment before he moaned softly against my mouth. His hand snaked down, his cock pressed against my own and suddenly caught in his grip as he stroked both of us in his fist. It was more beautiful and intense and perfect than anything I'd ever felt, and in embarrassingly short order it had me coming with a cry, my tail wrapping itself around his leg again. He kept stroking, his hand almost painful in its intensity, until I felt his seed splash against my chest and belly, joining my own there. He blanketed me with his body, curling his arms under my back as he breathed a satisfied sigh against my neck.

Worth it.

It had been maddeningly frustrating to stay myself from simply sheathing myself in his flesh again, but it was very much worth it to have him purring against me, to have his arms casually twined around me, to have him sated, and smiling, and willing. This felt right, as nothing had in days.

"What's your name?" I asked, breathing in the salt of fresh sweat, my face against the hollow of his throat, lips brushing the band of iron that rested there. He gasped at the question, and stopped breathing altogether for several moments. Odd, and more than a little troubling.

Of course, I had unceremoniously fucked him without having asked his name to begin with.

"Loskeph, sir..." he breathed, barely audible.

"I'm Makhamir," I replied, studying the point of his jaw for a moment before placing a long, wet kiss. Tasting the salt of his skin, breathing his scent. I could grow drunk on this lovely demon's flesh.

The kiss was sweet, but it was the way he melted, going limp beneath me, that made a pang of heat shoot through me. It was the way he whimpered, speaking in the only language my venom-madness knew, telling me more about desire and fear and need and confusion than a thousand words could. It was magnificent. I raised my head to meet his eyes again, hoping that perhaps he'd let me do so this time. His eyes were opened wide, and for the first time I had a clear view of them. Gray-blue, the color of a thunderhead, almost white where the blackness of a pupil should have been.

"You're blind."

"Yes," he answered, his far-off eyes closing again.

"So that's why you're in the gut... "

"No," he answered, flinching as if he expected a blow. "Well... perhaps. I fell to the gut after my eyes were taken, but being a slave of the Circles is my punishment."

"Punishment?" I asked.

"Gross dereliction of my duties. Showing undue mercy to mortals. I released someone who didn't belong in Hell. I was banished for that." He breathed sharply, eyes pressed tightly shut. "They sold me here."

"And the keepers of the Circles took your sight?"

"The Gray City is far worse a place than Hell, half-angel. Demons are not nearly so inventive nor so demanding as mortals. My superiors knew that when they chose this punishment for me. Eventually I'll be broken enough to return to Hell, I suppose, and be properly contrite about my place there. It's what I was put here to learn. I strangled the first man who tried to take me. They gave me to a cleric who put my eyes out with blessed needles. I remember what it felt like, when I realized that I was blind and would remain so—my mind shattered. I was broken beyond all usefulness. I fell to the gut, and woke there because no one gave a damn even enough to feed me." He paused for a long moment, then opened his eyes before asking, "Why did you choose me? You're an angel. You could have any whore from the tower for a song and a prayer. Why would you want me?"

I ran a finger along one of his curving horns, and he leaned fractionally against the touch. It made the corded tendons of his neck stand out in stark relief, and I found that I liked that quite a lot.

"I've been poisoned by the bite of an incubus. I need a demon. You suit me quite admirably."

His eyebrows rose, but he said nothing. I smiled a bit, gazing down at him. I'd been warned, as a child, that those who fell in sin spent eternity as the playthings of demons. I'd never considered having a demon as my plaything. I'd slain hundreds of demons for the glory of The One Who Is, but I'd never met one who'd writhe and moan and shiver at the simplest of caresses. I ran my fingers along the base of his tail, and it moved with all the speed of a viper to curl around my forearm as Loskeph flinched, eyes closed and teeth bared.

"Does it displease you to have it touched?" I asked, kissing his temple. The tension bled out of him, and his tail slowly uncurled.

"Those who touch it most often pull it..."

"That seems unpleasant," I said, electing instead to run my fingers carefully along the length of it from tufted tip to muscular base, venturing so far as to press my fingertip against the puckered hole beneath it. Loskeph drew his knees up at that, thighs readily parted, and a spike of desire crashed within me. Incubus venom was not something easily sated, it seemed.

But now I had a demon readily at hand, inviting me to do as I liked.

He was caressing me, apparently content with my supplication. His hands ran up along my sides, broad thumbs flicking over my nipples, and another cry died in the back of my throat. I was unused to such sensations, but I found that I craved them. Horrifying, that I'd finally found joy in my enslavement. Wonderful, that he should caress me, kiss me, touch me in ways that made me twitch and moan. It had been evil of him to remind me of how I'd come to this place. I'd withstood a thousand beatings with my pride intact, but a few well-placed caresses had me his willing whore. No, worse than that: whores could at least expect payment. A pair of tears escaped my eyes for the bitterness of it.

"You're weeping," he said, his voice clipped, almost a growl. Tears displeased him. It hurt that I already cared so much about displeasing him.

"I'm sorry," I choked, grasping for some answer that would please him, because as bitter as this was I wanted very much for it to go on. "You... you're so good to me."

And apparently that answer was perfectly acceptable, because his mouth was on mine again with the promise of tenderness and all thoughts of why this should hurt were gone from my mind.

He paused, rising up from me, and I heard the rustling of cloth and a warm, languid scent curled into the air, easily filling the small room. Slick fingers caressed me in the most intimate way, slipping into me with no resistance at all, finding that spot inside and toying with it. Oh, by all the power of The One who'd forsaken me, it felt good. Good enough to have my legs parted and my knees drawn up to grant him easier access, to have my toes curling in the sheets and my back arched. It hadn't been a lie. This was good enough to make me weep.

His fingers left me, and moments later he was inside me again, pressing inward in one long stroke. I tossed my head back into the impossible softness beneath me, overwhelmed by the sensation of being taken by one who meant it to be pleasurable. I wrapped my arms around him and pulled him close, bringing my hand tentatively upward along the back of his neck, nesting it in his hair. It was long, soft, and clean, a pretty luxury to touch. He purred approval, running his thumb in a quick circle around the head of my cock, making me buck and gasp appreciation.

All too quickly it was over—he was shuddering, his teeth pressing sharply into my shoulder, his seed spilling deep inside me. He lay still for a long moment, panting against my neck. I choked on another sob when he began moving again, fingertips moving down my chest and belly in prelude to soft kisses. I bit my lip against a scream when he took me into his mouth, and came much more quickly than I'd have liked because his mouth was a paradise beyond bearing. He drank me up, purring around me, running his hands in smooth patterns along the insides of my thighs. Eventually he moved up to lie alongside me, blanketing me with one enormous wing, humming tunelessly into my ear.

The venom-madness was sated, for now. Swallowing his seed had quieted it more than anything thus far; I'd have to keep that in mind. I felt half drunk, and wholly exhausted, and more satisfied than I'd ever been in my life. The demon at my side panted, looking up at the ceiling with an expression of quiet ecstasy.

At least there was that much solace then, that he'd had been able to enjoy it. This probably wasn't something he'd have chosen, but we were linked now, he and I. I really had no idea how long incubus venom left one so affected; those who were bitten did not generally escape the incubus' ministrations thereafter. I'd been lucky, more than once. Lucky to escape before debasing myself among demons who'd happily drag me to Hell and lucky again to find another who'd moan and writhe beneath me.

"You wanted food?" I asked, trying to draw my mind from the thought before I found myself taking him again right here and now.

It was strange, watching emotion play out in blind eyes. But that was guarded hope, plain as day.

"I would like that very much."

"Well we should see to that, then," I said with a sigh, forcing myself, reluctantly, to rise. I cast a searching glance around the room for my clothes. They were scattered, and my shirt was torn. My cloak was beneath him. He had nothing to wear beneath it. Another thing I'd have to remedy.

"I want to buy you. Whom would I go to?"

Loskeph's face held a look of quiet disbelief, eyes wide and shining, his voice catching again.

"Buy me?"

"You've done me a great service," I said, offering him a hand and pulling him to his feet. "And I sincerely hope you'll continue to do so."

That announcement was met with a burst of hysterical laughter, and Loskeph's arms were thrown around my back. My wings moved to wrap around him, pulling him close against me. He was trembling.

"I'm a slave of the Circles. You're an angel. I'm fairly certain that you could walk out the front gate with me and no one would have the courage to stop you."

The pastry was rich as butter, melting on my tongue. The meat inside was juicy, the spices creating little explosions of flavor. I hadn't expected anything so mind-shatteringly good as this. Slaves were fed on gruel. Often enough I was waylaid from receiving my share of even that. I'd been too long without food if something so simple as a pastry could draw such a response from me. Maybe it was just that his presence seemed to sharpen all my senses.

Two promises made, both delivered. He'd made it good. He'd fed me.

Worse than that, I found that even walking through the market I felt safe with his hand in my hand and his wing at my back. Safe in a way that I hadn't felt for even a moment since awakening in the gut. Oh, this was trust, and it was going to get me killed.

He wanted to buy me... to be my master. The concept rang in my head like a bell, awakening things in me that I'd thought long dead. Old training of mine, things I'd been taught through pain and humiliation during my first days in the tower that I had learned very well. Things I'd fought, then, with fists and teeth.

He wanted me. Wanted to keep me. I was banished from Hell, and Heaven had never wanted me at all, but this angel wanted me. An angel that walked the earth, but an angel nonetheless. An angel with human blood, who might well be as capricious and cruel as any

human, and had all the power of Heaven to back that wild abandon.

What did it mean for me that I was so happily submitting to his will?

This was probably a horrible setback in my progress toward earning my way back into Hell.

Even in Hell, no one had ever fucked me like that.

"It's hard to imagine you doing evil, Loskeph," he said to me, softly. Quite probable that he'd been watching me eat.

"I've done little enough of it," I answered. "I never was more than the least of the damned. Do you think banishment from Hell is meted out to those who are truly loyal? It's a thing done to half-breeds and mortal-lovers."

"But if you're not evil at heart, then what made you turn from the love of The One Who Is at all?"

I swallowed thickly, my mouth suddenly dry.

"It isn't a matter of goodness or of evil," I said with a derisive snort that was wholly beyond my station. Let him punish me for it, I didn't care. "It's a matter of obedience to The One Who Is. I do not belong to Him, and that He cannot tolerate. He is our maker as He is yours—demons are the children He does not love. How many demons have you killed without knowing that, angel? I've noticed that you carry a sword. What are you, in the wider world?"

"An Archon."

"A murderer of demons, then."

"I bring swift justice to those who do evil, mortal or otherwise," he corrected, and there was a tightness in his voice. It raised shrill panic in me, that he be displeased with me. I crushed that fear down with all the fortitude I could muster. I was after all a demon. I should not fear angels. Hate them yes, but not fear them. Not be supplicant to them.

Even when supplication meant gentle hands and burning kisses and fellowship and safety... when it meant all I'd ever wanted. I never had and never could belong to The One, but the core of me knew with terrifying certainty that I could belong to Makhamir.

"If we do evil, angel—and I will admit that most of us do—it is only that we learned at the feet of the master."

"I will not listen to you speak poorly of The One Who Is, demon."

He'd drawn very close to me; I could smell the heat rising from his skin.

"How will you stop me, angel?" I asked, bearing my teeth.

He lunged and crushed my mouth with his own.

Loskeph never failed to melt under my kisses. I took him from the pavilion where I'd bought the food and laid down coin for a room some ways above the gut, one with four strong walls and a locked door and an enormous feather bed, and I finished there what I'd started below.

He and I lived a tangle of sex and sleep and food and more sex for days.

More and more, as the days passed, we found ourselves lost in companionable conversation. I told him of my childhood in the holy city, my mother a temple virgin chosen to bear an angel's son, of my training as an Archon, and my adventures upon the roads of darkness and light. He told me of his life as a soldier of Hell, the wretched loneliness of it incomprehensible to me. Demons, it seemed, were not kind or loyal to one another. He'd known so much torment.

I woke on the sixth day and watched him sleep, sunlight poring over his face, and realized that I loved him as much as I loved any of The One's creations.

That was a problem that I did not know how to solve. I was obligated by honor to offer him his freedom for the service he'd done me, as soon as I was freed from the venom's curse. It was the least I could do to take him from this place and let him seek his fortune upon the road as a free man.

Loskeph stirred, sitting up, turning his head a bit as if to seek me out. I laid a hand on his shoulder and he turned to face me with a half-conscious smile.

"Do you know how long I'll be afflicted by venom?" I asked, twining my arms around his shoulders, pulling him back to rest against my chest.

"What do you mean?" he asked, leaning against me, tilting his head to offer me his throat.

"Not that I'm complaining, Loskeph," I said, placing a gentle kiss against the throat he'd so eagerly offered, "but for how many more days will I burn with the need to have you writhing beneath me? Surely you're growing tired of my constant demands."

Loskeph tilted his head a bit, as if I'd asked something very strange.

"You said it was an incubus that bit you, didn't you?" he asked.

"More than one, yes..."

"Then you'll need demon-lust for the rest of your life. It would hardly be an effective intoxicant for dragging immortals to Hell and keeping them there if it simply abated."

He might have punched me for the way the air went out of me then.

Damned. I was damned. The incubus who'd bitten me had damned me and cursed me with an insatiable need. I would go mad, or become a monster and be slain by my own comrades, or willingly consign myself to Hell for the amusement of demons. It was the sort of fate that befell Archons, I'd always known that, but somehow I'd never truly expected to face it.

"It's my duty to patrol the roads..." I said, still breathless, not entirely certain of my words.

"Well if you're to keep on with that," Loskeph said archly, "you'd need a demon waiting for you in your bedroll each night. One who appreciates the awesome power of your righteous wrath and has no desire whatever to see you fall into Hell. I suppose it would help if he'd once been a soldier. It's my understanding that the roads to and from The Gray City are dangerous."

"You would come with me of your own free will?"

"Where else would I go, angel, and find greater satisfaction than in your bed? Put a collar and a leash on me if you must for your conscience, but I would follow you to the gates of Heaven or Hell or anywhere in between. I don't think you could prevent me."

I pulled him into a fevered kiss in reply, my wings closing around us and cocooning us within.

Complications of Heaven and Hell be damned; this world between the two was ours.

Catch and Release
Sunny Moraine

People laugh at Suleiman when he tells them what he does for a living. Fisherman, eh? They roll their eyes in the dimness of the port's pub, cast knowing looks at each other, and he wishes that he hadn't said anything. There should be no shame in being a fisherman, he thinks sometimes. You do what you have to in order to live. Some people stay planetside and work there, in science, in industry, in finance. Even in service, they've got something to be proud of. Even the waitress in the pub. And him... fisherman, out there riding the solar winds in a ship that barely holds together, reeling in nets full of interstellar trash, rocks, pieces of broken satellites. Scavenger of the stars.

He came up here, he thinks, because it was all he could do. At one point it was all he wanted. Now he smiles thinly at the others in the pub and retreats to a far corner with his watery beer.

Yes, he's a fisherman. One of these days, he tells himself when he's feeling low and the black empty around him presses especially close, he'll catch something big.

The alarm sounds when he's on the bridge, on his back under a half-dismantled console, hands sticky with oil and the nutrient fluid that leaks out of the bionics. Suleiman sits up, cracks his high forehead on the console, swears richly and shoves himself to his feet. He scans the screens, the streams of incoming data. It's not large. It's dense. It's pulling things into itself, tiny things on a tiny level, and he knows that he'd never feel that pull himself, with his clumsy macro hands.

Later, he'll think about how wrong he was.

He sets the locks, puts the bioscan on auto, shimmies up the ladder to the intake deck. The central hub of the ship is turning in its slow grav-spin and he sometimes thinks that he can feel it when he's between decks like this, bouncing in the lower gravity with his hands on the ladder, so close to freefall he can taste it. He doesn't like zero-G freefall, but he thinks that part of him does, in a perverse way, the feeling of falling and falling and never coming to rest, like the stuff he picks up in the nets. A kind of connection, maybe, like a farmer up to his wrists in dirt and manure.

On the intake deck his boots hit the floor and there's the soft, comforting hiss of the maglocks. The room is dominated by a large central column ringed with transparent leaded aluminum. He turns to a console, taps out a command, watches as a tray slides up and into place in the center of the column. He moves to the window and puts his greasy hands heedlessly against it and looks.

Big things come in little packages. He doesn't know where he's heard that before, but it rings in his head, again, later. Not now. Because now, looking at the day's catch, what he primarily feels is disappointment. A small metal cylinder, not any longer than his forearm and no wider around than his fist. Space trash. Not even big enough to be worth the going exchange in scrap.

But there is that question of density. Nearly anomalous, as much as anything out here ever is. And as the scans run automatically, the console alerts him with a soft chime. He steps away from the window, bounces back to the console and peers down at the read-out.

Nothing. Or rather, an absence of something, which he's learned is not even close to the same thing as nothing. A gap in the data, coming from the inside of the cylinder. The scan can't penetrate it, and what's there is a blank space where anything might be hiding.

He steps away again, looks back toward the window. Could be anything, yes. Radiation. Disease. Something horrible from the black, all the more horrible for its mystery. He can imagine all sorts of things. A long time alone out here teaches one to keep the imagination under control or face insanity, but the mystery of the cylinder is coaxing it out of its bounds, teasing it to a fever pitch.

He punches up the command for a static forcefield, turns and shimmies back down the ladder again. The nets still furled, he thinks. He thinks for a long time, raking his fingers through his dark hair, unkempt and uncombed with no one here to see him. After a while he makes his way to his bunk, curls up on the cramped bed and tries to sleep. There, in the half-dark that guards him from the deeper dark, he dreams of Baghdad, gleaming and glorious, the graceful house-domes of Adhamiyah, the high minarets of Caliphs Street. In his dream he is his boy-self, lying on the hot rooftop of his father's house in the dying light, staring up at the stars and feeling his heart swell with them. Someday. Someday he would fly among them and see what he could see, and Baghdad would only be a distant jewel in a dark sea. Because Baghdad could hold onto him. Even so young, he can feel that. It might hold on and never let him go, and he wants to be away, high above it, free from that kind of pull. In his dream, he feels that pull, the spicy smell of the night and the beginnings of a sensual awareness, and he keeps turning his eyes back to the stars.

In his dream, she is there. She is floating above him, her long hair full of starlight. *Touch me,* she whispers, clutching at herself with transparent hands. *Ah, aiwa, touch me.* His boy-self twists, becomes confused; when he opens his eyes he's so hard it's painful, so hard he can't relieve it with his hand, and he lies in the little bunk and groans, his eyes squeezed so tightly closed that he sees stars behind the lids. It has been so long since he had anyone. Even a whore. So long he hasn't even dreamed about it, until now.

And who was she?

And when he can get up again, when he does a low-grav tottering stumble out the door and unhesitatingly back toward the ladder again, he somehow already knows the answer to that.

It takes him a second or two to get the field down with how much his hands are shaking, but he calms them, closes his eyes and takes a few breaths, and even the stale, recycled air is soothing when pulled in at that amount. When he opens his eyes again, the field is down, and it takes another couple of commands to lower the tray and open the column's panels with a soft hiss, making an opening he can walk through.

Everything echoes tinily once he's inside, and usually he doesn't spend much time in here, the air strangely thin and a profound feeling that he is somehow closer to the vacuum here than at any other point in the ship except the main airlock, which he knows isn't true, but he also knows by now that here, feelings count for a great deal.

And still he hesitates, standing over the little cylinder. It doesn't look like anything. He knows that technically, he could be bathing in radiation, though the scan at least hadn't detected any emissions of any kind. Still. He swallows hard, bends and picks up the thing.

It's astonishingly light for how dense it's supposed to be. It feels as though it might contain nothing. So perhaps it does. He turns it over in his hands, squinting at it in the bright lights that ring the inside of the intake column. It's smooth, metallic, featureless but for a small panel set into one end. He knows he shouldn't touch it. He touches it. It depresses very slightly. He knows he shouldn't press it. He presses it.

Later, he will decide that any number of things could have made him do it. The laughter of the people in the pub, the flush in his face, or the boy-self, lying on the rooftops of the new Baghdad, staring up and dreaming star-dreams. *Aiwa*. Dreams that stayed that way, only dreams melting away into the everyday slog that his life up here has become. To catch something big. To have a good story to tell, one that doesn't make them laugh or make his face burn. Yes, it could be so.

But he will also know that none of those things is the real reason why. He will know that it is her. And here she is, standing in front of him, her long hair full of starlight.

It's the hair that he sees, at first and most clearly. Then the rest of her comes into focus, though whether it's his eyes or reality he'll never be sure. Her long limbs, almost bizarrely slender, a half inch away from alien, the transparency of her flesh, her essential nudity. He can see the lights of the column shining through her cheeks. Her skin has a faintly blueish tinge. Her eyes are closed, and she is making no attempt to cover herself, though her hair floats around her and now and then passes over her small breasts. Suleiman looks down, momentarily unable to draw breath, and he sees that the tips of her toes are only just brushing the floor.

Her eyes open. There are no pupils there, and they are the color of the densest parts of the Milky Way.

Have you come to kill me?

Suleiman shakes his head. It's all he can think to do. Her voice is low, smooth, quiet, and does not even seem to be sound as he knows it, for it comes from the very center of his head. "I..." he starts, hands at his sides, though they already itch to reach for her with the same itch that brought him back up to this deck in the first place. "I found you."

It occurs to him to wonder if he might already be dead.

She cocks her head slightly, lifting her arms in a kind of supplication that becomes a dance that becomes an echo of flight that becomes merely her, if she can be called "mere" in any sense of the word, floating before him with her hands held out, palms up. *Then my term is not ended? Am I still to be imprisoned? Are you still angry with me?* She pauses then, and seems to look more closely at him. At another time and with another woman he would be ashamed of his rumpled clothing and his mussed hair, his face badly in need of a shave. But this is now, and she may not be a woman. He's sure she isn't.

She shakes her head slightly, and when she speaks again her voice is edged with slow realization. *You are not my adjudicator.*

"I am not."

She steps forward without stepping, her star-filled hair rising around her as if blown by a breeze he can't feel. Her hands lift with real purpose now, and the first time they touch him he thinks of ice so cold it burns. *Then touch me, would-be liberator. Aiwa, touch me...it has been such a long time.*

She does not have to tell him. She is already touching him, and to that he thinks there can only be one answer.

He manages to get them out of the cylinder and then they sink to the floor, her levitating body coming to rest on it at last, and he has time to wish that he kept this deck cleaner before she closes a burning kiss over his lips and he thinks of only her, her breasts curving into his palms as if they ache to be there, nipples so hard they no longer feel like flesh. When he pulls back to look at her beneath him, he can see light moving beneath that glass-like skin, not veins or organs but electrical impulses, tiny surges of power. He lowers his mouth to her, takes her nipple between his teeth and bites down and he could swear he sees sparks.

She moans and clutches at him, and it doesn't take very much to make himself forget how different this is, how strange this is, how remarkable that he remembers how to do everything and that what he does can give her pleasure. He's stripping off his rumpled clothes and she's helping him with her icy fingers; he's looking up for permission as he slides between her thighs and she's already shoving his head down, gone from so calm to so frantic in a matter of minutes. She tastes like lightly sugared milk and the succulent juices of a broiled hen. She tastes like he somehow knew she would taste. She comes explosively and this time he knows he sees sparks under her skin, lines of chain lightning shooting up into what would be her spine.

She doesn't give him time to rest and she does not take it for herself. She's pulling at him again, dragging him up against her, gone from frantic to ravenous, and part of him is beginning to be a little bit afraid. She reaches between them and grasps at his cock and he cries out, because it hurts, it hurts almost as much as it did when he woke in his bunk with dreams of her and of Baghdad still echoing behind his eyes. She strokes him and the pain is bowled over and forgotten. She is opening her legs for him, rolling up with her hips, her whole body like a hungry mouth. He falls into her and she hooks her legs over his hips and takes him, her long arms curled around his neck and the whisper of a hundred half incomprehensible demands and entreaties between his ears.

She is Baghdad, he thinks fitfully. They are one and the same, new, ancient, enticing, hungry. Baghdad rebuilt, center of the new world, rich with the wealth of the global economy, swelling with all the nations, reaching out to take him in. Trying to hold on. Which is why he had run, and now he is caught again. She is Baghdad, gleaming and seductive; she is the stars over him and the hot roof beneath, she is the lights and the noise and she is touching him, and this time he doesn't pull away.

Later, when they lie together in the tangle of his clothing and he notes that her skin shines without a drop of sweat, she tells him that she will give him a gift. She will let him choose how he dies.

There is a story behind it. Of course there is, Suleiman thinks as he turns restlessly, as if dreaming, and she whispers in his ear with her hot lips, smooth and organic as blown glass. *The first one who touched me, I offered him all the wealth of the Maghrayar trade routes and yet he did not let me go. The second one, I offered her her heart's desire and yet she would not let me go. Do you know how much rage that little jar can hold? I will give you the only gift I can bear to give.*

At length he rises, pulling away from her touch with an enormous effort, moving to the porthole and looking out at the void spinning around them. Mars is drifting past. They are homebound, if Earth is home, the course set long ago for when he had known that he would need to buy supplies from the orbital stations, and trade whatever he had found in the ports.

He looks back at her. Trade her? Can he even do that any longer? He slides his hands up into his hair as she looks back at him with her milky eyes. And would he do it? Would he let her go?

For wealth, for heart's desire... wealth holds no attraction. He had thought that he had already gained his heart's desire the first time he topped the gravity well and shot like an arrow out toward the asteroid belt. He might have been wrong, he sees that now—

but in any case, she is only offering him one thing.

And the ultimate point of it is that it is not truly even an offer.

He goes back to her, drops to his knees as though he might be about to offer up prayers that he hasn't spoken since he was a boy. He takes her into his arms and she goes willingly. He moves his lips across her skin, tasting her, that strange mix of alien and familiar. She tips her head back and sighs as he nips gently at her collarbones.

"I'll think about it," he says.

Take the time you need, she says. She drags her lips down his chest and belly, too soft from too much time in low-grav, but she doesn't seem to care. She closes her hands around the base of him, flicks her tongue against the head of his cock—her tongue as glassy and transparent as the rest of her, shimmering with electricity—and then she takes him in as far as anyone could and he arches his back and yells. It's a shock, a hundred tiny lightning strikes. His fingertips are tingling. He tries to push deeper but she holds his hips, presses him against the deck, keeps her own pace. She draws it out until he wants to scream. His hands are buried in her starlight hair.

He thinks he might die for this. He thinks it might be worth that and more. He thinks it might just be another dream, and somehow that is the cruelest possibility of all.

She moves through the ship, levitating, curious. She runs her hands over every surface, every console and bulkhead. She kneels on the threadbare carpet in his bunk, one of the few things he had taken with him from the city, lowers her face to it and touches it with her lips. *I can taste the years on it*, she murmurs, and he doesn't ask her what she means by that. He follows her, watching her, and she doesn't seem to mind. On the bridge she turns and laughs, spreading herself out against the central console in a way that would be obscene if she were human—and still is, somehow, but also, with her, it looks as though she could be no other way.

You could let me go, she says. *Take me down there*. She points behind her to the viewscreen, the blue globe of Earth growing fat in the distance. She lowers a hand between her legs and slips two fingers into herself, taking a delicate breath. All up and down her back, he sees the chain lightning crackle. He goes to her without a thought, turns her bodily over and fucks her from behind, hands in her hair again and pulling. This time he makes her cry out and it feels good.

You could let me go. If it's really that easy, if she really wants it to be that way, he doesn't know why she keeps doing this.

It takes Suleiman a day to decide. In the end it comes to him all in a rush. By then he's in high orbit, falling around the world, looking down at what he'd torn himself away from and hearing her offer in his ears. And her alternative, if it could even be called that. He can't consider it. Not while he's alive. He thinks about no longer being able to touch that crystalline skin, that hair, no longer being able to run the tip of his tongue over the lids that cover her milky eyes. No longer being able to kneel between her legs and taste her, no longer having her turn, arch against him, pull him into her cunt, her mouth, her ass. He could use her like this forever, he thinks.

She doesn't seem to eat. She basks in the sun on the bridge, stretching out on the floor like a cat and taking it in. Chlorophyll in her skin, perhaps, or the alien equivalent of it. Except he's not sure that her flesh is really flesh. That she is even really her. He does not know what he's really dealing with.

He doesn't think he has to know. He's pretty sure that it no longer matters.

In the night, he kneels on his rug and prays. Not the words he's been taught, and there is no way he can think of to prostrate himself towards Mecca. But that also doesn't seem to matter, and the god he feels he could pray to is not the god of his fathers. He is asking for guidance. He cannot let her go. He cannot make her let him go. He senses that this is what she is and what she does;

she takes and she grasps and holds, and she cannot let go either. Is that why she had been imprisoned? He has no idea how to ask her.

He asks for a sign. All at once he knows what to do. She has already given him a way out for both of them, the only generosity she can muster, the only gift she can bear to give. He can choose. He can make the one choice that matters, in the end.

He calls her. Goes to her there on the bridge. She opens herself for him on the floor by the pilot's chair, spreading her silver lips with her impossibly long fingers, her cunt glistening in the light of her hair and the chain lightning under her skin. He bends over her, braced up with his hands, and as the pleasure and the electric needle-pricks rock his nervous system, his sweat falls onto her skin like rain. She spreads it over herself, opening her mouth to catch the drops. She says it tastes like the red Kenaldor sea. She tosses her head, moans, comes with a small explosion and she drags him after her. He fills her. When he pulls away she lifts her hips and some of his come flows out of her in a slow drip, and he thinks of milk and honey.

He tells her what he wants. She has spoken of rage and he supposes that the lightning under her skin might be the evidence of it, but when he tells her what he wants, she weeps. Her tears are steaming. He doesn't know if it's grief or gratitude or something entirely other.

The pub is exactly as he left it. The port is, too, crowded and dirty. He docks with as little fanfare as usual and leads her through the airlock, draped in an old white *thobe*, her head covered by a blue and purple scarf given to him by his mother, the edges all gold embroidery; she wears it like a hijab. He thinks of women in the marketplace down the block from his childhood house, mysterious in their cloaking garments. He can't take his eyes from the flashing transparent blue of her skin.

So the pub is exactly as he left it, the entrance dim and murky down the concourse, and he leads her into it without a sound. Heads rise, give him a nod or two, and he hears muttered words and laughter. *Suleiman the fisherman.Wonder what treasures he's scooped up this time.* He takes her by the hand, leads her to the bar and orders them both small glasses of spacer's rotgut, burning and bitter. The bartender gives her barely a glance. She makes no move to take up her glass, but this, too, is nothing more or less than what he expected.

"Show them," he whispers. "Any time."

She nods once. She turns and he turns with her, to face the crowds at the tables, the rough traders with their thick coffee and their *h'uqqahs*, the bar women with their coarse voices, the port and dock workers, powerful and raucous. She turns and they all fall silent at once, though she is still veiled, her face hidden in the folds of her hijab. She raises her hands and pulls it aside, and as one they let out a sigh, a quiet moan.

This is what she is, he knows. This is what she does. This is why she had been locked away from the universe, and he can't feel sorry at having unleashed her on it once more.

She lets the scarf drop to the floor, and again they sigh. She shrugs the thobe off her shoulders and it slips down over her breasts, the swell of her hips and thighs, pooling at her feet. She stands naked before them and spreads her arms, palms up, beckoning. Not one of them moves, but one or two of them men reach between their legs with a kind of slow numbness. One or two of the women lay a hand against her breast, kneading softly.

She does what she had done when he had opened her capsule. She seems to dance and seems to fly both at once, her feet above the ground, turning and turning and all the people seem to be spinning around her like bodies in orbit, pulled in and held. She laughs, lightning crackle inside her and all around her, arcing over her like solar storms. She turns back to Suleiman and strips him there, slow and fast both at once, and he feels no shame at all in the act.

Wonder what treasures he's scooped up this time. Oh, he'll show them what he's found. He'll show them all. *And peace be upon them.*

She floats over him and pulls him into her arms, between her spread legs, her hand reaching between them to take his cock and slide it into her. He was hard when she began to strip and again the hardness is painful, but it's a pain that he loves, devours, wants more of. The pain of leaving, the pain of coming home. This is what she is as well; she is every place he has ever left, every place that has ever tried to keep him planetbound, *Baghdad*. Her cunt is a wet mouth, powerful, muscular, contracting around him and dragging him deeper as she arches herself against him. They are both in the air now, her strength impossible in her slim frame. He can feel the others still watching, but they no longer mean anything at all. She kisses him and he feels the air sucked right out of his lungs.

And it doesn't return.

There is a charge growing, in the air and in her. He can feel it under her skin, in her lips, on her tongue. He drives into her but the rhythm is lost; she is too strong for him, taking him in her own rhythm, in her own time, the beat of the sheer uncontrollable life in her. Another sigh from the watchers, a flash of bodies frozen in their own ecstatic poses. He is getting so close. He needs none of his own urging. She is dragging him along, rough and needy with her cold teeth against the base of his throat. But in the last, as the surface of his skin begins to crackle, she is carrying him gently over the edge.

She is giving him a gift. All she can bear to give. The only choice that matters, in the end. And isn't this what he wanted? The stars, and nothing holding him back any longer.

When the final bolt of their combined orgasm collects at the base of his spine and stabs up into his brain, the last thing he sees is the starlight in her hair.

And then only the light.

Where is he? Where is Suleiman the fisherman? All around the pub they are shaking their heads as if waking from a dream. Some of them are flushing, reaching down to gather scattered clothing. Some of the women are extracting themselves from the laps of their partners, their breasts swinging heavy, their cunts still wet. Suleiman is nowhere to be seen. Some of them have a memory of a woman made of glass and lightning with hair full of starlight and eyes milky as galactic arms, but they will question it and doubt it and later they will never believe that she was there at all. A dream, only a dream.

And that seems cruel.

In one of the lower spires of the port, a ship is disembarking. Passage has been given in trade for one of the other docked ships. It seems like a steal, really, though the ship offered in trade is a rickety fishing vessel, probably good for little more than scrap. The captain looks over at her passenger, robed and veiled. And isn't she lovely? The captain can see that much even with the veil. There is a kind of light on her, gauzy and soft, distant. There are her eyes, strangely milky, and as the captain turns away from the console to engage her passenger in a little friendly conversation, there are her hands, glassy and full of sparks, extended palm up as the ship falls toward the planet's surface and the feast that waits there, and all the worlds beyond.

Mirror
Clarice Clique

"Mirror, Mirror, on the wall, who is the fairest of them all?"

She stroked her finger over the gold frame as the surface shimmered into a thousand colors that no normal human eye could see. It was a question she had asked every day for the last hundred years of her life, and always the answer was the same. But today was not like any other day in the last hundred years of her life. In a far away Kingdom that was too small to have ever attracted her attention, a young woman had had a ball to celebrate her twenty first birthday, and at that ball she had met a prince who from the first moment he bent down to kiss her hand had made her spirits soar and her body glow. So the Mirror did not reply "Thou, my Lady, art the fairest of all", and the woman waited, staring into the shimmering surface, wondering if after all this time her magic was beginning to fail her.

"Mirror, Mirror, on the wall, who is the fairest of them all?"

She rested one finger at the top of the mirror and scratched her nail slowly down the surface. The noise reverberated through her castle. Something in her dungeon howled out in agony.

"O Lady Witch, though fair ye be, Snow White is fairer far to see."

She ripped the mirror off the wall and hurled it to the floor, but a moment before it hit the stone and shattered into a million lost pieces something made her click her fingers and freeze it in mid air. She moved a finger and the mirror was back on the wall.

"Show me this Snow White," she ordered.

She stared at the scene, studying every detail. The girl was in bed, the top of a white linen sheet resting on the curve of her bosom. The sheet was not as white as the girl's skin, though; next to her flesh the expensive material looked old and shabby. The girl's hair was polished ebony spread out over the pillow and shining even in the night light. Her lips redder than the most precious ruby were parted as she breathed gently in peaceful slumber. The witch watched the rise and fall of the girl's chest as if being hypnotized by the rhythmic movement.

The witch untied the strings on her corset, letting her robes fall to the ground in disorder.

"Mirror," she said, and the mirror transformed into an ordinary reflection.

She looked at herself, tracing a nail over her hard strawberry nipples. She cupped her hands under her breasts and squeezed their fullness. Her body felt the same as it always did. She touched the soft curves of her stomach and hips, but she wasn't satisfied. Her alabaster skin did not look as white as it had yesterday, her lips were not as scarlet and her long black hair looked dull.

"Snow White," she said.

The mirror shimmered; the vision of her own body transformed into that of the young princess.

She teased a finger between her legs as she gazed upon the image of the sleeping girl. The pleasure that others had to work so hard for but was so easy for her did not come. She licked her finger and pressed it against her magic spot; there was a tingle but nothing more. She stared hard at the girl, a small crease furrowing her brow. Then her skin was smooth again. She clicked her fingers and was dressed in her traveling robes.

"Mirror, we are going on a journey," she said.

She waited in the forest and wondered what she would do with the girl when she finally appeared. She had dealt with these types of damsels many times before: trapping them in towers, feeding them to wolves, sending them into eternal sleep, giving them as brides to beasts. She had felt her magic weaken the farther she had traveled from her castle, but she thought she still had enough strength to transform this girl into a swan. It had been a long time since she had done that, and it would suit this girl more than the last. She would be a perfect white swan.

Then Snow White was there in the clearing, skipping like a girl. She was wearing a short dress, not the usual attire for a grown up princess. The witch watched. There could be no harm in watching and waiting a moment before she cast the spell. As the girl skipped her dress rode up, giving a flash of white thigh. She sang as she picked the fruit off the trees and her voice was as sweet and natural as bird song. When her basket was full the girl turned and began to walk back to the palace.

The witch walked alongside her behind the cover of the trees. She watched as the girl took an apple from the pile of fruit and bit into it, a drop of juice rested on her bottom lip. The witch stared at the single droplet glistening on Snow White's red lip until the girl escaped from her view and disappeared between the palace gates.

If the witch had been in her own kingdom she could have waved her hand and the walls and guards and everything between her and the girl would have crumbled into dust. But she wasn't in her own kingdom. She would find another way. She pointed to a tree and the mirror appeared on it.

"Show me Snow White."

The vision was of the girl running into a chamber and hugging an old man. The old man was laughing and took the basket of fruit with another big familial hug. The witch smiled. She had found her way.

The King insisted on a grand wedding, and his bride-to-be smiled demurely and agreed with everything he said. In her thoughts the witch ridiculed what this tiny, insignificant man considered 'grand'. He talked more and more about the wedding night, telling her not to be scared and that he wouldn't hurt her. Once she had lost control and laughed in his face; she regained her composure enough to perform a memory obliteration and had ensured she didn't slip up again. Her magic was drained in this kingdom; ingredients were more difficult to find and it took all her concentration to pretend she was a twenty two year old orphaned virgin princess. But she managed it. The wedding took place, and some carefully chosen herbs in the King's meals meant the wedding night would never take place. Men had never been a problem for her.

When the King was in a sleep he would never stir from, the witch left her bedchamber and went to Snow White's. The King had never had the satisfaction of removing them so the witch was still dressed in the modesty of her wedding clothes, her whole body covered by the most expensive and finely crafted white satin and lace. The train of her dress rustled against the floor, but there was no one to be disturbed by it. Snow White's chamber was but a few paces away from the King's; the witch did not hurry. She took small steps, standing upright and staring directly ahead of her. She looked exactly as she had hours earlier walking up the aisle towards marriage with the King.

The heavy wood of Snow White's door creaked when the witch pushed it open, but the girl did not start. The witch stood for a moment and let her eyes caress the reality of the image she had first seen in the mirror. The tender white skin, the full parted lips, everything still apart from the gentle rise and fall of the girl's bosom. The witch's slippered feet made no sound as she moved to Snow White's side. A breeze stealing in the open window had blown a stray strand of hair over Snow White's forehead. The witch reached out a gloved hand and slowly stroked it back into place. This was the first time she'd touched the girl. She was used to hearing the minute movements of all around her: a rat scratching at a bag of flour in the cellar, the snore of a servant sleeping in the attic. It surprised her that all she could hear now was the beating of her own heart.

Snow White's eyes opened wide. She looked up at her new stepmother but she did not say a word. The witch stared down into the large blue eyes and was also silent.

Since the witch's arrival the girl had been skittering around the palace avoiding her; she had shown great skill in managing never to speak to the witch or stay in her presence for longer than a few minutes. Pleading illness and tiredness, she'd even escaped the ritual kissing of the new Queen's hand at the wedding ceremony. But now they were alone together and there was no King to concede to his daughter's every whim.

The witch looked away from the girl and down at her own body, wondering what those bright blue eyes were seeing. She could of course pluck them out and know for certain, but she found she had no desire to break the silence of this night with the girl's agonizing screams. She held her hand out in front of Snow White's lips, feeling the warmth of the girl's breath through the thin lace of her gloves.

"It is not proper for a Queen's hand not to have been touched by the lips of the Princess." The witch pronounced every syllable as if it was a rare delicacy in her mouth.

Snow White gazed up at her. The girl's expression was so blank that the witch considered whether the girl's beauty had made her miss the fact that the princess was dumb, but then Snow White's ruby lips trembled slightly, and the girl raised her head the small distance needed to make her lips touch the witch's hand. They stared into each other eyes and neither of them moved. This simple touch had caused a spark of pleasure to shoot through the witch's nerves, making her feel alive and scaring her. It had been a long time since another had given her even a hint of the sensations that a light touch of her own fingers in her concealed place provided. She knew now was the time to deal with this girl, before it became too late.

She broke away from the girl's gaze and looked down at her clothes. She suffocated the pleasure she had just felt and made the anger blaze inside her, focusing on her power and her age and the humiliation of the games she'd played merely to get into this chit's bedchamber.

"Once upon a time in a palace far, far away, I was just like you," the witch said, "but then I discovered that white just wasn't my color."

She yanked the right glove off and clicked her released fingers. The sound echoed around Snow White's room as if it was a living creature smashing against the walls. The witch's wedding clothes changed from pure white to violent red. She ripped at the neck of her gown, tearing the fabric away from her flesh. Snow White had not reacted to the transformation of color, but when the material fell away revealing the full curves of the witch's breasts, she cried out and pulled the covers tightly round her own naked body.

The witch smiled. She had not intended to destroy so much of the dress, but she pushed her shoulders back and her cleavage out. She was herself now, causing discomfort and fear in those around her.

"I am not scared of you," Snow White said.

The sound of the girl's voice made the witch pause. They did not normally sound like that, so calm. They normally pleaded for their lives in pathetic tones, they didn't speak with such confidence. And none of them had made her think of the scent of early morning and the taste of dew drunk from the petals of an angelflower. She closed her eyes for a moment before opening them again.

"You will be, my dear, when you see what I am going to do to you." She clicked her fingers and the mirror appeared on the wall.

Snow White did not move; she did not appear to have noticed the mirror. The witch pulled the glove off her other hand finger by finger and let it drop to the floor. The breeze that had stirred Snow White's hair was building into a storm. She laughed with exhilaration; the power was rising from deep in her womb. She raised her arms above her head.

"I am not scared of you," Snow White said. "I knew what you were the first time I saw you, waiting for me and spying on me in the forest."

The witch's arms dropped to her side; she tilted her head to one side and lines furrowed her brow.

"You are different. But you are like the rest. You think I am a child and do not know. I tried to warn Papa but he wouldn't listen to me. I knew you would be here one day, I've been waiting for you to come for me. I thought the Prince would stop it happening. But he didn't come today to protect me from you. Papa told him that I was ill and the illness was making me say things that it was unsuitable for a young girl to say, Papa told him it was best for him to stay away until I was better. He listened to Papa's messages, not mine."

"How did you see me? How did you know I would come? I don't sense the gift of futuresight in you."

The witch couldn't prevent herself from looking at Snow White. She gazed into those blue eyes and Snow White stared back at her, but her eyes seemed to be looking at something else beyond the witch.

"Before I was born they tell me my mother pricked her finger on a needle. There was blood. Droplets of blood fell on snow and they say she saw snow against ebony. She thought it was beauty and she wished that she would have a daughter with skin as white as snow, lips as red as blood and hair as black as ebony. I was born to her, and then she died." Snow White swallowed hard, the witch glimpsed white teeth biting down on her red lip. Then the girl took a breath and continued. "I know I wasn't meant to be. My mother wished for something she wasn't supposed to have and she lost her life because of it. I try, every day, I try so hard to be good, to earn the praise and acceptance of those around me. But I've always known what I really am. That's how I know what you are. We are the same. I'm not scared of you. I'm scared of myself."

A single tear was falling down Snow White's cheek, the witch did something she'd never done before: she bent over the girl and kissed the tear, holding it on her lips and then swallowing it into her body. She felt the droplet of the girl's sadness as if it were a thousand hailstones beating against her naked skin. The witch stood up straight. She looked sideways at herself in the mirror and she didn't know whether the reflection showed an old hag or a young blossoming girl. Every witch that had been defeated had been defeated by love. Love in all its many forms made people reckless, mad with courage. But more than that, love as a force silently untwined all the magics that witches need to weave to survive; it was the equivalent of dropping a shaving of unicorn horn into the most potent potion. All the power would be nullified. Nothing would be left.

The witch turned put her hand up to click her fingers together, but it wasn't the sound of magic that filled the room. It was the girl's voice:

"Please."

The witch had heard that word many, many times in her life but it had never before meant what it meant now.

She looked over her shoulder. Snow White was sitting up in bed, her hands by her side, no longer holding the bed sheets around her body. The witch gazed at her. Snow White stared back for a long moment before her eyes dropped to the floor.

The witch looked at the black hair framing the beauty of Snow White's face and the ends caressing Snow White's nipples. The witch looked at Snow White's nipples, perfect pink berries inviting a tongue to lick their round contours while a hand held the firmness of the breasts they decorated. The witch looked at the slight curve of Snow White's belly and the enticing dip of her belly button. The witch looked at Snow White's legs. Snow White looked back up at the witch, her big blue eyes wide, her lips parted, and she opened her legs.

The witch gave up. She fell on her knees before Snow White and buried her face in her moist pinkness. She breathed deeply, the scent of wild forests filling her nose. She hardly knew what she was doing, she didn't care what she was doing; she was all desire. She pushed her tongue deep between Snow White's lower lips, gasping as the girl's velvetness molded itself to her. The pleasure was so intense the witch struggled to contain her magic. As her tongue darted in and out of the secret place, Snow White's body floated and sparkled, a thousand tiny stars sprinkled over her. Snow White started to scream, and kept on screaming. The witch tasted the nectar falling on her tongue. The fire inside her was too strong. She pulled away from the girl and thrust her head out of the window into the cool air. She willed the rain to fall from it sky and it did, extinguishing the tiny flames that were igniting through her body. Her eyes were wild and the moon and stars flashed in and out of the sky. She heard a voice calling her.

"Come back. Come back to me."

Snow White was lying on the bed, one arm reaching out, fingers stretching toward her. She couldn't resist.

Snow White helped the witch lay down on the bed and stroked her hair. She lay down beside her and pressed the witch's head into her bosom. The witch glanced into the mirror; she did not recognize herself. Snow White moved down the bed and brushed her own cheek against the witch's.

"May I kiss you?"

The witch nodded without speaking.

"Thank you," Snow White said.

The witch closed her eyes and waited to feel the ruby lips against her own. Instead, she felt Snow White's hands tugging at her garments. The witch let herself be undressed, appreciating the cool air of the room on her revealed flesh instead of the layers of fabric. Snow White's hands brushed against her naked skin, making her breathe a little heavier and sending pangs of longing throughout her body.

"You are beautiful," Snow White said when the witch was naked.

The witch knew she was beautiful, she knew what every iota of her beauty cost in charms and potions and rigorous rituals and spells, but when Snow White said it her spirit soared and she floated a few inches above the bed.

Snow White giggled. "Is it always like this when you are intimate with another? I felt like I was experiencing all the joy in the whole world when you touched me and you had flames shooting out of your body."

The witch smiled, a real, genuine, relaxed smile.

"With a normal mortal they do not usually physically combust."

Unless I want them to, she added mentally to herself. "But if it is the right person you choose to be intimate with then it does feel like you are experiencing all the joy this world has to offer."

The witch sat up and moved to stroke Snow White's cheek but Snow White put her hands on the witch's shoulders and shook her head.

"Let me kiss you now."

The witch stared into Snow White's blue eyes as the princess's head lowered between the witch's spread thighs. Snow White's ruby lips disappeared and all the witch knew was pleasure. The girl's tongue flicked over the witch's sensitive spot and the witch screamed louder than Snow White had earlier. Snow White caressed the witch's thighs; she ran her tongue down the woman's legs to her toes and licked and sucked on them. The witch moaned and begged for Snow White's lips to touch every part of her body.

Snow White traveled up the witch's flesh, her mouth dancing and teasing over the witch's opened petals, then she thrust two fingers hard into the other woman. Her fingers fucked the witch, showing no mercy as the witch writhed under her touch. Her mouth continued to move upwards, stopping at the witch's breasts to suck on her hard nipples.

The witch felt like she was under the most powerful enchantment, that Snow White's body was controlling hers, forcing orgasm after orgasm to shoot through her leaving her flesh shivering and defenseless.

Snow White's movements became more tender; her kisses were like being brushed by butterfly wings. The girl let her long hair fall onto the witch's breasts and gently stroked them. Then Snow White smiled at the witch and wrapped her arms around her, drawing their bodies into a deep embrace. The witch looked into the mirror; the only difference she could see were the tears in her own eyes.

She left Snow White's room many hours after dawn broke. Before she closed the door Snow White called out to her, "Promise you'll look after Papa." It took the witch's most powerful magic to reverse the spell. She was drained and fell into a deep slumber, but her dreams were the happiest she had ever known. But when she awoke Snow White's final words haunted her. While she was sleeping Snow White had left the palace and gone to visit her favored prince. It was not known when she would return. The Kingdom buzzed with rumors of a forthcoming marriage. Had the turmoil of emotions she'd felt simply been the result of a simple seduction by Snow White to safeguard the life of her father?

The witch met with a huntsman and made it clear she did not want to see Snow White again. Then she called him back and told him there was in fact a part of Snow White she did want to see again. She ordered him to bring her the Princess's bloody heart.

The palace panicked, sending out search party after search party to find their missing Princess. The Queen sat on Snow White's empty bed holding a wooden box in both her hands. She traced the lid of the box with her thumbs but instead of opening it she placed it on Snow White's pillow and walked over to the mirror hanging on the wall. Her reflection stared back at her but she couldn't stop herself thinking of other images she had seen in its surface. This incident would vanish in the longevity of her life, an unnoticed rotten apple in an orchard of beautiful fruit. In the future she would forget Snow White; now she must focus on remembering herself. There were already fine lines at the corner of her mouth and eyes.

"Mirror, Mirror, on the wall, who is the fairest of them all." It wasn't a question, but the mirror answered her anyways.

"O Lady Queen, though fair ye be, Snow White is fairer far to see."

The breath caught in the witch's throat. The mirror shimmered into an image of the princess surrounded by dwarves. She was singing to them. The witch slowly exhaled then she clicked her fingers. She met the gaze of her reflection. The lines around her mouth and eyes had deepened.

The witch looked in the window and saw the same sight she had seen for many moons past. She drew her cloak tighter around her; she was not used to feeling the cold. Every day in the cottage was the same. The dwarves went to work, pretending they were going to toil in the mines, when in truth they earned their precious gems and metals through trickery and thievery. Snow White kissed each one on the cheek before they walked out the door and pretended she would spend the whole day tidying and baking, when in truth it took her only the time needed to click her fingers to transform the men's filth into cleanliness. One time she had experimented with the magic that the witch had unknowingly transferred to her in their moment of intimacy and had enchanted animal, birds and little elf folk to come in and do the chores. It had of course ended in disaster, but it had made the witch smile to see her try. The only other exploration Snow White made with her new powers was with her fingers delving between her velvet lips.

Whenever the dwarves weren't there, Snow White was naked. She spent day after day playing with herself. Sometimes lying down, sometimes standing up. When Snow White bathed herself in the chilled waters of the lakes the witch watched the princess staring at her own reflection in the water as she teased her nipples and breathed out her orgasm.

When the dwarves were there, Snow White was naked. She spent night after night playing with them. Sometimes on her back, sometimes on her knees. Whichever dwarves were not eating or sleeping were pulling on Snow White's hair, hanging on her breasts, biting on her buttocks and thrusting their prick into any of the princess's orifices which were available, and that they could reach.

Now all seven of them were there, taking it in turns to fuck Snow White's mouth and shoot their cream over her. The witch winced every time a globule of the dwarves' white spunk landed in Snow White's ebony hair. It was a debasement of beauty, but Snow White was moaning as loudly as the dwarves and the witch knew that if she herself allowed one of her hands to stray it would find the moistness between her own thighs. She knew she had to end this, even though it was already too late.

The witch had avoided seeing her reflection since leaving the palace but she was confident that Snow White would not know her. She had been too long away from her own home, but it was more than that; it was her connection with the princess that had drained her. It would be impossible for a mortal body to display the true age of her soul but whenever she glimpsed her own flesh she saw a vessel clinging onto the last embers of life.

After the dwarves left, whistling one of their crude songs as they journeyed off to find another victim to cheat and swindle, the witch knocked on the door. Snow White opened it with a smile. The look in those blue eyes was not one of surprise at getting a visitor when she was hidden so deep in the forest, it was the same look she had had when she had been in her own bedchamber and had looked up at the witch and parted her legs. Did she look at everyone like that? Is that why the huntsman had not killed her? Why the dwarves had given her shelter? Why the witch herself had failed in her own task?

"Greetings, respected elder," Snow White said, "how may I help you on this fine morning?"

"Would you be interested in the wares of a poor, old suffering woman?" The witch had not heard her own voice for a long while. It was aged but would Snow White be able to recognize the tone which still belonged to the younger looking woman who had covered the Princess's body in gentle kisses?

"I am sure I would like whatever you have to offer me," Snow White said.

The witch was ashamed of the tremor of her hand as she removed the apple from her basket. She held it out of the girl to take; the fruit was as red as Snow White's lips.

Snow White looked at the floor and then back into the witch's eyes. "I desire to taste that apple more than anything else, but I have no way to pay for such a royal fruit."

"Seeing your beauty is payment enough."

"I cannot refuse a gift." Snow White took the fruit from the witch and her fingers lingered, touching the witch's skin. "I cannot refuse anything you give me."

Snow White's lips parted, her tongue licked across her upper lip; she put the fruit to her mouth and bit into it. She chewed slowly, staring into the witch's eyes the whole time then she put the rest of the apple on the table and stepped towards the other woman. Her eyes were already glazed, her body was swaying. She leant into the witch, her breast pressing against the witch's chest. Their noses brushed. Snow White tilted her head and their lips were as close as lips can be without touching. The witch breathed in Snow White's warmth and felt she would never be cold again in her life.

"Kiss me," Snow White whispered and then she fell to the floor.

The witch leant over her and smoothed the girl's hair away from her face. She closed the lids of the blue eyes and then she left, closing the door of the cottage quietly behind her.

The witch had been dressed in her traveling robes through twelve full moons but she did not leave. Every day she watched over the glass coffin the dwarves had placed Snow White in; every night she stood beside it staring down at the princess's ruby red lips. Then one day the witch heard the cantering hooves and shouts of a hunting party. She clicked her fingers but the sounds did not fade away. One horse was coming closer. The witch knew who it would be before he appeared in the clearing and jumped off his mount beside the Princess. There were forces that bent the world to their will that the most powerful witch could not control, and she was not even the most powerful witch anymore. Without a word he broke the glass of the coffin and dragged Snow White's body out. He held her in his arms and pressed his lips down onto hers.

Nothing happened.

The witch laughed, it sounded like a cackle.

"Who is there?" the Prince shouted out, dropping Snow White

onto the forest floor and pulling his sword out.

The witch hobbled out of her hiding place.

"Begone from this place, foul hag, before you receive the punishment all your kind deserve."

The witch hardly heard his words. Fear had been holding her back. She had thought it had been the fear of dying, of giving the girl the last of her life essence, now she knew it had been a greater fear than the fear of losing herself. The Prince kicked her to the ground, she was barely aware of the blow, she crawled towards the Princess.

"Do not dare to touch her, you worthless creature, unless you wish to feel the blade of my sword hewing through your neck."

The witch put her lips on Snow White's and kissed her.

Both women clicked their fingers at the same time and the Prince's sword froze in the air. He strained to push it the remaining inch towards the witch's neck. Snow White offered her hand to the witch and the witch stood up, brushing the dirt off her gown. Both women clicked their fingers again and the Prince's sword sliced into the ground, sinking deep into the earth. He struggled to pull it out.

"Let go of it," the women said together, "and you will be released."

The Prince appeared not to hear them, his face turning purple with his efforts.

"It is time to leave this place," Snow White said. "We've been here too long."

The witch nodded. "It is time to go home."

"This is home," the witch said.

Her castle towered above them but the witch was staring at the Princess waiting for a response. She wished she had taken the longer route and approached from the more picturesque east side. She was suddenly conscious of how much death there was surrounding them; over the years she had cast many spells that required her to leach the life out of the earth and had never really cared or noticed until now. The Princess turned around slowly, looking up and down. The witch considered whether she would be able to chase the girl if she ran back to the greenness and ease of her own palace again. Then Snow White smiled and stared into the witch's eyes.

"This is home," Snow White said, pressing her hand against the witch's dress so the fabric formed a triangle at the top of the witch's thighs.

Then Snow White laughed and spun away from the witch. She began tearing her clothes off. The witch danced after her, her eyes mesmerized as the Princess revealed more and more of her flesh until all her garments were discarded around the forest floor and she stood naked a few feet in front of her.

"Come here," the witch said opening her arms out to receive the beauty of the girl's body.

Snow White shook her head, her hair tumbling round her face as she laughed at the witch. "You have far too many clothes on to interest me."

The witch clicked her fingers and her clothes disappeared. She smiled as the power surged through her. After her period of weakness when she thought the magic would fade from her, she felt stronger than she ever had before. She was at her home, her source, and she had found someone to love. It amazed her that she, as a witch, had been able to harness the power of love after all. But she would think about that later; right now she needed to chase Snow White who was running away from her giggling into the trees.

"Stop," the witch called out, "you don't know the dangers that are hidden here."

"Neither do you," Snow White said, appearing behind the witch and grabbing her around the waist. She bit down on the witch's neck and pinched her nipples before releasing her and disappearing again.

"You do not realize how much danger you are in! Let me show you," the witch said. Then, in another voice, she spoke ancient words that twisted around her mouth and fought with her tongue not to be released into the world. The earth trembled and trees that were older than the witch moved; Snow White was before her in a clearing, branches and plants tangled round her limbs, pinning her spread eagled to the ground. The witch walked slowly over to the Princess, and Snow White smiled up at her.

"Show me how much danger I am in then," she said. "What are you going to do? Kiss me and turn me into a frog?"

The witch smiled down at Snow White. "I could do, but you would be of no use to me as a frog." She clicked her fingers and a broken branch appeared in her hand. She licked her other finger and tapped it on top of the branch, and the wood transformed into a wooden phallus. The witch was rewarded by seeing that for the first time since they had met Snow White's eyes widened in something that might be a distant relative of fear.

"I saw you enjoy yourself with the dwarves and I imagined your pleasure if you had something," the witch paused and licked her tongue over her lips, "bigger to play with."

The witch rubbed the phallus over Snow White's cheeks and lips, Snow White's tongue darted out and licked the smooth end. The witch traced the outline of the Princess's body, running the hard wood down her neck, over her breasts and stomach, caressing the softness of her thighs and the muscles of her calves before traveling back up to the delicate pinkness between Snow White's legs. She held it so it touched the girl's lower lips and she waited, staring into the other woman's eyes.

Snow White smiled at the witch. "Fuck me," she whispered in her sweetest voice.

The witch plunged the wooden phallus into her, and Snow White yelled out.

"Is it too much for you?" the witch said.

"Fuck me harder," Snow White replied.

The witch responded by pulling the phallus out of her and then pushing it back in with one swift motion. The Princess screamed, but as the witch pulled it out the Princess raised her hips to keep it in her for longer. The witch used all her strength and magic to force the phallus in and out of Snow White, but the Princess did not beg her to stop - she begged her for more. The witch smiled. She left the phallus in Snow White, kissed one of her own fingers and touched Snow White's most sensitive spot. The girl writhed and moaned and pulled against her binds until finally she collapsed onto the ground and smiled up at the witch. The witch rested her head on Snow White's heaving bosom and gazed up at the stars.

"Are you going to release me now?" Snow White asked.

"You know you can release yourself whenever you want," the witch replied tracing her fingers over the Princess's lips.

The witch gazed into Snow White's eyes for a long moment, then the Princess clicked her fingers and wrapped her arms around the witch. The witch listened to the girl's heartbeat and realized that she would never be the most powerful force in this world, and this thought made her happy. It was together that her and Snow White were strong. She was no longer alone.

Many moons later they lay on the bed, both of them staring into the mirror. Their naked bodies were entwined and they were smiling.

"I always knew we were the same," Snow White said. "I should never have tried to run away from my destiny."

The witch squeezed her own and Snow White's nipples together with one hand.

"And perhaps I should never have tried to kill you," the witch said.

They both laughed at what had become their favorite joke.

"But we have the most fun when you're trying to hurt me," Snow White said and rolled on top of the witch pinning her arms down.

"We have the most fun when we're not talking," the witch said.

She jerked out of Snow White's grip and pulled the Princess's body against her own, tugging on the younger woman's nipples. She wrapped her arms and legs round Snow White and kissed her, pushing her tongue hard into her mouth before biting down on the ruby red lips.

And they lived happily ever after. (Although many other people didn't!)

A Vision In X-Ray And Visible Light

Nobilis Reed

Garrison arrived at his tiny cubicle, dropped into the chair, and stared at the screen in front of him. He checked his watch. Ninety seconds until he had to be logged in, or he'd be marked late and docked an hour's pay. With a sigh, he hauled himself forward, put his palm on the scanner so that it could read his RFID chip, and typed in his password.

"GOOD EVENING OFFICER HENCHLEY" appeared on the screen. "TODAY'S WORK ASSIGNMENT IS TRANSIT INSPECTION DUTY - BACKSCATTER"

"Of course it is," he muttered. "Same as always." He slumped down in his seat, pulling a little control unit to rest on his thigh. One finger rested on each of three buttons. The markings had worn off, but with four years of experience he knew their function without thinking, much less looking at the controller.

The screen lit up, shades of pastel blue and black. Ghostly human shapes drifted across the screen, hairless, naked, going about their business of getting from one place to another. This particular scene was a subway station somewhere. Garrison could see the dark black rails over the edge of the platform.

Everything metal was black. Easy to spot. Forbidden.

Female, height roughly one point five meters, standing on the edge of the platform waiting for the next train. Little circles of black spelled out "FUCK U TSA PERV" across her breasts and abdomen. From the size of the circles, they were probably pennies. He clicked over to visible light. The pennies weren't visible on her clothes; she had on a baggy sweatshirt and ragged black jeans. They were concealed. He captured the image and sent it to Facial Recognition with a description of the infraction. Metal wasn't allowed on transit.

A year ago, they wouldn't have reported this sort of invisible protest, but then some asshole smuggled knives shaped like the letter 'L' onto a train and caused a ten-car derailment in downtown DC. Two generals had been killed, and that was that. Even tinfoil was outlawed. The protesters gave cover to the terrorists.

Garrison wasn't sure what the protests were supposed to accomplish. The only people who saw them were cubicle jockeys like himself. It didn't bother him, didn't make him angry. If he was that sort, the constant stream of tits and asses and cocks and cunts that paraded past him all day every day would have gotten to him first.

She would be picked up for questioning when she reached her destination, perhaps not. It didn't matter. Garrison had done his duty, and had yet another silver star on his record for turning in a positive contact.

A new image came on the screen, a new camera somewhere else in the system. A bus stop this time, with people lined up, waiting. He scanned them quickly, then touched the button that declared that scene 'clear.' Another image came up. Clear. Another. Clear. Clear. Clear. Clear...

Eight hours later, the screen finally went blank. "Shift complete" it said, in large unfriendly letters. Below it, statistics scrolled up: Number of scans, number of reports filed, report confirmation rate. Garrison nodded. They were okay. Enough to keep his job, at least, though they'd never earn him a commendation. Losing the job would be bad.

He gathered up the remains of his lunch and stuffed it into the wastebasket under his desk. An uncomfortable emptiness gnawed at him, but it wasn't bad. Not like some nights.

He turned to find Lance Fergus hanging one lanky arm over the low wall of his cubicle. "Sam and Mickey and I are going over to the Panopticon for a drink. Want to come along?"

"Isn't that a strip club?"

"Yeah. It's across the line in the district, too, so they show everything."

"Dude. I just spent eight hours looking at naked people. Why would I want to spend even one more minute?"

"Come on. It'll be fun!"

"I'll pass." He grabbed his suit jacket off the back of his chair and wrapped it around his body, as if it mattered.

Standing in line for the bus, he glanced up at the camera cluster hanging from a nearby utility pole. It didn't look like much, just a black globe on the end of a short gray pipe, but Garrison knew that inside it was packed with sophisticated sensors on a swivel mount. He wondered who was looking at him right then, who was scanning him to see whether he was equipped for immediate, personal violence.

Then he took a deep breath and dismissed the thought. He wasn't carrying anything forbidden. He just had his clothes, the little wallet with his identification card, and the debit card that would get him on the bus and into his apartment.

Lance had already left on the bus going downtown, with his knot of friends. Garrison scowled. He shouldn't have been so dismissive, so rude. Would it have hurt to sit and have a few overpriced beers? He turned to the touchscreen on the side of the bus stop, tapped on the screen a few times to bring up one of the schedules. There'd be another bus going in that direction in fifteen minutes.

A bus pulled up. His bus. The doors opened, some of his coworkers got on, a few other people got off. He let the doors close.

There. It was done. No point now in going back.

By the time he arrived at the club, the sun was well behind the buildings, leaving the streets in shadow while the upper reaches glowed. The entrance to the club was a riot of swirling neon. A large bald man smiled as he approached. "Welcome to the Panopticon."

"Thanks."

Not entirely sure of himself, Garrison walked past him and pulled open the wide black door of the establishment. The space beyond was dark, and even after the shade of the street outside, he had to take a moment for his eyes to adjust.

A pretty woman in a bikini top stood behind a small counter to one side. "Twenty dollar cover charge," she said. Jazzy, upbeat music pulsed behind the walls.

He pulled out his debit card and touched it to the green payspot. A beep registered the transaction, with the amount showing on a nearby display. "I'm looking for a group? My friends from work said they were coming down here."

She shrugged. "I just take the money, sir."

"Okay, I'll just... mm. Look around, I guess?"

"Have fun!" She gave him a wide grin, and then turned her attention to the customer coming in behind him.

Garrison turned a corner into the club itself. Everything was dark except for the stage, a circular platform in the middle of the room raised to about table height, connected to the back wall by a narrow catwalk. A woman writhed and contorted herself on the pole, her body shimmering under the diffuse pink lights that came at her from every angle.

Stepping inside further, past a very large bald-headed man whose fists appeared to be superglued to the insides of his elbows, he spotted a bar running along the wall to his right. There were no stools there. It looked like it was just a place to pick up drinks.

"Can I get you anything?" said the bartender.

"Uh, yeah. Scotch please. Neat."

"Coming right up." A payspot on the bar lit up, and Garrison touched his card to it.

He sipped his drink as he wandered around the room, listening for the voices of his coworkers, trying to see a familiar face in the shadows and silhouettes that surrounded him. It was almost impossible to see anything but the stage. He was about to give up when the music changed, and a deejay's voice came over the speakers. "Big round of applause for the lovely Jayelle Kaye!" The woman on the stage scooped up her clothes and strutted down the catwalk towards a set of curtains along the back wall.

"And now," said the voice, "For your ecdysiastic enjoyment, the wonderful, the talented, miss Wyenne Ess!"

Another woman stepped out onto the catwalk. She looked vaguely familiar, but Garrison couldn't figure how anyone he knew would be dancing here. He walked closer.

She had dark black hair and pale skin, and wore a red sequined outfit consisting of a halter top and a skirt, both held together with long ribbons. He felt sure he had seen her face before, but couldn't place it. He found himself bumping into an empty stool at the edge of the stage.

"Hi there," she said, giving him a wink and a flash of a smile.

That took him back a step. Nobody had ever addressed him from a stage before.

"Sit down. I won't bite." She pulled out the knot in her skirt and held the ribbons out, making the skirt slide around her as she moved. The long slit between the two ends revealed brief glimpses of thigh.

In something of a daze, he sat. There was a payspot on the stage in front of him. He stared at it. It was labeled "Please tip generously" along the top and "One dollar per scan" along the bottom.

She was swaying to the music, strutting around the pole, making eye contact with the men around the stage one by one, but her attention lingered on Garrison. "First time?" she asked.

"Yeah."

She giggled. "Oh, I do love a virgin."

Garrison blushed. The guy next to him elbowed him in the ribs. "Go on."

He pulled out his debit card and waved it over the payspot. It flashed twice.

She smiled broader. "Thank you, sugar!" She dropped the skirt a bit, showing off the round globes of her ass, and the thin red g-string running between them.

"You're welcome." That was what you said when someone said "thank you." That was only polite. Right? Garrison felt uncomfortably out of his element. Ordinarily that feeling would have been more than enough reason to leave, but he knew this woman from somewhere, and he wanted to figure out where that was.

The woman wasn't really dancing, not in any way Garrison had ever heard of. She was just moving, with the pole as a prop and the music as a context. Even so, there was something hypnotic about her, and Garrison felt his gaze drawn to her hands as she reached behind her neck to pull out the knot. She held the ribbons out and above her head, playing with them, making her full breasts move like puppets on single strings.

Garrison had completely forgotten about his coworkers, and he didn't care. His world had narrowed to the woman in front of him, lowering the shiny triangular fabric in front of her breasts. Soon there was only the wide ribbon covering her nipples, revealing curves and shades he had never noticed before.

With a snap of her wrists, the dancer's halter seemed to disappear, suddenly transformed into a shower of red confetti, and she was dancing in nothing but the glittering red g-string. The music changed to an uptempo song with lots of synthesized rhythm. She moved energetically, swinging around the pole and doing splits and stretches that showed off her flexible physique. Garrison found his pants getting more than a bit tighter and shifted around to try to find a bit more room.

There were several flashes from around the stage as the other spectators swiped their debit cards over their payspots. The dancer smiled at each one, and Garrison found himself succumbing to the temptation to earn his own smile as well.

Now he knew what Lance had been talking about. This was fun.

The music changed again, a new song with a slower beat, with an energy that felt more intense than frenetic. The dancer sank to the stage practically right in front of him and slowly undid the knots on her g-string. She had almost no pubic hair at all, and Garrison found himself close enough to count the few strands that made up the narrow strip running from just above her slit.

Her inner lips poked out just the slightest bit, but as she swung one leg in a big circle, her labia parted and for a second or so he could see absolutely everything. No longer using the pole, the dancer prowled around the edge of the stage, gracefully and acrobatically giving each of the close-in audience members a good view of the most intimate parts of her body.

The tips came quickly, flashing from each station. Garrison found himself competing to tip her more than anyone else, and she gave him the lion's share of the attention in return. He thought he could almost smell the distinct musk of female arousal, as she arched her back on hands and knees, thighs spread out before him. Was this actually turning her on? Was there more than money going on here? Garrison couldn't imagine flattering himself that it was true, but he could see wetness glistening on her otherwise clean pussy, and what else was he to think?

When the music ended, she rose, gathered her things and disappeared backstage. Garrison finished his drink and decided he needed another. He made his way back to the bar, keeping his gaze turned away from the stage in hopes that his rather painful erection would subside.

Just as it arrived in front of him, he felt a gentle hand on his shoulder. "Buy a girl a drink?"

He started, almost spilling his drink, and turned.

"Oh, sorry," she said. She was wearing a loose-fitting white blouse with a plunging neckline that showed off her magnificent cleavage, and a matching knee-length skirt.

"No, no... it's fine, sure, what would you like?"

The dancer nodded to the bartender. "The usual, Hank?" She moved in next to him, elbow on the bar, standing a little too close.

He took a gulp of his drink. "That was some performance... uh... I didn't catch your name, I'm sorry."

"That's okay, you've got something else on your mind, I bet."

"Uh... yeah." He smiled sheepishly.

Her drink arrived, something pink and fizzy, and she took a long sip looking over the rim of the glass, staring into his eyes. "My name's Wyenne. I'm glad you enjoyed it. Nice to meet you...?"

"Garrison. Garrison... um." He wasn't sure whether he should use his last name. He wasn't sure he should use his first name, either, but it was too late to take it back. "I was supposed to meet some friends. This isn't the kind of place I usually go to. I didn't think it would be something I'd like." He was talking too fast, he realized, sounding like a nervous kid. He coughed to hide his embarrassment.

"Well, Garrison... maybe you'd like to take it a little further?"

Garrison stammered. "W-w-what?"

"A private dance, in the VIP room." She glanced in the direction of a door on the far side of the bar. "I promise a very intense experience."

Garrison's imagination flared. What was she offering? What could be more intense than what he had already seen? Was she a prostitute? What would happen if he were caught? Would he lose his clearance? Lose his job? He took another draw on his scotch and found the ice bumping his nose.

Wyenne put her hand on his elbow. "Come on. It'll be fun. I promise." She led him to the door, and pointed to the payspot next to the handle. "Fifty dollars gets you a tour of paradise."

With only a moment's hesitation, he ran his card over the payspot. He wasn't sure how much he had spent so far, but he knew he had enough to cover it. He made a good salary and lived a frugal, perhaps even spartan life, saving for—well, something. He was never sure exactly what, just that Good Americans Save. That's what he had always been taught. Perhaps now he had discovered at least part of what it was he was saving up for.

The VIP lounge had a couple of armless leather recliners and a long sofa. Wyenne went straight to a music console against one wall. "Make yourself comfortable," she said. The door closed behind them, shutting out the sounds of the club, replaced by a romantic saxophone solo.

Garrison stood, fidgeting, unsure what to do.

"One thing I need to say before we start," she said, coming up behind him. "You have to keep your hands away. No skin-to-skin contact."

He nodded. There were laws about these things? He never would have guessed. Not for the first time, Garrison regretted his sheltered upbringing. His parents had protected him from the corrupting influences that would have ruined his chances for a security clearance, but in making sure that he could get that all-important document, they had left him ill-prepared for the world at large.

Ill-prepared for Wyenne.

She reached around him, unbuttoned his jacket and pulled it off his shoulders. "Relax," she said. "Have a seat."

He sat in the nearest recliner, hands flat on the seat to make sure they didn't do anything they weren't supposed to do.

"What do you do, Garrison?"

Oh, boy. That was the question that soured everything, wasn't it? Whenever he met women, that question came up, and answering it never brought him any joy. The nice ones always seemed to go a little dark around the edges when they found out what he did for a living, and the ones who didn't weren't nice. They were always after something he wasn't able to give.

"I'm, ah... in law enforcement."

"Well, of course, sugar. That's the kind of place it is. Can you be more specific?" She smiled sweetly. "Can I see your badge? If you show me yours, I'll show you mine." She ran one hand along the collar of her blouse while she gave him a shy smile.

Garrison knew that there was nothing shy about this woman, and felt a sweat break out on his brow. He stuck a finger in his collar to loosen his tie, then realized he'd picked his hand up off the seat and slapped it back down.

"I don't really carry a badge," he said. "It's a desk job. We all just have RFID implants."

She straddled the chair, practically sitting in his lap. "Oh! Federal. Very nice," she cooed, deftly working the knot out of his tie. She glanced up for a moment, then returned her attention to her customer, sliding the satin fabric out from under his collar. "You just make yourself comfortable, sugar. Just let me... handle... everything."

On the stage, she had stripped slowly, taking a minute or two, at least, between removing bits of clothing. In here, she wasted no time. The blouse came off in one smooth movement, brushing across his face as it went. She tossed it to the side, and as soon as it left her fingers, she pulled off her skirt. Her underwear wasn't as flashy as it had been on the stage, just simple white spandex now, but up close they looked incredible. He could see the dark circles of her nipples and the little exclamation point of her pubic hair through the thin material.

... and he realized where he had seen her.

He looked up at her face. She was the girl on the platform, the girl with the pennies under her shirt. The girl he had reported for bringing metal onto the subway.

She popped open the clasp on her bra and slipped it down off her shoulders. Her breasts hung inches from his face.

He looked closely at her chest. There were very faint pink marks where the adhesive had stuck the pennies to her skin, just a few hours ago. It was definitely her. Why was she here? She wouldn't have gotten processed that quick. At the very least they would have kept her overnight.

"Something wrong, sugar?"

"No. No, not at all." He was afraid to shake his head, for fear that his nose might touch her flesh.

"Come on, sugar. I can tell. Something you'd like better, maybe?" She did something with the waistband of her g-string and that tiny scrap of fabric was gone as well.

Her naked thighs were on either side of his hips, and he could feel the heat of her skin on his face. A trickle of sweat ran down the back of his neck. His erection was back, in full force, and if she lowered herself even the slightest bit she would feel it. "I've got a clearance," he said. "I don't want to do anything that would endanger it." It wasn't really a lie, though it wasn't entirely true, ei-

ther. He did have some reservations about his clearance, but his curiosity about Wyenne's silent, mostly invisible protest and having no easy way to ask her about it was the real source of his confusion.

"Oh, don't you worry about anything," she said. "Half the guys out there have clearances, I'm sure. They don't care if you come downtown once in a while and have some fun. What happens in here never goes outside these walls. If it did we'd go out of business in no time!" She leaned forward and shimmied, and the soft skin of her breasts kissed the sides of his cheeks.

His eyes nearly rolled up into his head. Garrison felt weak, confused, and totally out of his depth. He gently pushed her back, swallowing down the lump in his throat. "I just wonder if maybe we could... talk? A bit?"

She settled down onto his lap, sitting right in the middle of his thighs, and her face softened. She looked, somehow, more sincere. "What do you want to talk about?"

"I want to know more about you. What you're like when you're not... this."

"Aw, sugar." She shook her head with a rueful smile. "I'm just here to make you feel good. And if this don't make you feel good, then maybe you're just not the strip club kind of guy? It ain't for everybody. I'm not here to give you the real me. I'm here to give you fantasy. I don't know you nearly good enough to give you any more than that. We're practically strangers. "

Garrison's mom had always told him that honesty was the best policy, that thinking up lies and ploys to manipulate people would only get you trouble in the end. He had to believe it was true. He took a deep breath. "I've seen you before," he said. "I work in the transportation surveillance section. Those cameras they got up in all the train stations and airports and bus terminals? I'm one of the people who watches those."

"And you saw me on one of your cameras?"

"Yeah. Saw you with some metal on you. Pennies or something like that."

Wyenne frowned and stood up. "So it was you that got me

picked up this morning." Mostly, her tone was neutral, but her professional friendliness had cracked, just a little, and Garrison could see through to the annoyance underneath.

"You had to know that would happen when you went into the station that way."

"Yeah." The beginning of a frown creased her forehead.

"Are you mad at me?"

She stared at him for a second. "Yeah, I guess I am. I don't like seeing my country all fucked up afraid, so that folks like you gotta be looking through everybody's clothes to see if they're carrying any pennies."

"But you work here. You...strip."

"Yeah, and it's my choice to work here. My choice to let people see my body. I ain't got a choice about using public transportation. Pays good to work here, but not so good I can afford a car."

He felt himself starting to launch into the justifications for his job, all the reasons he had told himself for why he had to do what he did, why it was right, but somehow they didn't sound so convincing anymore. After all, what kind of mayhem could someone do with a penny? Or even fifty of them?

Wyenne picked up her g-string and put it back together so she could slip it on.

"I hope they didn't give you too much hassle," he said.

Wyenne wrapped her bra around her body and snapped it closed, then slipped her arms into the straps. "One of the guys on the team they sent to get me knew me from here. One of the regulars. I was out again in an hour or so with a warning. Had to give them the pennies."

Garrison sat up and let the recliner fold down so he was sitting normally. "Why did you do it? Nobody was going to see your protest except me, and maybe the officers that intercepted you."

"It's complicated. And... not the kind of thing I like to talk about here." The skirt and blouse went on as easily as they had come off.

Garrison fished around in his head for what else to say. "Well, uhm. Maybe... look, maybe you want to talk about it over dinner?

I'll take you someplace fancy. I want to... I don't know. I want to know more."

"You're serious." She gave him an appraising look. "Alright. I'll meet you over at the Three Fourteen. You know where that is?"

"I'll look it up."

"Go on, then. I'll see you there. Eleven-thirty."

"Got it."

The Panopticon had some public internet terminals in a back corner that didn't have a good view of the stage. Garrison could remember when everyone carried smartphones and tablets around. It would have been nice, he supposed, to be able to look up the Three Fourteen and make reservations from his own device, but it wasn't so different using a public terminal. Besides, it was safer for everyone this way.

Five hours wasn't a long time to spend in a city like Washington. The Museum of Freedom was open until eight, and after that, Garrison found a sports bar not far from the Three Fourteen where he could catch most of the Orioles game. It was being played out on the West Coast, so it finished up late, which was just fine. He took it easy on the beer and had a couple cups of coffee along the way. Eleven was well past his usual bedtime. He wanted to be clearheaded for his chance to talk with Wyenne.

He made sure he was at his table by eleven twenty. Waiting too long would make him nervous, but he didn't want to get there after she did, either. He wanted to impress her, and if he couldn't be debonair or charming, at least he could be punctual.

The restaurant was fairly quiet, with just a few tables occupied. Potted plants lined the walls, in between tasteful oil paintings of landscapes and flowerpots, with more plants in between the tables to create little sheltered zones where no other diners were close enough to intrude.

Garrison was surprised to see her arrive in an elegant knee-length dress and simple shoes, rather than the street clothes he had seen her in that morning or one of the outfits she had worn at the club. With a simple string of pearls around her neck and a small handbag over her shoulder, she looked stunningly beautiful. He stood up as she came to the table, wanting to thank her for coming but finding himself unable to speak.

The waiter was there as soon as they were seated. He handed them menus and took their drink orders. He asked for a scotch, and she asked for a glass of wine. The waiter suggested a brand and vintage, both of which totally escaped Garrison's comprehension. She accepted graciously, and the waiter left them to their menus.

None of the items had prices. He wanted to say something, but he knew it would make him look like an idiot to ask, so he just scanned it for something—anything—he understood.

Steak. They had steak. That, at least, he could understand. He made his mental choice and set the menu down to find that Wyenne was also finished.

"You look nice," he said.

"Thank you." She smiled. "I'm glad you spoke up. I was beginning to wonder whether you'd had some kind of episode."

He stammered, then shrugged. "A bit surprised, is all. Having trouble finding my feet."

"I take it you don't get out much."

"No, I guess I don't."

"In that case, congratulations. It takes a lot of courage to do something like this."

The waiter returned with their drinks and took their dinner orders, giving Garrison a moment to think. He found himself smiling. For some reason, Wyenne's opinion mattered to him, more than it probably should. She was a stripper, just one step up from a prostitute, and yet she mattered to him. That thought puzzled him even more than anything else.

The scotch was better than he was used to; smooth and complex, with subtleties he had not noticed in his usual brand.

"You were going to explain your reasons for the pennies," he said, after the silence began to drag.

"Ah, right. Well... I think you have to imagine the scene. When the train came to my stop, I stepped off the train along with a dozen or so other people, walking in a big crowd toward the exit. Two big transit cops in bulletproof vests were standing there, and picked me out as I went by. They called my name, and asked me to come with them. Everyone had to go around us as they took me in. Nobody stopped to watch, or interfere, and I didn't expect them to... but lots of people saw. They saw that anyone could get picked up by the police at any time. They saw what we're becoming."

"Will you do it again?"

"I might. Though next time I'm not sure I'll just get off with a warning."

Garrison's first instinct, once again, was to defend his agency and their policies. He knew all the standard arguments, about how liberty required vigilance and how if they let their guard down, tragedy would result... and he knew what the result would be. Pennies. "You have a lot of courage, too."

"Hah! I don't know about that. I don't have a lot to lose. I won't get fired if I get in trouble with the law. It's not like they don't have plenty of women ready to take my shift, but I'm good enough that any time I want to come in and dance they'll make a slot for me. So I can run off and get arrested and all it'll cost me is a day's pay."

"Do you like working there?"

"As a matter of fact, yes, I honestly do. A lot of the other dancers are kind of desperate; they don't have much else they could do. Too crazy or too uneducated to get a job with more dignity. Me? I like it. Remember how I said I liked first-timers? That was the truth. Guys like you are so sincere, your eyes wide and mouths open. I like that. Makes me feel like I'm giving something really special."

The food arrived, and the conversation took another hiatus as they began eating. Garrison's steak was the best he'd ever eaten, and the red potatoes and steamed vegetables on the side were the perfect accompaniment. That, combined with the fact that he hadn't had anything substantial to eat since lunch, made him ravenously hungry.

When they were ready to talk again, they turned to relatively minor topics. They talked about hobbies, what kind of movies they liked, a few childhood stories. When the waiter came by to collect their plates and give them the dessert menu, Garrison found himself asking if she wanted to get some coffee.

"Are you planning on staying up?"

"I guess I'm a little sad this all has to end. It's been fun."

She smiled. "Let's go somewhere else for coffee," she said. "I know a good place."

Garrison paid the bill. He shouldn't have been surprised at the total, but it still made him shake his head to spend several hundred dollars on a meal. When they walked out, he offered his arm.

She gave him a crooked smile as she threaded her hand in his elbow. He let her lead him to the subway. She refused to tell him where they were going, except to say that she was sure he would like it.

He tried, several times, to guess where they were going, but every attempt failed. It wasn't her place, because she said the place wasn't tidy enough for company. He knew it couldn't be a hotel because they passed several stops where hotels were as thick as thieves in congress. Out of nothing but idleness and desperation he guessed his own apartment, knowing that it was wrong. She laughed and asked whether he thought she had the kind of access to information that he had. Finally he abandoned the idea and started a conversation about TV, which fell just as flat because she said she never watched.

They emerged in a commercial district and immediately turned down a side street into a row of smartly landscaped townhouses. They were quite new construction, with the new riotproof doors and the steel boxes on the roofs that indicated self-contained air systems. Wyenne walked up to one of them, waved her purse in front of the detector plate, and punched a long string of numbers into a keypad.

Beyond the front door a short flight of stairs led to an elegantly furnished living room, with a white leather couch sitting in front of a fireplace and a wide video monitor above the mantel. Everything was neat and spotless.

Garrison gaped. "Whoa."

Wyenne swept in, setting her purse on a side table. "How do you take your coffee?"

"Er, cream and sugar. Didn't you say you couldn't afford a car?"

"It's the truth. I can't. This place belongs to a friend." There was some hissing and burbling and in a minute or so Wyenne came out holding two steaming cups of coffee. She handed one to Garrison and sat on the wide couch nearly sideways, with her back up against the arm and her legs crossed, stretched out on the coffee table.

Garrison found a place on the far end of the sofa, scratching his head. "Well, you certainly are full of surprises," he said.

"You're lucky," she said. "I don't show this place to just anyone."

"I feel lucky." He sipped the coffee. It was quite good in spite of how fast she made it. He felt a little uncomfortable, in this strange place with this strange woman, but at the same time it felt like a great adventure, learning things and doing things he had never imagined himself doing. His thoughts about the risk to his clearance were fading quickly as his anticipation built for whatever it was that Wyenne had in store for him next.

The coffee cups weren't large and Wyenne finished hers in fairly short order. As soon as it was done, she set it aside, gently took Garrison's from his hand, and began unbuttoning his shirt. When she got to his belt she undid that as well, and then his trousers. He was quite hard by the time he got there and his cock practically leapt into her hand. She stroked it while she worked his shirt off his shoulders. Her breath was hot in his ear, punctuated by little chuckles whenever he moaned or otherwise showed a reaction.

When she slid off the side and took him into her mouth he thought he might faint. No one had ever done that for him, certainly none of the nice women he had dated from down at the sanctioned society. He'd heard of it, but never...

She worked his boxers and trousers down over his hips and around his ankles. From somewhere nearby she produced a condom and expertly slipped it into place. She rose up above him, lifting her skirt. She wasn't wearing any panties. Her body encased his cock with an easy grip that threatened to throw him over the edge immediately. Somehow, she knew how close he was, and waited there for his excitement to subside.

Her knees, sheathed in smooth stockings, lay on either side of his hips. Caffeine buzzed in his head, a spike of light in a bed of cotton wool. The pearls around her neck hung in his face. Tingles ran across his fingers and toes. His shoulders held the gentle weight of her hands.

He felt vulnerable. He felt confused.

He felt good.

Little by little, she moved. Not only that, she was doing something, making something happen inside her, some kind of muscular contraction that made it feel even better. There was something comforting about the way she stared into his eyes, about the way she caressed his face and neck, about the gentle smile on her face. It would be all right. It would all be all right.

Steadily, she built up speed, all the while doing whatever-it-was under her skirt. He was amazed by her stamina, but then again, she was a dancer. No doubt she would be fit. He tried to hold back, make the moment last, but he had no practice with the skill and clutched his hands around her waist as his climax poured through him, as unstoppable as a waterfall. His eyes clenched shut, his jaw tightened, and he threw back his head and growled, filling the condom, and emptying his mind.

It wasn't too bad, really. One master was as good as another. Technically speaking, he still drew his paycheck from the same place, but Lance had told him where the equities lay. He took his orders from the Apparatus now.

There was a recording. A well documented, clear recording, from several angles, of him with a prostitute. There was no doubt about what was going on, no doubt that it was him. Lance had showed it to him. Surveillance records showed him travelling from the club where she found her clients to a townhouse well known for renting out by the night. If that recording came to the attention of the security staff at his agency, his clearance would be pulled. Garrison didn't know whether Wyenne was in on the plot. Given that he had not paid her after they left the Panopticon, he suspected she was.

The funny thing was, they didn't want him to do his job any differently. He was to remain as vigilant as ever for terrorist activities. What they cared about was his social life. He was to get out more. Go on dates. Find a nice woman with a clearance. Someone from his social circle, someone young, naive, and sexually repressed. Lance told him that was very important. She had to be inexperienced. A virgin, if possible, or at least someone who didn't know much about sex. Someone who had grown up protected, like him.

They could get him a very good deal on a week-long vacation in the Caribbean. No computers, no schedules, no restrictions, and no cameras.

None that were connected to the Agency, at least.

Wood

David Sklar

These old bones aren't supposed to be climbing fences into someone else's field on a moonless night. That stuff's for young girls with a tingle between their legs, seeking out their young boys where their parents will not see. My creaky knees complain when my feet climb the fence, and when I land in the sod on the other side the axe handle bounces off my shoulder and thumps my collarbone. But Joe Burnham needs a reckoning for what he did, and if no one else will do it, it falls to me.

The tree is not hard to pick out. It stands very tall, a sycamore just a little south of the center of the field, and the shaft of it curves just a touch in the place where it rises from the low scrub. I put my hand on the tree, on the northern side, the inside of the curve. The bark is smooth; it feels good beneath my palm. I slide my hand upward. I know Burnham must feel that in his sleep. And underneath my hand, I blow on the trunk. Even over the noise of the peepers, I hear Joe Burnham whimper gently in the house at the edge of the field. I let my hand travel up the trunk, the backs of my fingernails slide up the shaft. The whole tree trembles slightly. Joe moans in his bed.

"Now sleep," I say, and I heft up the axe from my shoulder and take it down.

I let the tree lie where it falls, but at the base of the trunk, where I split it from the stump, I find a long thin knot that bores into the center of the wood. I cut this free and tuck it into the satchel that hangs from my hip. Then I dig up two handfuls of earth and toss them in with it.

At home in my cottage I set out two empty jars from under the bed and a third that is filled with mineral oils, distilled, as clear as water. The first jar I fill with soil from Joe Burnham's farm; the second I leave empty. From the knot of wood I carve a phallus with my knife. It is shorter than I would have liked, but sometimes it can't be helped. It takes me until the morning light to get the shape exact. Then I work the mineral oil in with my hands, rubbing it slowly along the shaft, a bit at a time, until it is smooth and supple to the touch, and I am intimately familiar with the penis I have carved, as if it had been born a part of me.

When I am finished with this task, I take the indigo candle out of its dusty box. I hold it in my hands and remember youth. I have not burned this candle in many years. But the work of today is the body's work, and it will not touch the heart unless it enters through the loins.

I light the candle with a match and call to the spirits entrapped within. The spirits issue from the flames, and they twirl in the smoke around the candle's shaft. I hear them whisper in the wind that moves through the room, and they blow around my hair. I call them by their names, Essimen, Erhifan, and others I will not mention.

They move around me in smoke, cool breezes and warm. They swirl up and down along my kneeling form, unbraiding my hair and opening the buttons of my skirt. They pass under my tunic and beneath my skirt, and they inspect my shriveled form, old withered breasts, and bones that push up against leathery skin. They cannot like what they see, but I am committed to this course.

A wisp of smoke dances up beside my head, underneath my hair, which still holds the twist of the braid. His whisper blows softly on the skin of my ear. "Why have you summoned us?"

"I have a working to do, and I need your help."

"Such workings are best left to the young."

"I am the age I am."

"Are you not afraid that your bones might break beneath the weight of a man?'

"I am resolute."

This breeze tingles down my neck and rejoins his brothers, who continue their dance around my form. They whisper to one another, but I cannot hear what they say. From a terrified place in the back of my mind, I shut out the thoughts of what they might do if they find me unworthy.

Airy fingers unravel the seams, and my tunic slips from my shoulders. They unbutton my skirt and remove my underclothes. A wisp of smoke whispers "Stand," into my ear. I rise to my feet and stand naked in the room. The spirits of passion twirl around me. I raise my arms straight out at my sides, and the spirits flow underneath and around, inspecting every inch of my brittle skin.

And even before they are finished I feel a tingle in my loins, a memory of the longings I used to feel when I was young. The tingle moves up my belly and down my thighs. I want to move, but I hold it in. A soft vocalization exhales through my mouth.

A wisp of smoke buzzes my ear and caresses my neck.

"So you find me worthy?"

They say nothing yet.

"You find me worthy?"

". . . ohhh. . . yes. . ."

"Then INTO ME!"

And they comply, twirling downward or upward into the core of my womanhood, where I once bore a daughter, long ago, wisps of smoke and spirit sliding between my nether lips, and I blossom inside.

"Thank you for coming to rest in this old crone. I promise you a ride you will not forget."

They do not answer, but I know they plan to hold me to my word.

I turn the empty jar upside down and place it over the candle to capture the last of the smoke that lingers above the flame. The candle fills the jar with smoke and then snuffs out.

I lift the jar up off the candle and slip the wooden phallus inside; then I screw the cap on upside down so that the smoke cannot escape. I put the jar in a leather valise and add a broad leather belt with a hole cut through the middle.

I wrap the candle carefully and return it to its box.

I light a fire in the hearth and I mix up a dozen oatcakes, small and flat and round. As they bake on the hearthstone, I mix earth and mineral oil in the empty pot. With this mixture I redraw the lines of my face, and by the time the oatcakes are cooked I am wearing a man's face above an old woman's naked form.

I eat three cakes for breakfast and toss the rest of them in a sack. Then I dress myself in men's clothes and walk into town to Harper's Inn.

By the time I arrive it is noon, and my shadow is neatly tucked under my feet as I step inside and approach the desk. "I want to see Miss Sally," I say.

"But it's early, sir," says old Charlie at the desk. "She'll be in bed."

"Well that's where I want to see her," I say, and I toss the bag of oatcakes on the desk. They clink like coins.

"But sir—" Charlie says to me.

"Ain't my money just as good as anyone else's?" I cut him off.

"Yes sir," he answers, and he stands aside.

The ladies let me pass as I walk up the stairs. Not much happens here by day, and of course Joe Burnham won't be coming here 'til late. I walk past yards and yards of red velvet until I come to Miss Sally's room.

I open the door without knocking, and Miss Sally lies sprawled on the bed, her tits hanging out of a negligee that wasn't made for the way real women sleep. She has kicked off the red velvet covers and dozes on rumpled satin sheets, but still she glistens with sweat from a restless night. She stirs as I enter.

"I'm not really ready," she mumbles, raising her head up from the pillow. Her hair remains skewed to the side, like the straw that sticks out of a field after harvest time.

With my finger I trace her outline in the air.

"What's this about?" She waves her arms around, vaguely imitating my gesture.

I open the jar a crack to let the smoke out into the room. I say, "Sleep," and I close her eyes from across the bed. Her head lands on the pillow like a feather on the road.

I close the door behind me and look around. I take a cut glass bottle of violet perfume from Miss Sally's vanity, and I put it in my valise. I approach the bed.

She flinches slightly when I touch the sole of her foot, but she relaxes into it quickly without waking up. As I slide my finger up the arch toward the toe, she sighs in her sleep. And up along the leg I glide my hand. The hairs on her legs, so faint that she needs not shave, stand at attention to my fingers as my hand slides up her thigh, under the negligee, brushing gently against her hair underneath the skirt on my way to caress that belly that was never stretched out by a child.

"Oh," she whimpers, her eyes still closed.

I want to curl up like a baby and suck at her breasts, but that isn't what I came for. Besides, I still have a few teeth left; I don't want to bite by mistake and wake her up. I open the jar again, and as the captured smoke escapes into the room I slide the wooden phallus down along the side of her breast.

"Oh, Joe," she says, and takes it in her hands, running her fingers along the shaft of it without opening her eyes.

I grip the wooden penis at the base and let her do what she will.

"It's so hard today, Joe," she says, and pulls it tight between her breasts, sighing as she squeezes them around it.

I know the sighing is for show, even in her sleep. But I'm not concerned. The sighs will be authentic in good time.

"Oh, Joe," she says, "you're harder than ever tonight..." She lets go of her breasts and moves her mouth toward the wooden dildo, but I slip it out as soon as she lets go.

"Why are you pulling away?"

"A moment, my dear," I answer, taking the strap from the valise. "I need only a moment." And I bind the penis between my hips, below my waist.

She lies slantwise across the bed with her head just leaning off the edge to reach my hips, and the bottom of her teddy has shifted away from the cheeks of her butt. The waiting has wakened a hunger in her—she sucks at the phallus fiercely when I let her have it again. I wonder whether the passion she shows me is genuine or a show to excite the man, put on through habit even in her dreams. I wonder, if I were a man, would I see it differently? And no, this isn't what I came for, but I wonder what it's like, and the spirits I called inside me will want their due. So I call for the soul of the wood to take root in my loins, and the arteries in my thighs to perfuse the wood. Within me, the spirits dance around the roots. And there, I feel it, her lips on my lingam, her tongue running furiously back and forth on the penis I built. And now that I know what it feels like, I understand why men come so easily. The wooden staff is throbbing, though it holds no juices to release.

She lets up for a moment to say, "I hope you're not done. I have plans for you."

But before she can take it into her mouth again, I straddle her on the bed and plunge inside.

There is no question now; her cries of pleasure are genuine, and she squirms, unable to contain herself as I slide it into her. "Oh," she says, and she twists in an effort to keep herself under control.

The wooden penis tingles. I glide it smoothly in and out.

"Oh. Oh."

I lay my hands on her hips and caress up her belly to her breasts.

"Oh."

I pull back for a moment, and I let her have just the tip.

"Oh." She rises to kiss me, but I cannot let her follow through. A kiss might wake her from her sleep, and it would almost certainly tell her I am not Joe.

I lay two fingers to her lips to hold her off, and she slips those fingers into her mouth and sucks on them eagerly, not noticing or not caring about the bony knuckles, and she plays with her tongue in the skin that stretches between. I imagine that tongue sliding into me, between my lips below, when suddenly she grabs me around the back and throws herself all the way on my wooden cock.

It is a struggle to stay upright underneath her sudden weight. She is not heavy, but she is not tiny either, and of course I am not the man she thinks I am. Of a sudden my body remembers how long since last I slept, and my mind slips loose into a mélange of sensations. The smell of perfume and smoke. The velvet blanket beneath my knees. Miss Sally's knees wrapped around my buttocks, her bare breasts slipped out of her nightdress, pressing against mine beneath the man's shirt I have on. Her sighs of pleasure muffled by her tongue between my fingers. The surging of the cock between my legs; the tingle of my clitoris underneath. The haze in my head, the exhaustion of my thighs. And as she pulls her mouth free of my hand so she can call out her building climax, I drop backward onto the bed and yield to a physical release that transforms my pores to light and scatters my essence out from my chest into the ends of the universe.

But I am still here.

Even as my soul expands, my body stays in place and awaits my return to myself. And as the pieces of my being fill the outline of my form, I remember who and where I am, and what I am doing. The task ahead reasserts itself. This is no time to rest. But my body cannot remember how to move. I feel the soft velvet bedclothes as if I were resting on a cloud. I would lie here forever, but my work remains to be done. And as I return to my body, I find I am not alone inside. The spirits of candlesmoke and passion I have invited to dwell within, they are emboldened by how easily I let them take the lead, and in the moment I let go they expanded their range. Now they squirm in my belly and throb in the arteries of my legs, inside my thighs. One rests at the base of the wooden phallus and sips at it like a drinking straw, tasting the nectar of Miss Sally's passions and siphoning off a bit of her soul.

I clamp down on the spirits with my will. *This was not in the deal.*

One whispers back. *But it was not excluded.*

I will not allow it.

You are in no position to negotiate now.

We shall see about that. I clamp off the wooden phallus with an act of the will, shutting all of them out. With my hand I squeeze the base of it, pushing back into Miss Sally most of what the spirit took. She squirms in this moment, responding to the rush of spirit that issues out of the wood.

"Oh, Joe," she says.

But retaking control is harder than I let on, and I am still woozy from the moment when I let the passions lead.

I unbuckle the leather strap and slip like a snake from between her legs, leaving Miss Sally still plugged with the wooden cock. And, taking the empty jar in my other hand, I slowly, carefully, slide the wooden phallus out, catching in that jar the juices that flow from her there.

It is not enough. I should have put the jar in place the instant she came. Now the fluids I need have soaked into the bed.

I reach inside her with my finger and work her some more.

"Oh," she sighs. "Oh Joe, you don't need to do that." But she continues to flow out, slowly, into the jar. I touch her clitoris gently, and she writhes on the bed. "Oh Joe." And I work the fluids from under the lips, from deep inside, from every crevice I find.

Just then my hand unsteadies and the cold jar taps her skin. "What?" she says and slowly opens her eyes.

In the moment her eyes need to focus, I put the cap back on the jar, and I slide the jar, the belt, and the wooden phallus back into my valise.

"Who are you?" she asks, and then she sees through my glamer. "Witch! Get out of here, witch!"

Such hurtful words. She covers herself with both hands and she squirms away to the head of the bed.

I have harsh words, too. "You tell Joe Burnham when you see

him, it was I who took his wood, and if he wants to get it back he needs to come and talk to me."

"Witch!" she shouts, and I take my valise and leave.

The ladies of the brothel step aside, and they cover themselves as I pass, like they would not do for a man, or for almost any other woman. Old Charlie looks at me at the base of the stairs. The glamer has dropped from the sack of oatcakes I left with him, but he dares not speak, and I am out the door before he gets the nerve.

Outside of my house in the woods, I meet a crow sitting on a wet post. I ask him to guard the house, then I mix the fluids I took from Miss Sally with the perfume from off of her dresser and dab a drop of the mixture onto the corners of the door. I walk inside then, and strip off my man-costume. And the rest of what I took from her, floral scent and woman musk, I work into my skin—into my face, my hands, my arms, my breasts, my belly, my back and buttocks, down my legs all the way to the toes, and of course between my legs, very deep inside, where I have invited the spirits to dwell. Then I go to bed nude and sleep out the afternoon until Burnham arrives.

I startle awake to the crow's call and, still in an afternoon's dream, I am my house and all the land around. I feel Joe Burnham's boots on the stones of the path toward my door, feel the small round stones slide roughly against one another. There is purpose in his step, and there is anger. I am not sure I want to let him enter at my door. A hollow thump—his fist is strong, but the wood is damp and old.

I waken slowly, turning my feet down off the bed, and as my knees move apart so the door slides open and he steps in.

"I see you at my door, Joe Burnham. What brings you here?"

"Miss Sally says it was you who stole my wood."

I glance down at his trousers. "It seems to me you have it where it belongs."

He glances down, then back at me, aghast. "Witch—you take it away when I need it and give it back to me when I don't."

I smile. "What makes you think you will not need it now?"

He stares at me, stunned.

"As fast as you go through the women in town, you might have known you would come to me."

He looks as if I'd asked him to eat a toad. I stand up.

"Is that what this is about?" he asks.

I approach him. "Yes, it is."

He turns to leave. I grab his arm. "You had best be sure, Joe Burnham. If you want it hard again, then I would advise you not to insult this old woman."

When he turns to face me again, he looks as if he has indeed swallowed that toad. "I don't know if I can."

I move close enough that he can smell Miss Sally on me. "You seem ready enough."

The bulge in his trousers continues to rise. "How—"

"Don't concern yourself with that." I unbutton his trousers and I take him in my hand.

Steeped as I am in Miss Sally's fluids, Joe Burnham does not stand a chance. Within moments of my touch he has leaned his head back. He is groping with his right hand for something to hold up his weight as I work him in my hand. "Oh," he moans, his deep voice cracking with the effort to keep control.

"You will be mine," I tell him, and he begins to pull away, but I shift the position of my hand, and Burnham throbs beneath my fingers. "Before this night is over, I will bend you to my will."

He reaches forward to push me away, but before he can touch me I slide my fingertips underneath his shaft and send him a tingle beneath the skin. His left hand closes gently around my arm as his right still clutches the doorframe behind his back.

"Oh... oh..." He no longer resists.

When he comes I do not waste a drop, but I rub it into my hands, my breasts, the sides of my mouth, as he crumples against the wall. The mingling of his fluids and his lover's makes old flesh young. My bony hands fill out, my breasts lose their sag, and I feel a gentle smoothness in the shape of my mouth.

Joe Burnham struggles to regain his strength. I watch him push against the wall to stand up. He stumbles, slides back down, stands up again, and fights to muster the will to walk away. "Well," he says weakly, "now that you've. . .now that you've had what you wanted, I'm going to. . . going to. . ."

"I'm not done with you yet." I kneel down on the earthen floor.

There are limits to magic. The energies I brought forth can make old skin supple, energize the body, fill out old flesh for a while, and give the illusion of someone else's face. But nothing I have done here is enough to regrow teeth. So I must be cautious as I take him in my mouth, not to snag him on the bony corner of one of the few that remain.

The tip is still dripping slightly, and salty on my tongue. I use this to augment my magic, to make my mouth young again. I find that place underneath, the one I worked with my fingers before, and he grows rigid again as I work him there.

"Oh. Oh." I hear him moaning but I cannot see his face. I run my once-more youthful hand along his thigh.

Now understand—Joe Burnham has magic of his own. He does not study the craft; most likely he does not know what he does. But a man can't seduce all those women, get a lady like Sally to love him free of charge, and even bed my granddaughter Thessaly, unless he has something special at work for him. I tempered it when I cut down his sycamore tree, but now I am calling it back out and I feel it call to me. And when he gently touches me on the back of my head, I feel a young girl's tingle between my legs. And the spirits I've summoned to dwell there—they feel it, too, and they hunger for more.

Slowly I slip him out of my mouth and kiss up the length of his body, unbuttoning his shirt with my hands just ahead of my lips.

And, when I am standing all the way up, with my arms around his shoulders, I wrap a now-youthful leg around his waist and rest my foot on the wood of the door.

"You are about to enter a temple," I whisper to him, so close that the sides of my lips brush the edge of his ear. "Be aware that a tribute may be required of you."

"You're all talk, old witch," he says.

"And you're all cock," I answer and slide him inside me. I feel his fullness in me, and the spirits I have invited to dwell inside grow excited. I hear them cackle between my nether lips.

He tries to kiss me, but I pull my head away; I will not let him take me as an equal. I knelt like a supplicant to set his mind at ease, and now, before I assert control, we stand face to face, but I will not let him bind me in this role. He nuzzles at my breasts. I let him suck. He takes them hungrily in his mouth one at a time, with a fervor that bears no restraining, like a man who has never known a mother's love.

I reach my hand up gently, and I cup the back of his head and stroke his hair. "There, there," I say. "It's OK. It will all be OK."

He throbs and surges inside me, and I feel his fluids fill me. And the spirits who dwell within drink it hungrily, and they take from him more than he realizes, so much more than he understands.

His legs seem ready to buckle, but I keep him pinned between me and the wall, my leg around his waist holding him upright. And at the point of collapse he continues to come, in short, slow bursts, his fluids leaking into my soil that will never again take seed, but which remembers richness, remembers an infant's growth inside.

A memory drifts into my head unbidden, of standing in this room when I was young, my lover propped between the door and me. My Edward. Black of hair, with a limp in his hip. But with hands that know where a body likes to be touched. I remember his caress on my buttocks, on my belly, swollen with child, and my breasts grown heavy with milk. And in the womb my ecstasy was heard by Heloise—the daughter who would grow up and bear Thessaly, who in turn is pregnant now with Joe Burnham's child.

Joe leans back against the door and begins to slide down the frame. "That was amazing," he says, his eyes half closed as if drunk. My hand that grips the back of his head moves down to clutch the hairs atop his neck. And with the strength I have taken from him, I lift him upright and bend him across a wooden chair.

"I'm not done with you." I tell him, and strap the wood phallus against my hips. He is not expecting me when I take him from behind, sliding that whittled replica of his manhood between his firm, round, strong, unready buttocks.

He moans like an injured man dying beside the road.

"You are mine," I say, pushing into him. "Understood?"

"Ohh," he moans, trying to flex the muscles in his back.

"You are mine to command," I repeat.

He tries to buck me off but lacks the will to pull away. He moans his pleasure even as he fights my will, and as I push into him, Burnham struggles to have it both ways, to take what I give him without bending to my will.

I lean in close, folding my body completely around him, my belly against the small of his back, my breasts on his shoulder blades, my chin stretched forward to rest on his shoulder, just at the base of his neck. I slide my hands slowly along his arms and grasp his wrists. "You will do what I tell you," I whisper. My breath stirs his hair.

And Burnham tries to buck me off, to resist my command, but his resistance thrusts the lingam deeper into him, and he gasps the way a woman gasps when a man is filling her fully, and then he submits. The tension leaves his shoulders and his back, and he rocks with me, moving his hips in rhythm with mine, a fluid motion that answers my command. I will the phallus to fill with veins, to plunge its roots into my body, and I feel myself in him, the penis that once again is completely mine sliding ever so gently in and out as the muscles of his back caress my belly and my breasts. His shoulder blades brush a tingle against my nipples, and the quiver runs across my skin. And my wooden phallus throbs.

And the spirits who dwell in the hut of my pelvis are

whispering down my veins. They are ready to take command if I lose control, but still I ride this moment like the surface of a wave as they egg me on. And the roots of the wooden phallus burrow deeper into me. "You are mine to command," I whisper again into Burnham's ear, though I am not as confident as before.

Burnham turns his head to the side and kisses my arm, down the inside of the elbow, along the forearm across the wrist. His back slides against my belly and breasts, his buttocks against my thighs. My head swims, and the indwelling spirits sound me out, prepare for the bright ecstatic moment that will let them take control. And, as he kisses between my forefinger and my thumb, a hand I had not been expecting reaches back between my legs and dips a finger smoothly into me.

I am on the crest of the wave, about to drown in the surging Now, and the spirits within me eagerly wait their moment. I think to clench, to pull in deeper what I have inside, so that Burnham will not find it hidden there, but what he is doing with his finger feels so good that I do not resist, but open myself completely to him, not concerned with what he finds. I am man and woman both at once, and both are being pleasured at one time. I moan my pleasure, I gasp for breath, I hear Joe Burnham moan and gasp, and all I have worked so hard for is about to slip away, but I don't care. The moment is too perfect to be anything but what it is. I feel the tingle in the front of the wooden phallus just under the tip, in the place where it pulses in men before they come. I do not break rhythm. I understand the cost, but I keep on. The roots of the wooden phallus dig deeper inside. The spirits wait. And as I am almost ready to give myself over completely, I hear Joe Burnham's come cry, his ecstasy screaming, and the roots of the wooden phallus plunge in an instant deep within me, driving their points into the centers of the spirits I let dwell there, and drinking them dry.

And when the spirits are sucked inside it, I seal them off. With a motion of the will, I trap them inside of the wood, and I leave it there, impaled through Joe Burnham between the legs.

He moans in submission, and I collapse upon the bed, an old woman again, an intensely pleasured old woman, home from the brink of a perfect moment where I did not step inside.

"That was amazing," Joe says, when he is able to speak again. And he tries to kiss me.

I sit up and take my lips just out of reach. "Yes it was," I answer. "Now what will you do for me?"

He pauses for only a moment. "Whatever you ask."

"Do you mean that?"

"Yes."

I smile. "There is a girl you have made pregnant. Thessaly. You will go to her and propose marriage. You will love her the rest of your life."

"What?"

"That is what I require."

"But you can't—"

"I already did. You agreed to it."

"My love is not a beast you can command!"

"Are you sure of that?"

He stammers. "But—but I was with you. I made it with you. And look—my love made you young."

"I am older than I look, Joe Burnham."

"Well, now."

"I have always been old."

He stares at me, uncomprehending. I have no heart to hear him say the truth cannot be true, just because his mind cannot fathom what I am. "The ancient sycamore I cut down in your yard—I planted it there. Before the records in the court say I was born, I planted it there. Old though I may appear, I am older still. When the mortal lass who thought herself my mother brewed tea in eggshells to confirm that I was but a cradled babe, I was old enough then that I had seen that before, and I held my tongue."

He looks down at his hand and sees at last the blood on his fingertips, where he touched inside of me.

"I have sounded your every note, Joe Burnham, and bent you to my will. And all I ask of you is to love the mother of your child."

"But how can you tell a person what to feel?"

I gently grind my hips against empty air. "Already you have wood at the thought of her." I clench my muscles and squeeze what I have secretly taken from him. Though he trembles, he tries to hide it, but it is obvious to the eye. "The thought of her touch brings you pleasure; the thought of her face gives you joy. You burn with desire for her, and if you resist, it will eat you within. You are beginning to feel guilty over being here with me." I touch his face, and he turns away in shame. "These barren lips hold nothing for you. Go where you belong."

Without looking at me, Joe Burnham reaches down and pulls up his pants. He buttons his fly without regard for the blood on his hands. He steps sideways and around as he buttons his shirt, still averting his eyes, and steps out through the door without ever looking back. Without noticing, for that matter, that he has a knot of wood in place of what he was given at his birth.

I look at that shut door for a moment then let myself flop on the bed, relieved to have the time at last to relax. Don't get me wrong. I feel a pang of desire. The spirits I trapped in the wood have left an ember rekindled in me, and the longings of my youth dwell in the space they cleared out for themselves. And a boy to sate my longings would be nice. But seeing to Thessaly and her child—that was my purpose from the start, and if I must live lonely, so I shall.

Slowly, carefully, I slide my thumb and forefinger up inside myself and extract, very gingerly, Joe Burnham's still-erect penis, which I have traded, unnoticed, for the one carved of wood from the sycamore tree.

The wooden cock will serve him well enough. It will not make new children, but it will stand at the ready to service my granddaughter's needs. I wind his penis up in a strand of my granddaughter's hair before I immerse it in the jar of clear mineral oils beneath my bed.

He will be a good lover to Thessaly—a good husband too. I have his manhood in a jar to make it so. And if once in a while I take it out and play with it myself—or if I wear it into town and go to visit Miss Sally again,-well, that's not Joe Burnham's business any more.

Devil's Masquerade
Michael M. Jones

As Grace's hand lifted to fidget with her mask for the twelfth time in as many minutes, I lightly swatted it away. "Quit it. You look fine." It was true. With the elegant white feathered mask masking her features, all I could recognize of my partner were her short brown hair, sharp green eyes, and scarlet-painted lips, currently pursed in a frown.

"I feel ridiculous, Starling," she grumbled, reluctantly lowering her hands while I gave her the once-over. "This job is ridiculous. We should be out on the streets in nice, sensible leathers and armor, beating people over the head until they stop misbehaving. Not tarted up like harem girls." Despite her obvious discomfort in the brightly-colored silks that draped her slim frame and hinted at the curves underneath, there was no hiding the fact that she cleaned up very nicely indeed, when she so chose. I reached out, retying the cord around her waist. We only wanted the illusion that things would come apart at the slightest provocation, not the reality. I stepped back, studying her before giving my nod of approval. Inspector Grace Wintersford, champion of the downtrodden, terror of the wicked, in as unlikely an outfit as you'd ever find her. Wrapped in gaudy, diaphanous clothing that fluttered with every movement, she looked like a tropical bird set free in an alien environment. I'd lost the argument when it came to jewelry; Grace refused to wear anything shiny or sparkly. It would have to do.

"I know." There was genuine sympathy in my tone. "This isn't my ideal assignment either. Nor my ideal outfit." While I wore something much like Grace's fluttering silks, I'd put more effort into artfully arranging them to show off my own generous curves, my long red hair teased into a bead-decorated waterfall of curls. Teasing and provoking without giving anything away: that was the only way we'd get anywhere tonight.

Grace's eyes flicked up and down as she eyed me, and I could feel her attention linger on my breasts, which currently threatened to escape their dubious coverage. As it stood, there was certainly plenty on display to ogle, nipples barely concealed. One wrong move on my part and.... I shivered, turning away after a few seconds, trying not to let the gaze get to me. Bad enough I felt all but naked dressed like this; I didn't need to go in already aroused. That would be... awkward. "You look a lot better than I feel," Grace said. "Clearly, you should have been a courtesan, not a Ducal Investigator."

"It was my third career choice, falling right after any-bloody-thing else," I replied. My hand on the hallway door, I paused. "Ready? Once we go out there, it's showtime."

"After you," said Grace, giving me a cocky grin. "Let's go find us a demon."

We exited the bedroom we'd been lent as a changing room and staging area and made our way through the opulent halls of Dressarie House, passing idealized portraits of long-dead people, sculptures that bordered on obscene, and knick-knacks worth more than the both of us made in a year. We passed one closed door after another, slowing whenever we heard a suspicious sound slipping through the cracks, speeding up once we were sure they were sounds of pleasure. One particularly enthusiastic squeal was enough to make my own toes curl with envy; I picked up the pace. Soon enough, after descending a winding marble staircase, we found ourselves downstairs. A moment later, a silently attentive butler ushered us into the ballroom. And that's how Grace and I entered the infamous Devil's Masquerade. Not as Inspectors Grace and Starling, armored both literally and figuratively with our authority as official representatives of the Duke, but as a pair of anonymous pleasure girls.

Grace whistled, low and impressed despite herself, as she took in the sheer decadent splendor of the ballroom. It was chock-full of the city's elite, the rich and powerful, mingling and drinking and indulging in various vices, a gathering unlike any other held all year long. On any other day, half of these people would be arguing with, ignoring, or dueling the other half. On any other day, they'd be dignified, maintaining their courtly manners and aristocratic demeanors. On any other day, they'd be unmasked... and wearing somewhat more clothing. But on the night of the Devil's Masquerade, all bets were off, no hunger too perverse and no desire too extreme. Here in this House, on this night, the people who ran the city were encouraged to indulge, as per ancient pacts and promises made to those who'd inhabited the land long before humanity settled here. And so the nobles danced and drank and fucked with wild abandon, glittering eyes framed by physical and social masks, their identities politely hidden even as they bared their bodies and souls.

It was early yet; the real debauchery didn't get going until after the Devil's toast at midnight. Sure, hands wandered along exposed skin, lips trailed lovingly over a stretch of shoulder, and the darkened corners were already occupied with writhing, tangled bodies, but this was nothing. Once the glasses were lifted and the lights all but extinguished, the wild revels would be underway.

Grace and I had no intention of being here that long. We'd never seen a Devil's Masquerade before, partly because it wasn't for the likes of us, and mostly because we had way too much class. We kept our vices out in the open and indulged like honest people. Technically, our authority gave us the right to be here, but realistically, it wasn't something that ever actually happened. Short of murder and rape, there were very few laws that could be broken or enforced on this night. If we made a spectacle of ourselves, blew our cover, it was likely that more than a few attendees would take offense to our presence. And not just because we'd pissed them off in the past.

Unannounced and unnoticed, we meandered through the crowd, side by side as if tied together. This was not a crowd in which we wanted to be separated. Time and again, Grace bumped my hip with hers, or jabbed me with an elbow to get my attention. "Lady Northgate really shouldn't wear that color," she hissed with evil glee. "Especially not while draped over—is that Magistrate Gabriel? His hands aren't where I think they are—oh, they are!"

I shushed her quickly. "Ours not to wonder why, ours not to give a damn. You know why we're here. Now hold still." I laced my arm in hers, letting her balance me while I called up my Witchsight. The room shimmered and blurred, the assembled masses of the city's elite becoming prismatic silhouettes, their emotions and thoughts flickering within them like so many bonfires. Unsurprisingly, greed and lust and gluttony dominated everything else; even those of more virtuous natures, like the aforementioned Magistrate, were indulging themselves tonight. Also unsurprising were the spells woven into the very fabric of the room, sorcerous cobwebs scattered over every surface to prevent eavesdropping, scrying, and other outside intrusions. Dressarie House took privacy and security very seriously, as befitting its status as the city's premiere brothel and discreet meeting spot. I saw beauty charms and protection spells on many of the individual guests, anchored to their masks and jewelry, and a few questionable-yet-legal allure charms, but nothing to cause alarm. What I didn't see, however, was the telltale crimson aura of a sex demon.

A sex demon. Believe it or not, even the Devil's Masquerade had standards, and incubi and succubae were strictly on the do-not-allow list. But one had been stalking the city for weeks, and everyone from the Duke on down was rightly confident that the demon couldn't bear to miss out on the fun and opportunities of such a night. It was like putting a buffet in front of a starving man. So a breach in the magical protections had been arranged, while two of the Duke's very best—that being Grace and myself—were sent in undercover, armed with magic and steel, with the understanding that if we ever talked about what went on tonight, there'd be trouble. The sort involving boiling oil and wild dogs, I assumed.

I dismissed my Witchsight, and reality slammed down around me. Grace held me tight as I reoriented myself, the feel of her arms around me rather more enjoyable than I let on. For an extra moment, I rested against her, savoring her unyielding air of protection. I pushed myself free once I realized I was enjoying it a little too much, immediately missing the way her fingers had brushed my bare arms. Another shiver, a deep breath to get myself under control, and, "It's not here yet."

"Damn. Let's get some punch, Star. I'm working up a thirst just standing around. It's blasted hot in here." The complaining was good-natured, but it was based in truth. The Devil's Masquerade was held at Midsummer, so the heat of a roomful of overindulging bodies was only made worse by the lingering heat of the day. I let Grace lead the way, watching the confident, authoritative way in which she moved, appreciating how her outfit accentuated her body more than she realized.

I wasn't her only fan. A noble I couldn't identify reached out to smack her on the rear, goosing her in the process. Grace tensed, ready to turn on the poor fool, but I cleared my throat, silently reminding her that we weren't here to make a scene. She subsided, still simmering, and I knew that the noble, should she ever discover who he was in real life, had best never misbehave around her. Grace held grudges like a champion.

The punch turned out to be both oversweet and slightly bitter; after a sip, I was ready to discreetly pour mine back into the bowl. Instead, the next time a groping hand reached my way, I pressed the glass into it while moving on. Grace drained hers, made a face, and muttered something about nobles having no taste whatsoever. We kept moving, constantly circulating through the crowd like dozens of other men and woman dressed as we were, here to give the guests a little extra variety in their... activities. Only difference was, we didn't stand still long enough to get dragged into any of the "games" that were already starting to take place. As the night dragged on and the drinks and drugs flowed, people were losing inhibitions and clothes at an alarming pace. At regular intervals, I paused to invoke my Witchsight, always with the same lack of results.

Everywhere I looked, there was something new to consider.

Swaying breasts, roaming hands, stiffening cocks, adventurous mouths. Kissing, licking, sucking, biting. One woman who I was sure was the Lady Farfield, one of the most dignified and elegant bastions of decorum at court, knelt in front of a domino-masked man, taking his cock into her mouth with the utmost of grace. I turned away as her head began to bob, feeling my own skin heat with an aroused flush. I was no innocent, nor a prude, but I preferred my bed games to remain private. It was one thing to disrupt a whore's transaction in a back alley, and another to see the most powerful men and women in the city fuck on the ballroom floor, surrounded by their peers. I glanced at Grace to see how she was taking this, and I was just in time to catch her looking at me, a guilty spark in her eyes. Her mask couldn't hide her wicked smile, either, one that fled as quickly as it had come. She cleared her throat. "Anything?"

I shook my head. "Nothing. Let's go check the other rooms before circling back here. Our 'friend' may want something more private."

Grace nodded. "Makes sense. Now that the festivities seem well and truly underway." With an uncharacteristically saucy sway to her hips, she threaded through the nobles, trusting I'd be right behind her. Knowing she couldn't see me, I took a second to readjust my clothes, plumping up my breasts a little more. My nipples ached with barely-acknowledged tension, my skin tingled with desire. This place was getting to me... and so was the movement of Grace's ass under those flimsy, gauzy silks.

Mind on the job, I told myself. There'd be time afterward to reward myself. A long, hot bath and a long, slow fuck were in my near future. Of this I was sure. Of course, that didn't stop me from wanting to grind my thighs together as I walked, to capture the silks between my legs and rub them against a traitorously wet pussy. The more I thought about it, the less I could ignore the tempting distraction. I stifled a groan of frustration and refocused. Find the demon. Deal with it. Get out of here. Never speak of this night again. Find out how the hell Grace could remain so cool and collected while surrounded by erotic displays of every nature and more than a few perversions.

The "private" rooms budded off a long hallway running behind the ballroom. It was easy to poke our heads into each room in turn, but it was harder to turn away after each new display, especially when invited to join in. In one, I counted at least four bodies, slick with sweat and undulating in a chain of ecstatic pleasure, breasts heaving and cocks sliding in and out of tight pussies. In another, a man cried in pained pleasure as a statuesque blonde whipped him with a velvet flogger, his body arching every time he was struck. Another man stroked himself feverishly as he watched, murmuring, "Yes, my Lord, yes." I was torn between lingering and fleeing; Grace solved it by tugging me away.

Room after room, scene after scene. In the space of an hour, we'd seen a lifetime's worth of sexual variations and would never be able to see the elite of the city in quite the same light again. We paused in the hallway to catch our breath and fan ourselves. I wasn't sure if I was sweating just because of the heat, or because my body was placing unreasonable demands on me. My silks clung to my curves, outlining me shamelessly, but I no longer cared. "Nice assignment," I said. "Remind me to thank the Duke."

Grace's chuckle was low and throaty as she placed a hand on my shoulder for a moment. "Beats scouring the sewers for wererats," she said. I shifted into the touch, letting my body rest against hers, breathing in the unique scent of her hair and skin. Even here and now, she was still Grace, a reassuring constant in this utterly bizarre environment. She kissed my forehead with cool, smiling lips. "I know, Star." I didn't even have to say anything, she knew me that well. "And yet, we were the best choice for the job. We know the value of discretion. Plus, I can't exactly see some of the other Investigators pulling off this look."

I giggled, pulling away again. "True. Hulking thugs, the lot of them. Two minutes out there, and they'd be killing innocent bystanders with their erections."

With only a few rooms left to inspect before we went back to the ballroom to start all over, we got back to work. I had to pull a mildly-protesting Grace away from the next room, where they were doing interesting things to a voluptuous lady involving candle wax and signet rings. "Were they really playing X's and O's?" I asked, the laugh bubbling up within me.

"Afraid so. I wonder what the winner gets."

"I've never known anyone to actually win that game."

"True." Grace pushed open the next door, and we paused, framed in the doorway, to check out the latest tableau of debauchery. Unlike many of the ones we'd seen of late, this one was deceptive in its simplicity. A dark-haired man, his features obscured by a simple yet elegant black mask, lay sprawled languidly on a chaise lounge, utterly naked. His head thrown back, lips parted, cock thick and erect, he was clearly in the throes of passion. The cause of the passion was evident: a curvy blonde was draped against him, one hand teasing through his hair, the other teasing along his hard length. With lurid crimson lips, kohl-and-red stained eyes, and decorative jewels pasted to her pale skin, she was both exotic and tawdry, a combination guaranteed to attract attention on a night like this. She was almost naked, the barest of flowing silks still covering her essentials; she might as well have been wearing nothing. She was beautiful. She was tempting. She was dangerous.

The woman looked up at us as we entered, eyes reflecting darkly against the light of the hallway, and her lips twisted in a wicked greeting. "Private party," she murmured. "Go peddle yourselves elsewhere."

Grace glanced to me, and I dropped into Witchsight, long enough to confirm what we both already knew: we'd found our target. The woman's aura blazed red, demon through and through. I dismissed the sight almost immediately, giving Grace the nod. "I'm afraid your party has been cut short," I said. "By the authority of Duke Blackstone, you're charged with unlawful predations and with breaking the Glassbridge Treaty. You will be taken into custody and sent back to the Dark Realms. If you refuse to cooperate, we'll be happy to do this the hard way."

As I spoke, I conjured silver fire, letting the flickering mystic flames envelop my left hand. Grace drew a short, slim sword from where she'd somehow concealed it, holding it with the casual ease of someone born to combat.

The succubus considered us with narrowed eyes, lovely features pinched in thought as she ran over the possibilities. She was outnumbered, and we blocked the only exit. Sex demons were not fighters—they survived on stealth and guile, using their charms to seduce their victims and steal their essence. No fool, this one, she clearly knew when she was outmatched. With a long, disappointed sigh, she nodded, climbing off her erstwhile victim, who moaned in sleepy, unaware frustration. Her magic had dulled his senses, but he'd recover soon enough. "I will submit to your authority," the succubus purred, "but under one condition."

Grace's eyebrow quirked, grip tightening on her sword. "You must be kidding. We made your choices clear. Go peacefully, or we send you home in pieces."

The demon laughed, a rich, dark sound sending shivers along my spine and tightening my nipples. "I'd rather do this the easy way, but I bet I can tear out this human idiot's throat before you dispatch me, darling." The endearment was anything but. "All I want is a little something for the road, and I somehow doubt you'll object." One hand flexed, fingernails extending into long ragged claws. Her other hand stroked down over her body, tracing bountiful curves, an erotic offering hiding the wicked nature underneath.

"We're not fucking you!" I blurted out. The flames around my hand blazed hotter and brighter, causing the demon to shrink back a little. My magic came from a higher plane, the antithesis of her infernal nature.

"Of course not. No, I merely want to see you two kiss." Dark eyes gleamed with evil delight. "Give in to the desire that flows within you both. One kiss. I swear by my Eternal Master that if you do this, I'll return home until summoned again." The air crackled as she swore her oath, an unbreakable binding.

Grace and I exchanged pointed looks before shrugging in unison. "Beats getting demon blood on my sword. That stuff's a pain to clean." She stepped toward me, closing the gap, even as I reached out for her, snuffing my witch's fire with a thought. Our bodies met, hers tall and slender, mine shorter and curvier, and I sank against her happily. Her lips found mine, and I gasped at the spark of contact. My every nerve tingled as her lips parted, tongue teasing out to taste my own lips, and I was lost. Hours of pent-up arousal burst free as restraint cracked, crumbled, and collapsed entirely. I found her tongue with mine, stroking and teasing, and she nipped at my lower lip in return. I moaned, and then it was over, one of us breaking the kiss before it could go much further. It might have been me, but I'm not so sure of that. I no longer felt capable of restraint.

The demon was openly ogling us, smile impish and satisfied. "Oh yes," she purred. "I saw the hunger in you. So moral, so upright, and so very, very hungry." She shook her head. "You humans. At least demons are honest about what they want. You hide behind respectability and nobility, but when given a chance to free your passions, you make us look like innocents." I spluttered with sudden indignation, but Grace's hand on my arm calmed me. "Don't get your tits in a twist, human. I'm leaving." The demon laughed merrily, the bell-like sound deceptively light. "I've had my fun. And the rest of my kind will have enjoyed themselves as well, watching your nobility and leaders indulge and fuck and run wild this night. Oh, you can't buy entertainment like this." She lifted her fingers to blow a mocking kiss. "I don't need to fight. I've already won."

By the time Grace's sword tore through where the succubus had been standing, the target of her rash anger had already vanished in a burst of fire and brimstone, leaving behind a groggy victim and a scorch mark on the carpet. Now it was my turn to soothe Grace, petting her cheek. "You know demons like to twist the knife any way they can," I assured her.

"No. It was right," she grumped. "If I ever meet that thing again, I'll chop it into a bucketful of tiny pieces."

I nodded. What bothered me, of course, was the bold-faced statement that all along, we'd been giving the demons what they wanted: a night of sin and indulgence for their amusement. Was this the open secret the nobility refused to acknowledge in daylight? And what happened if the circumstances ever changed? There was far too much we'd forgotten about the founding of the city, and I knew it was going to come back and bite us someday. I just knew it. But it was far too heady a topic to consider now. Not when I could still feel the kiss in my toes, Grace's skin under my fingers, her lips on mine. I ached with need, and a chance meeting of her eyes told me she was just as bad off.

"I know we wanted to get out of here as soon as possible..." I started.

"Report the job, go home, wash off the stink of the upper crust..." Grace continued knowingly.

"And fuck each other senseless," I finished. "But—" My words were cut off as Grace kissed me again, hungrily. Suddenly, my back was to the wall as she pressed me to it, the solid warmth of her body anchoring me as I melted into her embrace. I looped my arms around her neck, returning the kiss passionately, head tilted so our masks didn't interfere. I heard a distant clatter as she dropped her sword, and then her hands were roaming over me, tugging my clothes into new and more revealing arrangements. A quick yank and my breasts spilled free of their confines, heavy and full with need, nipples tight in the cooler air. Her knee thrust insistently between mine, and my legs spread a little in response, welcoming her advances. Could she tell how wet I was? How could she not?

"Grace," I moaned between kisses and nibbles. My hands busied themselves with untying and unfastening her clothes; since I'd helped her get dressed originally, I knew just what to do. Our silks slithered free, piece by piece, the bright colors pooling around our feet in a growing heap. I ran my fingers over each new stretch of exposed skin, as always marveling in her lithe, muscular build with its scattering of scars, each with a story behind it. She'd been a fighter long before I met her; five years we'd been together, and she still had tales of adventure and danger to tell me in bed. Lords, she was beautiful. And the things she did with her fingers were— "Oh!" I arched against her as she bit down at the junction of my neck and shoulder, something that never failed to turn me on. I clung to her as she nibbled and licked over sensitive skin, head flung back to expose my throat. Not that it took much at this point to make me writhe wantonly, grinding myself against the knee she'd wedged between my legs. My fingers dug into her back, pulling her against me, and I wordlessly begged for more, more, more.

In response, she slipped a hand between my legs, smiling against my neck when she discovered how hot and wet I was, primed for her explorations and ready to accept her. When she entered me, I moaned, muffling myself by once more capturing her lips in a fierce kiss. Muscles clenched tight around her thrusting fingers, I arched in time to her movements, demanding and driving her deep into me. I was in no mood for slow and gentle now, not after the lengthy buildup of the night, and she knew it. Those long fingers, so used to wielding a sword and dealing out death, were put to a much better purpose as she drove me to a quick, hard orgasm, my scream spilling free of parted lips. Here and now, no one at all would notice. I could almost imagine the answering shrieks of ecstasy, other orgasms echoing throughout Drasserie House in response, building on all the many years the building had hosted such things. There was no shame in this, just the knowledge of building on tradition, and so I gave myself wholly to the pleasure, Grace's fingers pushing me on to another wave, and another.

She finally slowed, pulling her arousal-drenched fingers free of me, and I sagged with release and relief, as boneless and satisfied as a cat in the sun. Slowly, wickedly, she licked her fingers clean, eyes half-lidded as she tasted the fruit of her labors and deemed it satisfactory. "A far better vintage than what they were serving out there," she teased me, voice low and husky.

"I think I need to sample some treats myself," I joked, still

shaking as I tried to regain my breath. Taking her hand, I tugged her to the floor, where I laid her out on a bed of our discarded silk disguises, the bright colors framing her tanned skin. Dropping a series of kisses from her throat to stomach, I teased her with my slow, steady progress. I kissed her breasts, ran my tongue around her nipples, slid my fingers over her thighs, and persisted in the game until she growled with frustration and dug her fingers into my hair, burying them in the curls. Then, and only then, did I oblige, parting her with my fingers and dipping my head in to taste her. As my tongue delved into her dripping depths, she released her hold on my hair, digging her fingers into the fabric under her instead. Her hips bucked, and I claimed my fill of her, licking and sucking, teasing her clit while she groaned and whimpered. By the time I added several fingers to the mix, she was thrashing from side to side, trying to take more of me. I fucked her with fingers and mouth, quickly pushing her straight over the edge into release. She shuddered and tensed, and when she exploded, I licked her clean. I could feel her very essence on my tongue, rich and full and pure, renewing me just as I'd done for her, and it felt perfect.

Afterward, I curled up against her, an arm draped over her chest, basking in our mutual content. Throughout it all, the man slumped on the chaise lounge hadn't stirred, lost in dreams, and I briefly pitied him, that he'd missed out on a lovely show. "Well," murmured Grace. "I suppose this assignment wasn't all bad. Nothing trying to kill us, no messes to clean up—well, none we mind."

I smiled an agreement as I kissed her. "True, that. I say we stay here for a little while longer. Not like we're in a hurry to leave, right?"

Whatever Grace was about to say or do was interrupted as the door opened, revealing a man and woman in the doorway. He was tall and well built, a black raven mask hiding his features but not his distinctive graying temples, otherwise stark naked save for boots and signet ring. The woman clinging to his side was heavyset but carried herself well, with large breasts and strong thighs. She had on a cat's-eye mask and a lot of glitter. Just another couple looking for a quiet place to tryst, and they didn't notice us at first. Not until they stepped inside and their eyes adjusted to the light. Then—

"Grace? Starling?" The man gaped at us, incredulously, frozen in his tracks.

"Your Honor," Grace greeted Duke Blackstone, our Lord and employer, politely, giving him a lazy grin from where she lay curled with me on the floor.

"Father," I greeted in return, turning bright red. "Good evening."

He cleared his throat. "Yes. Well. If your assignment is completed, I'll expect a report tomorrow." Pause. "It doesn't need to be... detailed." He and his companion all but fled the room, door slamming shut in their wake.

As Grace and I both collapsed in a fit of laughter, I found the strength to ask her, "Think we should request this assignment again next year? I'm sure we can find someone willing to summon another succubus...."

Fences
David Hubbard

Everyone expected the world to end with a bang: nuclear war, alien invaders, even zombies would've been fun. Instead, it was with a whimper; the smallest of sounds, really, a virus of all things. Dubbed the X1N1 virus, X for short, it was the most virulent strain of swine flu ever seen, and no one knew where it had come from or how it had become so lethal. I like to think it was just Darwinism at its finest. Survival of the fittest, and this time around humanity wasn't all that fit. Almost the entire population had already become infected before the virus had even been identified and named. But X was a clever little bug; it didn't always kill its host immediately. Sometimes it would just lay dormant: weeks, months, sometimes even longer. Like years, in my case.

The body count skyrocketed into the millions in the first few weeks after the initial discovery and diagnosis of the X virus. This of course brought on all sorts of responses: transportation was severely restricted in an attempt to slow the spread of the disease; the global economy crashed and burned; people panicked, and riots broke out at every grocery store and Walmart nationwide. News coverage attempted to continue where it could, though as time went on, it became more and more sporadic. Eventually only one network continued to broadcast, and all those fancy TVs were showing nothing but white snow or colored bars, in 1080p HD, of course. Martial law was inevitably declared, but unlike in most apocalypse-themed movies, it actually helped the situation.

Things finally settled into a kind of stunned calm. When the inevitability of the disease finally hit home, we all just learned to deal with it. There were several mass suicides among the scattered "End World" religious cults that sprang up almost as fast as the infection, but once they were gone, everyone else returned to their lives as best they could.

Even me.

"John would've loved the garden this year," I said with mixed pride and sadness. John and I had been partners for eleven years when the X virus arrived and changed everything. We had the 3,000-square-foot home in suburbia, two dogs, two cars, two incomes: every well-adjusted homo's dream. Then one morning, I woke up to find that reality had broken down the door.

I glanced up to the sun; it was a hot summer afternoon in Texas, not that there was any other kind. I stripped off my shirt, soaked through with sweat, and tossed it aside as I knelt back down and resumed pulling weeds from around the vegetables. John had always wanted a garden, so we had taken part of the backyard and turned it into one. Tomatoes, squash, peppers of all kinds, cantaloupe, cucumbers, okra: everything a Southern garden needed, and then some. Now it was paying off more than he would have imagined, providing me with plenty of fresh food to eat. This season had been especially abundant; ironic, considering there weren't very many people around to enjoy the fruits of my labor.

One of the benefits, if there was such a thing, to a disaster of this proportion was that there weren't any more bills to pay. No mortgage, no electricity bill, no water bill. It just didn't matter anymore when everyone was focused on trying to survive another day. Part of the healing process for me involved yard work, and the dogs certainly helped fill the void John had left behind. I had the best-looking yard in the neighborhood since I didn't have to worry about a water bill anymore. Not that there was an HOA anymore to appreciate it, the bastards.

That made me laugh out loud, and I had to stop weeding for a moment. I clambered back to my feet, still grinning, to get some water from the hose when I noticed I was being watched. The guy next door was in his second-floor window watching me working in the garden. I couldn't remember his name... Brian? Bret?

Something like that. John and I hadn't lived here very long and hadn't gotten a chance to really know the neighbors when the virus had sent everything to Hell in a hand basket. Still, I waved, trying to be neighborly. He just stared blankly and turned away from the window after a moment. That caused my smile to waver a bit, but I just shrugged, determined not to get depressed on such a beautiful day.

Hauling the hose out, I turned it on and took a long drink. The water was refreshing, cold and clear. In a fit of childishness, I put my thumb over the end of the end and pointed it toward the sky, letting the droplets rain down on me. I let loose a raucous whoop from somewhere in my childhood and tipped my head back, laughing. The dogs, female and male boxers named Pagan and Apollo, respectively, decided that they wanted to play in the water, too, and joined me in the impromptu shower. The water felt good on my skin, and soon I was soaking wet, my shorts clinging heavily to me.

"Screw it, who's gonna say anything?" I said as I dropped the hose and shucked off my shorts. I had swim trunks somewhere, but who cared if I was in my Calvin Kleins in my own backyard? "Not me, that's for damn sure." I turned the water off and got back on all fours to continue weeding. The dogs nosed around the wet grass for a few minutes before retiring to a shadier spot of the yard. A little while later, the hair on the back of my neck stood on end and I stopped and turned slowly to glance over my shoulder. Neighbor guy was at his window again.

Maybe it was the Texas heat frying my brain, but in a purely random moment of perversion, I pretended not to notice as I stood up and stretched languidly. Yard work did sculpt muscles quite well, if I did say so myself. I turned the hose back on and drank again; this time, though, I put the flow above my head and let the icy water sluice down over me. I was only half conscious that white underwear, when wet, became rather transparent. That thought and the chill of the water had my nipples hard in seconds. I shot a glance back at the upstairs window and caught neighbor guy staring. I waved again, beaming, and this time I got a reaction: his eyes widened like a deer in headlights and he stumbled away from the window so quickly I think he fell. I felt bad for about half a minute, but he didn't return the rest of the day.

Before it was completely dark, I jumped in the shower to wash off the day's sweat and dirt and then threw on some clean clothes. I had a basket full of tomatoes, peppers, squash, and ears of corn, and there was no way I was going to eat it all before it went bad. It occurred to me that maybe neighbor guy would like some, so I walked across my beautifully manicured lawn and up to his front door. I rang the bell and stood, smiling, holding my basket of goodies.

"Basket of goodies, indeed," I snorted.

What's gotten into you today, Jer? inside voice asked, amused.

When there was no answer, I pressed the doorbell again. I knew it worked because I could hear it, but no one came to the door. At least I didn't hear them come to the door. I got the impression that I was being watched again, through the peephole this time, so I just spoke to the air. "Hey, it's, uh, Jeremy... from next door... I have all these vegetables and I can't eat them all by myself... so I, uh... I thought I'd give you some... you know... to eat... so, uh... yeah... here." I finished abruptly and placed the basket on the step and scurried back home.

"Wow, you're a real master with words there, Jer... 'you know, to eat'... moron," I berated myself, shaking my head as I closed the front door.

A few days later I was making coffee when I heard a small sound on my front porch. I quietly set the cup down, grabbed one of the baseball bats I kept in every room of the house, and moved toward the door. Before the military had restored a semblance of order, it had been necessary to defend yourself, so I'd invested in some bats from a sporting goods store. It wasn't like there was any pressing need to play ball any time soon; the American pastime had become survival.

I peered through the peephole but didn't see anyone there. Moving to the side window, I pulled back the curtain just a fraction. Nothing. After another minute of silence, I unlocked the door and cracked it, peering out. No one there, but the basket I had used to deliver neighbor guy's veggies was returned, empty.

"Well, guess he liked them," I said, putting the bat down and opening the door to retrieve the basket. Once the door was secured again, I returned to my coffee.

Later that day, another Texas scorcher, I was back outside, shirt and shorts, working on the garden again. It was really the only thing that kept me sane. The nights were hard enough, but I had made John a promise that I would go on until it was my time, or until X decided it was my time. And, for the most part, I succeeded pretty well. It had been months since the last time I cried when I went to bed, so that had to be a good sign.

"Well, John, you sure would hate me right now, this garden looks fantastic. And it should, since I'm out here every damn day working on it," I said to the air. I had taken to talking to myself/John a few months ago as a way to give voice to all the thoughts that jumbled themselves in my head. I'd talk to the dogs, of course, but they weren't as engaging of conversationalists.

"My name's not John," said a quizzical voice from behind me, startling me so hard I went face first into the dirt with a yelp. "Oh god, I'm sorry. I... I didn't mean to scare you like that...."

I turned over and sat up, wiping the back of my hand across my face and searching for the source of the voice. I finally caught sight of a shadow behind the fence that separated my yard from neighbor guy's yard.

"Oh, it's fine. I just really like to get into my gardening," I replied, spitting mud. The sudden ridiculousness of my predicament hit me and I sputtered into laughter, which was soon followed by that of neighbor guy.

"Thanks," I said, when I could speak again.

"For... for what?"

"I haven't heard the sound of another laugh in a long time," I said, smiling through the dirt at the spot where I knew he was standing. I couldn't see him, but I knew he was able to see me.

"Y-yeah..." was all he could say, and I could hear the weight of pain in that one word.

"So you liked the vegetables then, huh?" I asked quickly—last thing I wanted to do was bring us both back to dark places. There would be ample time for darkness later.

"Oh, yes... very much. I wanted to say thank you, but...." he trailed off, and I realized how difficult it was for him to be speaking to me, even now. Poor guy, he didn't have anyone to talk to.

Neither do you, Jer, unless you count yourself—and that's just not healthy, inside voice chattered at me.

The silence was growing uncomfortable, so I quickly injected, "Well, as you can see, there's more where that came from. You're welcome to it any time; I can't eat it all by myself in any case." I finally had the presence of mind to get back on my feet, but I didn't move toward the fence just yet. Too many months of paranoia kept us both at safe distances from each other. "I'm Jeremy, by the way, Jeremy Petroklus." I waved at the fence.

"I'm... Bradley... Simms," he replied.

I was close. Bret, Bradley, whatever, inside voice mentally shrugged.

"Nice to, uh, meet you, Bradley," I said, even though we were about fifteen feet apart and an eight-foot wooden privacy fence separated us. "I think I'm gonna take a break, this heat can really be a kill—I mean—hot...."

You really are a moron, aren't you? inside voice seriously wanted to know.

"Uh, yeah, it's pretty hot again today. If you... if you ever want, I have a pool... in the backyard... you're welcome to it... least I can do for the vegetables." He stumbled awkwardly over the words.

"Thanks, Bradley, I just may take you up on that offer," I said politely.

"No, really... you can use it any time...."

I stared at the fence a moment before replying, "Thanks, I will."

An hour later, I was on Bradley's doorstep with my swimming gear: the trunks I'd finally located, towel, flip-flops, sunglasses, and sunscreen. I pressed the bell and waited. A few moments later, I heard the clicking of the locks and the door opened, giving me my first look at Bradley Simms. He was about the same height as me, six-foot-something, but where I was blond and blue eyed, he was dark with piercing green eyes. He was near my age as well, mid-thirties or so, with a wedding band on his finger. A day's worth of stubble stippled his strong jaw line, and the close-fitting t-shirt and shorts showed off that he wasn't the typical chunky married suburbanite.

"Good thing you have sunglasses on, your eyes are bulging out of your head," inside voice confirmed, causing me to blink several times before I smiled. "Hi there, neighbor."

"Hi," Bradley said with a nervous smile. "Come on in."

He led me through the hall and into the kitchen, where the sliding glass door opened onto his backyard. I took a moment to glance around, admiring the house. "Nice place, Bradley," I commented sincerely. My eyes stopped for a long moment on a picture of Brad and his wife, and I knew immediately why he had been so reclusive. I was the same way for months after John died.

"Thanks, you can call me Brad. All my friends do... well, they did back when I had friends...." He trailed off again, and I could see the darkness creeping back into his eyes, so I quickly moved the conversation forward.

"So, show me that pool you were bragging about earlier."

He came back to himself with a little jolt, as if he'd already forgotten I was there, and flashed that nervous smile again as he showed me out to the patio and pool beyond.

It was beautiful, landscaped all around with plants and decorative rocks. The water was crystal clear and very inviting.

"Wow, it's gorgeous, Brad." I whistled appreciatively as I laid my towel across the back of a chaise lounge that sat beneath an Italian-style pergola.

"Thanks, I work on it every day," he said, eyes moving critically, looking for anything that might be out of place or need work.

"Relax a bit," I said with a grin, playfully chucking him on the shoulder, "I'll feel really guilty if you start working while I enjoy the water."

He looked at his shoulder where I'd made contact as if he couldn't figure out what had happened and then shifted his gaze up at me with a confused expression.

I blushed nervously and grabbed my bottle of sunscreen, flipping open the top and squeezing out a liberal amount into my palm, then slathering it onto my shoulders and chest. Brad turned back to scan his yard, but I noticed he was watching me out of the corner of his eye.

"I'll be back in a minute," he said abruptly and walked quickly back into the house.

I watched him go as I finished with the sunscreen and took off my shades and flip-flops. I tentatively dipped a foot into the water; it was the perfect temperature for a sweltering Texas summer. Grinning like a teenager, I let out a loud "WOO HOO!" and did a cannonball into the deepest part of the pool. I came up for air, the grin and my hair firmly plastered to my face. The water was fantastic, and for a few moments anyway, I let all the horrors of the past slip from my mind and just enjoyed the moment.

Brad still hadn't returned after I'd made a few laps of the pool, so I hauled myself out and grabbed my towel, draping it across the lounge chair and then reclining on top to let myself drip dry in the summer sun. I picked up my sunglasses and settled them into place just as the glass door slid open and closed.

Brad strode to the chair beside mine and spread his towel.

"How was it?" he asked.

"Fantastic, thanks so much for inviting me over," I said, eyes closed, enjoying the feel of the water drying on my skin and the voice of another human being.

A moment later I heard a splash and opened my eyes to see Brad's head pop up above the water. I smiled and let my eyes slip closed again, suddenly drowsy from the heat and water.

"You're right, the water's perfect," he said, and I opened my eyes again in time to see Brad pull himself from the pool. It was like one of those slow-motion moments in a movie: Brad put both hands on the side of the pool, and I could see the muscles in his shoulders bunch as he heaved himself out of the water. His chest slid into view, water streaming down through the hair arranged in an attractive pattern that continued down in a small line to the top of his trunks. When those came into view, I think I actually gasped; they were the box-cut type, not at all what I would have pictured a married suburbanite like Brad would wear. They fit perfectly, outlining everything a guy like me appreciated.

And then some, inside voice whistled in my head.

As he moved over to the lounger, I had to put one hand under my chin to close my mouth and the other over my crotch to keep the rapidly growing hard on from becoming visible.

Been a long time huh, Jer? Inside voice was a master of the obvious.

"You... wanna beer, Jeremy?" Brad asked.

"Oh, uh, sure... yeah, that'd be great," I said quickly, and when he turned and strode to the kitchen, I watched the muscles play across his back, legs, and ass, then quickly took the towel out from under me and draped it across my midsection to hide the tent I'd made.

"Here ya go," he said and handed me an open bottle before straddling his chair and sitting back.

We sat in silence for a time, enjoying the sun, the water, and the company. After a while, I broke the silence with an invitation.

"Hey Brad, would you like to come over for dinner?" I asked tentatively.

"Oh... well, I don't wanna be a bother," he began.

"Oh no," I cut him off quickly, "it's no bother, I haven't had anyone to cook for since... since John died, and I'd really like to make dinner for more than one for a change." Until the words were actually said out loud, I hadn't realized how true it was. I was lonely, and had been for a long time. The dogs were definitely a help, but they didn't make up for real human companionship. I think Brad was lonely too, though he wouldn't admit it.

"Um... okay, sure. Why not?" he said, giving me a small smile as he tipped his beer back for a drink.

Slow down before you break something, inside voice said in exasperation. I was rushing around the kitchen like my hair was on fire.

"Okay, stop, deep breath," I said out loud, following my own instructions and trying to calm down. I hadn't had anyone over for any reason since John died, and while this wasn't a date, it sure had the feel of one, somehow.

I had the table set and the food ready by the time the doorbell rang. I was still so giddy, I had to stop at the door and take another deep breath to steady myself before I opened it.

"Come on in!" I said a bit too loudly as I ushered Brad inside.

"Here, I... I brought you this," he replied, offering me a bottle of wine.

"How thoughtful, you didn't have to do that, Brad, thank you." I smiled, and he blushed.

Before things could get any more awkward, I brought us into the dining room. "Have a seat, dinner will be ready in just a few minutes. Why don't you open that bottle you brought?" I said and took down two wine glasses and set them on the table along with a corkscrew.

As I finished preparing the salads, Brad poured the wine and took a look around the room; seeing a picture of John and me on the sideboard, he paused and took a drink.

"This is you and John, isn't it?" he inquired quietly.

"Oh, uh... yeah, we were together for eleven years," I answered as I brought the salad and plates to the table. Brad was still standing in front of the picture.

"Do you... miss him?" He said it so softly I almost didn't hear the question.

I stopped and waited for him to turn toward me in the silence before answering. "Every minute of every day. But life goes on, and that means I have to do the best I can with what I've got."

There was another long moment of silence as Brad's eyes stared into mine, then he tossed back the last of his wine and moved to pour some more.

"Sorry, I didn't mean to be such downer," he apologized.

"No, it's ok, it's been over three years now and it's good to talk about it," I said, "have a seat." I pulled out a chair and extended a hand in invitation.

We ate the salad in relative silence before I got up to get the rest of the meal. I don't think Brad had had a real home-cooked meal in quite a while, the way he went at it. After a few minutes, he paused and looked up at me across the table.

"Sorry, this is really good Jeremy, thanks." He flashed a real smile then, and a little color came to his cheeks.

"You're very welcome. It's nice to have someone over for a change, I was getting tired of eating alone all the time... well, the dogs are here, but I don't let them sit at the table with me," I said with a grin, but my heart clenched as I realized how true it was. I missed simple human contact; just conversation with another living being was hard to come by these days thanks to X, the tiny bastard.

We finished the meal and moved to the living room, where we sat across the coffee table from one another. I had brought the wine and refilled our glasses as I sat.

He took a long drink and then spoke. "Lisa and I were only married for three years before... before the virus. We had just bought this house after I'd gotten a promotion at the firm and were starting to talk about a family." I could hear the anguish in his voice, and his chin trembled with the effort to not break down completely. Suddenly, his eyes focused on me and he sat forward on the couch, the intensity in his voice taking me aback. "How do you do it, Jeremy? How do you keep going after... after..." he trailed off, unable to say the words, his free hand fluttering aimlessly like a wounded bird.

I looked at him, compassion welling up. "I just do, Brad. John made me promise that I'd keep living as long as I could, doing whatever I needed to do. So I do. I work on the garden, I read, I play with the dogs, I watch movies... I do everything I did on a daily basis when John was alive. It's what's gotten me through it so far, and I think it'll continue to get me through it until it's my turn."

He kept staring at me, past me, processing what I'd said and working through his own pain, his eyes wet and his glass empty. Suddenly he came back to the present. "I'm sorry... I should go... thanks again for dinner, Jeremy." He rose and headed to the door before I could say anything.

I reached the door as he opened it. "Brad, wait...."

He turned suddenly and embraced me, the breath he held released in a sob, but he stepped back quickly and tried to smile, then turned and headed across the yard to his house. I was left reeling in my doorway wondering what had just happened and struggling to think of a way to help my new friend work past his demons.

I waited a day before going over to use the pool again. Brad's car was gone, so I let myself in through the side gate and claimed the same lounger I had previously used. This time I didn't cannonball into the water, but slipped in and just floated along the surface, staring up at the cloudless Texas sky through the polarized lenses of my sunglasses.

After a while in the pool, I climbed out and moved the chaise to a sunny spot, laying it flat, and stretched onto my stomach to give my back and legs a more even tan. I usually wore a shirt when gardening, so the "farmer tan" was what I had ended up with. It wasn't long before I fell asleep, the sun adding to the drowsiness brought on by the sound and smell of the water.

I'm pretty sure the dream I was having was about John and I, but when I felt strong, gentle hands rubbing sunscreen onto my back, I couldn't help but let out a little groan of pleasure. The hands stuttered a moment but then continued to do their work, moving from my shoulders to my lower back. They skipped from there to the backs of my thighs, working down to my ankles, and when they came back up, the hands slid up the inside of my right leg, sending little bolts of lightning up and down my spine straight to my groin. That brought me fully awake, but I didn't move, afraid any sudden movement might only embarrass Brad more than he had already been.

Plus this feels fuckin' awesome! inside voice all but purred.

"Brad... what are you doing?" I said very quietly in my most nonconfrontational voice.

There was the sound of breath inhaled, but the hands continued their motion up the inside of my thigh, coming dangerously close to sliding beneath the mesh lining of my trunks. "You were getting red... I had to put some lotion on you so you wouldn't burn." His voice was husky and there was a tone I hadn't heard before. "Why, does it not feel good?" His hands stopped.

"No, no it feels good... great, actually. It's just—well, you're um... kinda turning me on...." I think I was actually blushing, so it was good my face was turned away from where he knelt beside the lounger.

Rather than stop, Brad took one hand and slid it across to my other thigh and began to rub gentle circles closer and closer to the edge of my trunks with both hands. I inhaled sharply as those strong, gentle fingers slipped under the mesh of my swimsuit, and the exhalation came out as a quivering moan.

"Brad," I hissed, breathless, "do you know what you're doing?" I was honestly worried. Here was this straight man, gorgeous, yes, but heterosexual nonetheless, rubbing his hands up the insides of my thighs.

He didn't answer, but when his hands made contact with that sweet, sensitive spot at the junction of my legs, I all but jumped off the lounger. I turned over so fast Brad fell over.

"What's wrong? Am I not doing something right?" he asked

with wounded concern. I was staring at his eyes, those emerald green pools, when I realized he was wearing that box-cut swimsuit from the other day. Only this time, the outline of an erection was clearly visible, along with a small wet spot.

"N-no, no... unless you count giving me a raging boner 'wrong,'" I replied, and blushed where he could see me this time.

Brad hauled himself up and straddled my hips, grinding his hard on into my own with such force I thought he would push us through the woven straps of the chair. He pressed his lips to mine before I could protest. I tasted the vodka then and knew what had helped bring about these lowered inhibitions. His tongue was insistent, prying my lips apart in a furious, hungry kiss.

When I could breathe again a few minutes later, I placed my hands on the furry pecs in front of me and pushed back gently. "Wait, wait... Brad, you don't know what you're doing," I protested, though maybe not strongly enough. It was difficult to think clearly with this gorgeous man on top of me; something made more so since it hadn't happened in a long time.

"Yes I do, Jeremy," he retorted, and moved to kiss me again, but I locked my elbows, holding him at bay.

You really are a moron, Inside voice was clearly irritated.

"You've been drinking, I don't think you know what you're doing... with me..." I said, concerned, but also trying desperately to ignore the throbbing in my groin.

"Yeah, so I've had a few drinks, but I know exactly what I'm doing. I'm sitting in your lap trying to kiss you," he replied matter-of-factly and leaned toward me again.

This time my elbows gave way, and I allowed him in again for several more minutes of deep, passionate kisses, then pushed him back to catch my breath once more. Both of us now had large wet spots in our trunks.

"Brad wait... you're not—I don't want to take advantage of you or our friendship," was my feeble-sounding excuse. Sure, I wanted him, badly now that he had gotten things so heated, but was it worth the risk of losing a friend, especially when you never knew when X would decide to claim you?

"Jeremy, I want this—I want you... I've been so lonely... after Lisa died... just being with someone, with you... you're so nice, and... and..." he trailed off, unable to form the words, and the pain in those green eyes almost broke my heart. I could certainly empathize with what he felt.

I held him back a moment longer, searching his eyes for deception. "Okay... as long as you understand that this isn't a pity fuck, for either of us, got it?" I gently ran my thumb under his eye, wiping away the tear that had formed there.

He smiled and nodded, and I moved my arms, letting that muscular hairy chest rub against my own as my arms encircled his waist and pulled him down on top of me. He groaned as my hands slid down to his ass and squeezed. He started to hump, grinding our cocks together, when I slipped my fingers into the waistband of his trunks and tugged them down over his muscular glutes. He stood up then, still straddling the chaise, and started to finish taking them off when I grabbed his wrists.

"No, let me." I looked up at him and he flashed his teeth wolfishly, putting his hands on his hips as I sat forward and slowly, slowly pulled those trunks down. His dick was so spring loaded, it almost put my eye out as it came free of the Lycra and swung toward me, trailing a sticky string of pre-come. I looked up at those green eyes as I stuck out my tongue and swiped at the swollen head, tasting the salty-sweet gathered there.

"Oh fuck, Jeremy!"

"I guess I'm doing something right, huh?" I replied, and with a wicked little grin, I showed him one of my many talents, swallowing him to the base in one long gulp that had him burying his hands in my hair to keep from falling over. I stayed down, inhaling the scent of musk and soap for a moment before sliding back up and letting him relax his grip on my hair a bit. His balls were big and hung down pendulously, perfectly. I scooped them up in one hand and ran my tongue over the fuzzy orbs, satisfied with the gasps that resulted.

"W-wait!" he gasped, "I-I wanna make you f-feel good too!"

"You are, Brad, you are," I assured him, but he wasn't convinced and moved back from me, stepping out of his trunks completely and then kneeling on the chaise to tug and pull at mine. He couldn't get them off fast enough, but when they were off, he sat there, staring at my stiff prick oozing pre-come. "Um... I'm not sure what I should do now," he said with a little embarrassment.

I laughed, but not unkindly, and sat up.

"Let me give you some pointers—so to speak," I grinned. "Here, sit in front of me just like this," I said, and guided him to straddle the lounger like I was so that our knees were pressed together and we could see and touch everything in front of us. "Brad, you've got the same plumbing—when in doubt, do to me what feels good on you."

He paused and cocked his head to the side with a little "hmpf" as if the thought hadn't ever occurred to him before. Wasting no time, he wrapped his hand around my shaft, giving it a good squeeze and sliding his hand up to milk a big dollop of clear slick. With his thumb he began to rub it around the head of my cock, and my eyes rolled back as I groaned.

"That feel good, Jeremy?" he asked huskily.

"Uh huh, keep doing what you're doing and I'll be there in no time."

"Well, I'd better slow down then," he teased, taking both hands and moving them up my sweat-covered chest to pinch both of my erect nipples as he leaned in to kiss me some more. Taking my cue, I moved my hands across his hairy chest, running my fingers through the soft, dark curls before finding his nipples and working them into two stiff pink nubs. Then it was Brad's turn to moan. Pushing him back from my mouth, I bent and swirled my tongue around first one nipple, then the other, pausing on the second to suck and bite gently.

We took turns stroking each other, finding just the right places, speeds, and pressures that made the other's eyes roll back and jaw go slack. Then I pushed him back onto his elbows so that his legs were spread wide, his beautiful curved cock was pointed up and toward me, and those plump balls were nestled underneath. I collared his cock at the base with one hand and leaned down, taking the head into my mouth and running my tongue around the edge. With my other hand, I cradled his balls, tugging them gently, and extended two fingers to rub the spot right behind them.

"Oh God, Jeremy, that feels so good," he gasped, legs trembling, barely able to remain propped up thanks to my ministrations. I continued working him over for several minutes.

Suddenly he sat forward, pushing me back so that I sprawled on my half of the lounger. True to his word, he did his best to make me feel good, and what he lacked in technique he more than made up for in enthusiasm. Doing his best to mimic what I had just done to him, Brad tentatively tasted cock for the first time, running his tongue up the side and over the head of my prick, following the trail of pre-come.

He locked eyes with mine when I managed to get up on my elbows and slowly took as much of me in as he could before his gag reflex kicked in. Not one to be deterred, Brad kept at it and quickly learned to use his hands to stimulate other parts of me as well: nipples, balls, and taint in equal measure. After a while he left off sucking cock to ask, "Are you ok? Is this good?"

"Oh, hell yes," I said. "For a straight guy, you sure pick this up fast!"

He grinned and his cheeks colored, then he swiped his tongue over the head of my cock again, sending shudders through my whole body.

"C'mere," I said with a growl and sat back up, pulling myself closer to him and hooking my legs over his so that our bodies could press fully against each other. Our arms wrapped each other in a tight embrace, hands moving as our tongues took turns exploring the other's mouth.

Brad was sucking my earlobe when I slipped my hand between us, groping for the pair of dueling dicks wedged there. We were drenched in sweat, and between that and what seemed like a gallon of pre-come, I didn't need any additional lube. Finding the prizes,

I squeezed them together, moving my hand up and down quickly.

"Fuck, Jeremy, you're gonna make me come if you keep that up," he breathed in my ear.

"Well, I'm not far behind," I said as he moved around and we began kissing furiously again, gasping and grunting into each other's mouths in time with my stroking. I increased the speed of my stroke and we both began to writhe, edging closer and closer to the point of release.

The sounds we were both making were steadily increasing in frequency and pitch when I felt my orgasm begin. Pulling away from his lips for a second, I looked into those beautiful green eyes and whispered, "Come with me, Brad." He stared back at me for that one perfect moment, and then our mouths were locked in their devouring embrace, uttering grunts, moans, and sobs as we came together on the chaise lounger. We shuddered and rocked, locked together with legs and lips and arms as I pumped all the fear, anger, and frustration out of us. We stayed like that, rocking gently, arms still wrapped around each other for some time after we'd crested the impossibly high wave and slid blissfully down the other side together.

It was two days before we spoke again. I thought it best to let things cool down a bit before trying to swim or make dinner again. I finally broke the silence by delivering another basket of vegetables. To my surprise, he opened the door and invited me in, leading me to the kitchen, where he took the basket and set it on the breakfast bar.

"Hey," he said awkwardly.

"Hey," I returned in equal measure.

An uncomfortable silence ensued, until finally it was Brad who broke the tension. "What does it mean if I want... if I want you around more?" he asked, fidgeting and not looking me in the eye.

"Um... I dunno, Brad. I just brought vegetables...." I replied.

He looked up then and snorted an involuntary laugh that

quickly broke the tension between us.

"Look, Jeremy... I'm straight," he said out of nowhere.

"Um... okay, Brad, I don't remember that ever being in question. Is it?"

"It's just—I've never—when we did..." he stumbled over the words and blushed, looking down at the floor.

I stepped a little closer. "Look, at this point, with everything that has happened to us and the world, I don't think your sexuality is really an issue. But that's just me." I put my hand on his shoulder and realized we were both trembling. "Brad, I haven't been with anyone since John died. I want us to be friends, and if we're more than that, so what?" I told him, realizing the depth in those words as they left my mouth. X had changed everything; now every day was completely uncertain.

He looked up and stepped closer to me, wrapping those arms around me and hugging me tightly. We stood there a long time, and when he finally began to loosen his grip, his face passed close to mine and he leaned in to kiss me, tenderly and with such intensity that my head reeled.

When we parted lips, he asked, "Jeremy... what does this make me?" genuinely concerned and confused all at once.

"Brad, I'm not sure, but... I think it makes you... human."

His held breath came out as a laugh, which quickly spread to me.

"Fuck you, Jeremy," he said playfully.

"Mmm... maybe," I retorted with a sly wink that made his cheeks redden but his nostrils flare with arousal. We stood there, in his kitchen, holding each other as the rest of the world crashed, ever so slowly, down around us.

The next day, after hearing the latest viral-induced body count on TV, we worked on tearing down the fence that separated our yards.

The Many Little Deaths of Cicilia Long
Shanna Germain

The first time Cicilia Long died, she was eighteen and had just enlisted as a Rift Jumper. In the tick-tock seconds before Cicilia's death, her mother was back in Illinois, standing on the slanted porch, looking up, lamenting the loss of her daughter to the forces of the sky. And Cicilia's girlfriend—former girlfriend, fuck-up of a girlfriend, fuck-and-dump-her girlfriend, the reason she was here in outer space girlfriend—was probably lying down on that super-skinny Darlene Shanka, not even thinking about Cicilia. Or maybe, hopefully, lying on her back under the pimple-faced Darlene, looking up at her constellation of zits and thinking about Cicilia flying up in the sky, past the sky, up in the universe, and thinking how she was the stupidest person ever for having passed her up for a little earth-bound nothing.

But that was all right for them, because at the moment before she died the first time, Cicilia was standing on the edge of a satellite station somewhere between the new moon and the old one. When Cicilia had enlisted, it had been because she was pissed at her former girlfriend and at her mother, who had said, "Well, perhaps if you dated boys instead..." and she'd thought she would have a desk job, making graphs or something like her Aunt Daliah. However, her superiors back at Base had quickly discovered that while she was athletic and intuitive, math was not her strong suit. So she'd been trained in rift-jumping, not in navigation, and had discovered she loved it. She was doing work that mattered—exploring the effects of time and space travel on the body—and so she barely even thought about the two women that had once been so important to her life. They were the reason she'd come here, a childish act of revenge, but they weren't the reason she'd stayed. It was beautiful up here. Wherever up here was.

For while Cicilia, through training and instinct, could tell the precise moment when the rift would open to let her through and the exact diameter of the rift, in both inches and centimeters, she wasn't exactly sure where she was in the world as she stood on the edge of it.

Which, as it turned out, was the problem. Because the girl who was trained in navigation, the one who was supposed to be watching Cicilia's back, was in lust or love or at the very least, like, with Cicilia. When she was supposed to be navigating the ship and its satellite to the exact rift-jumping spot, she was, in fact, looking at Cicilia's long legs wrapped in her high-tech atmosphere pants and at Cicilia's hair, which was longer than it should have been and so she kept it woven in three longs braids that fell out of the back of her helmet and rested against her back. Through the monitor, the shape of Cicilia's back and ass looked like an old violin, the kind that was perfect for playing, the kind that would make a perfect song if you just knew what to do with your fingers and her strings.

And in watching Cicilia and thinking about playing Cicilia, the girl who was trained in navigation forgot her training for a moment and lined Cicilia up, not at the very degree of the risk at which it was safe to jump, but one degree to the right, which was a place that was the exact opposite.

The rift opened, just when and how Cicilia knew it would and she gave the girl in the navigation room two thumbs up through the motion camera, noticing for the first time as she did so, the girl's perfectly heart-shaped face and her golden-green eyes.

And then she jumped.

Rifts are funny things, scientifically somewhere between black holes and worm holes, but looking more like ripped holes in a piece of sky fabric, a long jagged tear that let the underslip of the world show through. Sky fabric, unlike real fabric, is neither soft nor flexible, the sharp, hard edges opening toward a wide middle section. That very middle, wide-open center, was where Cicilia was supposed to do her rift-jumping.

Cicilia realized just how much rifts are funny things as she went through this one, but she didn't actually go through it. In fact, she was just two clicks to the left of where she needed to be, and her bottom half went through it and her top half hit hard enough against the edge of the rift that it dented her helmet, a sound so loud that even the girl who was trained in navigation heard it through the motion camera and drew in her breath, having realized at last that she had caused the love of her life, Cicilia Rachel Long, to have her first death.

Cicilia knew that this wasn't how rift jumping was supposed to go—at least not according to the hundreds of simulations she'd done at base. She had a moment of disconnect, her body going two ways and her mind going a third, and then there was a rather loud snap, like a door closing, and Cicilia was rift jumping, only it wasn't like any rift she'd ever seen, not even on the training video series "When Things Go Wrong, Which they Won't, But Just in Case, Videos I, II, III, IV and V" that they'd showed at base. This was kaboom and her whole body went whooshing. It was as though her body had been broken into an infinite number of pieces and she could feel each one all edged and tingly. Her body, in all of its separate units, beyond her nipples and clit, down to her cells, her neurons and dendrites and axons, all gave a collective gasp as if preparing themselves. The implosion and explosion were simultaneous, lightening the atmosphere with their collective heat.

Dying, thought the infinite exploding stars that once were Cicilia, was way better than sex.

The second time Cicilia Long died, she was, for the first time in her life, having good sex, and her death was both unexpected and unwanted.

The person she'd been having sex with was the girl who had been trained in navigation, but had been fired upon report of Cicilia's death, and was now managing a magazine for intergalactic travelers.

Cicilia didn't get fired. First the crew's standing priest physician resurrected her, which everyone said was a miracle and must have had something to do with her half-in/half-out of the rift death. Then she got promoted, for being the first Rift Jumper ever to die mid-rift. Cicilia wasn't sure that was a good reason to be promoted, but now she got to rift jump a couple times a month, which was more than anyone else was doing. She was, it turned out, far better at rift jumping than she was at doing math, and she liked it a fair deal more. There was never another jump like the first, of course, but they were thrilling all the same.

The former-navigator-turned editor's name was Alice, and in addition to her golden-green eyes, she had blonde hair shaved so short it was hard to see she had any hair at all. Cicilia loved to put her palms against its prickly softness while Alice was between her thighs, Alice's pierced tongue and the edges of her teeth tugging gently at Cicilia's clit.

They were on leave, or rather, Cicilia was—Alice didn't get leave, she just got days here and there where she didn't have to edit articles about the best interspace places to take your family and whether or not the popular shuttles were allowing pets that year—and Cicilia's last rift jump had brought her back here, to Alice's space and time. Alice never asked what happened when Cicilia rift-jumped, where she ended up or what she found or how it made her feel and Cicilia never told. It wasn't just the non-disclosure order she'd signed, either. It was that, mostly, Cicilia didn't know. She was some other person, some other entity, on the other side of the rifts, and that entity didn't always plug back into the entity that was Cicilia. It was an odd disconnect, and one that her superiors were especially interested in exploring, again and again, even though Cicilia didn't have any words for it.

So she was happy instead to sit on Alice's best chair, destroying Alice's best chair, in fact, with her wetness, eyes closed, not talking, with Alice kneeling between her thighs, her hands in Alice's nice, not-quite-there hair, letting Alice's tongue work her body open. The pressure was sweet in the way that berries were sweet—mostly good, a few duds here and there, but then every once in a while, the perfect explosion in your mouth.

This is what Cicilia was thinking and then not-thinking as Alice's tongue was finding its rhythm across her clit, as Alice's pointer finger slid slowly into her wet cunt. She had begun to think, especially with Alice's finger touching her soft, delicate insides, that she might be in love with Alice. She thought she might tell her, and see what Alice had to say.

Alice bit the inside of Cicilia's thigh softly, and all thoughts of speaking about anything went away. With her eyes closed, she saw stars and stars and stars, swelling into the bright spaces of her brain. Alice touched her in places, here and here, until Cicilia's breath caught from pleasure, and then Alice kept touching that place over and over, until Cicilia thought she might die of pleasure.

Cicilia Long did not, however, die of pleasure. Not that time. No, that time she died when she realized something—the stars in her brain were the same ones that she saw every time she went through the rift. They weren't constellations like here, but words, a language she realized she could read.

The discovery arrived pinpoint on time with her orgasm, which left her limbs wobbly and when Alice leaned too hard into her, Cicilia tipped over backward in Alice's favorite chair and bashed the wrong bit of her brain on Alice's just-cleaned floor.

This time, she didn't crack into a million pieces. She instead became a single line of lust and death, all corded into one. "Pleasure is a string," she thought, and then she was done thinking, at least for a while.

The former navigator, then intergalactic editor, now shaking blonde girl in a very small room, called the Base priest physician to resurrect the woman whose death she'd now caused not once, but twice. The woman whose cunt smelled like other worlds and tasted like a fresh breeze beyond the stars and who, while she slept, talked in a language that Alice had never heard before. Alice loved to fuck her, to lick those other worlds from her skin and her lips, to slide her fingers into the heat that was Cicilia's body. But nothing was worth this, not even those sleep-driven words that drove Alice into such a frenzy that she had to masturbate right next to Cicilia as she slept.

Alice waited patiently while the priest physician returned Cicilia to life. And then she dumped her.

The third, fourth, and fifth times Cicilia Long died, she wanted to. Perhaps the sixth time too, although by then she was coming out of her depression and starting to forget how soft Alice's hair had felt between her hands and was starting to remember the former navigator's last words to her.

"It's too much," Alice had said, handing Cicilia back her clothes after the priest physician had left. "I can't have you dying every time I'm not paying attention."

"It was just twice," Cicilia had said, holding her jumpsuit, her undies, her left rift-jumping boot. She refused to put them on. Alice wouldn't, couldn't kick her out if she wasn't dressed. But it turned out Alice would and could.

"Can I have my other boot at least?" she asked. Alice had already shut the door.

There were women to fuck after that, women who fit neatly between Cicilia's deaths, women with long red hair that covered their nipples, and women with curves that swelled beneath Cicilia's hands, women who fucked her with mechanical machines until her insides felt like they might burst, and women who begged for Cicilia's fingers inside them.

These women loved the way Cicilia smelled and tasted. It was a perfume, a food, a drug, an intangible thing that they all tried to make tangible with words. They loved it especially when she came back from a rift-jump, still in her suit, her long hair grown longer by time and space, her face whitewashed by the lack of light. They all wanted to keep Cicilia, to wrap her in their arms like a doll, like a huggable moon.

But they were just stopovers, ways to pass the time before she could jump again. And die again. Before she could see the star worlds in that other place and bring them back with her, if only in her dreams.

Those next four or five or eleven deaths weren't suicide, not really. Not when Cicilia knew she would come back. She just took the riskiest rift jumps, then took risks on top of that. She could read the stars in the worlds she went to, but she could never remember them when she got back. Death didn't do anything for her anymore, she noticed. No tingles. No explosions to turn her into stars. No direct line to pleasure. It was just something to pass the time.

The priest physician said, each time, "Don't do this again. I don't know how many times I can raise your ass." He only said words like ass with Cicilia, and only because she scared him. Anyone who'd gone somewhere he himself hadn't gone—he didn't mean the rifts, he meant the deaths—scared the gods out of him.

Every time, she said, "I know." And then she died again.

The last time Cicilia Long died, she was 145 years old. Which wasn't that old anymore; in fact, it was downright middle aged, what with all they'd learned about time-travel and time-holding, mostly from her rift-jumping work. She'd all but forgotten why she started—the overbearing mother, the cheating ex-girlfriend. She'd all but forgotten that first accidental death, that early accidental love and lust. What she remembered was the rift space, the stars, the sensation of dissolving between time and selves.

And when Cicilia wasn't working, which she wasn't much these days, she was dreaming. At night, the rift stars showed themselves, became letters of lust and love, spelled out how perfect she was, how everything and everyone wanted her. They promised the kind of death she'd had once before, that first time, when she'd read her whole life, her whole lust, in the pattern of the stars.

Cicilia was 145 years old and hadn't died in nearly forty years. Like sex, dying just wasn't worth it anymore. All the girls looked the same, all so young, wooing her for her achievements, for her discoveries, wanting her for what she brought back from the rifts. Sometimes she let a pretty girl think she was flattered, falling, and she'd take the pretty girl home and they'd fuck a new way, all toys and teeth and a whirlygig of tossing and turning in a bed or on the floor. They all looked a little disappointed at the end, as though they'd expected her to die post-fuck or were a little surprised to see her still standing before them, her hair turning white, handing them their shoes and clothes.

The last time Cicilia Long died, she planned for it fully. She talked to the priest physician, promised him it would be her last death. It was to be her last rift jump, a media thing, splashed across the sky screens for all to see. The retirement of a legend, a grand celebration. He'd balked, of course, but Cicilia could be nothing if not persistent, and in the end, with the enticement of never having to save Cicilia's ass again, he consented.

Cicilia stood at the edge of the rift, waiting for it to open. She knew where she was, exactly, and she knew that the woman doing navigation was just a little to the south of where she should be, but she could compensate for that now. The woman in the rig waved, and Cicilia waved back, smiling without opening her mouth.

Just when Cicilia expected, the rift opened, big and wide, and she slipped perfectly into the middle of it, letting it carry her through as it always did. Somewhere between here and there, she began to feel her other self slide in, the before time or after time Cicilia that wasn't really Cicilia. Just as it did, Cicilia popped the capsule between her teeth.

The drugs did their work, tick-tick-tick, biting her life back as she landed in the place that she always forgot. It was beautiful, as it always had been. The stars danced their light along her body, strokes as soft as fingertips, shines as hard as the edge of teeth. All her sensitive spots came to life, a flare of pleasure through her nipples, her clit, the soles of her feet. A million pieces of her, and each of them touched by light and pleasure. A thousand edges and all of them stroked by knowledge and joy.

Cicilia, dying, opened her eyes to the world. The stars whispered their sweet promises just to her, and in her final death, the smallest of them all, Cicilia Long whispered back.

The Dancer's War
N.K. Jemisin

The Ketuyae had wronged my clan, the Weavers-of-Cloud, some eighty years before. Something about a headwoman's daughter and someone's Third Husband; after so much time no one truly remembered. Honor-feuds had gone on for generations in our people's history. In the end, honor was merely an excuse.

Still, because of it I had spent my whole life training for the day when it would fall to me to defend the clan's honor. The one love we shared with the Ketuyae was dance. As soon as I could walk my mother's First Husband began schooling me in the Root, Stem, and Leaf patterns. By the time I was six I had also mastered Flower, Fruit, and Seed. We then progressed into the animal forms; I mastered the basic Twelve before I reached that age myself. The clan's elders watched my performances and nodded among themselves. "Here's a true Cloudweaver in the making," I heard them say. "If he bests the Ketuyae, we'll gain a worthy addition to our clan."

So they would, I promised them, and myself.

The gathering was held only once every ten years, so we set out as soon as we'd replenished our stores from winter. We arrived at the Evergreen's edge at summer's height, when the great forest was a-riot in color and life. Gathering City had already been cleaned and prepared by the clan which had the honor of hosting that decade's event. But to our great surprise, the living area to which we'd been assigned was right next to the Ketuyae's.

Our headwoman and her First were furious; they left at once to carry a protest to the hosts. I was more pleased than upset. I had been a child at the last gathering-of-clans, too young to fully comprehend the currents of anger and pride sweeping between us and our enemies. Now I was a man, albeit an unproven one. I wanted to see the Ketuyae through adult eyes and take their measure.

But the Ketuyae were prepared, having reached the City some days before us. In addition to surrounding their individual pavilas with thick curtains, they had built screens out of hides, each half again the height of a man, and positioned these about the perimeter of their camp. It was an insult, for it meant that the Ketuyae disdained even to acknowledge our existence. There was much murmuring as our elders debated an appropriate symbolic response.

As I dismounted to begin setting up camp along with the other unproven men, I felt eyes upon me. I turned slowly toward the Ketuyae camp and saw a sliver of a person gazing out at me from between two screens.

Startled, I moved away from my horse and walked to the edge of our camp, stopping with the tips of my sandals on their camp border. I could see only a little of the one who watched me—a strip of bronze skin, odd straw-colored hair, and one glowering blue eye.

I smiled, without humor and with everything of challenge, for I guessed at once who this might be: the Ketuyae's dance-champion. As I smiled, the glowering look changed to one of surprise, then corresponding recognition. I could see only a bit of his mouth but I saw that he smiled as well. How could we not feel delight in such a moment? It can be the fulfillment of a lifetime to meet a worthy opponent, no matter the outcome.

But was this one worthy? I had to know.

So I turned and began pacing along the border, heading for the far corner of the Ketuyae encampment where there was a gap between the screens. My counterpart turned and walked with me, vanishing behind screens only to reappear in tantalizing flashes. I kept my pace measured even though my heart was pounding. Then we reached the gap, and I faced my nemesis for the first time.

The Ketuyae were plainsfolk; I had learned that much of their kind from our elders. Their clan had left the Evergreen many centuries before and mingled with strange folk from the cold lands to the north. It was one of the reasons why we had never gotten along with them, for we Cloudweavers kept to the oldest traditions and our lines were pure. We still lived among the dappled shadows of the Evergreen, and other clans said the forest was in our blood—for we all had dark hair, pale skin, and eyes as green as leaves or brown as bark. We were slim-bodied so that we could run silently through the brush, and we wore close-fitting tunics and limb-wrappings so that we could climb swiftly through the trees.

I had seen already that his coloring was strange, but I did not fully comprehend the difference between our clans until I saw him in that moment. He was huge. Had he been a Cloudweaver, he would have been half useless, for no tree-branch could have borne his weight. He towered over me by a full head, and his shoulders—half again as broad as my own—were partially hidden beneath the mass of curling gold hair which tumbled over them. He had taken no trouble to bind or sculpt it. Or perhaps that was simply not his people's way, for there were no bindings on his arms, legs, or feet either; he wore only leather slippers and breeches. His torso was bare down to where the ripples of his lower abdomen flowed beneath the flap of his breechclout. No, not quite bare. Each shoulder and pectoral had been marked with stark black tattoos in bold swirls and chevrons whose meaning was known only to the Ketuyae.

He was so utterly alien that for several moments I simply stared. It was clear that I was just as strange to his eyes. I was gratified to see him frown slightly, puzzling over the layered cut and braiding of my hair and the bead-patterns of my short tunic. Then he spied my legs—bare but for calf-and-foot wrappings—and his eyes widened. His expression seemed almost scandalized for some reason. I could not help chuckling at such a foolish-looking stare.

This seemed to remind him of the matter at hand. He pulled his eyes back to my own and smiled again, this time derisively. "I've heard the Weavers-of-Cloud called Weavers-of-Grass by the elders of my clan," he said in a voice as deep as a bear's, "but I had no idea the men of your kind came this small. Are you a child?"

"Are you a termite mound?" I retorted. "How will you dance with such a lumbering body? Unless you mean to prove yourself by hurling rocks or some other barbarian craft."

"I dance well enough," he said. "You will have your challenge, never fear." Then he stepped closer so that he, too, stood with his toes on the border-line. This put his chest only a few inches from my nose. I was near enough to feel the heat radiating from his skin.

I craned my neck upwards to glare at his chin. "You try to intimidate me like a beast—all size and superficiality. Perhaps you think your shaggy mane helps too."

"Perhaps you think your beauty makes you a woman," he said softly.

I frowned at this, for at first I was not certain it was an insult. I had been named beautiful by others, though none would presume to call it womanlike; that would have been like comparing a pile of mud to finished sculpture. For him to imply that I thought so highly of myself... "Weavers-of-Cloud revere the old ways," I snapped, "unlike you grass-hopping Ketuyae. I don't claim to be the equal of a woman, but I'm more than equal to you."

He nodded, his smile widening as if I'd pleased him in some way. "We shall see on the proving field," he said then, and—another insult—walked away without so much as a bow.

I stood glaring after him, my fists tight at my sides. I was flushed, breathing hard as if I'd already danced a full Twelve. I wanted to run after him and attack him with my fists like an uncultured child. I wanted to run back to my pavila and laugh into my furs. I felt giddier than if I'd eaten honey-sweets.

Oh, this challenge would be everything I'd waited for. Everything I'd dreamed.

The proving tests began promptly at sun-zenith the next day. Not all the young men undertook tests of great importance. Some merely demonstrated a craft or some sort of cleverness, whose worth the Council of Elders would judge. A young man who failed to win the elders' approval on the first try could make another attempt later during the gathering. He would never earn high rank, but at least he could bring some honor to his clan, and perhaps earn himself a Third or Fourth Husbandhood.

But when a young man sought the ultimate test, he took up the Challenge Staff which stood at the center of the city's proving field. Any man could claim it, and by throwing it at the feet of another, invoke a challenge to which the other had to respond. When the challenge was between men of different clans, wagers were often made on the outcome. When the clans were at feud, as ours was with the Ketuyae, the whole of Gathering City might turn out to watch.

For the winner would bring glory and wealth to his clan. Women would bid high to have him as First Husband, so that he might sire strong daughters and sons. Mothers would solicit him to train their children in pleasure and craft; elders would gradually groom him for leadership in clan or even the Council. But the man who lost the challenge would damage the whole clan's honor. At best his clan might relegate him to permanent low status, where he would be forced to perform the most hateful tasks: fighting in battles, winter guard-duty, servicing the other low-status men whom no woman would favor. At worst he might be banished, forced to beg acceptance from another clan—or wander alone until death. There were no second chances for a man who challenged and lost.

My clan liked me; I was unlikely to be banished if I lost. But neither did I fancy spending the rest of my life putting arrows through barbarians or shivering in some remote guard-post. I wanted to be a First, but that was the least of it. What mattered more was that I had always believed myself to be the best dancer in all the clans. This was my chance to prove it.

I walked onto the proving field as soon as the sun peaked. Other performances were going on in the squares around me, but the central square—where the Challenge Staff stood thrust into the earth—was empty. The crowd murmured as I approached, for they knew the history between Ketuyae and Weavers-of-Cloud. There had been a challenge between our clans at every gathering since the feud began. Doubtless most of the City had already made wagers on this one. My heart pounded, but I smiled a madman's smile as I reached the central square. I would give them their wagers' worth.

The Ketuyae was waiting for me in the square. He'd oiled his body to make his skin shine, and tied up his hair in a high ponytail. He had traded his breechclout-flaps for long drapes which hung fore and aft, dyed in simple but lovely patterns. His smile was as fierce as it had been the day before.

I stopped at the edge of the circle and cast off my cloak. I heard a collective gasp from the crowd, for I too had taken pains to look striking. I wore no tunic. I'd had my mother's First wrap my waist in black leather straps instead, leaving my chest bare. Though I yearned to scandalize the Ketuyae further, I'd donned pants of flexible black fawnhide, laced tightly along the sides. My hair hung unbound and unbraided behind me, black as a raven's shadow and straight as a waterfall. Those who knew the Cloudweavers understood the insult that I sent by this, for we unbound our hair only among the familiar trees of our clan-home—or when we felt otherwise unthreatened.

He knew what it meant, I saw in his eyes. "You still think me a termite-mound?" he drawled.

I flicked my hair and stepped into the square, putting one hand on my hip. "As you said, we shall see."

He nodded, then assumed the Seed Growing position to begin. I raised my eyebrows; he moved gracefully for one so large.

"My name is Elan," I told him, and to his Seed I offered Leaves-in-Autumn to signify that I meant to smother him.

He laughed and struck another opening pose: Sapling Rising, in spite of my leaves. He turned as he did it and I saw that his tattoos met between his shoulderblades and tapered down into his breeches. Oversized or not, his body was magnificent. I almost wished this were not a challenge, so that I could just watch him move.

"I am Ansheara," he replied. "There's no real need for one of us to throw the Staff down, is there?"

I laughed and flashed a Choking Ivy that made my hair whip like a ribbon before it settled around me. I saw his eyes widen slightly. "Of course not."

The drummers took this as their signal, and we began.

From the beginning he took the lead—he had such natural power, such aggression, that I knew better than to contest him on that level. His muscles rippled like ropes as he rammed Trees up from the earth, slapped Leaves from them like a hurricane, stamped Seeds with such force that I felt the ground vibrate. His loin-drapes sliced the air like a swallow's tail. Before he was halfway through the Forest Cycle he was running sweat in rivers, his pale hair whipping in strings—and he had only just warmed up. But the true spirit was in him. I saw that in his outflung arms, his thrown-back face; a smile of pure joy was on his lips.

And I shared that joy. Since I could not best him in power, I countered with intricacy and speed. I flowed through the subtleties of Root and Stem, then rippled my whole body in patterns his larger frame could not have mimicked when I Flowered. Before long I was controlling the dance, though he led, for he had to shape his force around my gentler grace or the dance's beauty would be marred. So I stroked his arms like wind through his Branches, and he bent and swayed, helpless. He spun with me, entranced, as I Vined around his taller Trunk.

It was glory. Ecstasy. I knew that my own face reflected his joy, for I had never danced like this, with a partner who was my equal, my completion. When we drew close to begin the earthforms and rippled together in Rivers, I heard him moan very softly into my ear. The sound sent liquid heat through me. It was natural that I then flashed Lightning and sparked Fire in the Forest, for there was no other outlet for my feelings. It was a difficult posture, our legs intertwined, but we wove together perfectly. My thigh between his, his calf against mine, our torsos flickering back and forth as the Fire rose higher and higher... oh vessels of Earth, I could not think! It felt too good, his body against mine, this perfect melding of flesh and spirit. It came as no surprise that within my pants I was hard as stone, and when his breechclout brushed me I felt the same underneath the leather. The Fire raged in us both, and it sought more than one outlet.

Focus! I commanded myself, and drew away to take us into Fleeing the Fire, which would begin the animalforms. I could not help groaning as I put distance between his body and mine. I saw anguish on his face as well.

And so it went, for how long I could not have said. I lost myself somewhere in the beat of the drums and the pounding of my feet against the sand. I was lost, too, in the Ketuyae Ansheara. He was so perfect! I have no doubt that the Earth Herself moved through both of us on that day, a blessing in sweat and flesh.

But at last the glory ended, for we had gone through Forest, Beast, and Sky, and when we danced Moonset there was nothing left to dance.

For a long time afterward there was silence. Or rather silence was all I heard, for I gazed at Ansheara and for an interminable span I yearned to dance with him again. I saw the same hunger in his eyes. But then the spell faded and I became aware of the crowd, which was shouting and whistling and stamping and screaming around us as if they had been possessed by demons. My muscles began to tremble as soon as I relaxed from the final pose, and if my mother's First had not suddenly appeared to wrap me in an ecstatic hug, I might have collapsed right there.

Across the square, I saw Ansheara do just that, flopping onto the sand with no sign of his original grace. He looked dazed as three women who looked much like him—siblings, perhaps—descended on him with congratulations.

He did not take his eyes from me. And I gazed back over my Firstsire's shoulder, wanting to weep.

Then the crowd began to hush. I leaned against one of my girl-siblings as we turned to the elders who had sat nearby throughout our dance. There had been no clear winner of our contest, so they would have to render a judgment.

Even then, as I looked at their lined faces, I knew what the verdict would be.

"A draw," pronounced the Mother of the Council. "Either one of these men would be an asset to any clan."

The crowd went mad again. My mother and all her husbands joined my siblings in hugs. But just when I might have begun weeping from a sheer excess of emotion—not all of it happiness—I heard a gasp from the people all around us.

I looked around in confusion. Ansheara was on his feet again, and this time he held the Challenge Staff in his hands.

"I am not satisfied," he said. His voice was rougher than usual, husky. His eyes were not quite sane as they fixed again on me. "I desire a second challenge."

And he flung the staff down into the sand, at my feet.

There was an immediate protest from my family and clan, and not a few of the folk from other clans. Even some of the Ketuyae were upset, wondering what on earth Ansheara was thinking. It was not unheard-of for a verdict to be challenged, but never when the outcome was a draw. We had both won. What more could he want?

The Council Mother raised her hand for silence. "If you challenge again, Ketuyae, you risk a less-favorable outcome," she said. "Are you certain?"

"I am," he said, still gazing at me.

She looked at me, clearly uncomfortable. "Elan of the Cloudweavers, you have danced a fine challenge. It is not right that you should be forced to defend the honor you've just won, but—"

I straightened, shrugging off my mother and siblings. I should have been terrified, but I was not. Perhaps I had been infected by Ansheara's madness, but suddenly I was as eager for the chance as he was. Beyond the Staff, I saw my enemy's eyes gleam at me.

"I am a Cloudweaver," I said, and then I chuckled. "At least, for now. The challenge has been issued; I can but answer."

The Council Mother looked from one to the other of us, and sighed. "Men. So be it. What will be the method of the challenge? Another dance? I cannot see how either of you has the strength for that."

We didn't. I looked at Ansheara and spread my hands, passing the choice back to him. Dance was my only true talent, but I was not worried. He would not issue a challenge that I had no hope of winning, for that would dishonor both of us. We had danced the seasons together and felt the Earth move us both. I trusted him.

He saw this and blurted, a shade too eagerly to sound uncalculated, "A different kind of dance, Council Mother. By your leave, I ask the right to demonstrate my worthiness as a husband to the women of my clan."

There was a collective gasp. It was presumptuous in the extreme for any man to declare himself available for husbanding when his status was not yet secure. But that was irrelevant. I stared at him, too stricken to speak.

The Council Mother was too, but she recovered faster. "Elan has also won honor today," she told Ansheara sternly. "Such demonstrations may be performed using unproven or low-status men, but to ask this of Elan —"

"He gave the choice of method to me, Council Mother," Ansheara said, affecting a humility that I knew full well he didn't feel.

I must have been mad to trust you! I thought at him. Let him read my fury in my face if he could not hear the thought. But perhaps he did hear it, for he abruptly grew serious and came over to me. He stopped, as close to me as he'd stood the evening before. My family members were near enough to hear him, but no one else.

"Our clans are in feud," he said softly. I stiffened, for I knew then what he meant by his outrageous request.

Our dance had been a promise that needed to be fulfilled. That was simply the way of things. We had felt the Earth's spirit in both of us. Under ordinary circumstances I would have invited him to my pavila that very night... but the feud made usual methods of fulfillment impossible. Once we left the proving ground, we would never dance together again, in this or any other way. We could share only enmity—and I would spend the rest of my life wondering what might have been.

For the sake of my clan's honor, I could not refuse him. But as with the feud itself, honor was just an excuse.

So I raised my voice, keeping my eyes on his. "I accept this challenge," I told the Council Mother. Then, because I was Elan, I lifted my chin and added, "I too have potential wives to impress."

The crowd burst into an excited frenzy. Nothing like this had ever before happened in the history of any of the clans. The Mother conferred with the other councillors, then called for furs and rushes to be brought so that a bed could be made on the sand of the challenge square. Youths from a neutral clan were sent to find oils and other items that might be of use. While the preparations continued, Ansheara took my hand and led me toward the newly-made bed.

"You're afraid?" he asked me, half-smiling.

"Of course not," I snapped, though I pulled my hand from his so he would not notice its tremor. "I played this game as a boy."

"I too, but never in front of so many. And I have never been judged on my performance." He grimaced.

"You chose this challenge."

"You accepted it."

I glanced at him sidelong; he smirked. I hated and desired him so much that I thought I might go mad.

"So be it," I said, stopping beside the bed. The boys had finished bringing their offerings; an array of flasks and ceramic implements sat beside the furs. The crowd hushed around us; I tuned them out. "This is still a contest, Ketuyae. I mean to win it."

"If you can, Cloudweaver," he whispered, and came for me.

This dance was his to lead; we both felt that instinctively. That was fine by me. The contest would be decided not by who put what in whom, but by who yielded first to the pleasure of it. I sidestepped as he approached and we circled one another, measuring. The sweat from our prior dance had not yet dried. I could smell him, like loam and dry grass from the plains. And lust too; that scent was easy to recognize. I had only to compare it to my own.

"I saw you and thought of night orchids," he said.

"I've heard better flattery from virgins," I replied.

He reached for me, hooking me around the waist and drawing me against him. "But night-orchid seeds are delicious," he breathed, and then he kissed me.

I expected him to try and overpower me, but instead he was gentle, exploratory, tasting my lips with the appearance of great care. Testing my defenses. When I did not react (beyond lifting an eyebrow), he moved his lips over my chin, along my jawline, and up to brush the lobe of my ear. I smiled and bent my head back to allow access. Let him think he was making progress. In the meantime I took the opportunity to slide my hands over his back, which I had secretly yearned to do since our dance. As he licked about the leather collar on my throat—which I will admit sent a small shiver through me—I followed his tattoos down, sliding my hands under his heavy loindrape to explore his solid dancer's buttocks. He wore no breechclout underneath, and his pants had neither seat nor crotch.

He chuckled against my collarbone when I paused in surprise. "On the plains one must do certain things quickly."

No wonder he'd been so shocked to see me wearing only a tunic the night before. "In the forests," I whispered into his ear, "we believe in doing them well."

The Ketuyae's arms suddenly tightened around me, lifting. I was borne back and down, laid out on the bed with my hair spread over the furs. As he rose to secure his position he hooked his fingers into the waist of my pants, then stripped them off me in one fluid motion. I gasped as I was bared to all the clans—they cheered—then gasped again as he lay down upon me. To bare himself he had merely detatched and tossed aside his fore-drape. I felt his male parts nestle snugly against my own.

"Oh, but I mean to do you very well, Cloudweaver," he said. And then he began to thrust against me. Not hard, and not seeking entry; he had no need for that. Just a gentle swaying motion, one branch rubbing against another on a windy day.

I had underestimated him again. I had judged him by his size, assuming he would prefer swift forceful couplings—and perhaps he did. But I preferred subtlety, tenderness: the gentle graze rather than the hungry grind. Somehow he had intuited that from our dance, and now he used the knowledge ruthlessly. I inhaled as he caressed me with nothing more than that part of himself, delicate as a fingertip and heavy with promise. My body could not help responding, for too much of my desire had been left wanting by the dance. I turned my head away, trying to hide my excitement, but my hips lifted traitorously, offering. I heard him chuckle and felt him pull back so that he could torment me further; he was enjoying this. Our roles had reversed from the dance and now intricacy would be my undoing.

But perhaps power would be his. It took an effort to focus my mind, but I reached up and gripped his hips. With that leverage I pulled myself up to grind against him, so hard as to verge on pain. At once I saw him gasp, and knew that I had found his weakness as well.

But he changed his tactics at once, pulling back so that our parts were not in contact. No, you don't—I thought fiercely, but he bent his head to my nipples and tickled them with tongue and fingers to forestall me. I yelped and stiffened in spite of myself. But I had never before climaxed from that pleasure alone, so I relaxed and enjoyed his ministrations while he—overconfident fool!—groped one-handed for an oil flask.

Feeling mischievous, I reached out languidly and took the nearest before he could capture it. With a thumb I flicked out its stopper, tipping oil into my palm. "Allow me," I said. He looked up swiftly, no doubt surprised to see me still coherent. It was a simple matter to set my foot and push up with one leg while he was off-balance. Before he knew it I had rolled on top of him. Dimly, though I tried not to notice, I heard another cheer from the crowd.

Before he could protest—or begin an awkward struggle to resume control, which would make both of us look bad—I stroked him with my oiled hand, using a quick firm motion. He groaned and shut his eyes in helpless pleasure, his expression going tight and almost pained. I smiled, inching backwards. There was no doubt that he knew what was coming; he just couldn't bring himself to stop it.

So I pierced myself with him slowly, rocking back and forth to make the entry easier. Given his tastes, a swift claiming might have been better, but it had been some time since I'd played this role and I had to get used to it again. It did not help that his branch was nearly a trunk, compared to mine. He hissed in pleasure despite my slowness, and we both shivered as I finally sank to the roots. Then I rose up into the canopy again, and back down, and up; all the while I concentrated on making my muscles relax and my flesh soften. For the time being I had an advantage, for I could hardly yield to pleasure while enduring such discomfort. I had to consolidate my position quickly.

But I was too slow. The spell faded and then Ansheara lay quiescent, stroking my hips occasionally but otherwise making no move to engage me. He merely smiled up at me and waited for the ground become even between us again. He did nothing even when I felt the first twinge of pleasure and—unintentionally—caught my breath. Only when I stopped grimacing did he slide his hands up, over the strapping around my waist, to draw little circles around my nipples. This time the sensation caught me by surprise; it was as though lightning arced from my chest to my nether-regions. I flung my head back, just barely biting back a yelp. Too late I noticed the bunching of his muscles. He flipped us swiftly and hooked his arms under my knees, hauling my hips up so that he could stuff a wad of furs under them. The crowd went mad with delight at this, of course. I cursed their fickleness and my own folly.

He covered my mouth with his own to silence my curses. Then he began to ride me. As before, he was gentle, not so much thrusting as rippling his hips against mine. He slid in and out of me with the sinuousness of a snake and—vessels of Earth!—the accuracy of one as well, finding my pleasure center again and again. I could not help writhing, though I put a hand to my mouth to try and stifle my inadvertent cries. He grinned down at me, victory gleaming in his eyes.

No, Earth damn you. I will NOT fail!

I shifted one leg, putting them both onto one of his shoulders instead of separately propped against each. He raised his eyebrows and merely shifted his angle, rippling even more perfectly against my center. I whimpered like a child, but thought fiercely of winter guard-duty and managed to push back the gathering storm. Then I twisted my hips and flipped my legs to the side. It was an awkward position for him; he would have more trouble finding my center, or having any decent leverage at all for that matter. It was a gamble, but I had gauged him correctly this time, I was certain. He was a man who did not like losing control once he gained it. He would not tolerate this weak position for long.

With a grumble of displeasure he finally shifted, pushing the wadded furs aside and lying down behind me. He lifted my leg again and resumed his ripples, but I had leverage now. I propped myself on one elbow, gripped the furs, and began shoving myself back against him, forcing our rhythm faster, harder.

He gasped and tried to resist, our rhythm clashing for some moments as he struggled to keep his movements slow and sensuous. But he had been fighting his natural inclinations all this time. His lust slowly overwhelmed his intentions and soon he was grunting into my hair, thrusting hard to meet me, sweat slickening the passage between us even further as our pace quickened. Through a haze I saw some of the crowd leaning to one side to get a better view of our connection. It must have been a glorious sight. It felt glorious, like riding an earth-shake, and I was suddenly hard-pressed to keep my head even as he lost his. I had never enjoyed force before, but as in the dance, we were adapting to one another.

It was perhaps in desperation that he finally shifted again, rolling me onto my belly and then hauling us both up to our knees. I cried out in dismay as well as delight, for now he could reach my center with every great surging movement and I was helpless to stop him. Guard-duty, I thought frantically, but even that didn't help.

I was hard as stone, aching as he rode me faster, and in a few moments I was going to spill whether I wanted to or not.

But not first! I set my hands and knees and began ramming back against him. I heard him cry out, nearly a sob, but then I could spare no further thought for him. I tried to focus on my hair, which was stuck to my face by sweat and getting in my eyes; my legs, which ached after dancing and now this; my lip, which I'd bitten somewhere along the way. None of it helped. He was the Fire again, and I was the Forest. He was destroying me, renewing me, searing and stoking at once, and I was all but mindless with it.

As my defenses crumbled, I had only one trick left. Closing my eyes, I focused on the muscles within me and worked them in a silent dance, stroking and gripping him with my body.

He shouted into my ear, his hips pumping faster; I could feel him trembling, on the brink. Only a little more and I would win! But then—ah, Earth herself!—he reached around me and found my branch, so close to dropping its fruit. I might have withstood if he'd gripped me clumsily or eagerly, but instead it was the most tender caress I'd ever experienced. He cradled me lovingly, grazing the taut flesh with the pads of his fingers alone.

Thus did I lose the contest.

My seed was already coming into his hand when I felt him shudder and whimper and press tight against my back. He throbbed hard within me but I barely felt it, my mind frozen in horror, my body spasming in ecstasy. As I lost all strength and fell beneath his weight he fell with me, somehow managing to angle us both so that we landed on our sides. And there we lay, too spent to move. He, victorious. I, miserable. The crowd was raucous as a flock of summercrows.

Through their roar and my own mind's haze, I heard the Council Mother issuing orders. Someone threw a light blanket over us; night had fallen during our contest and our sweat was cooling in the evening breezes. Someone else knelt before me with a cup of water, for which I was desperately thirsty. I barely managed the strength to sit up and drink it. As I did so, the boy who held the

cup grinned at me. I could not imagine why.

Another boy was giving water to my destroyer. I heard him swallow it noisily and plead for more for both of us. He was magnanimous in his victory. As the boys went to fetch it, Ansheara stroked me under the blanket and took care in withdrawing from me, for I was already sore. It was nothing to the rawness of my soul.

"Congratulations," I whispered. I could not face him. I no longer had the right.

His caress paused, but before he could speak, the crowd hushed as the Mother held up a hand.

"An unprecedented event," she said, and then she was forced to pause as the crowd sent up another cheer. With a sour look, she waited until they calmed, and continued. "Two challenges, both equally difficult to judge."

There was no getting 'round it. Mustering my strength, I pushed myself upright—more or less, for I could not help hanging my head. My mussed hair at least helped to obscure my face.

"The latter should be no difficulty, Council Mother," I said. Pride made me speak loud enough to be heard, though I would rather have died than say this. "The Ketuyae is the clear winner of this contest."

I felt Ansheara stiffen behind me, and there were murmurs all around. The Council Mother looked momentarily perplexed. "Judgment falls to the Council, not to you, Elan Weaver-of-Clouds. While you might have been in a position to know..." and she could not help smiling at this, "...your reason was surely impaired."

"My senses were not, Council Mother. I felt his peak, and it came after mine."

"Elan..." Ansheara whispered behind me. I felt his hands on my shoulders, but I shook them off and forced myself to lift my head. I would not accept his pity. We had both fought too hard for that.

But he raised his voice to save me anyhow. "Council Mother, it seemed to me the peak came in the same moment—"

She had been staring at us. Suddenly she held up a hand and dropped her head, shaking it ruefully. "Enough! Enough. In Earth's name..."

She lifted her head, and I started, for she was smiling. So were several other members of the Council, behind her.

"Men," she said again. "Did you really believe the matter would be decided by such a foolish measure?"

I frowned in confusion. "I—"

"Be quiet, child, and stop trying to face defeat with dignity. You didn't lose—certainly not because you found your pleasure first. That's the most asinine notion I ever heard." She took a deep breath and made an effort to calm her irritation, then spoke more patiently. "You both set the terms. The test was to demonstrate your worthiness as husbands. So we judged you by your consideration of one another. By your affection—and your display of that was especially impressive given the feud. We judged you most of all by the amount of pleasure you gave to one another." She folded her arms. "We judged you by the things that would matter to a wife, little fool—not to young men whose only experience has been boys' games."

I could not comprehend what I was hearing. Ansheara did, for he laughed and wrapped an arm around my waist and pulled me against him to kiss my cheek. But the rest of me remained stubbornly in a daze.

I had to hear it aloud. "Then... which of us has won?"

The whole Council was enjoying the situation. The Mother glanced back at the other Council members; they cackled like a flock of gulls. I came near to going mad in the time it took her to stop laughing and speak.

"Both, of course. Another draw. Though it was a stupid contest to begin with. As long as you both enjoyed yourselves, there was no way either of you could lose." She grinned then, flashing the few teeth that remained in her mouth. "But you gave us a wonderful show."

Seventeen marriage offers awaited me by the time I awoke late the next morning. My mother's First informed me of this while I ate breakfast; he was so proud I thought he would burst. By the time I left my pavila to pay my respects to our headwoman, the number had risen to twenty. My sisters were having trouble finding storage space for all the courting-gifts I'd received.

Our headwoman praised me for my talent and courage and for my sacrifice in sharing pleasure with the hated Ketuyae. Then she probed to try and get some inkling of which marriage offer I would take. Some of the offers had come from other clans. If I took one of those, it would mean wealth for Weavers-of-Cloud in the short term—for my new wife would surely have to pay some exorbitant amount in compensation—but loss in the long term, for my seed would flower elsewhere.

I modestly told her that I would consider all my offers with due respect, and would inform her of my decision as soon as possible.

Afterward, I staved off demands for the tale of the legendary contest against the Ketuyae—so it was already being called—by promising to regale them later at the evening's dinner-fire. I told them I was tired, which was true enough; I was sore from limbs to nether-regions. But there was more to it, which they would not have understood, so I did not speak of the heaviness of my heart. The only one who did seem to understand was my mother's First, who once upon a time had also danced for the clan's honor against a Ketuyae man.

"But my dance was not a draw," he told me, smiling. And though he had told the tale many times before, this time I finally understood the faint sadness that always came into his eyes when he spoke of his great victory.

It was he who finally got the clan to leave me in peace for a time. I dared not leave our encampment; I would be mobbed by half the city as soon as I stepped beyond our borders. Fortunately, near the back of our camp where we'd stored our belongings and trade-goods in unused pavilas, I found a quiet spot which overlooked the nearest edge of the Evergreen. I stopped here, and stood awhile watching the forest grow.

"How long are you going to mope about?"

I had, of course, made certain that my spot was near the Ketuyae's boundary. I smiled and glanced over at Ansheara, who'd shoved aside a screen and now leaned against it. He glanced around to be sure that none of his clan were watching, but then returned my smile. It shamed me how much my spirits lifted at the sight of him.

"I have little else to do," I told him. "Go count my marriage-offers, perhaps. There's no need for me to practice dancing today. Or ever again, I suppose." I lowered my eyes.

"You do think you're a woman. Arrogant fool."

I looked up in surprise. He looked ready to reach across the border and grab me, though that would have started a war. Instead he folded his arms and gave me a scornful look.

"Go and practice. If you can't dance, I can't challenge you again."

"Challenge me?" I laughed, though bitterness was in my heart. "Weren't two draws enough for you, Ketuyae?"

"No," he snapped, "and if you have any wit they won't be enough for you either."

"We can't —"

"We can. There's no law to say we can't challenge again. We set the precedent ourselves, yesterday. We can challenge each other over and over, until we're doddering elders if we want. Do you understand?"

Through a haze of shock, I did. The notion was utterly foreign to every tradition I'd been raised to revere, but I could not deny its logic. I did not want to deny it.

A smile spread slowly across my face. "Then... after the summer gathering ends, we will have to choose a neutral location for our yearly challenges. It seems clear that one challenge per decade is not enough to contain our clans' feud."

He grinned. "I would say not. I still do not accept our draw, after all."

I reached up and tossed my hair, which was still unbound. "Nor do I. It is a matter of pride between men."

"Indeed. So it's settled." He straightened and put his hand on the screen. We had taken enough risk; it was time to part. "Next summer, and every summer thereafter. If you can bring yourself to wait a whole year." He smirked.

I snorted. "Anxious to taste loss for the first time, Ketuyae?"

"Anxious?" He looked at me for a long moment, his smirk fading. In that moment I remembered our dance, and the Fire, and the greater fire that had come later.

It would be a very long year.

"...Anxious, yes," he said at last. He spoke softly. "Though not for losing."

I grinned. "Prepare well then, you walking termite-mound. I'll have new tricks for you next time."

"Of course, Weaver-of-Grass." He stepped back to close the screen, then paused. "How many?"

"Eh?"

"How many marriage-offers are you going home to count?"

I stared at him. "Twenty, thus far."

He lifted a thumb to point at his own chest. "Twenty-two."

I burst out laughing; I could not help myself. He shut the screen and was gone, but I heard him whistling smugly as he walked away.

Insufferable fool, I thought as I turned from the border. But I was smiling as I thought it.

I would dance him into the ground, next year.

Ink
Bernie Mojzes

The Eldritch Horror sat quietly at the end of the bar, smoking and staring at the olive in an otherwise empty martini glass. One supple pseudopod held a Virginia Slim menthol to one set of lips. Another mouth drew on a Camel unfiltered, held in a withered claw of a hand. A third, hand-rolled (for want of a better term), smelled of cloves. With each exhale, smoke seeped from various orifices scattered around its amorphous body, both out of and under the cheap suit it had stuffed itself into.

A pencil-thin tongue snaked out of one mouth and twisted sensuously around the olive at the bottom of the glass. The tip prodded the pimento out of the olive, then curled the olive up into its mouth.

I wondered if it really disliked pimentos, or if this was the Eldritch Horror version of peeling labels off beer bottles.

The barstool next to it remained empty, even though it was a Friday night and the college kids were out in force. I made my way through the sea of earnest, drunken faces. The fragments of conversation I caught were less about sports and relationships, and more about contextual framing of meaning, and Hegelian dialectic, and one particularly ill-advised comparison of Umberto Eco with Dan Brown. Not even English and Philosophy majors wanted anything to do with the Eldritch Horror.

Or so it seemed.

Still, it was a public place, and it seemed safe enough. I settled in next to the Horror and waved for the barkeeper.

"I'll have one of what he's having," I said. I glanced at the Horror. "Or she. Or it. But with a twist. And his next round's on me, too."

Three of the Horror's eyes wandered over to regard me. "Thanks," it said, the word burbling through its body like a

Paleolithic tar pit. Even so, it managed to evince a sense of suspicion.

"No problem." I tipped my hat—a battered and rain-stained fedora, but all I could afford—and then stuck out my hand. "Name's Harry. Harry Levinson."

It extruded a soft, smooth, feminine hand with manicured fingernails. They were coated with black polish; the ring finger's nail was slightly chipped, and it had been long enough since the polish had been applied that the nail was exposed near the cuticle. One of the eyes stared hard at me, bobbing to catch my attention. It blinked, and when I looked down, the feminine hand was gone, and a strongly muscled and tattooed man's hand was squeezing mine. I was surprised how real it felt.

"We are pleased to make your acquaintance, Harry Levinson," it said. A disharmony of voices, raked over hot coals in unison. "You can call us Sam."

"Sam?" It seemed incongruously normal.

"It's as good a name as any, and better than some. And sometimes we play piano." It waved a protuberance toward the back wall where, through the sea of college kids, I could see a dilapidated upright piano. Plastic cups and empty beer bottles littered the top.

"Are you any good?"

"Ssssometimes." The word hissed like steam from a ruptured pipe.

The bartender returned with martini glasses and a large shaker. He dropped an olive in one glass, rubbed a twist of lemon rind along the rim of the other, and divided the contents of the shaker between them. The viscous liquid resembled bloody ink. I caught the bartender's eye.

"Vodka, cranberry juice, and black sambuca," he said. "Weird, but safe enough. That'll be sixteen fifty."

I handed him a twenty.

It was revolting. Sam chuckled through a dozen mouths, not all human.

"Just like mothers' milk," it said. "Tell us, Mr. Levinson, what is it you want?"

It had been too much to hope that I could just blend in with a crowd like this, that I could pass as just coming in for a drink after a long week. Men like me have our own bars, where we sit alone and try to find absolution for our sins in endless shots of bourbon. But there's no absolution for some sins, either in a bottle or anywhere else, and the best we can do is try to remember to shave at least once a week.

This was a bar for kids with all their hopes and dreams ahead of them. I'd buried mine many years ago.

There was a photograph in my jacket pocket. A girl with fierce determination in her eyes, holding a lacrosse stick like she might take your head off with it. It had been almost six months since she'd gone missing, just before midterms. I laid it on the table.

"Have you seen this girl?"

Several of the Eldritch Horror's eyes studied me, moving around to examine my face from all angles. "You are not with the police."

"They've given up looking. I'm a PI. I've been hired to find her."

"Who—" The voice cut off, and noises burbled under the thing's skin. I got the feeling it was conferring with itself. A tendril extruded from its flesh and tapped the picture. "We have seen this woman. She came to this bar on occasion. She sat and spoke with us." The tendril lifted the photograph gently, as eyes clustered to examine it. Abruptly, it crumpled the paper and dropped it in my lap.

"You will not find her, if she does not wish to be found."

"Her name is Angela." It sometimes helped humanize the victim if you used a name. Not that I was sure that any amount of humanizing would have an effect on a creature like this. "She—"

"We know her name." There was something akin to anger in its voice, and I waited for more, but it just turned its eyestalks away from me.

I took another sip from my drink. It was still awful.

In the sea of students, a murmur grew slowly into an encouraging cheer. There was a swirl of movement in the press of bodies, and a young woman, blushing and nervous, spilled out of it. She took a hesitant step toward the Eldritch Horror.

"You'll excuse us," it said. Eyebrows distinct from eyes hinted its intention, and I slid off the stool and stepped back, against the wall next to the Horror.

"Of course."

It patted the barstool next to it with a human hand and took the cash that she held out to it. Using its bulky body to shield this from her view, it quickly rifled through the stack of bills with the full attention of one eye, while other parts of it exchanged meaningless pleasantries. Her name (Meghan), her major (education, with a concentration in literature), her favorite band (Radiohead), her favorite hentai artist (she didn't really like that stuff).

And then it handed the money back to her. "We are very sorry. You are one hundred and fifteen dollars short."

The news passed like a wave through the crowd, and soon, fives and tens and even twenties changed hands and were stacked on the bar in front of the Horror. It re-counted the money and handed Meghan three twenties change.

"Are you ready?" it said.

"I think so."

"You should be sure," it said in perfect dissonance. "You must desire this for yourself. Not for them."

She managed a small smile. "Yes. Yes, I'm ready."

The Eldritch Horror gestured toward a door, next to the piano. The crowd opened a path to it. I reclaimed my seat.

"Go on, then. Remove any clothing you wish to remain undamaged, and then turn off the light. We'll be with you soon."

The Horror watched her until she closed the door behind her, then waved some of the cash at the bartender. "Does this cover our tab?"

"Yes, and then some."

"Good," it said, rising from its seat. "Mr. Levinson's next drink is on us."

"Thanks, Sam." The bartender turned to me. "Another inktini?"

I could feel my taste buds recoil. "Uh, maybe later. Whiskey'll do me just fine. Jameson, if you got it." I heard the door click shut behind me, and the bar erupted in a cheer. "Better make it a double."

"You're gonna want to stick around for this," the bartender had said, what felt like an eternity ago. He wouldn't say why. The jukebox and the chatter of the patrons drowned out most of the noises from the other side of the door. Other than the occasional squeal that pierced the air, it was as if nothing unusual was happening at all.

And it remained that way for over an hour.

When the door opened again, and Meghan stood wet and naked in the doorway, the patrons stood back and made way for her. She staggered on wobbly legs to Sam's piece of the bar, which had remained empty the entire time.

She sighed onto the bar stool and leaned back, arching her back until her head and shoulders lay on the bar. She closed her eyes and breathed deep, even breaths.

The viscous fluids that covered her were pearly white, and clear, and deep sea fluorescent blue, and swirls of the blackest black. They pooled in the hollow of her throat, between her breasts, in her navel. They seeped down her legs, dripped from her toes and her limp fingers, and slicked her hair.

The patrons in the bar gathered around, pressed close. One sucked fluids from Meghan's toes. Another knelt between Meghan's legs and delved deep with her tongue to receive what remained within. They licked her belly, her breasts, they tasted her lips, squeezed pearly rivulets from her hair. One woman perched on my lap and raised the limp fingers to her lips.

"What's so special about this?" I asked. "What does it do?"

"Hallucinogenic," she said, catching a drop on her tongue. She wore a t-shirt cut to expose her midriff. It had the word Yale stretched tight enough across her breasts to show her piercings.

Another of the patrons had climbed onto the bar and crawled

over to clean Meghan's forehead. His thin face was accentuated by a wispy goatee, looking for all the world like an escapee from the Mystery Bus, but for the horn-rimmed glasses and the wide-lapelled polyester shirt.

"Not hallucinations, man," he said. "Visions. It's like being touched by a god."

"Whatever," Yale said. "It's better than acid and less of a commitment."

She scooped some of the stuff that had pooled over one of Meghan's clavicles and brought it to my lips.

"Less of a commitment?" I asked.

"Half hour. Hour, tops."

When she slipped her sticky fingers into my mouth, I did not resist.

Visions.

I floated in a warm sea. Around me, strange creatures. Jelly fish. Bony fish with blocky, armored heads. Shelled things with tentacles that swam with bursts of water forced through soft bodies. Some of them I caught in translucent tendrils and brought into my center to be crushed and stored until they had decomposed enough to be consumed. Attracted by the blood of my victims, something huge and razor-toothed approached quickly, and then veered away abruptly, disappearing into the darkness of the depths.

The road wavered like moonlight filtering through the waves. Yellow lines to the horizon, and it would be an hour to the next stop. I shook my head and blinked my eyes until the lines straightened. Three days until I was home. The hands on the steering wheel in front of me were big. Strong hands with broken nails and rough calluses. I reached for my thermos. The coffee was cold, but I drank it anyway.

My face burned. Terrifyingly large, the hand swung again. Tears stung my eyes. She loomed over me, her face twisted in rage, the omnipresent cigarette dangling from her lip.

"I'm sorry, Mom," I said. "I didn't mean to...." I was crying so hard the words wouldn't come, and then spilled out in a tangled rush.

But there was no reasoning with her. And it didn't matter that I hadn't meant to be bad. It didn't matter, because I was bad, and I deserved anything I got. Still, I struggled, kicked and slapped and tried to bite as she pulled up my dress and yanked down my panties, and the cigarette's touch was worse than I'd remembered.

Something soft pillowed my head. Soft and sticky and warm, and moving under me like a placid sea.

I peeled my face from the tacky skin of Meghan's breast and sat up. People were strewn around the room, either face down on the bar itself, or on one of the few tables, or sitting on the floor, leaning back against a wall. Some lay on the floor with their heads in someone else's lap.

"Twenty-five minutes," the bartender said. "That might be a record. You must not have taken a lot."

"You didn't..."

"I'm working. And besides, someone's got to babysit. I lock the door and make sure nobody's taken advantage of."

"Makes sense," I said. "I should go. Can you let me out?"

"Sure. You find what you were looking for?"

"Could be," I said. "Could very well be."

I knew what had happened to Angela. At least in a vague sense. The question was, how to prove it? And could she be saved?

Only the Eldritch Horror could answer those questions for me, but it wasn't at the bar the next evening, or the evening after.

"Takes him a while to recover," the bartender said. "He's not as young as he once was."

I thought about the drug-induced vision I'd had, floating in ancient seas. Some of the creatures I'd seen had pre-dated the dinosaurs. I'd looked them up. Ammonites. Trilobites. I hadn't found anything in my admittedly superficial review of the fossil record that resembled Sam. But that didn't necessarily mean anything.

Sam didn't show the following night either, and nobody knew where it went when it wasn't at the bar. Maybe it had a house, a normal suburban house with vinyl siding and a manicured lawn, or maybe it lived in the river. It didn't matter. There were no other leads, so I just kept coming back.

The week went by, and, when I fought a driving rain and flooded creeks to reach the bar on Saturday night, I found it almost as packed as it had been the night I had first met the Eldritch Horror. Sam was there, perched on its high stool at the bar, sipping a bloody-black martini.

I settled in next to it, and the bartender met me there with my whiskey.

"Good day, Mr. Levinson," Sam said. "We trust you are well?"

I shook the rain out of my hat. "Just a bit damp."

"Yes, it has been a long time since we've had weather this good. The humidity does wonders for our complexion, don't you think?"

We chatted about the weather, about global warming, and the recent elections. It was surreal, discussing politics with an amorphous creature that was unimaginably old. We pretended that I wasn't there to find Angela and that it didn't have the answers I wanted.

In the end, I almost lost my nerve, but I fished in my jacket pocket and pulled out an envelope. There was a thousand dollars in there, the amount that Meghan had given it the week before. It was an advance on expenses, courtesy of Angela's mother.

"Why?" it asked.

"Because there's things you aren't telling me, and I need to know. It's the only way I know to get closer."

"For whom?" A pseudopod took the envelope from my hand and slipped it back into my pocket. "We must decline."

"Is it that I'm a man?"

It studied me. "That is of no concern. It is more often women, but that is their choice, not ours. Men are more restricted in their actions than women, in some ways, especially in front of their peers."

"Maybe it's just that the tentacle thing has a more direct appeal to women."

"Perhaps," it said.

Something slid across my foot and up my pants leg. It was cool and dry, like a silken snake, and its touch was so sinuous that I found myself getting aroused, even before it got past my knee. I almost pressed my hand against the lengthening molehill of my pants to stop it, but I'd offered to buy this, and I couldn't see trust growing if I didn't follow through.

It slid across my balls and down the length of my cock. And then, it opened. It took the head of my cock into it, first just the tip, and then a little more, until it closed on the shaft. I felt it stretch, like a snake swallowing an egg. Tough ridges of tissue gripped my skin, and the muscles rippled around my flesh, working me deeper and deeper inside, until it pressed against my pubic bone. Part of it began to stretch, then, across my scrotum. It began on the left, gradually encompassing my left testicle, and then...

And then it was gone, the thin tendril snaking down my leg, and I groaned out loud.

"If you'll excuse us," the Eldritch Horror said, and it took everything I had to bring myself back to enough awareness to realize a young woman stood with us, holding a wad of cash.

It was Yale, though today she was wearing a slinky black dress and stiletto heels.

"Of course," I said, standing to make room. My arm brushed hers as we passed, and I could feel her shiver of anticipation, and not a little fear. I understood perfectly. "Have fun."

I watched them disappear into the back room, feeling... What? Jealousy? Rebuke? Anger? The weight of forty-six years of bad choices?

The Eldritch Horror had chosen, and deemed me unworthy.

I pushed my way through the crowd, trying not to let my erection brush up against anyone.

Outside, it was still raining, and I stood in the middle of the parking lot, letting the wind gust waves of water across my body and watching the lightning.

And then I turned around and walked back to the bar, and waited for Yale's return.

The next day, I paid a visit to my client, Claire Cassidy. Angela's mother. She sat rigid on her sofa, in a deceptively bright and inviting living room, inhaling a Marlboro Light. She didn't ask me to sit.

I turned the easy chair around to face her instead of the television, and perched on the arm.

"So?" She set her cigarette in a recently cleaned and overflowing ashtray. Her voice was as tense as she was. "What have you found out about my daughter's whereabouts?"

What should I say? She's gone. She's—not dead, exactly, but gone forever, where you can never follow.

Instead, "Can you think of any reason why Angela might want to run away?"

"She wouldn't dare." Claire tapped a cigarette out with trembling fingers, pressed it to her lips, and drew the lighter's flame toward the tip with an unconscious inhalation.

I waited for her to put the pack back in her purse. "You've already got one burning," I said.

Claire flung the cigarette at my face. It fell short and landed on the carpet. "She... wouldn't... dare!"

I let the cigarette smolder. "Here's what I know. She wanted to change majors. She hated marketing. She wanted to do what she wanted with her life, not what you wanted. And you? You stopped paying her tuition. You sabotaged her financial aid applications. You canceled the lease on her apartment. The last time anyone talked to her, she was headed down to the river. She said she was going somewhere where you could never hurt her again."

"Is she..."

"Dead?" I shrugged. "I can't really answer that. All I can say is that in the three weeks I've been investigating her disappearance, I've learned a good deal about her, a good deal that you don't deserve to know. She was tough and resourceful and determined and, if she's alive, you'll never find her. And if she's dead, you'll never find her body. Nobody will."

Claire Cassidy stared at me. She fished another cigarette out of her purse, breaking it in the process. She lit it anyway. "You're fired," she said, her voice tight with rage. "Get out of my house."

Later, she would sue me for a refund. I wasn't worried. My standard contract is pretty air-tight. I went back to my office and typed up my expense report.

It was almost a month before I ventured back to the bar. That's how long it took me to scrape together the money after someone poured sugar in my gas tank, and my poor old Honda needed some extensive repairs.

The jukebox was off, and over the hubbub of bar talk, I heard the piano. It was pretty good. A Scott Joplin ragtime piece, I couldn't recall which one. When the song ended, I stepped out of the crowd and raised my glass.

"Play it again, Sam."

"Mr. Levinson. Still on the case, we see."

"Nah. Got fired before I could quit."

Many eyes swiveled to face me. "Then why are you here?"

I tried to give a casual grin, but my face refused to comply. Just a twitch of the lips. "There's something I need to know. Not as part of the case. Not for anyone else. Just for me."

"Something?"

I placed the envelope with the money on the soundboard. "Several things."

The Eldritch Horror regarded me silently, then passed the envelope back to me. I felt a moment of despair, and then it extended a pseudopod to the door knob of the back door. The door swung open.

"Remove any clothing that you don't want damaged," it said, "and then turn out the light. We will be with you shortly."

It wasn't what I expected. Well, I don't really know what I expected. Maybe a bed? The room was empty, except for a wardrobe, in which I hung my clothes and placed my shoes. There were mirrors on one wall, and a barre, like in a dance studio. Maybe at one time it had served that function, though that seemed odd for the back room behind a pub. The floor was linoleum tile, yellow and avocado. Very seventies.

There was a rusted drain set into the floor in one corner. I tried not to think about that.

Instead, I looked at myself in the mirror. No, not wise. It sucks getting old. There is little as unappealing as a middle-aged man. It was worse under industrial fluorescent lights. I'd left my drink half-finished on the piano. Maybe ten feet away, and impossibly distant.

I hit the light switch, and waited.

The light from the bar blinded me for a second, and then the door closed, and I was alone in the room with the Eldritch Horror. I heard it slither across the floor, felt something like snakes spreading around the room, encircling me.

It was too late to run.

Don't touch me. Oh god, don't let it touch me.

"Can I change my mind?" I asked. I heard my voice quaver.

The voices came from all around me. "Of course. Would you like to stop?"

Yes. "No."

Tendrils ran up my legs, and I shivered. Or shuddered. I'm not sure which.

"Are you sure?"

I reached down to touch the tendrils, which had reached my waist. They were soft, and twined between my fingers like cats at dinner time. "I was not. But now I am. Thank you."

I felt lips on my neck. Teeth grazing my ears. A soft touch on my back, circling me. Something running through my hair. A mouth pressed to mine, opening, the tongue probing my mouth.

My cock ached. The Eldri... No. Sam. Sam touched my face, my chest, my back. Wrapped my legs in what seemed like a hundred hungry mouths. Touched me almost everywhere. Everywhere but my penis.

The dark was absolute.

"What can I do?" I asked.

"Nothing." The voices surrounded me. "This is for you."

And then there was light.

Just a pinpoint of blue light, dangling at the end of a pseudopod, hanging in front of my face. Like an angler fish.

I pushed that image out of my mind. Better a Lovecraftian tentacle monster from the abyss than those teeth.

The light dropped, lowering until it hovered directly in front of my cock. It reached forward, touching the tip. My cock jumped; the glowing tendril followed it, a cobra's dance. Another touch.

And it slipped inside.

A hundred tendrils lifted me from the floor and bore me to the mirror as more dangling, bioluminescent lures appeared, allowing me to see myself in the mirror. The one that had pushed into my urethra intensified, until it glowed through the skin. I felt my cock swell as the blue glow slid down the length of it, disappearing under my balls. I watched, held motionless, as it slid in and out of me, very slowly at first, and then faster.

The tendril that penetrated me flowered, extending glowing petals that curled around the head of my cock, and then, as it had done before, slowly engulfed the entire organ, crawling down the shaft with pulsing ripples as it continued to slide in and out of me. The feeling was indescribable.

A chorus of voices by my ear: "We think you are ready now. Are we correct?"

I nodded. I was lifted, and lain down on my back on a bed that slid and slithered under me, that wrapped around my waist and pinned my arms at my sides. Things I could not see slid across my body and wrapped around my legs, pulling my knees up to my chest.

Something wet explored between my legs, pushing gently. I gasped and tensed.

"Relax." A dozen voices. A hundred. More.

I took a deep breath, let it out slowly. "Ok."

And it flowed into me. More than I could imagine. I felt myself stretching, not just my sphincter, but my belly. In the dark, I imagined things sliding under my skin.

"How deep can you go?" That was the last I said. Something slippery pushed past my lips and began to pump into my mouth. Tiny suckers caught at my tongue, pulled at my cheeks from the inside.

"We are infinite," it said, "but human bodies are fragile things."

Something pressed hard against my prostate. Something else took my balls into it and rolled them with what I hoped was a tongue. I felt the orgasm building, not in my balls, but between my shoulder blades. My body arched, involuntarily, and I groaned against the thing in my mouth. The thin tendril slid out of my urethra, just in time, and I spent myself into—what? Into a softly pulsing tendril.

Which detached itself from me. Miles of tendrils slid from between my legs, leaving me feeling stretched and empty. The tentacle in my mouth pulled away, and everything that held me in place loosened. I sat up on my bed of snakes.

"Wow."

Something whispered in my ear. "Now that you are warmed up, let us begin."

I wasn't sure how much more I could take. It was almost comforting when it wasn't a tentacle or tendril or pseudopod or strange glowy thing that touched me next, but human hands. No, not almost comforting. It was. And even when those hands brought my mouth down onto a very human cock, something I had never done before, I grasped at it like it was the most familiar thing in the world, pumping it with one hand as I sucked, until it swelled and emptied in my mouth. I held on to it until it softened and shrank, pulled back into itself, and warm lips pressed against my face.

I ran my tongue between them, from the clit down to the soft, wet opening and back. I sucked the lips into my mouth, flicked my tongue across the clit. Sam sighed and wrapped fingers into my hair, dug fingernails into my back. I slid two fingers inside her... it. Something tugged on my cock, warm and wet. Fingers cupped my balls, probed me where only tentacles had gone before.

I licked her until the fingers tightened in my hair and she clenched, clenched and moaned, and released. She? It. A thousand voices echoed, an almost infinitesimal delay.

I was hard again. In the dim blue light, I could see a clear pseudopod pulsing around my cock. Hands stroked my legs, massaged my shoulders, spread me open and fingered me. Women's hands, and men's also. Young and old, different colors. Some had hard calluses and thick nails, and dark, matted hair. Cro Magnon? Neanderthal? Older?

There were probably other things in there, in the multitude that called itself Sam, because it was as good a name as any. Tigers, and bears, and even prehistoric creatures like dinosaurs and woolly mammoths. I put that thought next to the angler fish. Best not to think of these things. Best not to give it ideas.

I took a deep breath and risked the question I'd come to ask. "Is Angela here?"

A thousand voices. A hundred languages. One answer: "Why?"

I took that as a yes. "May I speak to her?"

The hands pulled away, the bed of tendrils slipping from under me until I knelt on the bare linoleum. Only the one transparent tendril, wrapped around my cock, connected me to Sam.

The blue light increased. The tendril which stroked me darkened and thickened, became lips, a mouth, a face, a head. It extruded a body, arms, legs. She wrapped warm fingers around the base of my cock and pulled her lips away to gaze up at me.

"I needed to be sure," I said.

She brought her face up to mine. She even breathed like a human. "Sure of what?" The suspicion was back, and the hand that had stroked my cock now gripped it like it might want to rip it off.

"Sure that you were safe."

She smiled. "I am." She pressed against me until I lay back on the cold floor, and then crawled over me. She reached behind her and grasped my cock, pressing the head against her pussy, sliding it back and forth until it was positioned right, and then sank down.

She kissed me, then, with soft, eager lips. "Thank you," she said.

"For?"

"For caring enough."

"Was it worth it?" I asked. "All this?"

She pressed herself against me. "Oh, yes."

She rode me until I spent myself inside her, and then she curled against my chest.

"Would you do something else for me?" she asked. "When I used to... used to come to Sam, there was something I used to do that took them somewhere beyond ecstasy."

"Them?"

"Sam. Them. Us." I felt her lips smile against my cheek. "It's something that nobody has done since I merged. I think we would trust you enough."

"We?" The smile again. "Yes, for you. And... and all of you."

"Thank you," she said, and, before she slipped away into the chaos, she told me how they liked it.

The fucking began in earnest, then. Tentacles and cocks and cunts and mouths, breasts covered in sensitive nubs that rolled under my palms. I asked for more light. I wanted to see what I was doing, and what was being done to me.

The human body is not infinitely malleable, like some things, but can learn to accommodate far more than seems reasonable in the light of day. More than one thing penetrated my ass at one time. Things filled my mouth—male, female, and other. Tiny cocks fucked my nostrils and ears with rabbit-like speed. Things sucked my toes, rubbed against my thighs, rode my fingers like animate gloves.

Around me, bodies formed, fucked, melted into other things, into other configurations.

I pressed through the chaos, the madness that probed and fucked and sucked me, swam labial seas and climbed mountains of cock. And found, at the heart of the confederation that was Sam, a nub.

I touched it with my thumb, and a shiver ran through the room, through them all. I kissed it and licked it and sucked on it, and it swelled in response. I pulled at it with my teeth, biting gently.

"Harder." A voice. "Harder." Another, echoing, and then others, dozens. "Harder, harder, harder." And one voice, a voice I now knew. "Yes. Now."

I bit hard, and pulled. Something tore. Bitter, black ink spilled into my mouth, spread across Sam's surface, on my hands. Around me, the chaos of bodies convulsed. Hot liquid spilled on my back, across my face. It was in my hair and in my ass.

I bit again, even harder. I chewed the nub, tearing pieces of it off, swallowing them. More ink. More cum.

They washed through me, the collective memories of thousands, tens of thousands, of souls.

It was too much. Far, far too much.

When I woke, it was in a cradle of Sam's flesh. We lay that way for some time, me too shell-shocked to do anything, and Sam waiting on me. After a time, they spoke.

"You wish to join us," they said.

"You wouldn't want me," I said. "I'm damaged goods. More bad memories than good."

"We have tasted you," they said, and the dissonant chorus no longer tore at me. No longer felt wrong. "You are not ready yet to be us, but when you are, we will welcome you."

I nodded, trying not to let my disappointment show, and then stumbled to my feet. A tangle of snakes slid across the slick floor to make a path, and I stumbled naked out of the room on wobbly legs and into a sea of eager faces.

It was time to share the gift.

Ota Discovers Fire

Vinnie Tesla

As Ota picked his way through the underbrush, he ran his thumbs over the new calluses on his palms and smiled with warm satisfaction. He ran a hand over the week's stubble on his chin and thought of how frightened, how naive he had been setting out from the great coastal city. Now he was sleeping rough, finding his own way through the nearly trackless wastes of the inland forests.

Ota was musing on the gentleness and serenity of the forest when his stomach lurched as he realized that the thing about a yard uphill from his right side was not a rotten tree stump, but a fresh deer carcass, gutted and bloody.

It was just starting to draw insects and didn't yet stink noticeably. The head was largely intact, though the throat had been torn out, and a large predator had apparently eaten its fill from it. Ota looked around. As a child, Ota had had a book of engravings—seemingly landscape pictures—of richly detailed rocky cliffs and elaborately limned oak trees. Stare a little longer, though, and the engravings would reveal hidden pictures—faces, hands, leaping animals lurking in the patterns of light and dark. Likewise, the entire forest transformed in aspect as he stared at the carcass, each tree trunk potentially concealing a threat, each bush harboring the possibility of a seething horror.

He knew this stretch of forest still harbored wolves, bears, and occasional smilodons. There were rumors of creatures more dangerous still. Whatever had made this kill might well still be lurking nearby. He looked about to his left, then his right. There was a prickling at the back of his neck and he whirled to stare back the way he had come. A faint sound above him made him turn, and he staggered back in surprise until he fell and landed on his tailbone on the hard trail. Some sort of shaggy ape was crouched on a tree limb, staring back at his startled gaze.

It was only when it opened its mouth and succumbed to the peals of laughter that it had evidently been suppressing that his vision once again reorganized itself and he realized that what he was looking at was human after all, a woman with hair in matted black locks, a gray pelt tied in a rough kilt around her waist, chin and bare chest smeared with a dark, flaking paint that, a moment later, Ota realized was probably dried blood, presumably from the deer on the ground.

He suppressed the urge to run from this bizarre apparition. "You... speak Samath?" he ventured.

She dropped from her branch, landing soundlessly a little too close for his comfort. He backed up a step. Standing erect, she would have only been a couple inches shorter than he, but she crouched as if ready to spring in any direction.

"Enough," she said, "and I think you do not have Darsh." Her voice was accented almost beyond intelligibility.

The accent, and the name of her own dialect, stirred a memory—he'd heard it caricatured in numerous comic plays: the bestial autochthons of the eastern forests. He'd never tried to imagine a female.

"You're a thonnie!" he exclaimed, relieved to understand the situation a little better.

Her expression soured. "I am Nika Umu—the Moon People," she announced.

"Yeah, autochthons! Wow, I didn't think you guys ever made it this far west!"

Her expression clouded with suspicion. "You are not native to this forest, either, I am thinking."

"No," he said uncomfortably. "I came here from Ensa."

Her brow furrowed. "I have heard of this city...."

Ota hadn't been expecting such a tepid response. "Well, we are head of the Southern Confederation. I mean, that's a pretty big deal."

She ignored this. "Ensa is magic city, I hear. People there are wizards." She looked at him with sharpened curiosity.

For his part, Ota was baffled. "Magic...?"

"They make the fire speak, take on forms...."

"Oh, salamandry! No, no. I'm no salamander. I can barely even light a cheroot that way. Most of the time, frankly, I use matches."

"But you have the craft a little?" she persisted. "Show me!"

"Okay...." He pulled a crumpled piece of paper out of his pocket—it had an old shopping list on it—and held it out cupped in his hand. He tried to slow and steady his breathing, to feel the heat that his teachers had told him was always pulsing inside him. The autochthon watched steadily, and he found himself becoming acutely self-conscious. He squeezed his eyes shut and concentrated again.

After a time, he felt ready. He tossed the wad of paper up into the air, and reached out with a rush of heat. He opened his eyes just in time to see the paper flare up as it fell to the ground. It wanted to go out, but with the fire started, it was easy to coax it to sustain itself, flaring for several seconds before it subsided into fragile ash, latticed with creeping red sparks.

Red faced and sweating with effort, he released the last, unconsciously held breath (his instructors had always scolded him for that—it was poor technique), and looked back at his spectator. He was torn between embarrassment and pleasure at her awed expression.

"How you do that?"

"I'm sure you don't want the detailed answer, which I can't remember half of anyway. For little stuff like the paper trick, I can just draw on my own spirit-fire. If I needed to do something harder, I know a few breathing exercises that can build the fire up a little. Real fireworkers use much more dangerous methods to produce very large amounts of spirit-fire."

Her eyes were wide. "You know how to do this?"

He shook his head. "I have the basic ideas... this isn't stuff you try without expert supervision."

There was a moment's uncomfortable silence.

"I'm Palatine Ota" Ota said.

"Pa-la-"

"Just call me Ota," Ota said. "Palatine is—" he tried to envision how to concisely explain the nuances of rank and prestige expressed in that matronymic. "It's a family name."

She nodded. "Why is a man of Ensa wandering the inland mountains?"

"I'm on my way to Ivy City. There's family business I need to do there.

"You go west by walking east? That is a fine trick."

He flushed. "I—I don't know these mountains very well."

She waited.

"I was with a caravan," he continued. "I paid a group of merchants coming up with goods for the hill towns to let me come with them. I didn't choose my companions very well, it seems, since they decided they wanted more."

"They took your money?" the autochthon seemed oddly shocked.

"Well, what they could find. I—"

"No, no. They took your money for the guiding? You paid them?"

He chuckled ruefully. "Not enough, apparently. Or maybe too much. It made me look like an easy mark."

"Oathbreakers," she said, in a tone that suggested that she knew no stronger curse. "So now you hunt them for revenge."

"Ummm, no. Now I'm trying to get to Ivy City on foot, like I said."

"Ah! You wait for them to relax before you strike. Very cunning—I like!"

Debate was looking like a lost cause. "Thank you."

"I am Ulvzarger," she announced, pointing proudly to herself.

The word was vaguely familiar. "That's your name?" he asked.

"No. That is what I am."

Now he remembered. Other, darker plays had reveled in the exotic term. He'd always assumed it was mythical.

"You're a wolfma—uh, person?" he said incredulously.

"By night, when I choose, I become a great she-wolf. It is my power," she announced with obvious pride.

"Like... literally? It's not just a symbol or something?"

"A magician is surprised at this?" she said, cocking a dark eyebrow.

"I've met a few magicians—salamanders and artefactors, transformationalists, farspeakers, dreamsmiths.... I've never known of one that could transform himself, though."

Her expression became very serious. "I do not know all these words; but every magician transforms himself."

At this, Ota rolled his eyes. "Oh, sorry," he said, "all I know about magic I learned from scholars and work-masters. I didn't have the benefit of your thonnie koans to tell me how it works."

She glowered. "Do not mock the ulvzarg. Our anger is terrible."

"Are you threatening me?" Ota said incredulously. "I'm so much bigger than you I could—"

Something hit his coccyx, hard. To his surprise, he found that he was sitting on the ground.

A wave of pain washed through his stomach and he realized that the wolf girl had punched him in the gut.

"You hit me!" he exclaimed.

"You ever see a wire cut through a round of cheese, city boy?" she asked, standing over him.

"In the stomach!" he persisted.

"You must have been so surprised, the cheese was so much bigger than the wire."

"That wasn't a real fight," he said, outrage driving him on to speak through the waves of pain that still narrowed his vision. "You just suddenly hit me."

"Oh, and how do I really fight, cheesewheel," the girl spat back. "Do you need a parchment declaration, maybe a trumpet blast? A real fight starts with a knife in that soft belly, instead of a fist. You are older than I, I think. But you have much to learn about the world."

She stepped back. "You go now."

Where previously he had been intrigued by this half-naked

autochthon, now he was so indignant he could hardly speak. He pulled his pack back on with shaking hands.

"Well, uh...." The correct parting words for this situation were far from obvious. "Well, enjoy your deer," he said, but it came out far less biting than he intended.

He set out along the trail. He walked fast, devising devastating rejoinders he should have used. Then he remembered that she had said that he was heading west. He tried to make out where the sun was, but the bandits had taken his pocketwatch, so he wasn't certain whether the sun was now rising or setting, and the trail had so many switchbacks that figuring out its overall direction was impossible anyway. "I'm a good fighter," he mumbled to himself as he walked. "I got a commendation in Pugilism at the Academy. I could totally have taken her...."

She was probably wrong about the directions anyway. Either out of malice or simple ignorance. He continued walking, more slowly, for a long while, each step feeling more maddeningly uncertain than the one before.

Then he turned around.

When he had walked, it seemed, at least as far back as he had out, the spot where he had found the dead deer was nowhere to be seen. Oh well, he thought, I guess I overshot it somehow.

He kept walking, wondering if he should turn back again, the gnawing uncertainty growing with every step. Then, at last, he reached a spot where the dented, blood-stained shrubs showed where the deer had rested a little while before. Neither it nor the autochthon was anywhere to be seen. Including, this time, in the branches of the trees.

"Hey!" he called into the woods. "Please! I need a guide! I need to get to Ivy City, but I don't know these woods! I'm running out of food! I don't know what else to do...." Nothing answered his voice but a bird call.

He drew breath and tried again, "I'll make it worth your while! I'll pay! In gold!"

"How much?" she said, quietly, behind him, very close. He

whirled, infuriated that she was still taunting him like this, but more certain than ever that he had no choice but to draw on her skills if he could.

"How long would it take you to get me to Ivy City?"

"You walk fast, you see their walls in three nights. You walk slow, you take longer."

"'Three gold pieces to take me there."

"Three good gold pieces, I am your guide." With her left hand, she reached under her fur kilt and gripped her crotch vulgarly. Her right, she held out expectantly.

Hesitantly, Ota took it, and she looked significantly at his other hand.

Feeling ridiculous, he cupped his own groin.

"Bound by gold," she recited.

"Uh-huh."

"You say."

"Bound by gold," he quoted back.

"It is done," she said, and immediately darted off down the trail.

She set a challenging pace, pushing through the undergrowth so effortlessly that she rarely even bothered to lift a hand to push aside a branch, and often waiting with evident impatience while he picked his way around thickets she had seemed barely to notice.

"Isn't there a path we can take?" he begged.

Without looking around, she said: "Path is slow and dangerous. We do not need path."

After about an hour of this, with his back and feet throbbing, it occurred to him that, as his guide, it was entirely appropriate for her to carry his pack.

He jogged along until he was caught up with her and, breathing heavily, explained his logic.

"No," she said.

"I... I'm willing to pay a little more," he ventured.

"To keep you safe, I must be ready to fight," she said. "The snail is not brave fighter. The turtle is not feared by his enemies. I am not to carry big bag like pack animal."

"I didn't hire you to be a bodyguard," Ota protested. "You're a guide."

"And how I take corpse to Ivy City when you are killed for gold or for meat? I drag you? You carry your bag; I will guard."

She pushed ahead, with the phrase "for meat" echoing in his ears.

Shortly before sundown, she paused on a rocky hillock. "We stop here. You have food?"

"A little," he said. "I don't know if you'll want to eat it...."

He brought out a bag of milled grains mixed with honey, butter, and dried fruit—traditional Ensan travel fare. She tasted it. To his surprise, she pronounced it good, then proceeded to devour three days ration of it, leaving a rather scant final portion for his supper.

As she picked the last fragments of oats out of his bag, he gathered wood and built a campfire. Too weary for salamandry, he brought out a small box of matches and struck one on a stone to start the fire. She seemed to find this process nearly as engrossing as his earlier performance. Once the fire was blazing merrily, he leaned back, grateful to be off his feet.

"Tell me of these traders who robbed you," she said pensively.

"Well, it was a little caravan going up to Ivy City. My family's in coastal trading—we don't really do inland business.

"I was impatient to get going. I'd spent most of my life inside of Ensa's walls, and this was going to be my first important business assignment. For a lot of communication, we just hire farspeakers, but this was an actual credit transfer, so the documents are almost as good as gold. I was going to get to be the courier. So I went down to the marketplace and found some guys who looked like they'd be tough enough to beat off bandits and smilodons, asked if they'd let me go with them. It was four guys... I think they said they were from Tarr... and two llama carts.

"It was kind of awkward at first—me and those guys didn't exactly have much to talk about. They did a lot of muttering amongst themselves. Then about a week in, they got a lot nicer—

let me ride on the llama cart most of the time while they walked alongside, pitched my tent for me each night, things like that. Then, one morning, when I was getting ready to set out for the day, they suddenly punched me in the stomach a few times, stole my boots, and rode off laughing with all my stuff.

"It took me a couple days to find a village, barefoot and empty-handed. I'd hidden a little gold inside my clothes, so I was able to get supplies to move on."

"And now?" the autochthon asked.

"Now I walk to Ivy City, tell Fascian Lors what happened, and hope like hell that the traders are too ignorant or cautious to cash my family's chits. If they don't, I'm probably just demoted. If they do, I'm unemployed, and possibly disinherited as well."

"Four men, two carts," said the autochthon thoughtfully. "Weapons?"

"They've got machetes, and a couple crossbows," Ota said. "Why?

"I guard you," she said. "It is my business."

"What, you think they're going to come back and attack me again? It doesn't seem very likely."

"Probably not," the girl conceded, in a way that Ota somehow failed to find reassuring. He groped for a change of subject.

"I just realized," he said, "I don't know your name."

"I have no name," said the girl.

"That's ridiculous," Ota said. "How can you not have a name?"

"I was Zurok-sa. That means third from top of Zurok pack. Now that is not me."

"Sa means 'third most dominant pack member'?"

"Yes. Samath is a clumsy language."

"But that's a title, it's a role. It's not a name."

"Personal names are for children and the dead."

"But isn't there a name for a person without a pack?"

She frowned. "Nezkhad," she spat. "Do not call me that."

His eyes widened. "I don't think I could pronounce it, anyway."

There was a pause before he spoke again. "So did they kick you out of your... pack, then?"

Again she was on him so fast he didn't fully register it until they were rolling on the ground. He flailed ineffectually at her, uncertain even what she was trying to do.

With brutal efficiency, she rolled him onto his back, shoved his head back and clamped her jaws around his larynx. When he tried to twist away, she bit down harder.

He had to fight down a wave of blind panic as it occurred to him that this half-human creature might actually kill and eat him. He gasped for breath, her slight weight rising and falling with his chest, her sharp smell strong in his nostrils, her breath hot and damp against his neck. Her skinny legs held him as fiercely as her teeth.

She drew back long enough to hiss, "Apologize, cheesewheel," before her mouth was at his throat again.

"Um, I'm sorry," he began, furiously trying to recall what precisely had given such offense. "I'm sorry that I—" he hesitated, afraid that paraphrasing his earlier words might provoke her further. "—that I asked that question about your pack."

She immediately sat up, now resting on his hips. With odd, crisp formality, she said: "I forgive you. You are an ignorant sun-person."

Then she smiled that odd, closed-mouth smirk of hers. "Oh! You are liking this."

She ground her hips against his, and, mortified, he realized that she was referring to his erection, which he had not consciously noticed until that moment.

She squirmed her hips against him, producing startling waves of pleasure, and—unbelievably—giggled. "Perhaps I should make you apologize more often. Perhaps you are so rude because you need to be mastered, hmm?"

Before he could formulate a reply, she was off him, reclined against a tree on the other side of the fire, grimy knees high and wide. The remains of the fire cast wavering red light on her thighs. She was watching him intently. Without artifice or subtlety, she tugged her fur kilt up to her waist, displaying her dark pudenda for a moment in the dim, guttering light. Then her long hand was over it, squeezing and cupping, her hips squirming in counterpoint.

She smiled, and this time her teeth showed. He suspected that it meant a very different thing when she allowed herself to do that. "You no hear the stories about moon-women?" she asked.

He barked with laughter. "You don't have teeth down there—that's a stupid story for adolescents to whisper in the playground."

"There's teeth," she said, "and then there's teeth."

Feeling gingerly at his bruised shoulder, he found a raw spot where her teeth had broken skin, sticky with blood and saliva.

"You bit me," he said. "Am I going to become a wolf-man now?" He was uncertain what he thought of the notion.

She looked blankly at him for a moment, then began to chuckle. In a moment, she was hooting with laughter. When she was able to speak again, she wiped her tearing eyes. "Yes, yes. You are now ulvzarger like me. Also, if senator sneeze on you, you are then senator, yes?

He flushed. "Well I just thought—"

"Listen, chee—city boy," she snapped. "All moon people wish to be ulvzarg, very few can. First you must be accepted into the ulvhaaar—the wolf cult—then you must learn the seven public dances, and the three secret dances." She fingered the livid scar over her left eye. "One of those is not so easy."

"Then you must go into the forest alone and with your little knife kill your brother and take his skin. Then you must befriend his spirit, who you have murdered, win his forgiveness. Then comes another test, which you cannot know. Ulfharoo die every year trying on this test. Then you are ulvzarg. Not before."

Cowed by this furious speech, Ota was silent.

"Stupid city boy." Then a sly smile spread across the wolf-girl's face. "Pretty though."

Ota shook his head. "You are so weird."

Then she rolled onto her side, and within seconds she was snoring loudly.

In the quiet that followed, Ota found that his body was shaking from the dense combination of pain, anger, fear, arousal, and exhaustion he'd experienced that day. He realized that tears were prickling at his eyes.

Uncertain how authentic the wolf-girl's slumber was, he stood and stumbled off into the undergrowth, determined to get out of easy earshot of the campfire. Then he leaned up against a tree trunk and waited for the sobs to come.

The distraction of the walk through the uncertain terrain of the forest, however, had cooled his emotions enough that the tears wouldn't come. In this introspective state, though, he became aware that his arousal was still nagging at him. He hadn't masturbated in several days, and this suddenly struck him as a good opportunity.

He turned around and leaned back against the tree, pulled down his breeches, and began stroking his penis, which swelled cooperatively. He shut his eyes and summoned his favorite fantasy.

He was in a huge marble bathtub with a pair of pretty women—the particular casting had changed often over the years, reflecting the most desirable girls he'd encountered lately. This time it was Aventine Agen and Aventine Essa, a pair of cousins of excellent family who had demurely flirted with him at several recent events. They were soft and gently perfumed, with exquisitely colored fingernails and tasteful makeup with a fantasy's perfect resistance to bathwater.

The girls cooed and giggled as they lathered his limbs and torso, pausing occasionally to rub their perfect bosoms across his skin. They glanced, from time to time, with shy giggles, at his suds-shrouded erection, but he knew that they would never be bold enough to touch it until he demanded it of them—their nervousness and exquisite hesitation was often a point he dwelt on in great detail in this fantasy.

It wasn't working. His cock was rigid in his hand, but the images weren't connecting up to the sensations. He released the fantasy, let his mind drift....

Heat. Darkness. Skin slick not with soapsuds but sweat. Arms twined together, contending for control, teeth against—he shook his head no, his hand accelerating on his cock—against his throat. His own teeth sinking with bruising force into taut, salty flesh. An accented voice chanted curses and insults as he pounded furiously into clinging wetness.

He cried out, his voice sounding strange in the forest's hush. A moment later, he heard his semen spattering on leaves. He caught his breath and picked his way back to camp.

As he was pulling his blanket out of his pack, the wolf-girl said, "Feel better?" without opening her eyes.

He murmured something noncommittal and laid down on the far side of the fire, on his back. For a time, he watched the stars, trying to puzzle out what to make of her question.

Sometime in the late watches of the night, the cold woke him. It was a slow, unpleasant process. First he huddled fetally under his blanket, rebreathing the thick damp air that pooled there, neither asleep nor awake.

As he began shivering, he deferred taking any action, aware that any movement would dissipate the little pool of heat he'd managed to accumulate.

Finally, he sat up and looked around, his teeth chattering. Their campfire was reduced to a little pile of dimly-glowing embers. He looked around—the woods that surrounded their hilltop were daunting, depthless black. He stood, hands folded under his arms, teeth chattering, and forlornly assessed the spot where there had been a pile of firewood some hours before, hoping for some previously overlooked scraps. A small sound made him glance at the little grey mound that was the wolf-pelt covering his strange guide. She sat up. "You are cold," she said, with no trace of sleep in her voice.

He bit back the urge to say something sarcastic. "Yes... I was going to... see if I could find some more wood."

"In the dark?"

He was silent, save for the chattering of his teeth.

"You can sleep with me if you like." Her voice was flat. "For warmth," she added.

Suddenly he realized that she was nervous making the offer.

He gritted his teeth against the chattering and said, "Thank you. I'd like that." Then he fetched his wool blanket and carried it over to where the ulvzarger sat. Hesitantly, awkwardly, they pressed together. She was naked, of course, under their covers, and her hands and feet were icy, but her torso was warm.

He kept his hands closed in fists as they squirmed together. She seemed all elbows and knees, and he was hyperconscious of every shift of her body. They'd be lucky to get any sleep at all, he thought, but he was grateful nonetheless for the warmth that was starting to suffuse their pressed-together bodies.

Then it was morning. His mouth was dry, his eyes gummy with sleep. His shirt was rucked up under his armpits, and her cheek rested against his bare chest; there was a little damp patch where her saliva had puddled. His right arm, on which she rested, was completely numb.

He shifted and found that his joints were even more sore than he had feared.

Her eyes flickered open, and she leaped up, scattering both blanket and pelt, reaching her arms up towards the rising sun, yawning hugely as he scrambled to cover himself again against the still-chill morning air.

She continued her stretching, bending over to lay her hands flat on the ground, and accidentally—or deliberately—displaying her taut little bottom and dark, thick vulva. Suddenly he realized that she was watching him, face upended between her calves, with that closed-mouth smirk. She plucked up her wolf pelt from where it covered Ota and briskly knotted it around her waist. "Time to go," she said.

He stood, with many groans of discomfort, and packed his blanket.

To his great but unspoken relief, that day was rather easier than the last. Rather than cutting wildly across country, they spent much of the day following a dry streambed, which involved a fair bit of clambering over rocks but also some long stretches of straightforward hiking, where his longer legs could actually allow him to keep up with his agile guide.

Once again, the sun was beginning to set before she found a campsite she considered satisfactory.

As he squatted, building a fire again, she asked, "You have fire stick?"

"Matches? Uh, yeah. That's what these are."

"No, no. Big, loud. To kill with."

"You mean a musket? Of course not, I'm a—" Ota was going to say 'patrician,' but he realized that the protestation would be incomprehensible at best and offensive at worst to his half-naked autochthon companion. "I didn't bring one," he said.

"Then I must change tonight."

Ota was confused. "I thought that kilt was the only clothing you brought."

"Into wolf, cheesewheel. Then I hunt." She sounded downright gleeful at the prospect.

"Does it hurt? Changing?"

"Yes," she said. "But is such joy! We ulvzarg cannot live without the change. We do not change a month, we are very sick, then we are dead."

Intrigued despite himself, Ota pressed on. "So how do you do it? Do you just concentrate and it happens, or what?"

"We use old powerful chants, and secret hand motions, and special powders made by our elders. And there must be the skin to change into, of course," and she stroked the head that dangled from her kilt affectionately.

He nodded. "So we wait till sundown?"

"I will go now and prepare. I will stay close to guard you, but this is secret work—if you interrupt the ceremony, I must kill you," she said flatly.

He started at this, unsure how serious she was. "You mean, um...?"

"If you interrupt the ceremony, I will kill you. Is that clear?"

He stared at her for a moment, waiting for some gesture of explanation or apology. None came.

"Yes," he said at last.

She nodded. "Good." She went to the campfire and found a stick with a bright ember at one end, took it, and slipped into the darkening woods, staying close enough that he continued to catch glimpses of the ember's glow, though she herself was obscured from view.

He sat by the little fire, straining to hear whatever was occurring nearby over the fire's crackle. After a time, he could hear a faint, rapid chanting in Darsh, then a sharp, bitter smell reached his nostrils. It made his eyes water. He found that he was yawning a great deal.

His head snapped up—it was nearly dark, the fire was a little cluster of embers, and what had been chanting before was now a growling, snarling sound in which syllables could perhaps still be faintly discerned. There was also the rustle of leaves and the crackling of branches. Whatever was in the woods was coming out.

Ota had never actually seen a wolf outside of engravings, but he knew they were closely related to dogs. What emerged from the copse moved like no dog he'd ever seen. It was nearly as big as a man, as shaggy and gray as the pelt the wolf-girl wore around her waist, with hind-legs longer than its front, so that it moved with a curious rolling gait, its front legs touching the ground only occasionally.

It twitched its head about, sniffing the air audibly, then bounded off into the darkness, faster than any human could move.

He sat up, waiting for the creature to return so he could catch another glimpse.

Then it was gray early morning. He was stiff, and his blanket was covered with dew. The wolf-girl was curled in a ball by the fire. Next to her were two rabbits with their throats ripped out and bloody shreds of skin and bone from a third. He built up the fire from the night's embers and set out to find straight, green wood to make skewers for the rabbits. He eyed the soft, muddy ground around the copse, curious to see what sort of tracks the creature had left, but found only prints from the girl's bare feet.

He rummaged in his pack and brought out the vial of olive oil and pouch of salt he'd acquired in the village. Now out of ways to stall further, he squatted on the ground to undertake the cold and messy task of skinning and gutting the rabbits.

The sun was high in the sky before, arms aching, knuckles singed, and eyes streaming from the fire's smoke, he pronounced the rabbits done.

The wolf-girl had only stirred to pull the pelt over her face when the sun rose above the trees. She lay there still, faint snores emerging from under the shaggy gray fur, wiry calves and hard, black-soled feet bare to the sun.

"Breakfast," he called softly.

She groaned and pulled the pelt down to her neck to blink up at him blearily.

"Head... hurts" she groaned. With effort she managed to focus her eyes on the roasted rabbits on the sticks Ota held. She reached out a hand demandingly. "Hungry."

"Careful, it's hot," he said, handing her one of the sticks. "I hope you eat cooked food."

"This hungry? Yes."

She bit into one of the rabbit's legs, then yelped and jerked away and looked at him reproachfully.

"I said it was hot," Ota said.

She pulled off a strip of flesh and blew on it with comical delicacy before biting, more tentatively, at it. "Good!" she exclaimed.

By the time Ota had seated himself, pulled his own rabbit off its skewer, and taken his first bite, the girl had pulled most of the flesh of her rabbit's legs and devoured it and was starting to gnaw at the slightly charred bits along the spine. By the time he'd finished the second leg, she was watching him eat intently, her own carcass ripped bone from bone and picked scrupulously clean.

He passed her his own rabbit, and she fell upon it with apparently-undiminished hunger.

When she was finally convinced that there was no more meat to be had on the bones of either animal, she looked up. "You throw guts away?"

He nodded.

"Wasteful lowlanders. Good food there. Still: you could make a good second husband."

He goggled. "Excuse me?"

"Ulvzarg say...." She gazed into space as she improvised her translation.

First husband is tough and fierce. He has status and is good hunter.

Second husband is crafty and beautiful. He prepares good food and makes cunning tools.

Third husband is wise and patient. He knows all the old songs and teaches children.

All are strong and horny. All are good to fuck.

She frowned. "Only sound much better in Darsh. Has... rhyme?"

She thinks I'm strong? he thought. "You have a first husband?" he asked.

"Not anymore."

He waited to see if she would volunteer more. She did not.

"Shall we get going?" he asked.

She nodded and stood, then picked up the wolf pelt and knotted it around her waist again. Then her head darted up and caught him watching her movements. Her mouth quirked in a half smile, then she strode off into the forest.

He grabbed his pack and hurried after, hastily slinging it over his shoulders as he strode along.

That afternoon, they crossed a broad, shallow creek. Ota pausing before each shaky leap from mossy rock to mossy rock. From the other side of the creek, the autochthon, who had flowed across the water hardly breaking stride, watched with an expression which he suspected concealed suppressed laughter.

"We stop here," she announced when, with a final stumbling bound, he arrived on the muddy bank at her side.

"We do?" The sun was still high in the sky.

"There is water here, and a little food."

"'Cause I could still go another—" He looked at her face and noticed the dark circles under her eyes. She was still not fully recovered from last night's transformation, he realized.

"Okay, cool," he corrected himself. "We can get some rest." He set his pack down.

She picked a spot and unfastened her kilt and belt, setting them down on the ground. He forced himself not to stare at her broad pubic patch, her little high buttocks, as she settled herself onto the ground, curling into a ball on the pelt. "I sleep now," she announced, and she closed her eyes.

He sat down and watched the riffling of the creek beside them. For a moment his feet felt relief, then he was overtaken by a sensation he hadn't experienced in over a week—he was restless. His energy was still high, and he wanted something to do.

As quietly as he could, he rummaged through his pack and extracted a tiny, precious cake of soap, for which he had paid an extravagant sum at the village. Then he stood and made his way upstream. He found the experience of walking without a pack startlingly pleasant. After several days of its weight, there was a giddy lightness to bearing only his own. The sound of rushing water ahead drew him on, and he soon was at the base of a small cascade, the water pouring off a series of ledges into chest-deep pools floored in dead leaves and sparkling sand.

The day was warm and he hadn't bathed since the village the week before. He took off all his clothes and jumped into the water, biting back a cry at the cold, then began exuberantly soaping himself, groaning with pleasure.

"What are you doing?" came the Ulvzarger's voice, very close, behind him. He jumped and went down in the water, flailing and splashing. She was sitting cross-legged on a rock at the top of the little fall.

Suppressing his anger and embarrassment, he tried to explain about the new fashion for washing with soap that had started supplanting anointing with oil among the more forward-looking Ensans in the past few years.

"Show me!" she demanded, springing into the water beside him, leaving her wolf-pelt behind on the rock.

Well," he said hesitantly, "you work up some lather like this...." He demonstrated with the cake of soap, then handed it to her. She took it, but held still.

"Then you rub the suds onto yourself...." He demonstrated.

Instead of following suit, she raised her arms. "Show me!" she said again.

Throat thick, he stepped forward, and found that the water only came to mid-thigh where he was now standing. He ran sudsy hands over her ribcage and stomach. She smiled encouragingly, and he soaped the dark tufts under her arms, then reached up her arms to her wrists.

He could feel his penis lengthening and thickening as his hands ran over her body. She watched it unabashedly, with her curious little closed-mouth smile. "And, um, you can wash the rest of your body, the same way," he announced.

Her smile disappeared, and he tried to turn his attention to washing the remaining suds off himself as she clumsily turned the slippery cake in her hands, then spread the suds over her pubic triangle and small breasts.

She put the soap down and suddenly leapt in his direction with a terrifying roar. He flinched as she hit the water beside him with an enormous splash, then rose laughing merrily.

"Now both us are clean!" she announced. She stepped close, her nostrils flared. "You smell good." Her fingertips traced up his bare flanks. The head of his cock bumped against her navel.

He took a stumbling step backward, and her expression clouded. "You are not allowed? You must stay pure for marry?"

He flushed—calling an Ensan man of his age and class a virgin was an insult, though he knew her question was not so intended.

"I've been with plenty of girls," he said defensively, and he climbed out of the water to begin toweling himself off with his shirt.

She followed him and stood streaming and naked on the rock beside him. "You choose your women well?" she said teasingly. "They bring you much honor?"

"I'm.... really not sure what you mean."

"The women you have fucked: they are brave? Rich? Clever?"

"Um... I guess."

She sighed in exasperation. "Their honor is yours. Choose wisely, or you lose honor."

"I'll... um... keep that in mind."

She was still looking at him steadily.

"I just..." he began. "It's not right for women to be so... aggressive."

She looked taken aback. "I beat you in fight. Right of arva is mine, of fuck-choosing."

Now he was indignant. "You mean you think now you get to... to take me whether I want it or not."

"No." She smiled, and all her many teeth showed. "I am too... niiiccccccce." She drew out the word into a dangerous hiss. "I will not force you." She stepped forward again, and her nipples were brushing against his bare chest. "Lucky for me you are wanting it so much, hmm?"

The sun, now approaching the tree line, was failing to disperse the chill from the stream's water. "Look, I'm getting cold," Ota said. "Let's go back to the fire."

At their campsite, he threw a few more branches on the glowing embers and stood to watch them catch.

After a moment's silence, he turned to look at his guide. "I am not an autochthon," said Ota. "I am not a member of your pack, and I am not going to act like a member of your pack no matter how many times you punch me in the stomach. I am your—" She was watching him intently with an unreadable expression. He had been about to say 'employer,' but he bit the word back. "—equal."

A smile tugged at the corner of her mouth. "You do have the fire in you," she said, "I had fear you were soft all through."

Mollified somewhat by her compliment, he answered her half-smile with one of his own. "You can push an Ensan so far, but no further," he said, with a little pride.

Her smile was broadening as she stepped forward. "And then you push back?" she almost purred.

He wasn't quite certain how literally to take her, and, though he was determined, he had no particular wish to be punched in the stomach again. "Sometimes," he said cautiously.

She brought her arms up and shoved him, though so weakly he only staggered back half a step before catching himself.

"Hey!" he protested, and instinctively shoved back. She yielded with the thrust, her feet unmoving. Her face was cocked, her grin still growing. She put her hands on his chest and pushed harder this time, but now he was braced and her push propelled her own body backward a step.

She closed with him, and they grappled, the cool bare skin of their chests sliding together, warming rapidly. She was attempting to throw him to the ground, but gently this time, with only a portion of her strength. He felt a surprising flash of anger at this condescension, and with a surge of his own strength, tried to throw her instead. At the same moment, a smoldering branch caught fire all at once, sending a rush of sparks into the air with a loud crackle. She laughed a happy, full-throated laugh, twisted from him in some way he couldn't even follow, and then his feet were off the ground and his spine thudded against soft damp moss. She was straddling him, darting for his throat, but this time he grabbed at her matted locks before her teeth could reach him.

Her snarl was so terrifying he almost let go, but there was still a laugh underneath it, somehow, and her hips ground against his groin, teasing his half-erection fuller.

She was tossing her head against his confining hands, and he allowed her to work her head nearer until she was gnashing her teeth menacingly scant inches from his face. Gathering his courage, he then darted forward and grasped her lower lip in his own teeth. His nose slammed painfully against her cheekbone, but he ignored the discomfort, slowly increasing the pressure of his bite until her snarls gave way to harsh breathing.

He knew that many of the northern city-states considered kissing a perverse and decadent Southern custom. He released her lip, keeping his tight grip on her locks. "Your people kiss?"

"Sometimes," she said.

He ran his tongue tip over her lips, pressed his to them, felt the rigid barrier of her teeth. He tugged at her hair and her breath hissed. "Open," he demanded.

Her teeth parted, and his tongue slipped into her mouth, touched the tip of hers. Then her jaw shut again, trapping his tongue, just long enough to mark his own vulnerability before she opened and let him explore further.

As their mouths sealed together, he released her hair to run his palms over the long, lean muscles of her shoulders, to slide them down the length of her back. The campfire was still brightening as the wood continued to catch. He could feel its heat against his flank. Her shaggy kilt was rucked up to her waist, and he found his hands cupping her firm little bare buttocks as they circled over him.

She sat up, her face flushed, eyes unfocused and gleaming, continuing to undulate against his erection, sending waves of pleasure rushing up his spine so that he gasped and shuddered, working his hips back against her, squirming.

Then she reached back and took his wrists, pushed them up over his head, and swarmed up his torso until she was straddling his head and upraised arms. She angled her hips forward until her dark, swollen vulva was poised over his face, dense black hair spreading upward from it halfway to her navel. The thick smell made his nostrils flare. He was aware of his hunger to lick her, her hunger for his mouth, the fire's hunger for more wood to consume, and they were all one thing, new and yet familiar.

"Now you lick," she said, and it was somewhere between a demand and a simple announcement. Then the slippery heat was pressed against his face, her kilt falling around his head to block out the light and muffle the noise so that there was nothing but touch, taste, and smell.

He extended his tongue, and at once her clitoris was against it as she rocked against his face, the little shaft thick and swollen. Its taste was sour for a moment, then mild as fresh lubrication reached his tongue.

She unknotted her kilt and threw it aside, so he could see, in sharp perspective, her pubic tangle, her lean belly, her little breasts, her intent, flushed face bent down to watch him. She released his wrists and pulled roughly at her own dark nipples, the muscles of her thighs trembling against him as she sighed with pleasure.

Then she leaned backwards, and he felt a hand fumbling at the front of his breeches. She cursed quietly in Darsh, and he reached down and opened them for her. Her long, cool hand reached in then and grasped his cock, and an uncontrollable shudder ran through him. He felt a rush of heat against his side as the crackling sound of the fire intensified, its blaze bright in the corner of his eye.

For a minute, maybe two, she tugged at his erection with strong, unsteady strokes, then she let out a strangled cry and leaned forward again.

"Lick faster," she demanded, and he did. One of her hands rested on the ground; the other tugged at each nipple in turn. The bouncing of her hips was making his lock on her clitoris precarious. Slowly, he managed to kick his breeches off until they dangled from one ankle.

She began to wail, each scream accompanied by a tightening of her thighs around his head, her voice still loud through the muffling of that pressure.

At the height of one such cry, he twisted violently, throwing her to the ground in a tangle of kicking limbs, and flung himself on top of her, using his greater mass to press her to the mossy ground, his rigid cock sliding along the groove between her buttocks.

She bucked underneath him but he stayed in place, once more suspecting that she could have thrown him had she so chosen.

He bit down on her shoulder, tasting salt on her skin, and a shudder ran through her. He managed to angle his cock so that it slid between her legs, pressing against wet heat and scratchy hair. She locked her thighs against it and squirmed, both of them groaning at the sensation.

He held tight against her, only allowing minute movements, each thrust producing exquisite, almost painful friction on his cock.

"Give me fuck, you clanless fefzarger," the wolf-girl demanded. Her tone suggested that the term was not a compliment.

Ota decided to press his advantage a bit. "You have to ask nice," he said, and punctuated it with a slightly more emphatic thrust.

She looked back over her shoulder with that familiar mischievous grin. "Or you punish me by not fuck?" Her tone was amused and skeptical

This was an unexpected response. He hesitated, trying to devise an effective riposte. But she spoke first. "Please to give me fuck," she said, "you clanless fefzarker."

At that moment, an ambiguous victory was more than victory enough for Ota. He pulled back, gripping her hard shoulders in his hands, until the head of his cock was nudging against the opening of her cunt. Open and wet with his saliva and her lubrication, it gave way eagerly. Her hands were bunched into fists. She groaned long and low as he worked himself into her until his groin was pressed against the crease of her bottom, his cock buried inside her, where she tugged at him with her internal muscles.

She looked over at the fire, which roared white-hot and as tall as she now. "You do this?" she asked, wide eyed.

"We," he corrected her. "I think."

"Beautiful," she said.

Then the rhythm of their motion together took hold of him, and there were no thoughts, just heat and urgency, the taste of her skin as he gnawed at her shoulder, her groans which soon grew into ear-ringing screams.

He soon was roaring himself, pounding furiously into her, so uncontrollably that, as he approached orgasm, he slipped out, his cock sliding along the groove of her ass instead for several thrusts before he could persuade his body to pause so he could pull back and take hold of his slick, straining cock, angle it down, and—

He was on his back, she on top of him, growling and laughing. "Not yet, not yet," she said. "You not spurt yet."

A hot, hard hand gripped his inflamed cock, squeezed, and a frustrated half-orgasm surged through him. The flames were dying down for lack of fuel, but the campfire's heat was almost uncomfortable against his side. Steam rose off their writhing bodies as chill evening air hit their damp skin. His cock jumped in her tight fist, and one thick, opaque drop rolled off the head to puddle on her knuckles. She darted her head down, and a long tongue flickered out to lap at the fluid. Then she took the head into her mouth, her tongue almost too much friction on his sensitized head as her cheeks hollowed with her sucking.

She straddled his hips and angled his cock so that it slid along the crease of her vulva, working her hips against it. The sensation was delicious, but Ota craved more. Involuntarily, his hips jumped, trying to sink into the hot cunt that was so tantalizing him.

He glanced up at her face, and her intent, hungry, un-self-conscious gaze was mesmerizing. Their eyes remained locked as she lifted her hips to put the head of his cock against the mouth of her cunt once more, then sank slowly onto it, her mouth falling open in sympathy as her cunt opened to him.

Finally she sighed with pleasure and began grinding her hips in little circles against his pelvis, denying him the vertical thrusts that he craved.

He gripped her hips, tried to bounce her on himself, but she took his wrists and pushed them up over his head again, leaning down so that the points of her nipples brushed against his chest, her breath hot against his cheek as she continued to circle on him.

After a time, she released his wrists and pushed herself up enough so that he could see her face. She guided his hands to her soft little breasts, which he stroked with pleasure. "Pull my teats," she demanded, and he took hold of her prominent, dark nipples and tugged. "More!" she barked.

He pulled harder. She howled, sank forward, and sank her teeth painfully into his shoulder.

"Hey, you said to!" he protested.

"Yes," she said. "You pull teats, I bite neck, all is good."

"Maybe so," he grumbled, "but a little gentler than that is even better."

"Soft city boy. It is a good thing you are so pretty."

Then there was no talk—just the slow, deliberate building of speed and force, the waves of motion that ran through the two of them and moved them together as they found a common rhythm and followed it.

One of his hands was at her nipple, kneading and tugging at it, the other cupped one taut buttock, which rose and fell, flexed and relaxed as she shoved herself down onto him.

She was propped on one elbow, her other hand pressed tightly between them, moving furiously against her clitoris. His hand tightened on her ass as his excitement swelled. "Yes, yes!" she groaned, then screamed as if she was being gutted, locking tight against him, every muscle in her body taut.

Then she sighed and slumped on top of him. With his hands, he tried to urge her to continue her motions, but she was utterly limp now.

Frantic with need, he rolled on top of her and began pounding furiously at her. She purred in relaxed pleasure and spread her legs wide; he was making little sloshing noises in her cunt now. Through slitted eyes, he saw her reach up, smiling with her lips over her teeth. Then his head was held fast as her fingers gripped his scalp, and her suddenly bared teeth were across his throat.

He tried to freeze in place against this renewed threat, but his hips would not stop. He shuddered against her, groaning helplessly, then came in a series of convulsive waves. In seconds, the fire's amber light faded to a dim red glow. Not until he had stopped shaking did she release his throat, and he slumped, gasping, on top of her, sweat-slick skin against sweat-slick skin.

When he had gathered enough strength to lift his head enough to see her face again, she was smiling tenderly at him, her mouth pressed shut. "The oathbreakers are no more than a mile from here," she said.

He blinked rapidly. Of all the things he'd been expecting her to say next, this was not among them. "Pardon?"

"The merchants. Who beat and robbed you. They passed this way today. Almost for sure they camped near here."

He sat up, cross-legged, suddenly uncomfortably aware of his nakedness. "You're sure?" he said, looking around at the dark forest.

"Several men, at least two llama carts, and a donkey stopped at the stream, I think to repair a wagon wheel. They did not move until this morning. If they have no wings, they did not get much further."

Without choosing to, Ota found himself pulling on his shirt and leggings. "What, they've been sending you letters?"

"They did not try to hide their tracks. An ulvhaar not yet weaned could tell you what I did."

"Okay," he said, nodding slowly. "You didn't mention this before."

"My bond was to guide you to the city. Your honor was your own."

"And then you changed your mind," he said with some asperity.

"Now we are semen-bound. A part of your honor is mine."

"So what am I supposed to do with this information? Storm in and demand my money back?"

She gazed at him levelly. "You know what must be done to restore honor. They broke the gold oath—their blood is forfeit."

He stood up and began pacing agitatedly. "Look, it's all very well to say 'zer blood iz vorevit blah blah blah,'" he said, in an atrocious parody of her accent, "but they've got crossbows. I'm one guy with a machete!"

"You are one guy and an ulvzarg," she said.

He glared at her. "What, to restore your damn honor?"

"Not for honor." She grinned, showing every one of her teeth. "Grezhi pethni; the hunt is its own reason."

He continued pacing, finally whirling on her. "I'm not going to kill them."

"You wish that honor for me?"

"We're not going to kill them," he corrected himself. "They could have killed me, easily. Instead they barely even beat me up. They deserve to get fucked over, but they don't deserve to die."

"They are oathbreakers."

"Look, the insult is to me, right? We'll come up with something else. Thus far, no further."

Her look of disappointment was almost comic.

"You're right, though. We need to do something, and we need to get those chits back. Can you guide me to their camp without getting caught?"

"Yes," she said.

"Let's go then."

Following was physically not so difficult as Ota had anticipated—the ground was even here, the woods relatively sparse, but it was still a profoundly uneasy experience, hurrying through the dark, unfamiliar forest toward some unknown confrontation with the bandits who had previously betrayed and robbed him. And even if they should succeed in defeating the bandits—he trusted the autochthon's honesty and woodscraft, but did he trust her self-control? She'd made clear what her own honor demanded.

It seemed like many miles of silent walking that followed, fording several dark, icy streams, and at one point being startled by a terrifyingly loud and close bird that sprang into the air before him, beating its great wings furiously. At long last, she stopped abruptly, then sniffed the air in all directions. "Close!" she announced. "Quiet!"

They continued by minute, cautious steps. Soon Ota could smell woodsmoke, and, a few paces later, he managed to make out the red light of a low campfire through the trees.

His heart pounding furiously, he continued to edge forward until he was peeking around the trunk of one great, gnarled old tree right into the clearing, where, as the wolf-girl had predicted, the llama cart on which he had crossed into the mountains rested by the fire. From beneath it protruded four sets of boots; the men slept under it as a mobile shelter. Apparently they felt safe enough here that they had not bothered to post a sentry.

The llama train was tethered to a tree on the far side of the fire, and they were pacing and tugging at their ropes nervously, casting frightened glances back at where Ota and his companion crouched.

"Now what?" he said

"We kill."

"No!" he cried, then jumped as one of the merchants snorted and turned over in his sleep. There was a silence as Ota frantically tried to devise a scheme. "So I'm looking at that bonfire, and you know what I'm thinking?"

"You will use magic to defeat oathbreakers? You have power to do this?"

"Basically, yeah. But no, I don't. Or rather, I don't usually. I'd need you, um. You to...."

She watched him expectantly.

"To. Havesexwithmeagain," he spat out. He was glad of the dim light as he felt his face flushing.

"All right," she said at once, turned around, leaned up against one tree trunk, and flipped her kilt up over her waist, displaying, very faintly, the narrow pale orbs of her buttocks.

"Okay, hold on, let me get hard," he murmured anxiously, opening his breeches and tugging at his cock. After a minute he was half-hard again, and he pressed up against her, then slid easily into her cunt, still wet from their earlier coupling.

The heat and constriction on his cock was pleasurable, and it stayed moderately firm, but the anxious circumstances were sufficient to keep him from any real enjoyment. After several minutes of increasingly self-conscious thrusting and stifled gasps, he paused. "I don't think it's working," he said. "Whatever it was that happened before, it's not happening."

She turned, his damp cock slipping out from between her thighs to rest against the base of her belly as she faced him. "You need fire, yes? I have fire for you." She kissed him hard on the lips, then leaned forward to bite at his neck and shoulders. Shudders ran down his arms as she bit down, and his flagging cock began to stiffen again.

She growled very quietly in his ear and gripped his upper arms in her hands, holding him in place as her bites became harder.

By the time she pushed down on his shoulders, leaning back against the tree trunk to spread her legs wide, his cock was painfully rigid. His knees sank into the cold, damp mossy ground, and his face was pulled into the heat and pungent softness of her swollen cunt. He licked at her clit and heard her breath hiss in between her teeth. His head felt swollen, almost congested, but he wanted more. His hands gripped the firm little cheeks of her bottom, her fingers tugged at his scalp, then left it. He sensed but did not see her tug at her nipples. Somehow he could feel that if he continued at this rate, she would come shortly. If he slowed down now, the teasing would draw out and intensify her orgasm.

His tongue slowed, and she growled low, her hips shoving minutely against him, trying to extract more sensation from his mouth. The pressure in his head was almost painful, but he wanted more, more.

His middle finger found the mouth of her cunt and pressed inside slowly, effortlessly, and he felt the sensation of being penetrated. She made a furious hissing sound, biting the back of her hand to suppress her cries, and he felt the pain of the bite. The sensation of pressure flowed down his spine—heat, warmth, light, energy. He felt sensitized, hungry, like he had an erection across his entire surface. He felt it swirling and eddying inside him, straining to reach out.

He was standing now; he didn't remember the transition. Her black eyes were boring into his, her cool hand was stroking his cock with tantalizing lightness. The other hand raked slowly down his chest, leaving, he knew, livid red welts. He could feel the swelling in her labia, feel the constriction in her throat, feel the heat of his cock in her palm, could feel her feeling him feeling these things.

"Oh, yes, yes," he whispered, "yes, more. I'm—"

Her fingers pinched down hard at the base of his cock. The pressure, trying to escape through his cock, was terrible. "Please, please," he whispered, barely cognizant enough to continue to keep his voice low.

Her eyes tracked his face; she wore a fierce, cruel grin. Her grip on the base of his cock was unrelenting, the fingers of her other hand tugged roughly at his nipples, and—

—and his mind sprang outward like ripples from a tossed stone. He felt the burrowing things in the soil beneath his feet, the flying squirrel watching them in the tree above them, the beating hearts of the men in the clearing, the fierce little spirit of their bonfire, his brother, which knew him and loved him.

"Yes," he said. "I'm ready."

The wolf-girl needed time to prepare herself, but Ota welcomed the chance to stretch these new limbs of his awareness. He closed his eyes, slumped to the ground against a tree trunk like a marionette with its strings cut. He joined his mind to that of the bonfire in the clearing, made its rhythms his own, linked himself to its crackling, flickering life.

She disappeared into the dark woods but stayed close enough that he could make out her voice in murmured chants and catch whiffs of an acrid burning smell a couple of times.

In time, he was aware of the wild creature that was his lover moving from the site of its ritual. Its heart rate was faster than a human's; vaguely he could sense its powerful night vision as it flinched from the painful glare of the bandits' modest campfire. It crept along silently until it was in position on the far side of the clearing, crouching in darkness, waiting to play its assigned part.

Ota drew breath, held it. The fire in his chest swelled and brightened.

In answer, the bandits' campfire grew in brightness and size until it was twice Ota's height, the damp wood whistling and hissing as its moisture boiled away. Ota took hold of those sounds, shaped them with his will. The fire spoke in a chilling, unearthly voice, like a chorus of spirits.

"Thieeeevessss," it keened. Then: "Jussssstiicce."

Four men stumbled from under the shelter of the cart, stumbling and blinking blearily in the fire's suddenly-magnified brightness. From the leaping flames, Ota shaped a giant head, forcing the recalcitrant material into a wavering shape of a wolf's face, many times life-size.

At the sight, one of the men—Ota remembered that his name was Corach—bolted for the woods behind him, away from the apparition. Ota felt a little flare of disappointment in the ulvzarger's mind that her task was thus made so disappointingly easy. The man did not get far into the woods before meeting her.

Of the three remaining by the fire, two watched the bonfire with wide, frightened eyes. A third had apparently slept with his crossbow at his side. A large, taciturn man named Balato, he had always struck Ota as the informal leader of the band. He had his back to the fire now, scanning the dark woods with his crossbow at the ready, not far from Ota's true location, still hidden in the shadows.

"I'm sorry!" cried out one with a blond beard. His name was Seda. "I didn't know! She told me she was fifteen!"

Balato spoke: "Shut up, you idiot. Haven't you ever seen Ensan salamandry before? That patrician we rolled must have followed us.

"Come on out kid. Let's talk about this where we can see you."

"Even if it is," said the fourth bandit, a skinny, nervous man named Fethar, "he's got... powers. He could light us on fire or something."

"If he could do that," snarled Balato, "wouldn't he have done it already?"

Ota found that the fire's consciousness was blurring his own—its urgent hunger to feed, to consume made strategic thinking difficult. He decided to cut this debate short. The fire spoke again: "Yooou desssire evvvidencce?"

In the dark woods on the other side of the clearing, the ulvzarger removed one hand from the bandit's mouth. The other held a knife at his throat.

"You scrrream now," she said. "You not scrream enough, I give you help. You do not want that." She snarled then, loud enough to be heard by the bandits standing back from the bonfire, and bared her teeth.

Blood-curdling yowls of terror and pain filled the little clearing.

Fethar made as if to flee into the woods, but, confronted with the forest's depthless shadow echoing with the agonized screams of his companion, he stopped short.

The control of the fire was beginning to take its toll on Ota. His circle of awareness was contracting. He felt weary, and a throbbing headache was coming on. If this was to end well, it had best end soon. "Vengeanccce," the fire keened.

Fethar prostrated himself at once, whimpering that it wasn't his fault and it hadn't been his idea. Ota recalled that he had held back at first and then come over and given him a couple gratuitous kicks in the ribs when he was clearly down and helpless.

"Get up, you idiot," said Balato, gesturing with his crossbow. "You're just playing into his hands."

"Stop making it worse for us," Fethar said, standing to confront him. "We need to beg for mercy,"

"I'm not begging some Southland patrician with a couple magic tricks for mercy."

"Don't point that damn thing at me!" Fethar said, shoving the crossbow aside.

"Then get the hell out of my—"

But Fethar grabbed the crossbow with one hand and punched Balato in the jaw with the other, sending him reeling to the ground.

"Now," said the fire, and a gray, shaggy shape darted silently out of the darkness. It made straight for Seda, who, with surprising courage, stood his ground and collided with the sprinting shapeshifter.

A moment of grappling, and the burly man had pinned the smaller woman's arms at her sides in a ferocious bearhug. Lifting her feet off the ground, he waddled over to the fire, which reached out ineffectual tendrils of flame as Ota strained to intervene.

Two heads tossed about atop the ulvzarger's shoulders. Ota stared for a moment before realizing that the gray, muzzled one was just the wolfpelt's empty skin. The other appeared, for an instant, to be fully human. Then eyes and mouth opened in a furious snarl. Ota felt her surge of rage and bloodlust, and in the dying fire's uncertain light her eyes appeared to flash luminous amber, the teeth in her mouth appeared too sharp and numerous. Ota shuddered and the hair stood up on the back of his neck.

"Hey!" the bandit announced. "It's no monster. It's just a thonnie g—"

The howl of agony reached Ota's ears before his eyes could interpret the blur of motion as the autochthon darted forward in what looked almost like a rapid kiss.

Then the big man was writhing on the ground, his hands covering his face. The wolf-girl bent over him, her wide grin made macabre by the blood dripping from her chin. She spat a lump of something onto the man at her feet, and Ota realized, with a lurch of his stomach, that it was his nose.

The men who had been fighting watched, ashen-faced from the other side of the campfire, the crossbow discarded a few feet away. For a moment they and the ulvzarger stood. The only motion in the clearing was the writhing, whimpering man on the ground and the rapidly dying fire.

Balato took a small sideways step towards his crossbow, and the ulvzarger's grin widened and her crouch deepened. Her eagerness for more mayhem was palpable. In response, the bandit straightened his stance, moving his hands into a carefully neutral position.

Suddenly the ulvzarger was in motion again, an unbelievably fast blur that swarmed past the cringing men, over the llama-cart, and out of the firelight into the darkness.

In an instant the fire died down to red embers. Balato retrieved his crossbow, but in the darkness, the wolf-girl was tugging at Ota, pulling him away from his spot on the ground by one hand as she pressed a heavy sack into his other.

"Let's go!" came Balato's voice behind him. "That thing has all our gold!"

"I'm not chasing it," said Fethar. "I don't know what it was, but I don't think it was human."

"Fine, I'll— I'll—You chickenshit cowards! You've—"

Now out of earshot, Ota was stumbling through the darkness, aided by the ulvzarger's hot hand in his own and the last dregs of his expanded awareness that helped guide him on the forest's uneven surface.

"Is there any chance of their catching us?" he asked uncertainly.

The harsh barking sound that followed it took Ota a moment to recognize as laughter. "No," she said at last. "They not find ulvhaar in potato sack."

Some time later, after many stumbles and stubbed toes, the autochthon announced, "We rest here." Too weary by this time even to unpack his bedroll, he collapsed to the mossy ground, curled around the heavy sack of treasure. A moment later, she was twined against him, her wolf-pelt draped over their bodies. "In fire, at beginning, that was wolf?" she asked into his ear.

He nodded.

"Worst wolf ever," she murmured happily.

The wolf-girl was straddling him, her vulva grinding slowly against his cock, which was almost painfully hard. His arm was thrown across his eyes; strong morning sun warmed his face. "G'morning," he groaned.

"Yes," she said, and slid down on him, swallowing his penis up in one slow stroke, hot and wet, until her groin rested on his. There she held for a time, clenching and relaxing on his shaft, before she began to rock her hips minutely.

By the time he uncovered his eyes and opened them, squinting against the glare, she was bouncing vigorously, her little tits jumping about, her ragged fingernails digging into the skin of his chest. She reached a small climax, hissing through clenched teeth, and he felt a warming rush of spirit fire run up his spine.

Energized, he gripped her, rolled their coupled bodies over, and dug his bare toes into the moss for purchase to pound into her, pushing her knees up to her shoulders as he hammered his hips against hers.

He came, and he rolled off of her, hands running over her body affectionately. She leaned in and whispered into his ear: "My secret name is Yarot. Never say it aloud."

"Yarot," he murmured back, and fell back to sleep.

He awoke alone. He sat up; it was almost midday. The autochthon was nowhere to be seen. "Ya—?" he started to call, then caught himself. "Ulvzarger?" he tried. No answer. He stood and immediately saw Ivy City's famous ivied walls a few hundred cubits past the low shrubs that had concealed their resting place. By his side, the sack from the bandits' camp lay open. Gold gleamed inside, but it was the rolled sheaves of parchment, stamped with his family's seal, that made his heart leap. When he lifted it, it seemed to be about half the weight he recalled from the night before. The far-smaller money pouch at his belt was also open, he realized. When he looked inside, he felt little surprise to see its contents diminished by three gold coins from the last time he had looked.

He stood, pulled on his clothes and boots, donned his backpack, and started towards the walls. Then, seized by a sudden intuition, he turned around to the great forest on whose outskirts he stood. "I don't think you're really gone yet," he called out. "I think you're still watching me."

The forest answered nothing. Not a leaf stirred.

"Thank you. For everything," he continued. "If you ever need something from the Settled People, go to Ensa and ask for Ota of the Red Palatines." He paused again. "Goodbye," he called out, then turned around, and began to walk to the gates of Ivy City.

Contributors

Frances Selkirk lives with her family, cats, and chickens on the outer edge of suburbia. She has worked as a technical writer for many years, but for even longer, she has written stories for her family and friends. Her first known work was a very tame squirrel romance, dictated at age four. "The Beauty of Broken Glass" is her first published story.

Elizabeth Schechter is a stay-at-home-mom who lives in Central Florida, where she enjoys seeing the looks on the faces of the other playgroup moms when she answers the question "What do you do?" by describing herself as a pervy fetish writer. Her first novel, *Princes of Air*, was published in 2011 by Circlet Press, and her second, a steampunk novel entitled *House of the Sable Locks*, is forthcoming.

Elizabeth can be found online at:
http://easchechter.wordpress.com/

Kierstin Cherry was born in a tiny village in northern New England. Forced to attend an all-girl parochial school, she led the other girls in a revolt against the nuns and escaped into the wild. Raised by wolves and fairies, she found her calling as a semi-shy erotica writer and editor, and has recently graduated with her MFA in Writing Popular Fiction from Seton Hill University.

Although Kierstin has a quirky, irreverent sense of humor, she is very serious about her work as an author and editor. She puts the romance back into necromancy with her erotic vampire stories including "Graced" featured in the Lambda-nominated anthology *Women of the Bite*, by Circlet Press ebooks, and in print by Alyson Books.

Eros is a ribbon, silky, shining, supple. More than a flat line of color; it delineates space and cuts a delicious, shimmering demarcation on a plane of infinite variety. Passion is the ribbon's texture and imagination its material, and the ribbon itself is endless, a radiant path that cuts through the known and the unknown. The shadowed spot on the plane it binds might be a secret vampiric lover, or something darker. The splash of velvet might be burning incense to attract a heroine to a secret meeting with mystery. That yellow patch might even be funny, if you are in a mood for something lighter.

Erotica doesn't have to be nice or fair; it can be dire and dangerous. **Angela Caperton** writes stories about all the colors of the plane, but the ribbon, Eros, is essential.

Look for her stories published by Cleis, Circlet Press (including her sexy scifi novel *Man's World*), Coming Together, eXtasy Books, Exite, Mischief, Renaissance eBooks and in the indie magazine Out of the Gutter. Visit Angela at http://blog.angelacaperton.com

Sacchi Green's stories have appeared in a hip-high stack of publications. She's also edited eight erotica anthologies, including Lesbian Cowboys (winner of the 2010 Lambda Literary Award,) Girl Crazy, Lesbian Cops, and Girl Fever (all from Cleis Press.) A collection of her own erotica, A Ride to Remember, is published by Lethe Press. Her alter-ego, Connie Wilkins, writes science fiction and fantasy, with work in Circlet Press's Best Fantastic Erotica and Best Erotic Fantasy and Science Fiction. On the editorial side, she's the editor of Time Well Bent: Queer Alternative History and co-editor of Heiresses of Russ 2012: the Year's Best Lesbian Speculative Fiction, both from Lethe Press.

Kal Cobalt lives in Portland, Oregon with two partners, a menagerie of pets, and one very serious muse. For robot erotica, check out

K.C.'s Circlet Press anthology, *Robotica*. Another K.C. tale of bits and bytes in Circlet's *Wired Hard 4*, "Parts," was shortlisted for the 2010 Gaylactic Spectrum Awards. K.C.'s literary libido has also been spotted in *Best Gay Romance*, *Country Boys*, *Hot Gay Erotica*, *Boys in Heat*, and splattered all over the internet. K.C. in the flesh has often been spotted hula hoop dancing, knitting, and obsessing over tea when not agonizing over the current novel-length project or trapped beneath a cat training for the Sleeping Olympics.

Check out kalcobalt.com or @kalcobalt on Twitter to read 10 things you always wanted to know about robot sex, see what life as a pornographer is really like, find a twisted take on Christmas in Vegas in the future, explore two years of columns on (mostly human) sexuality, lurk furtively in the internet shadows, or hey, make contact! I promise I only talk about myself in the third person in author bios.

Elizabeth Reeve lives in the Sonoran Desert with her husband, a pair of standard-issue writers' cats, an extremely belligerent parakeet, and a backyard full of wild-growing nightshade. She re-reads all of Austen's books regularly, and will watch any adaptation—even the really bad ones—at least once. Usually more than once. Okay, always more than once. You can find her online at: http://elizabethreeve.com

Kathleen Tudor is a writer, and editor who sometimes walks on the wild side. Her work has appeared in *Anything for you: Erotica for Kinky Couples* and *Best Bondage 2012* from Cleis Press, *Hot Under the Collar* from Xcite Press, and other anthologies. She is also co-editor of Circlet Press' anthology, *Like Hearts Enchanted*. Kathleen can be contacted at PolyKathleen@gmail.com, and watch out for news of new releases as well as hot stories on her blog, KathleenTudor.com.

Monique Poirier lives and works in Providence, RI. Her works appear in Circlet anthologies *Like Clockwork*, *Like a Prince*, *Like Butterflies*

in Iron, and *Like An Iron Fist*. She can be reached at: Poirier.Monique@gmail.com.

Sunny Moraine is a humanoid creature of average height. They're also a PhD student in sociology and a writer who has published short stories in *Strange Horizons*, *Jabberwocky*, and *Shimmer*, among lots of other places. Their first novel *Line & Orbit*, cowritten with Lisa Soem, is forthcoming from Samhain Publishing. Their days are spent in balancing teaching, research, writing, and healthy doses of nothing whatsoever. Their life is a trick of light, so don't blink.

Clarice Clique has published one erotic novel, *Hot Summer Days*; a few standalone works, *The Transformation of Claudia Thomas* and *In This Moment*; and has had many stories in anthologies, including *Partner Swap* and *Explicit Encounters*, both published by Xcite. She is particularly pleased to be part of *Fantastic Erotica: The Best of Circlet Press* 2008-2012 as 'Mirror' was one of her first published pieces of erotica and gave her the confidence to continue writing.

She is currently finishing her second BDSM novel.

She can be followed on twitter and at: http://friendsofclariceclique.webeden.co.uk/

A few years ago **Nobilis Reed** decided to start sharing the naughty little stories he scribbled out in hidden notebooks. To his surprise, people actually liked them! Now, he can't stop. His wife, teenage children, and even the cats just look on this wretch of a man, hunched over his computer and shake their heads. Clearly, there is no hope for him. The best that can be done is to make him as comfortable as his affliction will allow. Symptoms of his condition include three novels, several novellas, numerous short stories, and the longest-running erotica podcast in the history of the world. His website can be found at: www.nobiliserotica.com.

Some artists take their industries by storm. **David Sklar**'s career has been more like an ill-conceived siege in which he misestimated which side would be first to run out of supplies. His publication history is a litany of unalike oddities, ranging from erotica to children's stories, with all sorts of things in between. Still, he has somehow managed to get work into *Strange Horizons*, *Bull Spec*, and other places, including pending works in *Ladybug* and *Scheherazade's Facade*. He lives in New Jersey and tries to support his family with freelance work. For more on David and his work, visit http://davidwriting.com.

Michael M. Jones is a writer, book reviewer, and editor. Previous Circlet appearances include *Like A God's Kiss*, *Masked Pleasures*, and *Like A Mask Removed*. Upcoming appearances include *Like Myth Made Flesh*, *Lustfully Ever After*, and *She-Shifters*. He is also the editor of *Like A Cunning Plan*, and *Scheherazade's Facade*. He rarely sleeps standing up. He lives in Roanoke, VA with a pride of cats, way too many books, and a wife who somehow understands him. For more information, visit him at: www.michaelmjones.com.

A lover of fantasy, table-top RPG games and, of course, erotica **David Hubbard** lives in a suburb of the Dallas area with his partner of 12 years, Bruce, and their two boxers, Pagan and Apollo. He completed his BA in English with a minor in Medieval Studies this year and is looking forward to devoting more of his time and energy to his writing and gaming projects. He is thrilled to be included in *Fantastic Erotica* and hopes to continue writing for Circlet for years to come.

Shanna Germain wants to have the word "wanderlust" tattooed somewhere secret on her body. Her writing has appeared in places like *Best American Erotica*, *Best Lesbian Romance*, *Like a Thorn*, and more. Visit her star constellation at: www.shannagermain.com.

N. K. Jemisin is a Brooklyn author whose short fiction and novels have been nominated for the Hugo and the Nebula, shortlisted for the Crawford and the Tiptree, and have won the Locus Award for Best First Novel. Her latest novel, *The Killing Moon*, will be published in May 2012 from Orbit Books. Her website is nkjemisin.com.

If **Bernie Mojzes** has one failing (and I've got it on good authority (references available on request) that he's got quite a bit more), it's that he doesn't understand genre. He writes stuff. Sometimes it's "What if Gomer Pyle was an ambiguously gendered, shape-changing, British swamp faerie fighting the Nazis?"; other times it's "You know, caterpillars could be the new cephalopods." He lets other people tell him whether it's steampunk or dieselpunk or whatever. Some of it (he's told) is apparently erotica, and you're holding one of those stories now. There are others, in Circlet's *Like a Vorpal Blade* and *Like a Treasure Found*, and most recently, in *Stretched*, his first dead-tree format pr0n. It's not all smut, alas: he's got a short, illustrated book called "The Evil Gazebo," and stories in *Daily Science Fiction*, *Crossed Genres*, *Dead Souls*, and a passel of other places. In his copious free time, he co-edits *the Journal of Unlikely Entomology*. If you're so inclined to learn more, and/or to register a complaint, please visit www.kappamaki.com.

Vinnie Tesla is the author of *The Erotofluidic Age*, a tongue-in-cheek pornographic Steampunk e-book, published by Circlet Press. He has a bunch of short stories and a badly-neglected blog at vinnietesla.com. His current project is a crime novel set in the world of "Ota Discovers Fire."

Best Erotic Fantasy & Science Fiction

edited by Cecilia Tan & Bethany Zaiatz

ISBN: 978-1-885865-61-8 $19.95 pb

"Circlet has given us a wonderful sampling of exactly what they're about, demonstrating the extraordinary outcomes possible when writers push the boundaries of genre to create works defying convention."
—Rise Reviews

The editors at Circlet Press present a cherry-picked collection of only the best of erotic fantasy and science fiction. From over 300 entries, they have chosen the top 16, including the stunning winner by Allison Lonsdale "Vaster Than Empires." The stories in the anthology span many genres and sexualities, at times defying such categories. Entries were judged on writing quality, originality, and eroticism, the three virtues Circlet Press values most in all publications.

Best Fantastic Erotica

edited by Cecilia Tan

ISBN: 978-1-885865-60-1 $19.95 pb

The best erotic science fiction and fantasy as determined by the annual contest run by Circlet Press. Rewarding originality and positive sensuality, the contest inspires well-known and unknown writers alike to excel in this provocative genre. Erotic sf/f combines erotic and sexual themes with magic, futurism, high fantasy, cyberpunk, space opera, magic realism, and all the many other sub-genres. The 2006 winner is a multi-genre writer from Canada Arinn Dembo, whose "Monsoon" draws on the mythic tradition of India.

Scheherazade's Façade
edited by Michael M. Jones
ISBN 978-1-61390-058-1 $14.95 pb

First book in Circlet's new imprint for gender-exploratory fiction, Gressive Press. The gender lines are blurred and transcended in twelve tales of magic, self-discovery, and adventure, penned by some of today's most intriguing authors. In these pages, you'll find heroes and villains, warriors and tricksters, drag queens and cross-dressers, tragedy and triumph. Featuring all-new work from Tanith Lee, Sarah Rees Brennan, Alma Alexander, Aliette de Bodard, and more, Scheherazade's Façade is filled with surprises and beauty, and may just challenge the way you see the world.

One Saved to the Sea
by Catt Kingsgrave
ISBN: 978-1-61390-069-7 $9.95 pb

Winner of the 2012 Rainbow Award for Lesbian Paranormal Fiction! In the Orkney Islands, seals shed their skins to dance on land. Lighthouse-keeper's daughter Mairead has watched the selkie girls secretly and longs to join them. Her brothers have left to fight in the war, her father is invalid, and Mairead feels alone. But a selkie girl has been watching her, too. What wildness will the shapeshifter draw her into? One Saved to the Sea by Catt Kingsgrave will sweep you away to a past that never was, and into a love story just this side of impossible.

All titles available in ebook formats also.

Simulacrum

by Rian Darcy

ISBN: 978-1-61390-070-3 $14.95 pb

"This is another winner for Circlet and I've added a new writer to my must read list. I found the story to be well thought out, characters well developed, and the sensuality strong"
—Baryon Reviews

In Simulnet, no one knows who you are: the perfect playground for the imagination... or a serial killer. The police ask Shaun to partner with an enigmatic programmer to hunt a murderer in the sex clubs and ramen shops of cyberspace. But as they investigate, Shaun finds himself wanting to know more about his partner. Ultimately the questions Shaun needs to answer are the ones deep in his heart.

Chocolatiers of the High Winds

by H.B. Kurtzwilde

ISBN: 978-1-61390-050-5 $14.95 pb

This rollicking adventure puts the steam into steampunk as we follow young Mayport Titus while he and his cohort seek to supply the world once more with that elusive and tricksy treasure known as chocolate. Mayport is the heir to the Titus Chocolate fortune–or what is left of it after his parents were lost on the high winds when he was a boy and the banks and handlers have had their way since. Perhaps the young Titus heir takes after his father in some ways, for he is no conformist to social moires. As soon as he is of age, our hero slips the bonds of institutional education for an intercontinental adventure in search of his father's old airship, The Dutch Process.

The Prince's Boy: Volume One

by Cecilia Tan

ISBN 978-1-61390-058-1 $19.95 pb

Winner of Honorable Mention in the Rainbow Awards and the NLA Writing Awards! In a fantasy world where male/male lust fuels Night Magic, Prince Kenet lives a sheltered life. Isolated from the war that threatens the kingdom, he and his whipping boy Jorin are of age, but still sneak forbidden pleasures in their bed at night. When a dark mage tries to bespell Kenet into sexual submission, the prince and his boy are thrust into the world of intrigue, sex, and war. Orginal published as an online serial, The Prince's Boy chapters 1-56 are collected in Volume One. Every chapter, by design, features a sex scene pushing the plot forward to the next installment!

The Prince's Boy: Volume Two

by Cecilia Tan

ISBN: 978-1-61390-069-7 $19.95 pb

In this conclusion to the gay fantasy saga begun in Volume One, in Volume Two thwarted lovers Jorin and Kenet must reunite in order to defeat their common enemy, the scheming mage Seroi. Seroi has twisted Kenet's father's mind and is set on ruling the country for himself... as well as making Kenet into his magically bonded sex slave. But the bonds of love, not only between Kenet and Jorin, but between other characters as well, may be stronger than the magical chains Seroi would use to enslave them all. Includes chapters 57-96, epilogue, and the bonus short story Sergetten's Tale.

All titles available in ebook formats also.